William C. Richards

Great in Goodness

A Memoir of George N. Briggs, Governor of the Commonwealth of Massachusetts,

from 1844-1851

William C. Richards

Great in Goodness
A Memoir of George N. Briggs, Governor of the Commonwealth of Massachusetts, from 1844-1851

ISBN/EAN: 9783337094102

Printed in Europe, USA, Canada, Australia, Japan

Cover: Foto ©Raphael Reischuk / pixelio.de

More available books at **www.hansebooks.com**

GREAT IN GOODNESS;

A MEMOIR

OF

GEORGE N. BRIGGS,

GOVERNOR OF THE COMMONWEALTH OF MASSACHUSETTS,

FROM 1844 TO 1851.

BY

WILLIAM C. RICHARDS.

" Justum et tenacem propositi virum."

"Only the actions of the just,
Smell sweet and blossom in the dust."

With Illustrations.

BOSTON:
GOULD AND LINCOLN,
59 WASHINGTON STREET.
NEW YORK: SHELDON AND COMPANY.
CINCINNATI: GEO. S. BLANCHARD AND CO.
1866.

ROCKWELL AND ROLLINS, Printers,
122 Washington Street, Boston.

PREFACE.

HERE are perhaps not a few lives, in the great annals of our age, which are invested at their close with sufficient interest to entitle them to immediate commemoration by some friendly hand, and to secure for the service rendered a meed of approval more or less general and cordial.

It is of rare occurrence, however, that a life which has ceased for several years without any adequate memorial, will, by the force of its inherent excellence and by the charm of its unfading beauty, not only justify but compel a tardy portraiture.

The life of GOVERNOR BRIGGS is of this exceptional order. The silent lapse of five years has served not to cloud it with the mists of forgetfulness, but rather to brighten it into the pure and steady radiance of a meridian fulness. The long continued reticence of the biographer concerning this noble life has proved to be less an injustice done to that, than to the public outside of the wide sphere which it filled.

It is needless to recount here the causes of this delay, and certainly it is more grateful to him, from whose hands the Memorial at length proceeds, to express his deep sense of the advantage he has gained for the adequate fulfilment of his pleasing duty, from the necessity he was under of contemplating the character of his subject at a period when wise impressions had ripened into convictions, and when he had not to forestall, but simply to follow the judgment of the wisest and best concerning him.

In tracing his history through an extended and eventful career, as the poor boy, the young lawyer, the wise counsellor, the eminent statesman, the upright judge, the useful and consistent Christian, it becomes more and more evident that his was a remarkable life, and his name one which "the world will not willingly let die." The need of this formal biography to preserve it from oblivion is not half so apparent; and it is given to the public with as much of hesitation as of hope: with hesitation, because of the manifold imperfections of its doings; and with hope, that these will be lost sight of in the surpassing interest of its theme.

It could not have been done, without more and indeed fatal blemishes, had not filial love and generous friendship ministered largely to the work of its preparation. The biographer should justly disclaim having done more than to carefully edit the copious materials supplied to his hand.

He commits the book, which is the record of one emphatically "*Great in Goodness,*" to the public, and especially to the Christian community, with the confidence that it contains for all a beautiful example of honorable achievement and incorruptible virtue — an example too shining to be overlooked.

PITTSFIELD, *August* 30, 1866.

CONTENTS.

CHAPTER I.

CHAPTER II.

CHAPTER III.

CHAPTER IV.

CHAPTER V.

CHAPTER VI.

CHAPTER VII.

CHAPTER XII.

CHAPTER XIII.

CHAPTER XIV.

CHAPTER XV.

CHAPTER XVI.

CHAPTER XVII.

CHAPTER XVIII.

CHAPTER XIX.

CHAPTER XX.

CHAPTER XXI.

CHAPTER XXII.

CHAPTER XXIII.

CHAPTER XXIV.

CHAPTER XXV.

CHAPTER XXVI.

CHAPTER XXVII.

CHAPTER XXVIII.

CHAPTER XXIX.

CHAPTER XXX.

CHAPTER XXXI.

CHAPTER XXXII.

CHAPTER XXXIII.

APPENDIX I.

APPENDIX II.

APPENDIX III.

Illustrations.

MEMOIR OF GEORGE N. BRIGGS.

CHAPTER I.

GEORGE NIXON BRIGGS was born at South Adams, among
the hills of Berkshire, Mass., on the twelfth day of April,
1796.

He was the last but one of twelve children, ten of whom
grew up under the healthful influences of his father's humble but cheerful home.

Both his parents were born in Rhode Island—his father,
Allen Briggs, in Cranston, April 27th, 1756, and his mother,
whose maiden name was Nancy Brown, in Cumberland,
Jan. 11th, 1762. His mother was of Huguenot descent;
and if we should seek his ancestors, we might find them
among the Pilgrims who sought these shores in the ship
"Fortune."

His father was a blacksmith by trade, and might have
sat for not a few features of the picture drawn by Longfel-
low, in his well-known poem, "The Village Blacksmith:"

> "The smith a mighty man is he,
> With large and sinewy hands;
> And the muscles of his brawny arms
> Are strong as iron bands.

.   .   .   .   .

> " His brow is wet with honest sweat,
>   He earns whate'er he can;
> And looks the whole world in the face,
> For he owes not any man."

His parents were of a simple but noble type of character, which was subsequently illustrated in a beautiful outgrowth in the life and work of their son.   They inherited
more of the sterling than of the simply stern characteristics
of their Pilgrim progenitors.   Their industry and frugality
sufficed to exalt them, not indeed out of the estate of the
poor, but, certainly, in it, to a position of social respectability, which their contentment and piety combined transfigured, for themselves at least, into true domestic happiness.

To a clear and vigorous judgment, his father added a
degree of intelligence which gave his opinions force among
his neighbors, of whom he was ever highly esteemed.

The remembrance of his parents was always dear and
fresh in the heart of the son.   His tributes to their excellence were frequent and fervent; and never, throughout his
varied career did he cease to acknowledge, with filial gratitude and pride, his immeasurable obligations to the fidelity
and force alike of their parental influence over him.

Long after they were gathered to the dead, and when
his own life-labor was fast approaching maturity, he traced,
in a letter to one of his children, a portraiture of his
father, so beautiful in its delineations, so touching in its
filial tenderness, that it not only deserves, on these ac-
counts, a place in these memorials, but depicting, more fitly
than any language of the biographer could possibly do, the
human sources of that sturdy yet gentle virtue which dis-

THE HOUSE WHERE HE WAS BORN.

tinguished his life, and constituted indeed the great motive-force of his admirable character, could not be omitted here without injustice. The letter was addressed to his only daughter, then residing with her husband, at Lawrence, Mass. It bears the date of a day which, as the reader will discover, was of no small interest in the family : —

PITTSFIELD, 27th April, 1851.

MY DEAR CHILD :

I suppose you were disappointed in not seeing me last night. Right glad should I have been, if I could consistently have been with you at Lawrence to-day, but it was *not* so; and the longer I live the better I learn, I hope, to be content with what it seems to be the will of Providence I should meet, whether it is the thing most agreeable to my wishes or not.

The day has been one of much interest to me. It is not only your birthday, but it is the birthday of my own father and of our little one here at home.[1] Ninety-five years ago to-day your Grandfather Briggs was born at Cranston, in the State of Rhode Island. He reached his threescore years and ten, and two days afterwards went the way of all the earth, to " that country from whose bourne no traveller returns." His mother was early left a widow, with four young sons, of whom he was the third. Their names were Oliver, Benjamin, Allen, and Elisha. He told me once, that when a boy it was decided he should go from home, to learn the cooper's trade. When he left, his mother went some part of the way with him; and when about to separate, they sat down on a rock by the wayside, where she gave him a mother's counsel, wept over him a widowed mother's tears, and then returned to her lonely home, while he passed on to his new home.

But it seems he did not stay long with the cooper, for he learned the blacksmith's trade. He was a first-rate blacksmith, and followed the business all his life, or as long as he was able to work. He had no early education, never having entered a school-house till after he was twenty-one years old, and then not as a scholar.

1 George N. Briggs, eldest son of H. S. Briggs, youngest son of Gov. Briggs.

His life was one of labor and toil. He was the father of twelve children, ten of whom reached maturity. He possessed a strong, discriminating, logical mind, was an observer of men and things, and in general information was behind very few men belonging to his class of life in his day,—I mean mechanics and farmers. He had a heart full of kindness and benevolence, and an integrity of character worth more than the gold of California without it. I never heard him utter a sentiment that I could wish I had not heard from him; and I never heard him speak an indecent or vulgar word, or a word that I should now think would be improper to speak before a family of children.

In religious sentiment he was a decided Baptist, though his mother was a Quaker. I never heard him say an uncharitable thing of other denominations. He heard preachers of all religious sects; and the pleasure of hearing them depended not upon the name of the preacher, but upon the soundness, piety, and unction of the sermon. Subject to the frailties of human nature, he lived the life of the righteous and died his death.

The last of August, 1813, in my eighteenth year, I left his humble but comfortable and hospitable mansion in White Creek, Washington County, New York; and, with what few extra clothes I had tied up in a cotton handkerchief, went out, I then knew not whither, to see what a kind Providence had in reserve for me. Just before I left the house I looked into that venerable face, then hung around with locks white as the driven snow, and saw the full round tears falling fast over it. Often, before that, from my infancy, I had seen the perspiration drop from the same face and brow upon the hot iron that his strong arm was beating upon the anvil. The hard blows thus given were to earn bread for me. When I cease to remember and venerate that dear parent who wielded them, or to respect the occupation in which they were given, may my fellow-men cease to respect and my children to honor me. On his tombstone is written, "An honest man is the noblest work of God." I believe all who knew him think it belongs there. I have no wish to see or have a different one in its place.

I was born in April, but fifteen days earlier in the month. You know my poor history. Your birthday was the same as that of your grandfather. How much more sunny have been your days than his! Till the recent, and I hope fast-dissolving cloud that has shadowed you for a few weeks past, your life has been one of brightness. I hope and believe there are yet for you, and your dear husband, many years of sunshine and prosperity. The incidents of your birthday I have heretofore given you, and they need not now be repeated. Our little George N. is now the representative of the generation of our family for the 27th of April. You were sixty-three years behind your grandfather; and the boy is thirty-one behind you. What there is for him we cannot foresee. My first and great desire for him, as it has always been for my own children, and as I hope it always will be for all that shall succeed me of my own family, is, that he may early be a true and humble disciple of the Saviour. If he lives, may the great truth sink speedily and deeply into his heart that "the saint is greater than the sage, and that discipleship to Jesus is the pinnacle of human glory." May that glory belong to every individual of all the generations in whose veins my blood may run.

You see this letter is taken up by talking of your grandfather and father, of yourself and your little co-natal of the 27th of April. Think you that she, who, on the 27th of April, 1819, after hours and days of agony, gave birth to my first-born child, will ever cease to be the dearest one on earth? All my children grow dearer as my departing years bring me nearer to the point of separation from them. God bless you all.

Affectionately your father,
GEORGE N. BRIGGS.

Mrs. HARRIET C. B. BIGELOW.

This tribute to his honored and beloved father was not a mere artificial expression, such as a man risen by the force of his own will and wit, to public eminence, might choose to make concerning those from whom he had sprung. It was in perfect harmony with other utterances upon the same theme, and no less with the spirit he continually manifested in his remembrance of his parents.

His friend, the Hon. Charles Hudson, having asked him,

upon one occasion, for some written reminiscences of his life, he began his letter in reply with an almost epigrammatic and equally modest expression of his own estimate of it, " A full length would be only a sketch."

He then proceeds to speak of his father, in terms of honest pride, adding to other tributes these words : —

"He was all his life a hard-working, poor, and honest man — a real character of Seventy-Six. His poverty never made him bow his neck to any man. He died leaving to his children a legacy worth more, and dearer far to me, than the wealth of Crœsus, — a name as pure and spotless as the snowy locks he carried to the tomb. His epitaph is, —

" 'An honest man's the noblest work of God.' "

It is remembered of him, also, that when he was informed of his nomination for the office of Governor of Massachusetts, he said, eagerly, to his daughter : " What honest pride my father would have felt in the honor offered to his son."

Amid the simple attractions and pleasures of his unostentatious abode, he would say to his children : " I could desire nothing more to make my enjoyment of this home perfect, except the power to share it with my parents. But, then, they have a better home than I could give them."

Reverence and love for these excellent and faithful guardians of his childhood were but the legitimate emotions and experiences of his nature and spirit ; the one uncontaminated by the world, which yet paid him tribute ; and the other preserving, amid the cares and honors and burdens of public life, the simplicity of his early days.

He was but seven years old when the family removed from South Adams, and made a new home in the village of Manchester, Vermont. There, in sight and within the shadows of the Green Mountains, the most susceptible years of his young life were passed; and it can hardly be doubted that his natural surroundings conspired with home influences to fashion his childhood to a lofty standard.

Less is recorded of that childhood than those who knew and honored and loved its maturity into a large-statured manhood, could wish to have perpetuated in these memoirs. That it was a period of natural and ingenuous happiness, is evident from his own recollections, and from the testimony of his brothers. They describe him as "a fair and always happy boy." He was emphatically "the favorite of the family." His was a gentle and sunny nature, characterized withal by such intelligence, vivacity, and shrewdness, that his mother, with a true prophetic forecast, not far removed, it may be, from simple maternal instinct, was in the habit of calling him her "little lawyer."

She was justly proud of that character and of that career, of which her mother's heart had sufficient prevision, to be interpreted by her fondness and faith into a verity.

Doubtless George's childhood was toned and shaded, to some extent, by the narrow material resources of his home. But these, on the other hand, by necessitating the employment of every hand in the household not really too feeble to help, served as a stimulus to those energies in the boy's nature which might have lain dormant in conditions of affluence, and which, unstirred in his early life, might never have been aroused to that efficiency which marked their exertion and their products in his after career.

The demands of a large family upon the father's and mother's toil had these opposite effects; that while they developed the physical and moral forces of the man into a stalwart and noble strength for endurance and action, they consumed the life energies of the gentler woman ; and there is left for us, to awaken our sympathies, the picture, from a granddaughter's hand, of "the self-sacrificing devotion of the overwrought mother, whose toils and hardships made her prematurely a little child in her age."

But George's childhood felt not the shadows of this final wasting away of his mother's strength. Her smiles and her benedictions fell upon all its progress with their sunny and invigorating influence, giving fresh sweetness to the ringing but not boisterous music of his laughter, and calling forth, even in the boy, the gentle and genial tempers and manners, which in the man, the statesman, and the Christian, were matured into assiduous, and in their measure and persistence almost exceptional courtesies and amenities, in every phase and position of his life.

The twofold spell of the parental power—the unswerving and sturdy manliness of the honest toiling father, and the unselfish and vigilant tenderness of the no less busy mother ; and these diverse but inter-active agencies, both intensified and sanctified by the grace of God, moulded the boy's character into a fixedness of right purpose, which no subsequent temptations of personal or public circumstances availed to pervert into evil courses, or even to warp into proclivities to unlovely habits.

"Who is able," asks Goethe,[1] "to speak worthily of the fulness of childhood?" Certainly, it would be a task of no common magnitude to define and exhaust the meaning, the prophetic signs of that particular childhood which is here passed in review. The completed life, the broad and

---

[1] Autobiography.

lofty development into which it advanced, steadily, if not with splendor of progress — these alone can express the true comprehensiveness of it. Every part of the unfolding and maturing process must, therefore, have its peculiar interest and profit.

3

CHAPTER II.

ANOTHER CHANGE OF HOME—EARLY RELIGIOUS TRAINING—EXPERIENCE OF RELIGION—RELIGIOUS EARNESTNESS—BOYISH ELOQUENCE—REMARKABLE SCENES—AN OLD BALLAD—PRAYER EXTRAORDINARY—APPRENTICESHIP TO A QUAKER HATTER—ANECDOTES—AT SCHOOL—INCIDENT OF LATER LIFE—LETTER TO THE CHURCH HE JOINED IN HIS YOUTH.

THE sojourn of the family in their Vermont home was brief. At the end of two years after their removal thither, they left it for the State of New York. In 1805 the village of White Creek, in Washington County, became the place of their abode, and the scene of important experiences to the young subject of this memoir.

His training had always been of a decidedly religious character. The strict, though by no means sombre piety of his parents, controlled the moral discipline of the household. The Bible was to them a book of meaning and of authority, and their children were taught to honor and obey its precepts. From its decisions, as they were conscientiously interpreted to them, there could be no appeal; and their consciences, unscared by worldliness and victorious passions, were easily impressed with a sense of the fitness of that standard of life which the Bible proclaims.

The spirit and practice of piety in the parents thus reproduced themselves, as if by an inevitable law of sequence, in the children. The inspired philosophy, embodied in the precept, "Train up a child in the way he should go, and when he is old he will not depart from it," had a remarkable exemplification in the development of religious tendencies in the mind of the amiable and gentle boy. While he was in his fourteenth year he became the subject of personal religious experience, and was soon after baptized and received into the Baptist church at White Creek.

This happy result was, undoubtedly, induced chiefly by the development and progress, in the place where he lived, of one of those apparently phenomenal epochs in the life of the church which are called Revivals. These were now of frequent occurrence in this country, and sometimes of such striking power as to excite wonder and awe outside of the pale of the church.

George entered with characteristic eagerness into the new and almost fascinating interests of the religious services which attended, with growing frequency, the progress of the work of grace in White Creek.

It is not surprising that he so speedily yielded himself to the growing influence, or that when he did so he should give himself up, with boyish enthusiasm and sincerity, to the service of Christ. In his after life he looked back upon this period with a profound interest, and often realized how little he could then have known of the true character and power of sin in his nature, as compared with those profounder views and convictions of it which evermore quickened his apprehension of the grace of Christ in His work of atonement.

No sooner was the boy numbered with the young converts, than he began to exhort others to seek the salvation of their souls. His extreme youth gave to his ardent appeals an extraordinary charm, and carried them to many hearts with resistless effect. He says, in reference to this period : " I was then a white-headed little boy. I used to attend all the meetings with the gray-headed old men, and felt as old as any of them."

In this naive acknowledgment of his self-imagined equality of age with the men of gray hairs in regard to religious experience, the ingenuousness of his character appears; and not less manifestly the secret of his remarkable boldness in the part he took in the exciting scenes around him.

For a graphic and deeply interesting glimpse of the boy at this time, the reader is indebted to the reminiscences of the Hon. Hiland Hall, of Vermont, who was, in his youth, George's occasional companion, and not much his senior. Their subsequent association in Congress advanced their early, though slight, acquaintance into warm friendship. Mr. Hall writes to Mrs. Bigelow, under date of North Bennington, December 23, 1861. He says, —

"The first remembrance I have of your father was about the year 1810 (possibly 1809), when he lived at White Creek, some five or six miles from my own residence, and when he was from thirteen to fourteen years old. It was during the excitement of a religious revival, when his eloquent and what were deemed almost miraculous addresses in religious meetings drew together great crowds of people, and elicited very general and extensive appreciation and admiration."

Numerous as are the remarkable points and positions in the public life of the subject of this memoir, there is probably none so well calculated to excite surprise as this extraordinary representation of him in his young boyhood.

We behold a scene of singular and marvellous interest. A mere child stands before us, in the midst of a great throng of people, many of them as old in years as he was young, whom he holds, as in a spell, by the strange fascination of his speech, as he dwells, now, perhaps, upon some grave and perplexing doctrine of theology, or, anon, pleads in impassioned strains with the impenitent around him to "flee from the wrath to come," and take shelter in the arms of that Saviour whom he had found. Not a little is added to the effect of this almost unique representation by the fact that his venerable father was in the assemblies, and one of the most eager of his auditors.

The granddaughter, writing of these occasions, from her recollections of her father's words, says, —   .

"His father in these meetings was the sweet singer of this Israel. His voice and patriarchal presence were exceedingly impressive. None who ever heard him sing, —

> ' The day is past and gone,
> · The evening shades appear;'

or those other scarcely less familiar lines, —

> ' I saw one hanging on a tree,
> In agony and blood,
> Who fixed his dying eyes on me,
> As near the cross I stood!' —

could ever forget the rich pathos of his tones. My father could sing only with his soul. He had little ear for music, except as blended with sentiment; but all through his life sang some of his father's hymns. An old ballad, which we older children remember hearing grandfather sing with almost dramatic effect, and which father sung for us when we were little, is out of print, but is still sacredly preserved in the family."[1]

---

[1] The reader may be gratified to find at his command a copy of this ballad, and it would seem to have a right to a place in these memorials. It is entitled

THE SACRIFICE.

> " The morning sun rose bright and clear;
> On Abram's tent it gayly shone;
> And all was bright and cheerful there, —
> All, save the patriarch's heart alone.

3*

It is difficult for us, perhaps, to comprehend the reason, or rather the process, of this strange power of the boy over

When God's command arose to mind,
  It forced into his eyes a tear;
Although his soul was all resigned,
  Yet nature fondly lingered there.

The simple morning feast was spread,
  And Sarah at the banquet smiled;
Joy on her face its lustre spread,
  For near her sat her only child.

The charm that pleased a monarch's eye
  Upon her cheek had left its trace,
His highly-augured destiny
  Was written on his heavenly face.

The groaning father turned away,
  And walked the inner tent apart;
He felt his fortitude decay,
  While nature whispered in his heart,—

"Oh! must this son, to whom was given
  The promise of a blessed land,—
Heir to the choicest gifts of Heaven,—
  Be slain by a fond father's hand?

"This son for whom my eldest-born
  Was sent an outcast from his home,
And in some wilderness forlorn,
  A savage exile, doomed to roam.

"But shall a feeble worm rebel,
  And murmur at a Father's rod;
Shall he be backward to fulfil
  The known and certain will of God?

Arise, my son, the cruet fill,
  And store the scrip with due supplies,
For we must seek Moriah's hill,
  And offer there a sacrifice."

The mother raised a speaking eye,
  For all a mother's soul was there;
She feared the desert drear and dry,
  She feared the savage lurking there.

the minds of adults and venerable men. It is not to be supposed that he uttered remarkable things in doctrine, or

Abram beheld and made reply, —
  "On Him from whom our blessings flow,
My sister, we by faith rely;
  'Tis God's command, and we must go."

The duteous son in haste obeyed,
  The scrip was filled, the mules prepared;
And with the third day's twilight shade
  Moriah's lofty hill appeared.

The menials then at distance wait, —
  Alone ascend the son and sire;
The wood on Isaac's shoulder's laid,
  The wood to build his funeral pyre.

No passions sway the father's mind, —
  He felt a calm, a death-like chill;
His soul was meek and all resigned,
  Bowed quickly, though he shuddered still.

While on the mountain's brow they stood,
  With smiling wonder Isaac cries:
"My father! lo, the fire and wood,
  But where's the lamb for sacrifice?"

The Holy Spirit stayed his mind,
  While Abram answered, low and calm,
With steady voice and look resigned,
  "God will provide Himself the lamb."

But, lo! the father bound his son,
  And laid him on the funeral pile,
And then stretched forth his trembling hand,
  And took the knife to slay his child.

While Abram raised the blade full high,
  To execute his Lord's command,
An angel's voice, as from the sky,
  Cried, "Abram, spare thine only son."

But let no pen profane like mine
  On holiest things too rashly dare, —
Turn to that Book of Books divine,
  And read the precious promise there!

in experience. A simpler conclusion would be more in keeping with the facts. The exceeding youthfulness of the speaker, the rarely paralleled boldness of his position, the fluency of his language, the nature of his themes, and, superadded to these things, the tumultuousness of emotion which seizes upon the multitude in times of powerful religious influence, make up a very probable explanation of the effect produced by the ardent and persuasive harangues of the zealous child upon a primitive and simple-minded people.

It is hardly to be questioned that the interior force, behind these efforts, was strong and real. It is in striking evidence of the justice of this conclusion, that the religious life of the boy, thus commenced in fervor of demonstration, progressed with the steady force of principle, and finally matured into a symmetrical, controlling, and productive Christian character, of sadly infrequent manifestation in these days.

Beyond a doubt, to the Christian men and women who were moved to tears and praises by his words, if not to the heedless ones who heard him, but regarded him only as a boyish phenomenon, his labors in those district and village school-houses seemed to verify the language of the Psalmist, " Out of the mouth of babes and sucklings hast Thou ordained strength."

These recollections of his childhood were always a source of pleasure to him ; and he dwelt with interest upon the

> Ages on ages rolled away;
>   At length the time appointed came,
> And on the mountain Calvary
>   God did Himself provide the Lamb!"

3*

simplicity of the Christian people of the period and of the locality to which they refer.

There were not wanting, moreover, amusing and ludicrous incidents in connection with the school-house scenes and services, which appealed irresistibly to his acute sense of the humorous.

On one occasion there existed a neighborhood misunderstanding, and the difficulty was not forgotten in the place of worship. Indeed, it may have been purposely brought into it. At all events, one of the aggrieved parties, and a prominent leader in the circles of prayer, thus emphatically expressed himself in an address to the throne of grace: " Thou knowest, O Lord, that ——— is a great liar."

In far later years, one of his children, hearing this incident narrated, said to him: " Can this be true, father?"

" True?" said he; " I heard it myself!" and then proceeded to give the names of the parties to the quarrel.

It must have been soon, if not immediately after this period of religious excitement, that George left his father's house, to live with a Quaker by the name of John Allen, that he might learn from him the hatter's trade. In this service he spent three years, and always cherished for " the excellent Quaker," as he calls him, a sincere feeling of respect.

Although the lad must have made such proficiency in his art as would have enabled him to pursue it on his own account, he never resumed it after leaving his Quaker master. That he did not hold his trade in contempt, is clear from the fact that he always prided himself rather upon his knowledge of it.

It is related of him, that when he was holding the highest office his native State could confer upon him, being on one occasion in a brilliant company, a lady said to him, "May I ask, Governor, at what college you graduated?"

With great gravity and courtesy of manner, he instantly replied, "At a hatter's shop, madam."

Beyond that period of his youth passed with John Allen, he himself gives us a brief glance in advance : —

"Then, in an irregular manner, I attended for a year a respectable grammar school, my studies being very much interrupted by other indispensable occupations."

During this year he lived again with his father, "doing chores," as he phrases it, "for a family of ten or twelve, going to school as I could catch it." In these words we have the key to what he says about the interruption of his studies by "indispensable occupations."

The energy and resoluteness which carried him at all available intervals of his toil to the school-house, doubtless gave to his studies, however interrupted and fragmentary, a measure of success, which does not always crown unintermitted and protracted opportunites for acquiring knowledge. The boy was in earnest in the hatter's shop and at the academy-desk alike ; and his spirit, while at the latter for only a few brief months, doubtless compensated, in great part, for much bodily and unwelcome absence from it.

Akin to the incident just narrated, and illustrating the absence in his character of all foolish pride about his early life and experiences, is another, which also occurred in 1846, when he was Governor of Massachusetts.

He was one day in Methuen, and visited the large hat manufactory of Mr. Ingalls. When in the vat room, he saw the old familiar processes of the trade going forward —

COLLEGE FROM WHICH HE GRADUATED.

the workmen surrounding the vat, their sleeves rolled up to the shoulder, and going through the usual manipulations. He stood looking on with eager interest, and after leaving the shop told those with him, that, but for the apparent affectation of the thing, he should have taken off his coat, rolled up his sleeves, and joined in the work, adding, as he said this with a genial smile upon his fine features, " I believe I could make a good hat now, in the old way. I always liked to do it. It was comfortable work."

The love which the young disciple bore to the little church in White Creek was not extinguished by his early separation from its services and fellowship. A whole generation of men passed away in the interval which elapsed between the time of his departure from White Creek and his earliest subsequent communication with the church there. After he settled in Pittsfield, he applied to his early Christian associates for a letter of dismission, and the epistle he addressed to them breathes an affection so tender, and displays so strikingly the loving spirit of the mature Christian, whose boyhood we have been tracing, that it cannot but be deemed an appropriate close to this chapter of White Creek reminiscences. It will be noticed that its date is thirty-one years later than the times just reviewed. It is addressed to the church through its pastor, Rev. D. Tinkham : —

PITTSFIELD, March 28th, 1844.

MY DEAR FRIEND :

I suppose you are yet the pastor of the church at White Creek. Far back in the records of that church, I think in the year 1810 or '11, will be found the name that is at the bottom of this letter. Never having transferred my relation from that body, I should be glad, even at this late day, if consistent with their views, to have a letter from them.

4

As a period of time greater than that allotted to a generation of men has passed away since in my boyhood I became a humble member of a band of believers, I conclude that most of the beloved ones who were then its members have gone to their rest. The names of Parker, Curtis, Smith, Center, Fowler, and Shed, are fresh in my memory as in the morning of youth. They were to me fathers in Israel. Their venerable forms and hoary heads are, I suppose, all laid low in the peaceful grave. Their spirits, I doubt not, are with Him who once wore a crown of thorns, but who is now the light and glory of the New Jerusalem, and the joy of the saints in heaven. Into the service of that Prince of Peace who has taken them home, I enlisted at the age of fourteen years. He is the best Prince and Master that was ever served. Truth compels me to say that I have been a poor soldier; yet I hope I may say, with equal truth, that while I have lacked zeal, I have never denied my allegiance, even in the enemy's country; nor have I ever, for a single moment, regretted that I so early entered so glorious a service.

Since I left White Creek in 1813, I have never met with the church. My thoughts have often, very often, in the midst of the varied scenes in which I have been placed, gone out toward them with a warmth and an affection that belonged not to earth. I have frequently sighed to visit and hold communion with those friends who remained of the number with whom I united my destiny, and to mingle my sympathy with those who have joined them since. Whether, in the Providence of God, I shall ever have this happiness on earth, I know not. But whether I do or not, I wish them the richest blessings of the Great Head of the Church, and pray that He who keepeth Israel, and who neither slumbers nor sleeps, may be with them and have them in His care. Though personally a stranger to nearly every one of the present members, they are a continuation of the church of which I was a member in the morning of my days, and which had my first love. As brethren of the church they have my warmest Christian affection; and they, I trust, will continue to have it till the pulsation of my heart shall be stopped by death.

With highest regards to yourself and family and to the church,

I am your brother and friend,

GEO. N. BRIGGS.

CHAPTER III.

THE boy of our narrative has now reached the bor- ders of young manhood, at the threshold of his eighteenth year, as he commences, in remarkable circumstances, the study of law.

In the same letter in which he speaks of his departure from the shop of the excellent Quaker, and of his brief school life, there is found also this passage, which dis- closes the undaunted courage and noble independence of the young hero : —

"In August, 1813, with five dollars I had earned at haying, I left home to go to studying law or medicine. I had a brother living on the Hudson whom I visited in September, and then, with my trunk on my back,[1] came into Berkshire County, penniless, and a stranger to all, except a few relatives and friends, most of them as poor as I was, and that was poor enough. My brother aided me some until 1816, when he died."

The brother to whom he here alludes was Rufus, the eld- est of the family. He was the confidential business agent

---

[1] This little trunk he carefully preserved, and only a few days before his death repaired it with his own hands, and affixed to it a card, giving its history, up to the time he began to study law. (See page 41).

of Chancellor Livingston, whose sincere respect and cordial
friendship he enjoyed. He was a man of spotless integrity, of great executive talent, and of a just and generous
nature. With only limited means, and a considerable
family, he was not able to offer his younger brother lavish
help, which, indeed, he would not have accepted, and, happily, did not need. His wants were easily supplied, and
the kindness which answered their calls was abundantly
repaid in kind.

Only three years was George the beneficiary of his elder
brother, when the death of the latter threw him entirely
upon his own resources. They proved adequate to his
needs, and, beyond providing for himself, he became the
sympathizing helper and friend of the widow and fatherless
children his brother left behind him. When his brother's
estate was settled, its value was so depreciated that the
family were impoverished. The mother died soon after,
leaving four sons, and one of them a hopeless invalid, as a
sort of special trust to their young uncle. After he married, his house was more or less the home of these orphans.
Two of them were with him seven years, and both of them
have since achieved an honorable career. The other two
found early graves.

As Rufus Briggs was the chief patron of the young
aspirant in his professional adventure, some of the letters
which passed between them at this time will find a fit place
in these pages.

The following letter was written soon after George's
visit to his brother : —

ADAMS, Oct. 15th, 1813.

RESPECTED BROTHER:

I arrived at Adams the day after I left you. Being anxious to
commence my studies, and preferring law to physic, I thought it

In Sept. 1813 I brought this trunk
on my back into the town of Adams
Mass. It contained my, entire wuldy Estate;
all of which was not worth ten Dollars
($10) I was in my eighteenth year & fell
rich in hope & prospects. Gods mercy have
been great to me ever since Augt 1861
Geo. N. Briggs

(See page 39.)

best, with the advice of Jesse Whipple, to converse with Esquire Kasson on the subject, who informed me that the law, in this State, requires four years' study without a classical education, and three years with; and finding his terms to be very reasonable, and Jesse recommending him to be an honorable man, and a man of talents, I have concluded, and I hope not prematurely, to enter his office on these conditions. As he had no personal acquaintance with me, he had rather not positively determine any further than this: that for tuition, use of his library, candles, and firewood, he should charge not more than forty dollars, and not less than thirty, and he thought not much over thirty; whereas the customary expense in this State is sixty-two dollars per annum. . . . . .

With respect, I am yours, &c.,

G. N. BRIGGS.

Mr. R. BRIGGS.

A month seems to have exhausted the first bounty George received from his brother, and with much delicacy he ventures to ask for a little more : —

ADAMS, Nov. 18th, 1813.

DEAR BROTHER:

Having been disappointed in your not being here ere now, I hasten to drop you a line by mail. I have heard nothing from White Creek since my arrival at Adams. By paying pretty dear for some part of my passage from Hudson, and being under the necessity of procuring some few necessaries pertaining to my study, and some few articles of clothing, of which old Boreas taught me I stood in need, I have expended what money you gave me. Necessity requires some other things, both for clothing and office. A little more cash would be gratefully received, if convenient, without incommoding you. Thanks are the only return I am at present capable of making; but hope, the anchor of the mind, reaches to the time when I shall be enabled to refund the *money*, though not the favors of so kind a brother and so generous a friend. A trifle will answer my purpose for the present. If convenient to favor me, be so good as to send it immediately.

> With respect, I remain
>> Your brother and friend,
>>> G. N. BRIGGS.

Mr. R. BRIGGS, Saugerties, N. Y.

The following letter is from a brother-in-law who resided in Adams, and, while supplying a link in the chain of the arrangements made for the inauguration of the young aspirant in a law office, bears testimony to his economy, manliness, assiduity, and amiability : —

ADAMS, Jan. 18, 1814.

DEAR BROTHER RUFUS:

I received your letter requesting me to board George, and to furnish him with necessary clothing and some pocket money. He is boarding with me. His calls on me for clothing and cash are as yet so small, that they seem scarcely worth mentioning. George is uncommonly steady, and attends to his studies very closely. He has gained the esteem of both old and young in the village. Mr. Kasson informs me that he progresses rapidly in his studies, and thinks he bids fair to make an eminent lawyer. Mr. Kasson is considered, by men more competent to judge of talents than myself, to be a man of ability.

You have the best wishes of your brother and sister for the welfare of your wife and family.

>>> JESSE WHIPPLE.

Mr. RUFUS BRIGGS.

In the next letter the elder brother speaks for himself; and the tone of his utterance is the ring of good metal. His kindness of heart, his sagacity, his sound judgment, his far-sightedness, are all tokens of a wise and good character. He evidently appreciates the nature of law learning, when he suggests to his young brother a period of twenty years' study as the conditions of " fame and fortune " : —

SAUGERTIES MILL, 24th Nov., 1813.

DEAR BROTHER:

I have this moment received your last letter. You will please call on Jesse for what money you may want before I see you, which will be at the first good sleighing; and I will repay him then. You must pay every attention to your studies; indeed, I have no doubt in my mind that you will. In order to insure to yourself fame and fortune, you must study hard for at least twenty years, and digest well what you read, and must know the why and the wherefore. My Lords Coke and Littleton must be your particular and intimate friends. You must read and well digest all the Reports, and study well the practice, not only of law, but of justice. And now I charge you, never to undertake what you believe to be an *unjust* cause for money; but at all times be ready to assist, with all the powers the God of nature has given you, the poor man in a just cause, for the love of justice, and to acquire for yourself immortality and fame.

Your dear brother,

R. BRIGGS.

Mr. G. N. BRIGGS.

Of the young student's life at Adams, only here and there a reminiscence is to be gleaned from letters written at that period, or from allusions to it contained in some brief autobiographical notes made at the wish of his children and friends. It was a brief period, not much exceeding a year, for in 1814 he removed to Lanesboro', another village of Berkshire, not less picturesque in its surroundings than Adams, and becoming to him in later years the centre of many happy memories and fond associations.

There he pursued his law studies in the office of Luther Washburn, Esq., which he afterwards said was "the rendezvous of the village, where its discussion and news-gossip and excitements were all carried on."

It would seem that this must have been a most unfavor-

able place for the young student, whose mind, as yet
undisciplined by habits of close application, would be
almost inevitably distracted, and effectually hindered from
study, by the hubbub around him.   It is remarkable in his
mental characteristics, that he was able almost at once to
conquer these disadvantages, and to fix his attention upon
his reading with a closeness that isolated him from the
groups in the office as entirely as if he had been in another
room.   He says of himself that he " never engaged in conversation, or even *heard* it, unless personally addressed,"
and adds, " I have read hundreds of pages entirely unconscious of the brisk conversation carried on in my hearing."

This almost spontaneous faculty of abstraction, and
equally the power of mental concentration, were in part
the product of his simple earnestness of purpose.   He was
at work with a will ; and from the beginning to the completion of the preparatory labor of his profession, he was a
close, hard student.

His letters, during his student-life in Lanesboro', were
addressed, chiefly, perhaps, to his brother Rufus, until his
death in 1816, and then he transferred his correspondence
to his widowed sister-in-law, and became her adviser, her
sympathizing and faithful and affectionate friend.

Some of his letters to his brother would afford interesting paragraphs for these pages, as unfolding the spirit and
temper and modest self-confidence of the youth, while yet
acknowledging his constant dependence upon his brother's
generosity.   On one occasion he writes thus : —

    " DEAR BROTHER :

    " You have the most sincere effusions of my grateful heart for
your earnest solicitude for my well being and prosperity, and
especially for my progress in legal pursuits. . . . . . I am fully

convinced that without unremitted application to books, there can be no proficiency made in study, and that without a sincere attachment tó virtue, no man can be happy. So beneficent has the Creator been to his creatures, that the instance is rarely to be found, perhaps, of a man not possessed of an ability for improvement, and even proficiency, in any science to which he will give his *attention.* . . . . . Perfection is what I have no idea of attaining while shackled with human nature; but consistency is that after which I am resolved to reach. Candor shall be my bosom companion; justice shall be my guide; and nobly to *fill* the sphere in which I move shall be the great end and aim of my labor."

These just and lofty sentiments were no mere rhetorical utterances. They were the reflections of his soul, of his conscience. The germ of a grandly useful life was springing up with a beautiful vigor, unchecked by the circumstances, unchilled by the atmosphere around him, although these were of a far less encouraging sort than most young men would have pined for.

He did, indeed, find sympathy and congenial associations in his Lanesboro' life. He boarded much, perhaps most of the time, in the family of a truly excellent physician, Dr. W. H. Tyler, whose subsequent personal and professional relations to him and his family were intimate and most felicitous.

In one of his letters to his brother Rufus, his ignorance of Latin is the theme of a touching plaint, and of a no less touching plea, that he should be approved in his desire and plan for obtaining a knowledge of it. He says, —

"I find my situation similar to that of a man ignorant of the art of reading, who should attempt to travel through a strange region by the direction of guide-boards. He would have no difficulty in finding the boards. He would clearly see the index and inscription; but, unable to *read*, he would not be in the least benefited by his silent guides. The ancient law books abound with Latin, and to these the modern authors refer; our maxims are wholly in that language. I feel very deeply my need of some knowledge of it."

In a later letter to his brother, this Latin question is thus satisfactorily disposed of: —

" As it seems to be your opinion, that if I study Latin, I had better get into some priest's family, and as I could find no suitable one, I had concluded, considering the additional expense it would make, and the deduction of time from my law studies, I would renounce the idea. But, as we have a very good school here, and Mr. Washburn says, on reflection, it is optional with the judges, whether to admit or reject the time,[1] and he thinks, under the circumstances, they will allow to me the time I devote to Latin. I shall therefore commence immediately."

The satisfaction of the rightly ambitious youth in this termination of his doubts, will be shared by the reader of these reminiscences.

In the same letter which dismisses the Latin problem, the writer appears, also, in the important department of finance. He writes, —

" The doctor says he is not anxious for the avails of my board until fall; but I think, if convenient for you, the amount might be paid before it rises to any considerable sum. If you have a little *loose cash*, it would be welcome to me at the present time to receive a few dollars, as I shall need a new book or two. What you gave me when I was at S., has found holes in my pocket, and has gone the way of all — money. Some for cravats, some for pocket-handkerchiefs, some for books, some for maps, some for sandals, some for a *head-cover*, some for travelling fees, and some,

---

[1] That is, whether to count time given to Latin as a part of the necessary time given to law study, or otherwise.

when the cold, wan hand of want has asked for a pittance, has freely dropped into it. And, further, as it is *my* province to ask, I am fast approaching a shirtless condition. I wish you would write soon, and tell me how I am to replenish. Conscience says, ' Stop now.' Be patient, my dear brother."

In this catalogue of expenditures there is nothing superfluous. We smile at its frugality, and rejoice at the beautiful gleam of charity which irradiates the cloud of poverty lying behind the picture. In later days that gleam brightened into a steady glow — a perpetual radiance, in the light and warmth and tenderness of which many heavy hearts were made buoyant, many tears were transmuted into smiles, many sighs were translated into thanksgivings.

In 1816, his kind and faithful brother Rufus died, and the prop upon which he leaned for his narrow income was almost suddenly withdrawn from him. In this emergency, he found help in his own hands, and earned some means by copying wills, deeds, and other documents in the office where he studied, and which was also the office of the Registrar. During a brief part of the year he taught in one of the town district schools, and filled his temporary office as pedagogue with credit.

Early in 1817, a remarkable work of Divine grace manifested itself in Lanesboro'. The place had not been thus specially visited since its settlement, although during all the time there had been a minister settled there. The people were moral, but irreligious. For some months religious conference meetings had been held, by a few professing Christians, without exciting any special interest. In March, it was evident that an increased solemnity existed in the congregations, which became large and crowded.

5

Many were convicted of sin, and numerous hopeful con-
versions gladdened the hearts of God's people.

At this time there was, as there had always been, only
one minister in the village. This was Rev. Mr. Collins,
whose long control of the spiritual interests and of the
theological opinions of the place had made him somewhat
dogmatic, perhaps, in his manner, and certainly did not
incline him to be tolerant of the Baptists, " a sect everywhere spoken against " in that region. So dominant was
he in the religious matters of the borough that few, if any,
ever ventured to dispute with him. He was not, it may
be reasonably supposed, inclined to look at first with favor
upon the little band of baptized believers, whose practice
was a silent denial of *his*.

It happened upon one occasion that a conversation took
place in the law office, in which Mr. Collins betrayed a
serious misapprehension of the faith and tenets of the
Baptists. · With great simplicity and modesty of manner,
the student answered him, and made a clear statement
of Baptist views. A prolonged discussion followed, in
which the young man did not forget for a moment the
respect due to the character and position of his opponent,
but at the same time abated nothing of his characteristic
sincerity and zeal, as he defended the church he loved.

To the great credit of his Christian temper, Mr. Collins, after his first surprise and vexation were past, treated
the young disputant as his friend, and, ever afterwards,
they co-operated with cordiality and mutual regard in all
good words and works. Whatever reproach upon the Baptist name lingered in the hearts of men, it never grieved
the ear of their staunch young advocate while yet he lived
in Lanesboro'.

These facts are gleaned from a long letter, written to his young sister, in which he appeals earnestly to her own conscience.

In September of the same year he writes to her in grateful response to the tidings which had reached him, of her conversion and baptism. His letter is full of affectionate and judicious counsel, given with much frankness, but with equal modesty.

"We," he says, "who take upon us the name of Christians, profess to renounce the vanities of the world. The delusive paths of youth are to be avoided, and we should live and act as though we were living for heaven. On this point it ill becomes me to admonish you, for my way since I loved the Saviour has been a dark and devious one. Yet I continue to *hope in Him*."

In this revival the young law-student labored with all the gentle enthusiasm of his nature, under the influence and restraint of grace. His appeals and exhortations were always fervent, and frequently of visible effect. He was at this period the warm friend and loving co-laborer of a young Baptist preacher — the Rev. Augustus Beech — who was settled in the village as a teacher. This friendship was perpetuated into the mature life of the young men.

Among the blessed results of the revival referred to, was the formation of a Baptist church in Lanesboro', in the year 1817. Only twelve members were gathered into its communion at the time of its constitution, and of these twelve one was a gay young girl, who subsequently became the loving wife of George's youth, and who is now the honored widow of the good man gone to his rich reward, and the beloved mother of reverent children.

CHAPTER IV.

COMMONPLACE-TRUTHS VIVIFIED—A STRIKING CAREER—INFLUENCE OF EARLY FRIENDS—HENRY SHAW—LETTER TO MRS. SHAW—DEATH OF HIS MOTHER—LETTERS FROM MR. SHAW.

COLERIDGE somewhere says, "To restore a commonplace-truth to its first uncommon lustre, you need only translate it into action." There may never have been any "uncommon lustre" in such an immemorial truth as that of the homely English adage, "Where there's a will, there's a way." But the logic of the philosopher applies to it, nevertheless. We discover very little force in the hackneyed and worn-out phrase. It has lost its primal sharpness, and lies, in our memory, a dead letter. But let it be once and again translated into action, and the dull truth instantly glows with meaning, not perhaps new, but newly burnished, attractive, and impressive. The proverb in speech, and its truth interpreted by deed, appear quite different' things, however really the same.

The youth, who rose from the drudgery of the hatter's shop to the dignity of the magisterial bench; who advanced resolutely, step by step, from a precarious pupilage in a village law office to the power of the judicial ermine; who climbed out of the obscurity of humble birth and burdensome poverty to the shining eminence of the national council halls; who translated a childhood almost unprivileged from the meagreness of its opportunities, into a manhood of broad and beneficent influence ; — the youth who accomplished such results as these, thus translating his resolute will into steps and progress and attainments and achievements that compel our admiration, has undoubtedly glorified with an " uncommon lustre" a commonplace-truth. And not one such truth only, but yet another, less homely in its expression because it is embellished with the drapery of the poet, —

> " Honor and shame from no condition rise ;
> Act well your part, — there all the honor lies."

The career and character of George Nixon Briggs give to such precepts as these the force and fervor of principles, of potency enough to inspire mighty purposes and lofty aims in souls struggling beneath a mountain-load of discouragements and disasters.

There is really nothing extraordinary in his case, except his singleness and steadiness of purpose. His abilities were not exceptional, nor was his application excessive. In respect to the former, he has thousands of peers amid the rising generation of this day, and in the latter virtue, it would not be difficult for any one of them all to match the noble example he has set. His is no impossible excellence ; his whole career no phenomenon to be wondered at, but rather to be nobly and broadly emulated.

In estimating the forces which combined to shape his character, the friendships he enjoyed are of no secondary value. His life in Lanesboro' was strongly influenced by others, with whom he was closely bound in mutual regard.

Of these, two have been incidentally named — the worthy physician whose house was his home, and the young Baptist preacher, with whom he was leagued in a warm Chris-

5*

tian affection, and in labors that made them both unselfish
in the exact ratio of their earnestness and measure.

There was yet another friendship vouchsafed to him in
those early days, the strongest of them all in its force,
and, unquestionably, that which most powerfully influenced
his mind and affected his after life. It was the friendship
of Henry Shaw, a man remarkable even among remarkable
men. He was a gentleman of wealth and commanding
social position in Lanesboro', but was far less indebted to
these conditions than to his intellectual pre-eminence for
the power he exercised in the community, and to which,
especially, the young student of law rendered enthusiastic
homage.

The disparity of their ages, and indeed of all their personal surroundings, made the beginning of their intercourse
an affair of generous courtesy on the part of the elder.
He sought the young man in his office, and won his regard
most effectually by counsel, which was as judicious in the
way it was given as it was excellent in itself. To advice,
made sweet by sympathy, he added the offer of help in
obtaining a library for the embryo barrister.

When he had secured the esteem and confidence of the
youth, Mr. Shaw so kindly and wisely veiled the disparity
of their circumstances from him, that the friendship became
rather that of equality than of patronage. Its mutual
force grew fast, and ripened into a degree of strength, and
even tenderness, which makes it one of the most luminous
points in the life here contemplated.

To pass it by with a mere allusion would be an injustice
done rather to the subject of this biography than to Henry
Shaw, whose name was early inscribed upon the heart of
his friend, and remained legible till the tablet crumbled

into dust. The actual records of their friendship are only fragmentary — the remains of active and long-continued correspondence ; but such vivid recollections of it linger in the hearts of those to whom this Memoir is to supply the place of husband and father, that it would seem to them defective without clear reflections of him who was faithful to that husband and father in affection and service, in word and in deed.

Twenty-six years after this beautiful friendship germinated in the little law office in Lanesboro', and when the young devotee of Blackstone was in the political metropolis of the land, no longer a law-student, · nor even a law-expounder, but a law-maker for the nation, he wrote to the wife of his early and constant friend, what he had been all along desiring, but hesitating to say to his friend himself. There is no fitter place for this tribute than here, just in advance of the letters which well reflect the man to whom it is so delicately paid.. It was written during his sixth and last term in Congress : —

WASHINGTON, Jan. 3d, 1843.

DEAR MADAM :

I have your kind letter of Dec. 25th, and am glad to know you prize the little picture of Mr. Adams, with his autograph, which I sent you last summer. A double motive induced me to send it. I thought you would be pleased with what I considered a good likeness; and, then, I intended it as a memento of regard to one whom I have been happy to consider my friend from the days when I was a poor and stranger-youth, in the old "Boro'," up to this time.

Twenty-six years ago, you kindly presented to me two volumes of Mr. Adams's lectures on rhetoric. Then I did not dream I should ever have the opportunity of sending you his likeness, or any other acknowledgment from this city. That token of your

good wishes, which was esteemed by me on account of the feelings which dictated it, more highly than rubies, though it has not
been talked about, was recorded on the tablet of a grateful heart,
and it will be remembered till that heart shall cease to beat.
None but a young man, struggling against the billows of embarrassment and poverty, could know how to estimate such an
expression of friendship. It is the time, circumstances, and manner, which make its value. Nor was it from you, alone, that I early
heard the voice of encouragement and hope. For more than a
quarter of a century your husband has been my friend. He was
the first person who suggested to me that I should ever be where
I am now. I am sure, I then deemed it among the most improbable of all events. Here, my dear madam, I hope you will not
think it improper for me to say to you what I have often said to
others, though not to your husband, — that he has shown me more
acts of friendship *than any other man.* Not to acknowledge such
favors, would be unjust to their author; not to feel them, would
make their recipient an ingrate. I have often wished to say this
to him. But the apprehension that he might look upon it as affectation, or mere profession (which I know he detests), has deterred
me from it.

In an hour of gloom, when on a bed of sickness, I told my little
family, if I went down to the grave, to remember that their husband and father, through every vicissitude of his life from youth
till that time, had at least *one true, one fast friend,* and that friend
was Henry Shaw. The pleasing, grateful recollection of that fact
will go with me to the tomb. The *fact* cannot be changed. I am
glad of this fitting opportunity to speak of it to you; and I speak
of it more freely because I feel there is no motive but a right one
that prompts me to do it. In leaving Lanesboro', where the most
interesting portion of my life has been spent, these, with a thousand
other affecting emotions, rushed upon my mind. I wished for
some proper occasion to express them to you and to Mr. Shaw,
but it did not offer itself. Perhaps the long-existing intimate
relations between us made it my duty to have done so. It was
not from disinclination, but for want of opportunity, that it was
not done. The people of that town have treated me as a brother.

If any breast there harbors feelings of enmity towards me, such a feeling finds no response in my bosom. God bless the good old Boro,' with all and every one of her children. They have dealt kindly and truly with me. Her rich valleys and verdant hills will long be cherished objects of my memory. I love her beautiful scenery, and dwell, with delight, upon the recollection of the enchanting prospects from her mountain-tops. Her quiet and marbled graveyards are dear to me. There repose the aged ones I venerated, the middle-aged I respected, the youth I admired, and the little ones I loved. There they will sleep till the resurrection morning.

With the best wishes for the happiness of yourself and family, and with great esteem,

I am your friend,

GEORGE N. BRIGGS.

Only a few years elapsed, after George left his father's home, before his mother sunk rapidly under the burdens of life, and died — died before the happy anticipations in her fond heart, of her boy's success in life, had received more than the first gleams of fulfilment. On the occasion of her death, Mr. Shaw, then in Washington, from which place he so often afterwards addressed his friend, wrote thus to him at Lanesboro' : —

CAPITOL HILL, Jan. 18, 1818.

DEAR GEORGE:

Laura informed me only yesterday of your irreparable loss, in the death of your mother. I do most sincerely mingle my tears with yours; but though to me a loss like yours would be the greatest of afflictions, to you it must be otherwise, for you are sustained by the consolations of that religion which gives hope and peace. The mind that has some stay to rest upon, permanent and indestructible, looks with comparative unconcern upon the waywardness of fortune and the ravages of death. This is your happiness. I am every night a believer; and every morning make haste to sin. Be consoled by the reflection that the change in your mother's condition is probably to her advantage; and suffer your grief to be lessened by your friend's participation.

Yours, faithfully,

HENRY.

Probably the intimation to which there is allusion in the letter to Mrs. Shaw had not, at this time, been made to the young student, or if it had, the dream of becoming a member of Congress, and of mingling in the scenes and with the personages described in his friend's letters, had hardly possessed his imagination. Yet such a description as the following, of Clay's impassioned eloquence, must have stirred his soul : —

CAPITOL, Jan. 21, 1818.

DEAR GEORGE :

We are in the midst of the debate on the Seminole war. H—— has made a speech that I presume will be read with applause, but you can scarcely imagine how disgusting his manner is. He was barely tolerated. Clay, yesterday, opened the *flood-gates* of the most powerful and captivating eloquence. His manner is without parallel. The whole house was held, for two hours, with breathless interest. The tears fell not alone from the eye of beauty, but chased each other down the cheeks of many a hard-faced veteran. Yet I presume, after all, the former[1] will read the best. So much is manner to be regarded in an orator. Study to make yourself master of this art. Language is something, but manner is everything. I will send you the debate. Let me have letters from you, often and long. Remember me to all my friends.

Yours, with sincerity,

H. SHAW.

The admirable sketch in the subjoined letter, of one of the ablest members Virginia had ever sent to the House of Representatives, is a good example, perhaps, of Mr. Shaw's

---

[1] H——'s speech, just before referred to.

fine power both of discrimination and description. In harmony ·with his estimate of Judge Barbour's intellectual force, is that of his illustrious friend and associate, Judge Story, who said of him that " he was not only equal to all the functions of his high station, but above them — *par negotiis et supra.*"

WASHINGTON, Jan. 24, 1818.

DEAR GEORGE:

. . . . . I told you something about Henry Clay. He is not however, in my judgment, the ablest man in the House. Philip P. Barbour, of Virginia,[1] is about the average height, very spare in person, has a keen, penetrating eye, and a sort of *violence* in his whole countenance, which, while it indicates strong passions, warns you that his head is the habitation of genius. In debate he is all on fire, and lights up in his hearers a corresponding blaze. · His action is vehement, irregular, and of course ungraceful. His voice is shrill, and gives you pain rather than delight. His mind flashes upon a subject with the vivacity of lightning, and leaves it surrounded with the light of the noonday sun. He is, beyond comparison, the most logical reasoner in the House; and, perhaps, is not surpassed by any in the nation. His language is pure, figurative, and flows with the rapidity and fulness of a mountain torrent.

Add to this, that all the members respect him, and consider him an *honest man*, and a sound constitutional politician. He is very plain in his appearance and manners, without ostentation. Considering his age, which is only thirty-five years, and the power of his intellect, I should not be surprised to see him, at no distant day, filling some distinguished station in the country's service. . . . .

Yours, ever,

H. SHAW.

The next letter was written after he had given his vote

---

[1] Appointed by President Jackson, in 1829, Judge of the Circuit Court for the United States for the Eastern District of Virginia.

in the House for the admission of Missouri with her slave constitution, — a vote which gave general dissatisfaction to his constituents, and involved him in no little censure both public and private.   Unwelcome as this course was to his young friend, the latter was persistent in the opinion, and no less in the expression of it, that it was the result of Mr. Shaw's inflexible convictions of duty.   He said frequently to Mr. Shaw's political opponents: " Shaw was honest in that vote. •He knew it might ruin him politically ; but he did it nevertheless, because he thought it was right."   It is not improbable that this letter compelled this positive testimony ; though it could scarcely have been needed to convince the young student of the conscientiousness of his admired friend in his course, in an act and upon an occasion of such magnitude.   Because he would have desired, if living, to give Mr. Shaw's memory everywhere all the vindication for his vote which conscientious convictions in casting it could carry with them, this letter is here associated with his commemoration in these Memoirs.

CAPITOL, Dec. 24, 1819.

DEAR GEORGE:

. I have this moment received your letter. It breathes the spirit of friendship. You ought to be my friend; not because I have contributed to advance your interest, but because from principle, alone, I have wished to do it. In my nature there is no disguise. The world will always see the worst side of me, because it is the *outside*.

I have written to you once, and have said but little on a subject that lies with weight on my mind. I refrain from saying much to any of my friends on the *Missouri Question*, for fear, as my popularity rests in some degree upon it, I may be suspected of sinister views. ' Before God, I have on this question nothing but the good of my country, as I understand it, at heart.

" To you I may speak with assurance, but what I say, let it be in confidence. I will not condescend to defend my motives to any man when called upon at a time and on a question like the present, and, at the same time, I know those motives are and will be impeached. I am firmly persuaded that this question will, if persisted in, have two effects : the first will be to reinstate Federalism in power; the second, and most frightful one, will be the separation of the States. . . . . .

" *Power* is the real aim of the men who are agitating this question with so much zeal. I hope they will be defeated; but the excitement which prevails here is prodigious, and the Southern people have no pledge, if the question be settled against Missouri, except the *forbearance of party,* that all the slaves might not be *emancipated !* Most *unfortunate* are those who are honestly, and from principles of supposed humanity, leading the country into this unprofitable discussion; most criminal are those who are doing it from design. Now I leave it to its course. I am willing to be tried by it. I might hope that the judgment of the community might be stayed till after the discussion in Congress. There is too much at stake to be in haste."

Here follow some extracts only, from sundry letters of the frequent correspondence with which Mr. Shaw freshened and stimulated the mind of his young favorite, still hammering away at Coke and Littleton : —

" Randolph ! I must reserve him for description by word of mouth. He is, George, the most extraordinary man living; the most bewitching and correct speaker. He is in fine health, and seems not to have lost any of his genius, though I suspect his fire is a little mellowed.

. . . .

" Pinckney is making one of the most eloquent and argumentative speeches ever delivered in any deliberative body. He began on Friday, will continue on Monday, and probably finish on Tuesday. He is the most astonishing man, uniting almost all the qualities of greatness with the most contemptible vanity. He is at the same time the prince of eloquence and dandies, his ambition bal-

6

ancing itself between the desire of eclipsing the first orators of the
world, and surpassing in extravagance the greatest fop! Clay will
try to outdo him, and he has the advantage in voice and manner."

Of much later date than the letters quoted, is that from
which the following extracts are made. In 1828, when Mr.
Shaw was in the State Legislature, he, without any knowl-
edge on the part of his young friend, urged his name upon
Governor Lincoln in connection with the office of District
Attorney. In allusion to this, he writes from Boston : —

DEAR GEORGE :

I have taken the liberty of presenting your name to his Excellency for the post of District Attorney. I have no hopes of success, but thought it would do you no *harm* to have your name
offered for consideration. I presented it in a *proud* manner, and
placed it entirely on the ground that the public good would be for-
warded by the appointment. I did not beg as a favor that which I
told his Excellency would reflect credit on his administration.

We have been three days on the Salem Theatre bill. It is a
contest between the moral and religious part, and the liberal and
spirit-of-the-stage folks. I am of course found here, where I am at
home, on the side of piety and good morals, and *we* shall beat them.
Be diligent, be popular, and hereafter thou shalt come to *great honor.*
I salute you all.

H. SHAW.

Further glimpses of the intercourse of these devoted
friends will appear as the biography proceeds. Mr. Shaw
never remitted his earnest kindness to him whom he sought
when a stranger and almost friendless. When he was sick
and for a long time confined to his chamber, he was with
him daily, ministering to his needs, soothing him by acts
of loving sympathy, and cheering him by smiles and words,
making of his mere presence, indeed, sunshine and balm to
the sufferer.

CHAPTER V.

IN the autumn of 1818, the first eager ambition of the young and persistent student, and the playful vaticination of his mother, were realized together, in his admission to the bar. He was now a lawyer, and his career and success in this profession demand a chapter or two of these memoirs for their record. The mother — who so fondly and proudly called him, in his childhood, her "little lawyer"—was not living to rejoice in the consummation of his hopes: inspired, it may be, by her own familiar epithet.

But while her happy congratulations were lacking to celebrate the event of his accession to the bar, those of

"a nearer one
Yet, and a dearer one,"

made up in no small measure for their loss. A few months earlier he had been united in marriage with Harriet Hall, the only daughter of Ezra and Triphena Hall, of Lanesboro'. Beyond the qualifications of a fair and happy girlhood, vivacity of mind and manner, and an amiable temper, his young wife was in perfect sympathy with him in his earnest and demonstrative religious character. She was likely, therefore, to be a helpmeet to him in all his progress; and this, indeed, she proved to be, — surviving him to mourn, though submissively, a bereavement in which the sources and the chief ends of her own life-inspiration were at once exhausted.

That his marriage was a happy one, his whole domestic life bears witness. Through more than forty years it poured sunshine on his daily paths, which no shadows of misfortune or sorrow could obscure. The veil which hangs before the domestic shrine must not be rudely torn aside, though every glimpse we could obtain behind it, in the home of the lawyer, the statesman, the philanthropist, the judge, the parent, the Christian, whose life is the noble theme of our contemplation, would reveal only the beauty and harmony of wedded hearts. If the young lawyer delighted in his fair companion, when she was in the freshness of her bloom, that delight certainly knew no abatement in any after period, although its immediate sources must have undergone successive changes. She was his good genius, and by her ready resources, her vigilant care, her admirable tact and sound judgment, ever embellished his home and strengthened his heart.

The following tender expression of his sense of obligation to her was fitly made to one of his children, and is perhaps only not too sacred for public repetition : —

"Your mother loved me when I was poor and young, and to her true and constant affection, her watchful carefulness and economy, her wakeful and delicate smypathy, I owe all I have or am."

Her widowhood is hallowed into a serene beauty by her memories of his life. These sweeten its natural bitterness, brighten its unavoidable gloom, and throng its loneliness with visions of delight. More than this, they interpret themselves, by the power of a divine faith, into anticipations of renewed fellowship with him who is, to her expectant heart, —

"Not lost, but gone before."

Here let the veil, drawn aside hesitantly, drop to its place over the sacred wealth of wedded and domestic peace and bliss, of which glimpses only are so beautiful and affluent.

The two years immediately preceding the young law student's admission to the courts had been a period of struggles with poverty, — less severe, perhaps, than other conflicts with the same adversary which have yet been crowned with victory, — but sharp enough to be depressing to any but a resolute soul. He bore himself well in the battle, and achieved his end.

But the strife did not end with his first success in it. His early professional career was not a realization of bright dreams of plenty of cases, and fame and fortune coming in like a flood. The young lawyer had yet "to labor and to wait." His purse was slender, and seldom full at the best. His daughter recalls one of his playful reminiscences of those trying times, when he made, as he described it, " a pedestrian excursion over the hills, in order to borrow a horse, that I might ride ten miles to pay five dollars of borrowed money."

When he was admitted to the bar, he took his young wife to his native village, and there he opened an office. Here, the majestic beauty of Greylock[1] rose up continually

---

[1] The highest mountain in Berkshire, at the foot of which nestles the little town of South Adams.

6*

before him, inspiring his heart and mind alike with lofty ambitions. His deep admiration of that noble hill,. and, indeed, of all the beautiful and impressive scenery of Berkshire, found repeated expression in his conversation and in his correspondence. The loveliness of nature and the diviner beauty of grace wove each its spell about his heart, and his reverent spirit always made perfect harmony of their influences and teachings.

His poverty proved, at a very early period of his life, a bar to his public advancement. His native village received him with welcome and respect, upon his return to dwell there. His character, his intelligence, his probity, were all recognized, and as a tribute to them, his name was suggested in a village caucus held for the nomination of a Representative in the Legislature. By the single, but effective opposition of a political leader present, who based his objection to the nomination on the ground that "George owned no property," the young man missed an early seat in the council-chamber of the Commonwealth.

It was well for him that he did so. He aroused himself afresh to the work of his profession. His attention to it, his candor and ingenuousness and good nature, secured him friends. Business came to his hands — not in magnificent measures, but still enough to yield him a support, and to enabled him to furnish and keep a little green cottage, over which Greylock was the grand old warden.

The gentleness and peaceableness of his nature, moulded early, and always strongly controlled by his piety, seemed likely, in the beginning of his practice, to have an untoward influence upon his fortunes. He was not one who "stirreth up strife," but, on the contrary, he adopted for his motto the Apostolic precept: "As much as lieth in you, live peaceably with all men." What he practised he taught, and practice in this direction did not tend to increase his *practice* in another direction. It is currently reported of him, that he always received his clients with persuasions to them to avoid the law, telling them they had better settle the matter among themselves, and that the lawyers would make the most out of the case, and " skin " them.

If he could prevail upon any one, coming to him with a deep sense of his supposed injury, and eager for legal redress, to look at the other side of the case, and incline to a quiet adjustment of it, he always rejoiced in such a result, and even offered to persuade the lawyer, retained on the other side, to give up the case to private settlement.

This course did not seem the wisest to all, as it did to himself. His father-in-law, being on a visit to him, went much into his office, and, seeing one of these *illegal* settlements effected, proceeded to the house, and exclaimed, with considerable feeling, —

" Really, Harriet, I am sure George will never make a living by his profession. Why, he seeks to persuade every one to keep out of court."

The perverseness of human nature and the implacableness of many minds often defeated, however, the good-will and peace-making efforts of the Christian lawyer. He tried the causes he could not hinder from coming to the issue of the law, and these were numerous.

Experience did not make him more flexible in this respect. Through all his legal practice, he carried out the wise man's philosophy of " letting alone strife before it is meddled with," and probably he did not try half the cases he might have conducted before the bar, if he had taken all the fish that came to his net.

It is related of him that, in the last year of his life, his professional advice was sought by a very sensible and practical citizen, who thus approached him, —

"Governor, I am excessively perplexed in the settlement of an estate of which I am administrator. I am afraid I shall be greatly embarrassed by the technicalities of the law, and make great blunders."

"Look here, D.," returned the Governor, "in two minutes I can tell you how to be a good lawyer — as good a lawyer as anybody. Just look over your case carefully; *understand* it, and then *do* what you think is *right*, and, in nine cases out of ten, you will have the law on your side."

The broadest review, as well as the narrowest glimpse of his life as a lawyer, would constrain the acknowledgment from the observer that he won the beatitude of the peacemakers.

Allusion has been already made to his generous hospitality in his home. Besides his nephews, who were with him for years, the parents of his wife came, in their age and pecuniary misfortune, to the happy and ungrudged shelter of his abode. The mother-in-law was, much of the time, a confirmed invalid, but never felt the want of unwearied care and kindness. After a second marriage she was again widowed, and was entitled to a portion of her husband's estate, which would have afforded her a handsome income. But as her union with her second husband was short, and formed late in life, she was persuaded by her son-in-law, on whom, without the property, she must be dependent, to relinquish all claim to it, and become again an inmate of his house and a sharer in all his possessions.

His was a generous heart and an open house. Especially was this true in the experience of travelling ministers, who,

before the era of railroads, always went in their own vehi-
cles. To them he extended, as it was facetiously said of
him, "both hospitality and *horse*pitality." The families
of these perambulating clergymen were often guests at his
table for days, and sometimes for weeks. "Every agent's
horse," testifies one who knew, "seemed to know, by
instinct, where Mr. Briggs lived."

So serious, at times, were the encroachments upon his
fireside, on the Sabbath and in the intervals of public worship, by distant comers, that there was literally no chance
for his children to get near it. His kitchen was thronged
by the colored people, who were as welcome as those who
crowded the parlor and the chambers.

These broad Sabbath courtesies and bounties were extended to the members of both of the village congregations,
without distinction. His was not merely a "House Beautiful" for his Baptist friends, but for the Congregationalists,
also. His practice was to have a bountiful lunch prepared
for them on the previous day, that there might be no Sabbath work in his dwelling, and thus the commandment be
honored.

It was scarcely probable that a lawyer, who dissuaded
clients from paying him fees, and a Christian philanthropist
who kept open house for neighbors and strangers; who
supported, with generous bounty, dependent relatives; and
who fed the hungry, clothed the naked, and soothed the
sons of sorrow in their lowly homes, — should grow rich.
He did not. Great possessions never hindered his progress
heavenward. The treasures he carried thither were hearts
he had gladdened and comforted and helped.

His reputation at the bar was achieved almost upon a
single memorable occasion. An Indian was charged with

murder, and, when the trial came on, the Judge appointed
Mr. Briggs as his counsel.   Fully convinced, by a careful
examination of the case, that the accusation was unjust and
the prisoner innocent, he entered, with all the ardor of his
soul, into the cause, and left nothing undone that he could
honorably do to secure the acquittal of the unhappy man.
In the management of this somewhat peculiar case he
developed powers and tact surprising to his friends, and
scarcely familiar to himself.   His argument was logical
and powerful, and his plea truly a model of jury eloquence.
The impression produced upon the court and audience was
profound, and the report of the case was speedily spread
throughout the county, echoing from hill to hill, and the
fame of the rising lawyer from dwelling to dwelling.

   It is a curious illustration of the fallibility of human
judgment and of the uncertainty of law, that, in spite of
all his counsel's eloquence and zeal, the poor Indian was
proved guilty, and suffered the penalty of death.

   An associate of Mr. Briggs says of his law life : —

   "He rose rapidly in his profession, and soon stood, as a jury
lawyer, at the head of the bar in his native county; the eloquence
and power of the young advocate being, in all that region, admired
and applauded."

   In a long night conversation with one of his sons, late
in life, he narrated the incidents and details of causes he
had managed and argued in the early part of his professional life, pitted against such able men as Senators Mills
and Bates, out of his own county.   Among other things,
he said that, from his earliest case to his last, he never
commenced the trial of a cause without an effort, and a
mental struggle, to subdue his own self-distrust and diffi-

dence, and that his power over juries and his frequent success was always a matter of surprise to himself.

At a later period in life he was engaged in a capital trial in his own county, which he managed with marked success. The case involved the life and reputation of an individual above the ordinary class of criminals. It was one that excited great interest, and called forth his full strength. One, who was present, relates the magical effect of his eloquence, evinced by the hushed silence, the thrill, and the awe of the crowded room. Many in the jury box and in the audience wept, and many faces became pale with emotion. His argument, illustrations, and appeals seemed to have carried his hearers with him; and in the closing sentences, delivered almost in a whisper, he seemed to be uttering their thoughts and feelings, as well as his own.

CHAPTER VI.

OF the numerous tributes to the ability and fidelity, and no less to the singleness of aim, which characterized the subject of this Memoir, in the successive phases of his life and career, kindly supplied, for the use of the biographer, by the memory and hand of admiring friends, there are two which have such particular reference to his early manhood and to his legal practice, that, although they glance at later epochs of his life, they find their most appropriate setting in juxtaposition with the chapter which presents him to our notice at the bar. The prominence and enviable distinction which marked him as a lawyer, in his office, in the courts, and especially before the jury, are not a little remarkable, when the disadvantages under which he struggled upwards to that position are considered. The circumstances and accessories of that fortunate struggle are graphically pictured in a sketch from the pen of the Hon. Increase Sumner. In showing us the condition of the bar, and of the community contemporary with the young lawyer's entrance into legal life, and his rapid elevation to the summit of his profession, he prepares us to make an intelligent and just estimate of the forces at work, and of the credit won, in the achievement so proudly and yet so humbly wrought.

This consideration avails with the biographer to withhold

his own hand for considerable space, and to present the tribute now referred to without abridgment : —

"When Gov. Briggs came to the bar, a state of things, in regard to business and practice, prevailed differing from what exists now. Since 1818 changes have been wrought considerably affecting, in Western Massachusetts, the legal profession.

"Berkshire was then mostly an agricultural county, having only a single banking institution; and manufacturing was limited in amount. Masses of business always involving the increase of litigation, did not then exist. Hence the practice of the lawyer was restricted mainly to the collection of debts, drawing of written instruments, and giving such advice as the comparatively few clients required. It was an isolated section of Massachusetts, containing about thirty-seven thousand inhabitants. The number of practising lawyers was about forty. Residing in different towns, much dispersed from each other, they were only brought together by the courts at five sessions a year; no session continuing, ordinarily, more than two weeks. It was the custom of the members of the bar to convene at the shire-town on the evening or day before the actual sitting of the court; and in respect to most of them, their quarters, for many years, were at a private boarding-house, — comfortable, pleasant, — kept by the late Bradford Whiting, Esq. When not occupied in court or in the preparation of their causes, they thus met at their quarters, incidentally, as it were, — constituting a kind of social professional club. The facilities of railroads being unknown, and all public conveyances limited, convenience, if not necessity, compelled them to remain at court till the term ended. This state of things produced amongst the brethren of the profession a friendliness of feeling, and tended also to promote an interchange of sentiments and ideas, adding to the intellectual acquirements of each. Legal questions, the history of the times; the conduct, lives, and merits of public men; — in a word, all the variety of topics appertaining to the day, were suggested and discussed.

"Hence the bar formed a kind of unorganized lyceum, not subject to precise system or rules, but with all its proprieties and advan-

7

tages. Many of the senior members had mingled in association
with such men as Caleb Strong, Theodore Sedgwick, Daniel
Dewey, Ephraim Williams, and others of honorable professional
fame in Western Massachusetts. It is not too much to say of the
Berkshire bar in 1818 and onward, that, for intellect and elevation
of individual and professional character, it was highly respectable.
One cause of this was found, perhaps, in the fact that the rules for
admission were very exacting, requiring of those liberally educated
three years of faithful study; and of those not thus educated, five
years in the office, and under the guidance of a counsellor-at-law,
before they could be admitted to the Common Pleas; a restriction
of some years' practice in that court before admission to the Supreme Judicial Court; and in the latter, a practice of two years as
attorneys, before attaining the degree of counsellor, a still further
advancement requisite before they were allowed to argue or
conduct a trial of a cause in the latter court. It was on the whole,
perhaps, a pupilage too exacting, though a process of thorough
training.

"An incident in regard to Mr. Briggs, in this connection, may
be given. On the day of his admission as attorney of the Supreme
Court, and directly after his taking the oath, he united with his
senior associate counsel, the late William C. Jarvis, in the trial of
one of his causes, and began introducing his evidence. The Chief
Justice, who presided, inquired who was interrogating the witness.
'It is Mr. Briggs,' replied Mr. J., 'just admitted as an attorney of
this court.' 'He is not a counsellor,' was the stern response of the
judge, 'and cannot be permitted to examine witnesses;' doubtless
little dreaming that the attorney thus repulsed would, in due time,
be elevated to the Chief Magistracy of the Commonwealth, with
the power of nominating the chief officers of the Judiciary.

"He was not learned in the books; yet he was a well-educated
lawyer. There are more methods than one of acquiring legal
knowledge. Cases in which he was employed he thoroughly and
faithfully examined and understood, not only as to the facts, but
the law, evidence of which is shown in his cases that are reported.
It was his habit, while attending court, always to listen to the trial
of cases, and to all legal questions which arose, whether he was

engaged in the suits or not; and his good memory retained facts, points, and decisions, with tenacity and exactness. This habit, connected with his clear judgment, contributed greatly towards making him a good lawyer.

"His manner of examining witnesses was excellent. He loved truth, and loved its development, for its own sake. No honest witness ever received from him rudeness. He never attempted to prevail, in a poor cause, by seeking to entrap or by assailing. Whenever a witness, honest but mistaken, gave testimony, in a manner alike kind and adroit, he would almost invariably succeed in exposing, in gentle and playful manner, the error, by the lips of the witness, generally to the amusement of the court and jury, and frequently of the witness also. On the other hand, if he confronted a witness apparently perverse, in a calm and serious manner, he probed him by an examination which almost always exposed the perverseness.

"In his addresses to the jury, and in his arguments to the court, he was lucid and methodical, seizing upon the true points, not burdening the cause by introducing such as were weak or immaterial; and his views were ever presented briefly, seriously, and impressively. Fond as he was in colloquy of relating anecdotes, as well for illustration as for pleasantry, he wholly abstained from them in his forensic efforts. He was grave, candid, earnest. For fidelity to his clients he was most exemplary, and it was a fidelity not based upon the position or wealth of his clients, but upon a stern sense of duty, founded upon professional obligation. The poor accused one in the criminal's box, friendless and penniless, would be aided by him with as much zeal and alacrity as though he were possessed of money and friends. If an accused outcast, forlorn and destitute, came under his notice, and if he deemed him wrongly prosecuted, he would without solicitation tender his services, and see to it that no rigors of the law needlessly harmed the poor victim.

"His intercourse with his professional brethren was not unlike an entertainment, where profitable sayings and pleasant humor and sweet music and decorated scenery are commingled. He took a generous interest in their welfare; and probably not one survives

him who does not hold in precious remembrance many instances
of his valuable friendship. The junior members he always approached with welcoming embrace, showing his kind wishes in
acts as well as in language. Whenever he perceived them, as often
he might, embarrassed, or at fault, because of inexperience, and a
suggestion of his could relieve or aid them, it was at once prof-
fered, and in such a manner as real kindness always dictates,—
especially towards those who, like himself, had struggled through
disadvantages, and, by dint of self-culture and unaided application,
forced their way to the bar. Congeniality of circumstances in his
own life, with that of others of his own profession, ever awakened
within him sympathies alike strong and amiable.

"In delineating the character and history of men over which
plays the shadow as well as the sunshine, the biographer often
finds it expedient as well as just to depict both, lest he should
fall under the imputation of partiality. The smallest hair casts a
shadow (' *etiam capillus unus habet umbram suam* '). But he whose
tastes lead him to descry such shadows must be better pleased
with the littleness than greatness, more gratified in perceiving a
speck on the disk of a flower than in the contemplation of its surpassing beauties. Only such will ever seek to discover a shade
upon the professional or other fame of Gov. Briggs.

"Comparing him with others of his profession, no one seems so
truly parallel as the late JAMES SULLIVAN. Each, in early life, pur-
posed to pursue a different calling from the law. Neither had the
advantages afforded in the higher institutions of learning, or was
trained under the guidance of legal sages. Both depended, under
the favor of Providence, upon their individual exertions for advancement; both were successful and distinguished in their profession; and the character of their minds, in regard to comprehensiveness, order, and force, was similar. Both made an early
profession of Christianity, and were eminently exemplary in the
performance of its duties in every relation of life, and each, for his
virtues and talents, was elevated to the Chief Magistracy of the
Commonwealth.

"It is exceedingly fortunate, whenever one of beneficent life and
ennobling example enters into the legal circle, for it cannot be

otherwise than that a strong attachment towards him should be formed, and his influence ever tends to elevate and purify the minds of those with whom he associates.

"This reflection, applied to the character and life of Gov. Briggs, whether as a lawyer, a citizen, or a magistrate, heightens our regard for his memory, and inspires a strong desire that it may be preserved. We, who had companionship with him and loved him so well, can visit his grave with thoughtfulness, not sadness; for voices seem to whisper, 'Lo! the good man has risen!' Pleasant remembrances warm our hearts, and we are comforted!"

The early friendship between the young law student and Dr. Wm. H. Tyler, of Lanesboro', has been already referred to as advancing into the most intimate relations, involving both personal and professional confidence, until death severed the ties that bound them together.

Soon after the melancholy tidings of the death of his beloved friend reached him, he wrote to his son the following commemorative letter, with which this chapter and the review of his active life at the bar, may be properly brought to a close : —

NORTH ADAMS, Mar. 4, 1862.

MY DEAR SIR:

I have been intimately acquainted with your father for forty-seven years, an intimacy that I count among the best things of my life. He commenced the study of law with Luther Washburn, Esq., of Lanesboro', and became a member of my family at the same time, — November, 1814, — being, as I suppose, seventeen or eighteen years of age. He was a very sociable and companionable inmate with us for two years, during which time he was a remarkably close applicant to his studies. Nothing diverted his attention, unless, sometimes, a law question came up among the social friends who visited the office. He then would exhibit his tact and skill for argument. His natural endowments were of a high order; his mind active and brilliant — intuitively grasping and mastering

7*

any subject presented to his contemplation. He obtained acquaintances and made friends with remarkable facility. I never saw or
heard of his being angry; and, being always cheerful himself, he contributed much to the cheerfulness of others. His vivacity rendered
his friends social and happy. He was sometimes merry; and often
related anecdotes and incidents in such a fascinating manner as to
charm and interest his hearers; but he always possessed so much
prudence and gravity, as never to trespass against anything sacred.
He had a better knowledge of the Scriptures than any man of his
age with whom I was acquainted; and his accuracy in quoting Scripture, I have had opportunity of witnessing several times. When
other lawyers had misquoted, he very readily and happily corrected
them. He made a profession of religion when a youth; and perhaps I have been more interested in his society from his having
embraced sentiments in unison with my own. I have enjoyed many
happy hours with him in social religious meetings. His brethren
were always gratified when he engaged in the public performance
of religious duties. You are aware of his having been called the
Apostle of Temperance. The first temperance meeting of which I
ever heard in Berkshire County or elsewhere, was obtained by
him at a public house in the north part of Lanesboro', I think in
1824 or 1825 (there were some twelve or fifteen persons present).
It was a novel affair. A constitution was formed, but as our obligations were not very strict, we soon formed another.

His benevolence showed itself in daily acts of quiet kindness to
everybody about him; his sympathy and well-timed efforts for the
benefit of the sick and afflicted in his neighborhood and elsewhere,
exceeded any with which I am acquainted. I have experienced
much of his kindness in my own family. I suffered from an accidental injury to one of my lower limbs for more than two years,
and then had to undergo amputation. During all that time he
would often visit me, cheerfully relate some story or anecdote,
and perform all the kind and consoling duties, so well known and
appreciated by those who are suffering on a sick-bed. Those personal qualities that made him the idol of his friends, gained more
and more upon me while he lived.

As a lawyer and advocate, I have known but few, if any, above him. A few years since, when he was in full practice as a lawyer, it was often said he made the best argument and address ever made in Lenox Court House. Conversing with him, at one time, with regard to a plea of great power and success which he had recently made, he said to me, that "for more than an hour he had no consciousness of there being any one present except the twelve men who constituted the jury."

The last time I visited his family, I rode with him to the Pittsfield Cemetery. On our arrival, he desired me to get out of the carriage, and to step on the ground which he had selected as the place of his own burial. Our conversation on this occasion, as also in many of our later interviews, was on the subject of our departure from this world to another. He was often recurring to the friends and acquaintances of the past, and recounting those whom death had called away. Language would fail me to express my high admiration of his great social and Christian virtues, and my deep sorrow and anguish at our irreparable loss.

Truly yours,

WM. H. TYLER.

GEORGE P. BRIGGS, Esq.

CHAPTER VII.

ELECTED TO CONGRESS—HIS CONGRESSIONAL DISTRICT AND CONSTITU-
ENTS—ANTICIPATIONS AND AMBITIONS—JOURNEY TO WASHINGTON—
LETTER, *en route*—CORRESPONDENCE WITH HIS FAMILY.

FOR twelve years Mr. Briggs steadily, and always successfully, pursued the path, his progress along which we have just reviewed ; gaining all the time, in greater degrees, the confidence and regard of his neighbors. The distinctions which marked this period of his life, were chiefly those he achieved for himself by his tact and his fine forensic powers. He was indeed chosen, in 1824, town clerk of Lanesboro', and two years later he received, from Gov. Lincoln, an appointment as Chairman of the Board of Commissioners on Highways for Berkshire County.

In the fall of 1830, his popularity found a demonstration in the voice of the people, by his election as a member of Congress from the Eleventh Congressional District, includ-ing, besides the County of Berkshire, a part of Hampshire County.

The whole of this district is a hill region, and more than a generation of years ago it was somewhat sparsely inhab-ited by a people, characterized less by refinement and wealth than by the steadiness of industrial thrift. They were chiefly farmers, who had such education as the common school supplied, with here and there examples of mental culture, which served to give force to the aggregate of the public intelligence. This was eminently moral, and indeed of an exemplary force of virtue.

Their excellent Representative in the National Legislature said of them, in after years: "I doubt if one among my early constituents kept a carriage in the proper sense of the word ; and yet scarcely one was without a vehicle of some kind or other."

The general parity of social condition among the people, indicated in this remark, might have been traced in other directions. They were of simple habits and tastes, and equally of a sincere character — appreciating moral and intellectual worth, and gladly seizing upon these in rare and felicitous union, in the character of him to whom they gave their honest and hearty suffrage at the polls. His predecessors in Congress were, perhaps without exception, examples of men whose remembrance among the people was a guaranty for the continued prudence and wisdom of their choice in any successor.

Mr. Briggs was thus sent to Congress at a very important epoch in the national history. Great questions were springing up out of the agitations and conflicts of popular and party interests, and a new era of legislative activity and distinction was about to be inaugurated in the council halls of the nation. Hitherto a stranger to all this sort of life, except as he read of it in the few newspapers to which he had access, and of a scarcely broader experience than that of many of his constituents, the young lawyer looked forward to his new position with mingled emotions of ambition and apprehension. It was not possible that his active and earnest and independent mind and nature should be unmoved with a strange delight, at the prospect of fame thus opening before him. At the same time his humble

and conscientious spirit shrunk with ingenuous apprehension from the contemplation of a sphere of action so new,
so strange, so remotely linked, up to this time, with his
personal expectations, and so exacting in its requirements
of the man who should aspire to fill it worthily and
well.

He girded himself for his work, however, without profounder misgivings than those which befitted a strong, but
surprised character, and armed with a consciousness of
rectitude in his motives and in his purpose alike, he went
manfully and hopefully up to the broad and distinguished
theatre — where the grand and impressive drama of National
History was to be enacted, with himself as one of those who
were to bear a part in it.

He was now in the thirty-fifth year of his age, and in one
sense well prepared for the new arena upon which he was
to cope with great minds and subtile spirits. He was self-
disciplined and self-poised. This advantage came of his
independent life-struggle. He did not go to Washington
quite as unknown as many do who are heaved up unexpectedly by the waves of political strife, and precipitated,
almost as unexpectedly to themselves as to their constituents, upon the shore of public office. His honest, homely
fame went in advance of him. His prominence at the bar
and his probity in all walks of life were known out of
Berkshire, and generously accredited at the National
Capitol, so that when he modestly apppeared among
his colleagues he gratefully found himself in the midst of
friends.

Chosen at the congressional election of November, 1830,
he did not take his seat until the beginning of the next
session of Congress in December, 1831. While in Wash-

ington, and indeed always when absent from his home, he was a constant and punctual correspondent with his family. His warm domestic affections were never chilled by the exciting scenes and events in which he was so often a participant. This almost voluminous correspondence affords a panorama of his life as a statesman — and will be drawn upon freely for the pictures to be framed into this Memoir.

"His first journey to Washington," says his daughter, "was commenced in the midst of one of the fiercest of the New England snowstorms, which proved to be the beginning of a *winter of snow* that continued till April; not leaving the surface of the ground exposed again for six months. The warm and covered stage-sleigh due at midday in the old Boro', on the route over the mountains from Greenfield to Albany, arrived this day at nightfall, coming through the trackless roads in a lumber-box open sleigh. How well I remember the dreary evening, and see again with childhood's eyes the large black trunk in the rear of the sleigh, and the muffled form of my father, sitting beside the driver, as they disappeared with the plunging horses in the blinding snow. The watchers at home had heavy hearts that night. Washington was far off in the vision of the children, and the storm and cold were fearful."

His first letter was addressed to his wife, from New York : —

NEW YORK, Sunday evening, 27 Nov., 1831.
MY DEAR HARRIET:

We had rather a cold time of it after we left Lanesboro' until we reached Hancock, when the weather seemed to moderate, and we came to Troy in a coach on wheels. Between Troy and Albany no snow was to be seen, except on distant hills. We took the steamboat at Albany at ten o'clock, yesterday, and arrived at New York at eleven and a half, and stopped at the "Atlantic," in Broadway. At Albany, we fell in company with Judge Prentice, Senator from Vermont. Judge P. is a very sensible and agreeable man. Being very much of a domestic man, his feelings about home and leaving his family, corresponded with my own. We have laughed some about backing out and going home, but concluded that we will have *grit* enough to go on to Washington and see how the land lies, before we entirely give up the chase and abandon our trust. I am in good health, and could I take a peep into the old tabernacle on the hill in the *Boro'* and see how my *better half*, the dear children, and the rest of the family are, I hope I should see you all in such circumstances that all my anxieties would be quieted. I hope for the *best*, as it is I quietly yield myself to circumstances.

Have been to church all day.[1]

Tell all the dear children that their father expects, while he is absent, they will be kind, affectionate, obedient, faithful in their studies, and good children. Mother and Alfred and Betty and Sally must be good children, too. Tell the doctor to look well to his charge, and *cure* you immediately. I shall write you often. In in the mean time, I am

Your affectionate husband,

GEO. N. BRIGGS.

He had not been in Washington more than a fortnight when he found leisure, even amid the novel and exacting engagements into which he was plunged, to write to his daughter a letter of true parental affection and solicitude. His anxiety for the right education of this only daughter, made him constantly assiduous in his care and watchfulness in all things that seemed likely to influence seriously her mind and character. The affectionate counsel of this letter is not yet out of date, though in this artificial age, and in the garish light of modern and fashionable female education, it seems certainly almost as homely as it is excellent.

---

[1] It was only just before the previous midnight that he arrived at the city.

WASHINGTON, December 15, 1831.

MY DEAR CHILD:

I was pleased to receive your letter, and when you learn that by devoting, occasionally, a few leisure minutes to an absent father you can contribute to his pleasure, I have no doubt you will find many opportunities to do the same thing. It gives me joy to learn from you your determination to give all vigilance to your studies. Let not the good resolution drop. A thing half learned confers no benefit on the learner.

Remember, my daughter, that, with the right state of mind, you may gather wisdom from everything that surrounds you. It is not from those persons alone whose appropriate business it is to impart instruction, that we are to obtain knowledge; but from everybody and everything we may receive instruction. There is nothing in the great field of knowledge which will be learned in vain, if properly improved, whether it be in the physical, intellectual, or moral world. Listen to the words and receive the counsel of age; it is the voice of experience, the oracle of wisdom. Remember, also, that one way of benefiting ourselves is to impart of our stock of knowledge to others, who may be in need of information which we possess and they do not. Whilst we communicate to them we mature our own views, and learn not only to think correctly, but to communicate aptly.

Recollect, that things you have learned and which may appear exceedingly simple and plain to you, may yet be mysterious to them. Take the most apt and agreeable means, then, to do them a kindness, in imparting to them every aid in your power. Learn never to be too confident in your own opinions, nor too bold in expressing them; especially in the presence of those older than yourself. The most costly jewels and the richest ornaments, when indiscreetly exhibited, or improperly worn, render their possessor an object of disgust. Finally, my child, let this great truth be ever present to your mind, that the highest personal accomplishments and the greatest intellectual achievements will eventually avail nothing if they are not connected with, or do not flow out of, a pure and virtuous heart. . . . . .

8

The following letter, besides bringing up a picture of court-life in Washington of a past generation, will remind the reader of the time when sketches of scenes and celebrities at the Capitol, drawn by the facile pen of Mr. Shaw, were affording the poor young pupil of the law such delight in his village home : —

WASHINGTON, 20th December, 1831.

MY DEAR WIFE:

The President of the United States, from long established usage, invites the members of Congress to dine with him, once or more, during the session of Congress.

Dinner parties consist of from thirty to forty members. As a matter of convenience, the names of all the members are arranged alphabetically, and so beginning with the first letter of the alphabet a sufficient number are selected to compose the usual party. Being high among the letters in their order, I had the honor of being detailed for the first dinner party. The invitation was given and accepted last week, and to-day being the time appointed, after the House adjourned, I began to set myself in order. Now, for the first time, the *new black coat and pantaloons* were brought out and put on, and with a most *ministerial* air I marched off for the President's, in company with Mr. Bates, of Northampton, and Messrs. Barstow and Babcock of New York. Having reached the house, we were ushered into the presence chamber of the President, where we found, standing in a room, magnificently furnished, the " old chief" with about thirty guests and four ladies seated upon a sofa. The first move was to pay our respects to the President; shake hands, and pass the usual compliments, and then be introduced to the ladies.

General Jackson is a man apparently more than seventy years old, very thin and slender in person, about six feet high; his face very long and narrow; his hair combed up and back, so that it stands erect all over his head, and is about three inches long. He has, for an old man, a pleasant *blue* eye, I think; though, under his spectacles, I could not precisely determine the color. His manners are easy and graceful and dignified. His movements are sprightly, though they have not the firmness and vigor of a man in the full strength of life. He talks freely and pleasantly on the ordinary subjects of conversation which arise in a mixed company. The lady of the palace is a Mrs. Donaldson, whose husband, I believe, was a nephew of Mr. Jackson. She, I should think, is about thirty-five years old, — a plain, agreeable, and elegant woman, appears free from vanity, and does not, in any of her airs or manners, indicate a consciousness that she is a *court lady.*

Mrs. Jackson, a newly-married wife of an adopted son of the General, appears next in rank, and is very pretty. Then there was a sister of Mrs. Donaldson, — a young lady of a fine form, with a sensible and engaging countenance, and most unassuming and agreeable manners. There was a fourth young lady, whose name I do not recollect. The modesty of demeanor, and modesty of attire of all these ladies, in the midst of the showiness of the mansion of the chief magistrate of the United States, made a very agreeable impression on me.

At six, dinner was announced. Were I to attempt to describe the table, its rich and splendid service, or the number and variety of the dishes, I should fail. Suffice it to say, after sitting an hour and a half, the party withdrew into the room we had left, where coffee was served; after which ceremony the company took leave.

The statesman, amid his official cares and responsibilities, — which his habitual conscientiousness and his simple self-respect did not allow to sit lightly upon him, — yet forgot not the individuality and interest of one of the dear household band his separation from whom was the greatest drawback to his happiness in Washington. In proof of his continual and particular remembrance of the children who were dear to him, and in all whose concerns he was accustomed when at home to take a lively interest, are the following letters, written during his first month in Congress : —

WASHINGTON, December 24, 1831.

Well, my dear little sons, George and Henry, it is now Saturday

night, and I want to inquire of you both if you have been very good
boys through this week? What have you been studying, and how
much have you learned? Have you let any of the scholars outdo
you in lessons and in complying with the rules of the school? Are
you dutiful and affectionate to your mother, respectful and kind to
your good grandmother? Do you love one another and your dear
sister? How comes on that beautiful calf? Do you take good care
of her this cold weather? I want to have you write me every Saturday night, and your sister every Tuesday, so as to send by
Wednesday's mail. What should you think to see little black girls
carrying pails of water on their heads? The black women carry
tubs of water on their heads, from the pumps, without touching
them with their hands, and so they carry the baskets from market.
Be very good boys. . . . . .

The young Alfred, to whom the next letter is addressed,
was a son of his brother Rufus; and one of the two who,
after many years' enjoyment of the bounties of his home
and hand, went out to make successfully their own way in
the world. The picture of the greedy youths and the perplexed waiters is hardly antiquated yet: —

DEAR ALFRED:

. . . . Mr. Adams is found in his seat, and in as constant
and regular discharge of his duties as any other member of the
House. He is a plain, unostentatious man, as purely republican in
his appearance and manners as any man on earth. He is treated
with the utmost respect by men of all parties.

To-day has been the first levee at the White House, and it occurred by accident. The *Globe*, supposing it usual to hold a levee
on Christmas (which, by the way, is never done), without any
authority, inserted an article stating that the President's house
would be opened. This notice being issued, it was too late to
recall it, and a levee was held in due time. It was as motley an
assemblage as the multitude at a cattle-show or fair.

A set of hungry, voracious boys and young men pressed around the servants who bore the trays of cookies, cakes, and wine, and followed them as a company of sharks would follow an infected ship. The waiters would, in vain, try to escape them and offer their refreshments to the ladies; they would rush on and devour the whole.

The President took his stand in the ante-room, and received all who chose to pay him their respects. . . . . .

The following letter may fitly conclude this chapter, as bringing the Washington life of the yet inexperienced statesman to the close of its first month, and also as bringing these memorials to the mile-stone of a closing year.

His Berkshire home had afforded him no opportunity of witnessing such pageants as those of Christmas in the Romish churches, and it is not strange that, brought up as he had been to the simple and almost barren ritualism of the Baptist church, he should find very little solemnity in the performance of High Mass : —

WASHINGTON, December 25, 1831.

WOMAN OF MY HEART:

This being a high day at the Catholic church, I attended their service of High Mass this morning. Two priests officiated, one at the desk, the other at the altar. The one at the altar was attended by four little boys about George's size, clad in white robes, two of them with scarlet sashes about their waist, the other two with scarlet sashes over their shoulders and down their backs. The priest at the altar was dressed in the gaudy style of a play-actor. Upon the altar stood a silver crucifix about eighteen inches high, with an image on it four or five inches long; the foot of the crucifix resting in a very gay cluster of artificial flowers.

Six candles, four or five feet long, were burning in large silver candlesticks. The priest in the desk informed us that the candles represented the apostles performing mass in the caverns of rock and subterranean retreats, where they were driven by persecution.

8*

To me, there was the least solemnity of anything which I ever
witnessed in the form of religious worship. . . . . . A very
excellent discourse was delivered, by the priest in the desk, upon
the duty of charity to the poor. A contribution was taken up for
the church.

A merry Christmas to you all. . . . . .

CHAPTER VIII.

IN THE "HOUSE"—PARLIAMENTARY KNOWLEDGE—HIS AFFABILITY AND
POPULARITY—INDUSTRY—HIS POSITION AS A SPEAKER—AN EFFICIENT
SPEECH—SPEECH ON THE APPORTIONMENT BILL—FIRST IMPRESSIONS
OF HENRY CLAY—HIS DENOMINATIONAL POSITION AND FEELINGS.

THE Berkshire lawyer was very soon transformed into a practical, trustworthy, and efficient member of Congress. His uncompromising fidelity to congressional business; his unobtrusive and genial manners; his diligence and success in learning, not only all the special duties which belonged to his place, but no less the whole method and process of conducting the affairs of the House,—made him popular, not with those alone who were of the same political creed, but with the members of the opposition, also.

If there was—as it not infrequently happened—a dispute in the House upon any undetermined point of order, none were so competent as he to bring method out of the prevailing disorder, for he had examined all available sources for information upon such points, and precedents were as familiar to him as to the most efficient Speaker who ever sat in the chair.

The uniform urbanity and graceful suavity of his manners disarmed all who might have otherwise subjected him to personal, or political ill-will. In confirmation of this point, is his daughter's testimony:—

"My father has often said that he never received discourtesy

from any member of the House; and never found any difficulty in
arguing with the most fiery Southerner, upon the most exciting
topics upon which they disagreed.' On the contrary, among the
gifts of friendship and respect which he received in Washington,
he had several beautiful and valuable canes from gentlemen whose
States recently stood with the enemies of the Government."

While thus making friends in Washington, he was deep-
ening the regard of his friends at home, and justifying, by
his earnest attention to their interests and the broader
interests of the Commonwealth he represented, the confidence they had so cheerfully reposed in him. From the
first to the last term of his patient and patriotic services in
the House, he subjected himself to no reproaches from his
constituents by any remissness of duty, or by any officious-
ness and presumption in guarding and advancing measures
involving their advantage.

He was not a frequent speaker on the floor of the House;
and yet he could not be charged with being simply a worker.
He spoke on various occasions; and if his oratory was not
as splendid as that of the men who inspired many of his
letters with enthusiasm, he was always heard with great
interest and unqualified respect.

It might have been, not unreasonably, the expectation
of those who remembered the strange eloquence of his boyish tongue, in the religious meetings to which reference has
been made, — and who, in later, days, heard him, it may
be, addressing a jury in his native county, that he would
take a high position as an orator in Congress. It is not
important that his failure to do this should be specially
vindicated; but it may be accounted for, perhaps, by the
modesty of his character, which, affected powerfully by the
consciousness that he was upon the arena where the highest

genius and noblest oratory of the country were displayed, constrained him to propose to himself no daring competition with the masters he was content to hear and admire and extol.

While then it is not claimed that he was a great speaker, in the ordinary acceptation of the phrase, it is nevertheless simple justice to his congressional career and fame to insist that his protracted services in the House of Representatives assume, in the light of a fair review, an aspect of eminent representative ability. His speeches were always thoughtful, consistent, earnest, and effective. He did not allow himself " to speak to Buncombe," as mere *ad captandum* oratory has come to be defined. He proposed to influence opinion by his efforts on the floor, and if he failed of this end, it was not because he sacrificed reason and logic to mere sound and nonsense.[1]

In the discussion of questions that arrayed the parties in the House in distinct antagonism, he avoided all acrimony of speech or manner, and was so fair in his estimate of the views of his opponents, and so catholic in his judgment and in his expression of his own views, that he never lost the chance of influencing the mind of his political opponents by arousing their passions, and so blinding their perceptions by his own indiscretion.

His very first effort in Congress was, perhaps, as fair an example of his force and depth in argument, and of the

---

1 The *National Intelligencer* said of his speech upon the Apportionment Bill, quoted immediately hereafter, — " He is probably the first member who ever changed a vote by a speech on the floor of Congress. A member from Kentucky said, after the close of Mr. Briggs's speech: ' I had made up my mind to vote for the bill; but the speech of the young member from Massachusetts has convinced me that the bill is unjust to the old Revolutionary States, and I shall vote against it.' "

kindness of his spirit, as any of the speeches which he
made during his early service in the House. It was delivered while the bill for altering the ratio of representation
in the House was pending. The special question under
consideration was the motion to strike out 48,000 as the
ratio, and to insert, instead, 44,000 in the Apportionment
Bill.

He took the side of the reduction party, and advocated
it with nice discrimination and equal kindness of manner.
With some omissions, the following is his speech upon that
occasion : —

"This, sir, is the most important question that has been presented during the discussion of the subject before the committee.
I consider it so because it proposes the highest ratio, which will
save to each State its present number of representatives upon
this floor. If 48,000 prevails, you take from the Southern States
and from New England, two of the sections of this country, two
members each. The same thing, as it respects New England,
occurred under the apportionment of the census of 1820. If the
bill as reported becomes a law, the operation of the two appor-
tionments will be to reduce the number of representatives from
the New England States more than one tenth. The gentleman
from Tennessee, I presume, could not have been aware of this
effect, when he adverted to the operation of the last apportionment
to sustain the report of the committee. This bill strikes from
New Hampshire one sixth of her representation on this floor;
from Massachusetts, one sixteenth; from Virginia, one twenty-
second part; from Maryland, one ninth. If these consequences,
so unfortunate to the individual States, and so undesirable to their
sections of country, can be avoided without the introduction of
greater evils, I trust that the justice of this Congress will see
that it is done.

"Mr. Chairman, are there not reminiscences connected with the
history of these old States worthy of consideration in the settle-

ment of the question? The four States most deeply to be affected by the decision which we are about to make, are numbered among the immortal thirteen. May they not point you to those great transactions which gave birth to this free republic, and ask you to remember the days of their trial and the deeds of their valor? May they not, in the language of kindness and affection, say to their younger sisters, ' Do not, in your prosperity, unless some great principle demands it, or some great interest makes it necessary, drive one of our members from this floor whilst you are so fully represented?' May they not say to their sisters of the West, ' The great domain which constitutes your rich inheritance was purchased by our blood and treasure, flowing as full as the rushing fountain. We envy not your prosperity, nor would we check the rapid growth of your population. Our children and our dearest friends are among you, participating in the success of your unparalleled fortunes. But we ask you to remember that, in the days of your minority and weakness, we successively took you by the hand, upon the principles of equality and justice, and introduced you into the great republican family. We are gratified with your increasing wealth. We are proud of your advancing greatness, for you are a portion of our common country.' Sir, may not old Massachusetts and old Virginia ask their elder sister, New York, — that great nation in itself, — to remember the perils and conflicts of by-gone times? In the great struggle of the Revolution the State of New York — which now appears upon this floor with a phalanx of representatives equal to the whole of New England — was comparatively small, and stood in need of the aid of her powerful neighbors. In every part of her territory, which was then inhabited, may now be found the bones of their sons whose blood crimsoned her invaded soil. Their relative condition has now changed. She has become populous and powerful, and they comparatively small. When she can at once be just and generous, will she be unmindful of her ancient friends? Can she forget Virginia and Maryland and Massachusetts and New Hampshire, the associates of her youth, the sharers of her toils, the companions of her glory?

.　.　.　.　.　.　.　.　.　.

" An honorable gentleman from North Carolina has told us that if

we increase our numbers, we shall approximate a mob. The representatives of the people constitute a mob! Sir, I have yet to
learn that mere numbers constitute a mob, however great they
may be. I had supposed that it was the character of an assembly
which would entitle it to that appellation, and not its numbers.
Let it not be said that a great and enlightened people cannot
increase their representatives for fear that, when assembled, they
should degenerate into the character of a mob. The spirit of our
institutions, and the true principles of democracy, demand a full
representation of the people in this House. It was a great question with the Congress which formed our Constitution, whether
the members of this branch of our Legislature should represent
the States in their corporate capacity, or the people of the States.
The latter principle prevailed; the former was adopted in respect
to the Senate. This is the only department of our Government in
which the will and opinions of the people can be brought directly
to bear upon their public servants. A democrat by birth, by education, and from choice, I fully concur with the eloquent gentleman from Rhode Island, that the best interests of the people of
this country require that this principle should be carried into full
and perfect operation. The representative and his constituents
ought to be brought as near each other as possible. To secure
the great object of the elective franchise, the citizen should know
the personal and political character of the candidate for his suffrages. It is this particular acquaintance, this personal intercourse, which fastens on the mind of the public agent an abiding
sense of his responsibility to the power which created him. The
representative ought to know his constituents, and be intimately
acquainted with their wants and their wishes, their manners and
customs, their business and pursuits. As you increase the ratio
of representation, you lessen the facilities for acquiring this
knowledge."

The " country member" carried with him to the political
metropolis a most unsophisticated nature, and took a fresh
and almost boyish interest in the phases of social life
which were from time to time revealed to him. He had

been in Washington only a few weeks when he attended a congressional party, of which he wrote the following account to his wife — thinking, no doubt, to beguile for her the weary hours of his absence from home by these glimpses of his new life : —

WASHINGTON, Jan'y 4th, 1832.

DEAR HARRIET :   .

For the first time, last evening, I attended a Washington party. It was at the house of Duff Green, editor of the *United States Telegraph*. All the members of Congress were invited, and great numbers of citizens. There were probably four hundred persons present. Seven rooms above and below were thrown open. The ladies were mostly below. The rooms were crowded as closely as men and women could stand, much of the time; and yet they would contrive to make a ring large enough to dance a cotillon; but it was what I call a squeeze of a dance. Yet dance they would and dance they did. The thing would have been well enough for boys and girls; but to see men, and men of families and gravity, crowd into a compass scarcely large enough to turn in, engaged in dodging and sprawling about with giddy girls, is, to my mind, extremely ridiculous. Whatever may be its pleasures in a suitable hall, in such a place as this I can imagine no rational enjoyment in it. However, every one to his liking; and if gentlemen and ladies reap pleasure from such an exhibition, they have my perfect consent to attempt it. I crowded and squeezed around among them till about nine o'clock; and home I came, took an excursion to Lanesboro', went to bed and slept away the night, and dreamed I had a quarrel with you.

There is reason to suppose that, much as Mr. Briggs valued the opinions and judgment of his able friend Mr. Shaw, one estimate of that gentleman was greatly qualified, if not indeed reversed, by his own maturer judgment. Mr. Shaw said, in one of his letters to the young student: "But Mr. Clay is not, in my judgment, the ablest man in

9

the House."   The following mention of the great Kentucky
statesman conveys an estimate of him more nearly in harmony with his paramount abilities, than the one referred
to, — though this may be due to the difference of time between the two observations.   Mr. Briggs writes to his
wife : —

WASHINGTON, Jan. 11th, 1832.

DEAR HARRIET:

We have had in the House, to-day, a very splendid and masterly
speech from Henry Clay. Notice was given that he would speak
to-day. At a very early hour the Senate chamber was filled to
overflowing. A great concourse of ladies — all the beauty and
fashion of the city — were present. Our House was depopulated;
so that we were compelled to adjourn two hours before the usual
time. He fully met the highest expectations of his friends. He *is*
a wonderful man. I called on him this evening. Such is his
frankness and suavity, that one immediately feels that he is in the
presence of a friend to whom he can unbosom his thoughts without reserve. He lives near, and I see him at his house often.

There is a General Griffin in Congress, from South Carolina, — a
Baptist deacon. He seems a very worthy, pious man. He says
that in his part of the State there have been great additions to the
Baptist churches during the last year. He is one of the right kind
of Baptists. Though he regards with charity and good-will the
name and character of *Christian*, under whatever form it exists,
yet he manifests a *peculiar* love and good-will and brotherly attachment to all those who stand in that endearing relation to him
which arises from sameness of opinion and harmony of feelings
and sentiment. A gentleman who belongs to the Presbyterian
church said to me, the other day, "Briggs, do you not think that
the Baptists love each other better, and have more *Christian*
fellowship for one another, than most other denominations?"
"Why," said I, "do you ask me such a question?" "Because," said
he, "I have observed it, and believe it to be true." This remark
gave me much more pleasure than to have heard him say, the Bap-

tists were the most respectable and prosperous people in the United States.

Love to all.

Ever thine, GEORGE N. BRIGGS.

The glimpse which the simple-minded statesman here affords the reader, of his equal ingenuousness in his religious opinions and preferences, may justify a brief comment. He was, notwithstanding his proverbial liberality of feeling towards all Christians, very firm in his own faith. When sometimes met with the apparently crushing accusation from some one who opposed his views of communion as a Baptist, " But you will not consent to commune with us," he had a short-hand answer at his command: " I do not refuse to commune with any Christian. The Bible, as we all agree, fixes the terms of communion, and I *dare* not change them. *You* do not comply with the terms required. You banish yourself."

His solicitude to impress upon the tender minds of his children, the watchful care of their Father in heaven for their interest, is beautifully exemplified in the following letter, addressed to them upon their recovery from sickness : —

WASHINGTON, Feb. 7, 1832.

HARRIET, GEORGE, AND HENRY, —

MY DEAR CHILDREN:

I was very much concerned to hear from Dr. Tyler, a few days ago, that you had the measles; but it gave me pleasure to hear, by letter to-day, that you are doing well. You must remember that the disease is one frequently of much danger, and that the mild manner in which you have been affected by it, is because our Heavenly Father, whose tender mercies are over all His works, was kind and good. Now that you have passed by the period of danger, you should remember His goodness with gratitude, and resolve to obey His laws, and serve Him all your days.

YOUR LOVING FATHER.

CHAPTER IX.

THE year which began with him so auspiciously and hopefully, amid the new and exciting occupations of his congressional life, was speedily clouded by a deep personal sorrow.

His son remembers that his father, on leaving home for Washington, in November, was strangely and irresistibly impressed with the belief that he should never see his youngest child again. He mentioned this impression to his travelling companion.

" He left the child," says his daughter, " in blooming health; the charm and joy of his home, a lovely little girl of two years. In February she sickened, and in a week her little life on earth was completed. The tenderness of the grief he felt in losing this youngest one was not affected by the long years that passed before he was reunited to her, though they had kindly plucked from it the sting and bitterness."

It was this grief that shadowed his spirits when he thus wrote : —

WASHINGTON, February 25, 1832.

MY DEAR DAUGHTER :

When I last wrote you and your little brothers, you had just been restored from a sickness which I then told you was, in many

100

instances, dangerous. I wished to impress upon your minds a sense of your obligations of gratitude to the Creator for His goodness in carrying you safely through. I little thought, then, that your baby sister was so soon to fall a victim to the same disease. But the wise and good Being who gave us for a while that interesting little child, knew best when it was proper to recall the gift, and has taken her to himself. Undoubtedly, my child, one of the designs of Providence in removing one who was so deeply interwoven into our affections, was to warn us of the importance of being prepared to go into that world where she has gone. How should the thought that she is in heaven, and all her infant powers employed in the holy occupations of that place of happiness, stimulate her surviving sister and brothers to endeavor so to spend their lives, that, when they die, they may join the angel spirit of their little sister? Whilst governed by this delightful motive, your conduct towards each other will be full of affection and tenderness, and towards your parents dutiful and kind, and towards all respectful and obliging. Let your time be actively employed in the culture of your minds and in the improvement of all the faculties with which you are endowed for the honor and glory of your Creator, and for the promotion of the happiness of those with whom you are placed. I have been pleased with your letters since your sister's death. Whilst you remember the interesting incidents of her short life, never forget that she was removed by the hand of infinite goodness and wisdom, and earnestly pray Him to prepare you to meet her in heaven. Write me often, and let me know of your progress in school.

Your affectionate father,
G. N. BRIGGS.

In the next letter the bereaved, but still courageous and trusting heart of the Christian husband and father, thus speaks to the absent wife and sorrowing mother.

WASHINGTON, February 26, 1832.

MY DEAR HARRIET:

Yours of the 17th did not reach me until this evening. Meditation upon our loss, and reflections upon your lonely and sorrowful heart, make my own melancholy. Let us not look too much on the dark side. While we, from the disappointment in the unexpected death of our child, indulge ourselves in grief, let us reflect what she has gained by being thus taken from an evil world. I send you a sermon which I have received from my friend Judge Lyman, of Northampton, preached from the same text Elder Johnson used at the funeral of our little daughter. The curl of that flaxen hair was a mournfully precious keepsake. It brings fresh to my mind the appearance of that beautiful head, whose shining locks I have so often, with such peculiar delight, combed and parted. But, my dear Harriet, I fear by dwelling on such thoughts and associations I am led too deeply to lament the visitation of Providence, at which I hope I do not repine or murmur. I inclose a ring, which I know will be rendered precious to you for the bright little lock of Anna's hair which it contains. The few lines from our dear mother gave me peculiar satisfaction; what a miserable world this would be to that poor woman, if there were no hereafter! Her life has been little else than a succession of sorrows and sufferings; though time moves tardily on, a few weeks, I hope, will bring us together.

God have you in his holy keeping, and comfort you by his spirit. Love to all.

Thine,   G. N. BRIGGS.

Into the shadow of this grief his faithful friend, Henry Shaw, advances, and, in his kind manner, makes this characteristic attempt to comfort his friend : —

BOSTON, February 17, 1832.

DEAR GEORGE :

The melancholy tidings of your loss reached me yesterday. To attempt any suggestions that might assuage your feelings would be, just now, a mockery of my own. With the full heart of a parent, I sympathize and mourn with you — consolation can alone be found in the reflection that an all-wise Providence has done it. My own little pet was, at the same date, ill, though rather improving. She may also die, I thought; and I selected a brilliant star, and called it the

home of my child, and with this fancy I looked and still look, when
evening comes, toward the heavens, and in dreamy imaginings
people the orb with a race of kindred spirits, pure and spotless as
the angels. Can you profit by the conceit? After all, my friend,
how selfish are our *sorrows!* For what end would we recall the
departed spirit of an innocent babe? That it might tread with
sorrow the vale of tears, and after having tasted every bitter cup,
sink, worn down with care, a victim to the untold wretchedness
of life? No! but we would make it happy, — this belongs not to us
to accomplish, — we would *keep* it because it ministers to our pleasure. Its innocence delights us. Its opening intellect flatters our
hopes. We love the child, but we love ourselves more. The end
of life is death, and if that end come before the image of God within us is tainted by vice or marred by evil developments, ought we
too deeply to deplore it? Rather let us submit to a destiny that
places in heaven an angel, to persuade us thither and to welcome
our coming. If I could console you I would, for I feel how void
must be your heart, how deep its loneliness!

The winter has been to us all a dreary one, while sorrow and
mourning afflict our village. However, I shall not stay long.

Your friend, sincerely,

H. SHAW.

He thus tenderly writes to his old friend and family
physician, in reply to his letter announcing the death of his
child : —

WASHINGTON, 18th February, 1832.

MY DEAR FRIEND:

The messages of sorrow and friendship, which the mails of the
last few days have brought me from you, have made a deep impression on my heart. They were not the cold despatches of the
physician conveying, in technical terms, the condition of his suffering patient. They came fraught with the feelings of anxious
friendship. I read in them all the stifled wish to save the feelings of an anxious father, the life of whose darling child was pois-
ing between life and death, and the faithful intention of communi-

cating the unwelcome truth, but in such a manner as not roughly to inflict a wound upon a parent's heart. Your *first* letter told me the fate of my dear little daughter. From the hour of its reception, I endeavored to prepare my mind for the fatal intelligence of the last. You have watched, with parental solicitude, the dying moments of a charming little child, and therefore know the difference between a parent's feelings when expecting the event, and its fatal occurence. I was present at the funeral of your lovely C——. I loved the child, and thought I entered into your feelings and sympathized with your sorrows. But the tender ties which bind a lovely infant to a father's heart had not then been mine and suddenly torn asunder. I knew nothing of your grief. As well might we attempt to judge of the exquisite sounds of a high-toned musical instrument, whose strings remain untouched, as to judge of the deep agony of a parent's soul at the loss of his tender offspring without having felt the rude touch upon those strings which bind that offspring to his heart. I feel, very sensibly, the deep interest you took and the unremitting care you bestowed upon our child. It is a matter of regret that my absence should have imposed so heavy a tax on my friends at home. But I am sure the recollection of their kindness will be long and gratefully cherished. In the midst of chastisement our benevolent Father has remembered mercy. . . . . .

Your faithful friend,

Geo. N. Briggs.

Dr. W. H. Tyler.

The following letter is addressed to his nephew, and includes some interesting pen-and-ink portraits of prominent men : —

Washington, March 25, 1832.

Dear Alfred :

. . . .

The Vice-President, John C. Calhoun, is nearly six feet high, a little round shouldered, and stoops; rather slim, though he appears as if he were made of nail-rods; face thin; cheek-bones somewhat high; dark blue eyes; very quick in his motions; and seems at one glance to pierce you through. No one can encounter that piercing eye without involuntarily experiencing a wish to retreat from its gaze. His hair is very long and black, and stands erect in every direction upon his head. He has more expression of face than any man I ever saw; is remarkably free and familiar in his manners and intercourse; makes no effort to put on, or maintain, an artificial dignity, when in the chair or out of it. He speaks with great rapidity. His voice is clear and sharp and shrill. He is a man of uncommon intellect, and evidently bears the marks of disappointed ambition. His opinions, whether right or wrong, are avowed with great fearlessness.

Gen. Smith is eighty-two years old, and is about as large as our neighbor Mr. Miles Powell, whom he resembles more than any man living. The scene between him and Mr. Clay has been misrepresented in the grossest manner. At the opening of the first speech, Mr. Clay said he felt sensibly the approach of age. To this Gen. S. had alluded in a taunting, rude manner. On another occasion he charged him with ignorance, in not having seen a law about which he spoke. There was not the slightest irony in Mr. Clay's manner or language, with the exception of the couplet from Pope. During his splendid speech, before the altercation, there was a burst of eloquence, which all felt to be irresistible, and which produced a cheering and clapping from the vast multitude thronging the gallery. Upon this, the General arose, and, in a perfect rage, called on the Vice-President to put an end to the disturbance. No one heeded his petulance, and the orator proceeded.

Your friend and uncle,

G. N. Briggs.

The uncle continues his pen-pictures for the gratification of his nephew : —

Washington, March, 1832.

Dear Alfred :

You inquired, a few days ago, if Col. Johnson is not a Baptist. I learn, upon inquiry, that he is not a professor of religion, but is friendly to the Baptist denomination. He is a man of hardly middle stature, light complexion, a mild, pleasant countenance, light-blue eyes, rather inclined to stoop, — and his whole personal appearance directly opposite to that which one would expect to meet in the person of the soldier who has the reputation of killing Tecumseh.

Judge Marshall is said to be seventy-seven years of age. He is a plain, venerable-looking man, has long, gray hair, parted from the top of his head, and tied in a heavy queue behind. I should think him about six feet high. His dress is that of days that have passed away, — long waisted, single-breasted coat, small-clothes, and old-fashioned, round-toed shoes. He boards nearly two miles from the Capitol, but walks back and forth, whether it rains or shines, without an overcoat. His step is strong and elastic. His voice is extremely feeble. In delivering an opinion, he cannot be heard, even in perfect silence, twenty feet distant; but his mind retains its unimpaired vigor. His whole appearance is venerable and imposing. His manners are very plain, easy, and dignified. Let me hear from you often. The absence of that dear little girl must leave a lonesome house. God bless you, my dear fellow.

Yours, truly,

G. N. BRIGGS.

The following letter contains an interesting fragment of history, which may be properly supplemented here with the reminder that the State of Georgia disregarded the judgment of the Supreme Court, and visited its displeasure upon the missionary by long imprisonment, from which he was finally released by the clemency of the Governor : —

WASHINGTON, Mar. 4th, 1832.

MY DEAR HARRIET:

I had letters to-day from George and Harriet. George reminds me that to-day, the fourth of March, is his birthday, making him ten years old. The fact irresistibly recalls many interesting associations.

The Supreme Court, yesterday, delivered their opinion in the case of Mr. Worcester (a missionary among the Cherokee Indians), against the State of Georgia. The State of Georgia passed a law making it a state-prison offence for any white man to reside among the Indians without a license from the State. Mr. Worcester, being a missionary among the Indians at their request, and under a license from the United States, refused to quit the country; upon which the State of Georgia caused him to be prosecuted, convicted, and imprisoned for a violation of the law. Mr. Worcester brought a writ of error in the Supreme Court of the United States, to have the judgment reversed. The court decided that the laws of Georgia, under which he was condemned, and the laws by which the State claimed a right to control the Cherokee Indians, were unconstitutional, and therefore void. They also decided that the Cherokee nation is a separate and independent nation, and that the State of Georgia has no right to interfere with them in their lands. I hope this just decision by the highest tribunal of the United States, in favor of a much-injured race, will be the means of restoring to them that justice which is their due. Tell the doctor that all the principles which the advocates of the Indians contended for last winter, in our lyceum, have been sustained, by the court, in the fullest manner.

May the best of heaven's blessing fall on you, and the dear family that are spared. Love to all.

G. N. Briggs.

The Representative in Congress was not yet, it would seem, so much of a hero to his own children but that one of them was saucy enough to play a First-of-April trick upon him. Of this he writes: —

Washington, April 7, 1832.

My dear Harriet:

A letter came to-day in an envelope, which induced me to think it contained something precious. On taking off the envelope and breaking the seal, I was amused to read the words, " April Fool," and at the bottom of the sheet, " Your dear son, Geo. P. Briggs." It reminded me of a boyish trick which, you will remember, was played by his father upon a certain young lady some fifteen or six-

teen years ago. How rapidly, and with a more than eagle's swift-
ness, time flies away. How difficult it is to realize that the parties
to the little "All Fools" trick to which I have alluded, who, at the
time it was played were in the freshness and gayety of youth, have
passed the meridian of life and become the parents of a family of
children old enough to begin to repeat the tricks of their youth.

. . . .

Two days ago Mr. Cook, of Ohio, received a note preliminary to
a challenge, for words used in debate. Give yourself no apprehension, for I think there is no danger of your husband getting
into a duel.

The year 1832 will long be remembered as the dreadful
cholera summer. In the following letter its appearance is
first mentioned : —

. . . . . "The cholera does not, thus far, prevail extensively. I hear it is in Albany. I think you have not much to fear
from it in the country.

"Lorenzo Dow is among the curiosities and oddities of the city.
He is rather a patriarchal-looking man. His hair is very long,
and parted like a woman's. His long gray beard gives him a
strange appearance. He has small, gray eyes, quick and intelligent. I have heard him preach, and was pleased with him. His
sermon was more serious and methodical than I expected. He is
a queer being.

"Tell Uncle John Farnum that I will thank him not to take all
the trout out of the brook that runs through the meadow, before I
come home. Should he be disposed to catch any, my mark is a
multitude of little red spots on the sides of the fish, and they have
black backs and white bellies." . . . . .

This allusion to his trouting tastes will find its proper
sequence in what his daughter says concerning it : —

"His excessive fondness for trouting never abated. Many a
summer's day has he fished down the beautiful Housatonic, quite
from its source in the north part of Lanesboro', through the

'Happy Valley.' The great mountain on the north, and the undulating wave-like hills on the west, casting over him their lengthening shadows, — the velvety meadows beguiling him with their softness, — the more fascinating trout holding him in successful dalliance, till, with a full string, at the appointed rendezvous, he met my mother, who, in the carryall, driving the veteran Billy,[1] had passed the long hours with her book and knitting, following along the road, while he angled in the winding stream. Arrived at home, perhaps, with a cramp in his leg, and over-weary, he would first dispose of his trout among the invalids in the neighborhood, and then he was willing to be refreshed."

The following personal reminiscence of a remarkable woman will interest the reader : —

WASHINGTON, May 27th, 1832.

DEAR HARRIET:

I attended church at the Capitol this morning, and heard the celebrated Harriet Livermore, of New Hampshire, preach. In her person she somewhat resembles Ann Rexford. . . . . . I have heard but few better models of correct speaking. . . . . . She is, without exception, the sweetest singer I ever heard. Her voice is inconceivably sweet, and though not loud, was distinctly heard by probably a thousand people, and every word was perfectly articulated. She said she was going among the Indians. . . .

He had a constitutional fear of disease and death, which all his life, as his family say, caused him much mental suffering, and which often required all his fortitude and power of will to throw off. His friends sometimes amused themselves at this timidity, and he by no means resented their raillery on the subject when he was in good health. His daughter says : —

"They tell a story of him and Rufus Choate, which, making some allowance for embellishment, I heartily believe. After the

---

[1] A favorite horse, still doing service for the family.

cholera commenced its fearful work on our shores, Mr. Choate
and himself were exceedingly apprehensive of its appearance in
Washington, as the session was prolonged into midsummer. It is
said they were in the habit of calling daily upon Dr. Sewall, whom
they knew intimately, to ask if there were any cases in the city.
For a long time the cheering answer was, ' *No.*' When, at last,
there occurred cases in town, and Mr. Choate received the information, he immediately said, ' Don't tell Briggs, doctor; he will
have an attack before night.' A few minutes later the same intelligence was communicated to my father, when he exclaimed,
'Don't tell Choate; it will frighten him to death.' "

The following letter to his wife illustrates the habitual
religiousness of his mind and feelings : —

WASHINGTON, 26th June, 1832.

DEAR HARRIET :

. . . . . I am not surprised at your alarm on the appearance of the cholera. There is much in it to appal. But still it
becomes us to remember that mortality is stamped upon all things
in nature; and though it is uncommon to see our fellow-mortals
swept off by scores at a time, by a resistless disease, yet, when we
reflect that by the certain operations of nature's laws, a few years
would do the same work; and when we consider that one is a more
sensible exhibition of that power which controls life and death
than the other, we should bow with reverence to the majesty of
that power, and tremble and adore the Being who exercises it in a
manner so signal. I told you something of an alarm we had,
that a ship-load of diseased emigrants had arrived at Alexandria,
and of its utter want of truth. Its ravages at Montreal and Quebec
are truly terrible; how soon it may make its appearance in different parts of our country I know not. Our ingratitude and trans-
gressions, as a people, deserve the severest visitations of Divine
judgments. . . . . .

We ought to endeavor to resign ourselves to the dispositions of
His providence, and calmly await and *meet* whatever His goodness
and wisdom appoints. It is our duty to use all means in our
power to avert sickness. . . . . .

Let the drains about the house be perfectly cleaned, and as little filth collected as possible. Throw about chloride of lime Persons should often bathe, and avoid evening air. Eat no vegetables of any amount. Live temperately, but well. A firm reliance upon the protecting care of that Providence in whose hands we all are, will do much to preserve our health, especially from attacks of contagious diseases. The mind should make itself familiar, by reflection, with the worst, and cast itself on Him who can alone sustain, and trust in Him for the event.

Our labors are very severe in Congress. I am quite well. May a kind and good God preserve us, soon to meet, and rejoice in His goodness. Do not imagine that this letter is written in agitation. It is not so. I hope to help quiet your mind, which I trust is not greatly excited. God bless you all.

Yours,   G. N. BRIGGS.

CHAPTER X.

THE last of July of this year brought him again to his home in the Boro', and to the welcome of friends and neighbors, after an absence of eight months.

"We children," says the daughter, "knew only *joy* at his return, and could not understand the distress our parents suffered, even in the happiness of a reunion. Neither did we understand why our father could not *look* at the picture of little Anna, which was so living in its truthfulness and loveliness, that it seemed almost herself. For weeks we wondered that he could not hear her name nor be told the story of her sickness, nor go, as we had, with our mother, to the place in the church-yard, where her little form had been so peacefully sleeping all the spring and summer."

"We all," continues Mrs. Bigelow, "have vivid recollections of the *cholera remedies* which were brought home, including a tin vapor-bath of formidable dimensions, and round boxes of numbers 1, 2, and 3, besides sundry powders, to be administered in various stages of the dreaded disease. I remember, too, hearing him describe, years after, that dreadful night in New York, which a most characteristic and amusing letter from Mr. Choate commemorates. He said the stillness of the tomb reigned in the death-struck city; and at an alarm of fire no response came from the usually alert firemen. Nothing, literally nothing, was heard, save

112

the footfalls of the man who uttered the cry, as they fell rapidly on the echoing pavements."

The following is the letter to which the daughter here refers ; and the picture it presents of his excitement, under the contagion of fear, is well worthy of a framework that may preserve it : —

SALEM, Aug. 12, 1832.

MY DEAR COLLEAGUE:

I rejoice to have it under your hand that you got home so well, and have thus far escaped the fell destroyer of so much of our peace at Washington. Like you, I had formed various projects for stopping at Newark, Jersey City, Long Island, and where not; all ending in an infernal, long, sleepless, and terrific night, at the Atlantic Hotel. The doctor and I found quarters in the same room. The moon shone as upon the city of the dead; and the only sounds from the streets I took to be the footsteps, or the slow wheels, of the bearers of the suddenly sick, or those, more happy, whose sickness was all over. Between you and me, I came once or twice in the night to what old people call hysterics — a sort of rascally nervous inclination to *squeal* and kick up my heels, fancy ministering to fear and fatigue ; and when the morning-star rose at length, it seemed to glitter and sing as on the day of the creation — so long and full of horror had been the night ! So I sallied down to the wharf to take the New Haven boat, and was told it was quarantined at New Haven, and that it was doubtful if any mode of leaving the city for the Eastward would be provided while the cholera continued. Having the premonitory symptoms very bad, I cleared for the Albany boat, shot up to Poughkeepsie, and came home, leaving my umbrella and twelve shirts (my wife says fifteen) at Jarvis's, in Poughkeepsie. There I called a doctor, who proved a modest, clever, sensible fellow, a friend of Pendleton and Clay, and a most decided, prepared foe of all cholera. He said nothing ailed me. Whereupon I went to bed, gentle as a lamb, and slept like a rock. Our people here are cool on the occasion. They send me my last year's bills to pay with as much punctuality

10*

as if all was straight, and receive my United States' bills, as if they expected to live a thousand years. I am shocked at such conduct.

Yours, in all love and honor,

R. CHOATE.

The reopening of Congress found him promptly at his post again. During the recess and his sojourn at home, his daughter made a public profession of her faith in Christ, and he writes to her this New Year's letter, — the only fragment of his Washington correspondence during that session which these memoirs include : —

WASHINGTON, Jan. 1st, 1833.

MY DEAR DAUGHTER :

I have only time to write you a few words this evening, and to wish you a happy New Year. This, I have no doubt, my child, will be a New Year's day which you will regard with peculiar interest. Within the year just passed away, you have taken upon yourself a profession and a character, which you have the deepest possible interest to sustain during the remainder of your life. To maintain, especially by young persons, the consistent and beautiful character of a disciple of Jesus, is a thing of first importance. Though at the present day the Christian profession has many aids, yet to the young and inexperienced every path is strewn with snares and evils. Caution, prudence, and reflection should direct and guard the way. A humble reliance and dependence upon the great Author of our being, and the Rock of our Salvation, should be our constant support. . . . .

On the 14th of January, he delivered a speech in the House, in opposition to the bill " to Reduce and otherwise Alter the Duties on Imports." In this speech he displayed his wonted fidelity to the interests of his constituents, and argued his cause with much force and felicity of language. A single passage will suffice to show the style and the spirit alike of this performance : —

"Mr. Chairman, has it been seen in nature that the flowers of spring bud and blossom and beautify the earth, under the influence of perpetual frosts? Is the earth green and verdant, and does it yield to the husbandman a plentiful harvest, where the poisonous simoon blows its withering blasts? And, sir, will it be contended that under the operation of unwise, imprudent, and oppressive laws, the people of any country, no matter what may have been their natural advantages, ever advanced rapidly in population and wealth, in all the arts and improvements that adorn and embellish private life, and add dignity and consequence to national character? Such an assumption would set at defiance every principle of political economy, and call in question the truth of all history. Why, then, is a policy under which the country has reached an unrivalled prosperity, to be rashly assailed and destroyed? Are we growing impatient under too much good fortune? Has great success made us restless and eager for a change? Let us take counsel of experience, and learn wisdom from the past, before we take a step that we may not be able to retrace."

The Christian father approves and encourages the pious determination of his daughter to withhold herself from the temptations of the gay and frivolous scenes of society. Writing to her from his Berkshire home, he says, —

LANESBORO', June 12, 1833.

My dear Child:

Yours of the 4th is at hand. We are glad to hear you are settled in a pleasant, convenient boarding-place. Your resolutions are right ones. I hope, by divine aid, you will be enabled to keep them. While Christians should always remember that they are not *of* the world, they should bear in mind that they are *in* the world. All the active duties of life can be performed, and yet the "followers of the Lamb" may keep themselves unspotted. We are made for society, and it is the duty of Christians to exercise a purifying influence upon the society in which they may be placed. You know the good part is to be *chosen*. It must be chosen with sincerity, and loved and cherished with all the powers of the soul.

All other things should be made subordinate to it. When chosen, it will exercise a controlling influence on the life and actions of its possessor.

His daughter's pen supplies the following interesting account of her mother's skill at the loom, and of her father's beautiful pride in the products of it. She says, —

"At a time when our manufacturers were not doing what they now are in supplying our people with fabrics, and in a district where one of the accomplishments of the fairest girl was *to spin*, beside cunning embroidery and kindred fine arts, our mother was by no means in her youth deficient in her attainments, as the snowy linen, *Holland* and damask, 'fine twined' and beautiful, the soft woollen blankets of blue and white, and *chiefest* coverlet of brilliant scarlet and white, are proofs. These are kept, with care and quite innocent pride, among our heirlooms. It was one of the affecting incidents of the last week of his life, — of the very morning, indeed, before he died, — that my father moved his hand fondly back and forth on the soft, light blanket thrown over him, and said, 'Made more .than forty years ago, by her own hands.'"

The allusion, in the next letter to his daughter, will be appreciated with this explanation : —

LANESBORO', Oct. 5, 1833.

DEAR HARRIET :

. . . . . Your mother took the first premium on her cloth at the fair (Berkshire Agricultural Cattle Show and Fair), which was an eight-dollar set of teaspoons. She has made a beautiful piece of cloth, — one I shall feel proud to exhibit as a specimen of household industry and ingenuity. . . . . .

While at Washington this year he wore, on state occasions, a suit of clothes made of this really beautiful cloth.

Had the fair solicitors referred to in the following letter

been far less fair, they would hardly have failed in their charitable quest : —

WASHINGTON, 8th Dec., 1833.

DEAR HARRIET:

This is the evening of the third Sabbath since I parted with you and my little family. Time and distance do not abate my solicitude for your welfare.

This evening, two beautiful young ladies called on me for charity to one of the Baptist churches of this city. They said the church was poor. I told them that was one of the characteristics of Baptist churches; — poverty was one of their jewels. The solicitors were so *fair*, and evinced so much zeal in the cause, that I could not turn them away empty-handed. I promised them I would go the next Sunday to their church, and hear Dr. Hall, of Kentucky, preach. When I have heard him, I will say more about it.

Tranquillity, health, and happiness to you all. I send special greetings to mother. Love to the children, and kindest remembrance to our neighbors.

In strong bonds,

G. N. BRIGGS.

To his youngest son, he writes thus playfully : —

WASHINGTON, Dec. —, 1833.

Well, my dear Henry, you continue to write me often, — that is right. I hope you will not cease to do so. You don't quite remember what I told you about beginning the names of persons with a capital letter. You see it don't look well to begin henry with a small *h*. If you wish to write about hens, why, you begin with a little *h;* but if you wish to write the name of a *smart, likely* boy, you begin with a capital H, and write it *Henry*. Tell Harriet we do not spell *writ, rit*. I think such a "*rit*" would hardly sue a man. How do the old cow and *heifer* get along? What are you studying at school? Do you learn well? Does Squier learn fast?

Do you take good care of your mother and grandmother? Tell
me all the news.

Your father,

G. N. Briggs.

His honest and hearty admiration of simplicity of manners is continually displayed in his sketches of persons : —

Washington, 3d Jan., 1834.

My dear Wife :

I dined with Mr. Adams last evening at 5 o'clock.   The whole
of the Massachusetts delegation were there, and it was a very
pleasant party.   I called on Mr. Adams the day before, and was
made acquainted with Mrs. Adams.   She is a *lady* — very intelligent, affable, and agreeable.   While she has the manners of one
who, from education, intercourse with the world, and position, is
far above the great proportion of those women who move in the
first circles of society, her appearance is marked with the ease
and simplicity indicative of an elevated and refined intellect and
an amiable temper.   Though somewhat advanced in years, she has
the vivacity and cheerfulness of youth.   Her dress is plain and
becoming.   Mr. Adams is yet plainer in his personal appearance.
He is a singular and a *wonderful* man.   When he opens his lips in
conversation, his words seem the very oracles of human wisdom
and learning.

To his nephew, he writes : —

Washington, 14th Jan., 1834.

Yours of the 28th, my dear boy, saying that you had made up
your mind not to go to Cleveland till spring, came to hand this
morning.   I was sorry to learn that you had yielded your purpose
of commencing the practice of law in the place you had contemplated according to your previous determination.   Remember, my
boy, "there is a tide in the affairs of men, which, taken at its flood,
leads on to fortune."   There is nothing in the simple fact of delay-
ing, for a few weeks, the time of executing any purpose of consequence; but it is the danger of falling into the habit of irresolu-
tion or wavering, if a fixed purpose is permitted to be shaken

without sufficient reason. When Washington, after having been detained late at night at his office, the last time he was ever in it, was asked by Mrs. Washington why he remained so late : "My dear," said he, "you know it has been with me a maxim, and one I have always practised, never to leave till to-morrow what may be done to-day." The wisdom of that maxim was never more clearly shown than in the case which then induced him to avow it. If the business that detained that great man had not been done then, he would never have performed it, for death put an end to his labors in a few brief hours. His practice was a beautiful enforcement of the Scripture injunction, to do with our might what our hands find to do. You will not consider these remarks at all intended to condemn your course. They grow out of an imperfect knowledge of the case, and are only intended as the hints of one who feels a deep interest in your prosperity, which may not, perhaps, be unprofitably in your thoughts, as you look over your plans and lay down the maxims on which you design to act through life.

An extract from a letter to his daughter affords an illustration of his religious solicitude for his children : —

"I am glad of the account you give of your brother George. I hope, indeed, that he has learned to love the Saviour, and that his future life will be adorned, not only by the Christian profession, but with the Christian *character*. It pleases me to hear that your little brother Henry "remembers his Creator," and learns to pray to Him in early childhood. The late eccentric John Randolph, of Virginia, in a letter to a friend a few years before his death, said, "At one period of my life, I was upon the point of yielding to the influence of the French philosophy of 1794, and becoming an open infidel. I was only saved from the fatal error by recollecting that when a child my dear Christian mother used to have me kneel, and, taking my little hands between hers, teach me to say, ' Our Father who art in heaven.' "

Under the date of Jan. 14th, he gives, in a letter to his wife, the following account of a remarkable sudden death which occurred in the House : —

"The regular and beaten round of business in the House to-day was broken in upon in a manner that produced such a sensation as I never before witnessed in a public assembly, and hope *never again* to witness. It was the sudden death of one of the members. Judge Bouldin, of Virginia, took the floor upon an all-absorbing question, which has been under discussion the whole session. The House was full, and the galleries thronged. In the ladies' gallery was the wife of Judge Bouldin, who had come up, full of expectation, to listen to his speech. He began to speak, by remarking that he had been rebuked by one of his colleagues for not announcing to this House, at an earlier period, the death of John Randolph,[1] late of Virginia. He said, 'I must state to the House the reason why I have not before done so.' Here he paused, as was his manner; seemed much agitated, threw his head back, looked partly round, then fell forward, and was caught in the arms of a member before he reached the floor. It was hoped by the horror-struck assembly that it was only a fainting-fit, but all efforts to bring him to life failed, and, after a few convulsive gasps, he expired. His distressed wife rushed from the gallery, but, before she was able to reach the place where her dying husband lay, she was carried to another part of the hall. Her shrieks of agony reached every part of the chamber. I was not in the House at the moment, having gone to the President's, to present a bill for his signature. When I returned, a deep gloom pervaded the whole multitude about the Capitol. I went into the Speaker's room, and there saw the lifeless corpse of my much-esteemed friend, with whom I spoke the moment before I left the hall to go to the President's.[2]

"How true, that 'in the midst of life we are in death.' He was a man of great ardor and warmth of feeling. I never heard him speak when I did not feel apprehensive that he might meet the event which has terminated his life to-day. He spoke with great effort, and the blood rushed to his face and head as though it would burst through every pore. It was a singular coincidence,

[1] Mr. Randolph was from the district Judge B. represented.

[2] His daughter remembers him to have said that he invited Judge Bouldin to stand at his desk while he spoke, as it was one of the best localities for being heard in the hall; and he thought the Judge had taken the place and died there.

that at the very moment he was speaking of the death of his friend, he should himself have ceased to exist. All these lessons teach *us* to be ready.

" Always thine,

" G. N. BRIGGS."

The funeral of that distinguished man, William Wirt, who died Feb. 18th, 1834, is the theme of the following graphic letter : —

WASHINGTON, 21st Feb., 1834.

MY DEAR WIFE:

I told you of the death of Mr. Wirt, two or three days since. The funeral of the great and good man took place to-day at 12 o'clock. I doubt whether, since the death of Washington, there has been in this country a death which has produced a grief so universal and profound as that now felt by the people throughout the republic, at the announcement of that of this excellent and upright man. While his varied, rich, and brilliant talents commanded the respect, his bland and amiable manners, his benevolent and pious heart, won the affection and esteem of all who knew his person and character. His face was a good index to his character. It was full of mildness and intelligence. His family are spoken of as sharing largely in the qualities of their deceased parent. Both Houses adjourned for the purpose of attending his funeral, — a token of respect, I understand, never before shown to any private citizen in this country. In this case, it was worthy the character it was intended to honor.

I was early at the house where he died. His family I only saw as they mournfully passed from the house to the carriages as they moved away to the tomb. . . . . . I saw none in the multitude who exhibited more evidence of being deep and sincere mourners, than the Indians who are delegates from the Cherokees. There were six of them, and they sat, I should think, an hour before the procession was formed. The gloom which deepened the natural gravity of their dark and swarthy faces, their downcast looks, and total abstraction from everything that surrounded them, testified how sincerely and solemnly they participated in the

11

sorrows of those who mourned the loss of him whose death had
called together such a company.   They lost in him a professional
and national friend, — a friend who in years past has stood by them
in the most trying circumstances.   One of them told me, last evening, that in Mr. Wirt the Cherokees had lost their best friend.
There were present, on this occasion, the President of the United
States and all his Cabinet; large numbers of both Houses of Congress; all the Judges of the Supreme Court; the most distinguished members of the bar from many of the States; several
foreign ministers; great numbers of private citizens of this District, and, probably, from most of the States of the Union. . . .

In the House, this morning, Mr. Adams pronounced a short
eulogy on the life and character of Mr. Wirt, of surprising ele-
gance and beauty. . . . . .   When his death was announced
to the Supreme Court, the venerable Chief Justice, in a few words,
before the adjournment of the court, paid a rich tribute to his
memory.   .   .

Mr. Wirt now quietly sleeps in the "house appointed for all the
living."   He is beyond the reach of human praise, but his reputation belongs to his country and his race; and now, as long as virtue
and talents shall be honored and revered, his name will be honored
and resplendent with glory.

Love and good-will to all.

Ever thine,

GEO. N. BRIGGS.

The following sketch of Rev. T. R. Stockton, at that
time, and also at a subsequent period, the eloquent and
beloved Chaplain of the House of Representatives, is a fit
and beautiful tribute to the character and congressional
service of the man and the minister : —

WASHINGTON, Mar. 9, 1834.

MY DEAR WIFE:

Having, as my custom is, attended public worship twice to-day,
I seize a moment to communicate with my dearest earthly friend.
Mr. Stockton's text at the Capitol was in John iii. 3: "Except a

man be born again, he cannot see the kingdom of God." He preached such a sermon as I think should be preached from that most important and interesting text. After showing what the new birth is, he proceeded to show its necessity. He described the kingdom of God as applied to the kingdom of grace here, and as also applied to the kingdom of glory in heaven. After giving a most enrapturing and eloquent description of the kingdom of heaven, — its throne, its vast extent, its inhabitants and effulgent glories, and contrasting its employments and happiness with the honors, riches, and highest acquisitions of this world, he said he seemed to hear his audience say, "Let us leave this earth, and enter upon the glories of that blessed kingdom. But stop, my friends," said he, " I hear a voice from that world, saying, 'Except a man be born again, he cannot see the kingdom of God.' " The audience was very large indeed, and the most perfect silence and attention were observed through the whole sermon. He is a reformed Methodist; I judge from twenty-six to thirty years old. His form is tall and slender. He has on his face the *death*-stamp of consumption. In prayer, his manner is drawling and too monotonous, probably induced, in a great measure, by the state of his health; but when he has proceeded a while in his sermon, he becomes animated, and breaks forth into the most fervid and brilliant strains of eloquence I have ever heard from the pulpit. There is in all his services the deepest solemnity, and, unlike almost every other preacher I have ever heard in the Hall, when he preaches I have never seen the least thing in his manner or language or sentiment that indicated a consciousness that he was Chaplain to Congress, or that he was preaching in the Hall of the House of Representatives. I understand he sustains a character without reproach, and his demeanor is meek and unassuming. This evening, Mr. ———, a Unitarian minister, is to preach a sermon upon regeneration. Those who are more pleased with the rationale of the modern Unitarian religion than with that old-fashioned religion preached to Nicodemus by our Saviour, will hear him. Those who reject what we consider the great truth of religion, — I mean, the new birth, — because they cannot understand the process by the light of reason, seem to forget that they

do not disbelieve that the wind blows when they can neither see
it, nor "tell whence it comes, nor whither it goes. So," says He
who knew, "is every one that is born of God."

Health good. Love to all.

Thine in strong bonds,

G. N. Briggs.

The preacher referred to in the next letter was one of the
two clergymen who were sent out from England in 1833,
as a deputation to the American churches, and whose
"visit" was made the theme of a popular volume : —

WASHINGTON, Mar. 11, 1834.

My dear Wife:

. . . .

Mr. Reed, from London, preached this morning. He is a man
of the very first order of talents. His text was Luke ix. 56: "For
the son of man came not to destroy men's lives, but to save them."
His design was to show the benevolent object of the Saviour's
advent into the world. This, he said, was manifest from early
indications of the designs of mercy towards the human family by
the Creator, as appears from the first promises of a Saviour in the
Old Scriptures. But, above all, the benevolent object of his advent
appears in his life and mission, in his acts and death. He noticed,
in the most appropriate and touching manner, numerous instances
of the kindness, mercy, and condescension of Christ towards the
suffering, the needy, and the guilty. "My friends," said he, "the
Saviour was *poorer* than you. He was more destitute than you
are. He was more *friendless* than you are. His sorrows were
greater, more numerous and severe than yours are; and, above
all, he died for you. Yes, the *Saviour died* for you. We may suffer much and sacrifice much for our friends, — but who would
die for his friends? Yet the compassionate Redeemer *died* for us.
He not only died for us, but the manner of his death made it more
agonizing than any death ever before or ever since witnessed. It
was not the nails in his hands nor the spear in his side that killed
the Saviour; it was intense agony of soul that terminated his life.
He suffered in intensity what we deserved to suffer eternally."

His sermon was entirely extemporaneous; and, for purity of style, and correctness and vigor of thought, deep pathos, and thrilling interest, I don't know that I have ever heard it equalled. He hardly quoted a passage of Scripture to which he did not add new and deeper interest, by his peculiar rendering. To show the active and all-pervading benevolence of the Saviour, he said, "He went *about* doing good. He did not sit down and wait till some object of distress called on him for relief, but, full of mercy, *He went about* — doing good."

I would that you could have had the pleasure of sitting with me and listening to that admirable sermon. I heard, last evening, what was called a most eloquent Unitarian sermon, in which the Saviour was spoken of as a person of high moral attainments and dignity, and declared to be nothing more than human, endowed with great powers. His life was represented as a glorious *model*, calculated to raise men's opinions of their own moral power, and thus to lead them to a course of mental and moral improvement. The life of *the founder of the Christian religion* was spoken of as eminently calculated to raise the character of man; but he was not spoken of as the *Saviour and Redeemer* of man. No declaration that he *died* for us, and purchased us with his own blood, was made to cheer the heart, and open a way of relief and escape from the bondage of sin and death. While others hailed that sermon as the perfection of preaching and a fine specimen of pulpit eloquence, to me its assumptions destroyed all hopes of salvation for ruined man. . . . . .

But I am making this letter too long.

Most affectionately, thine own,

G. N. BRIGGS.

11*

CHAPTER XI.

CHARACTER OF HIS LIFE IN WASHINGTON — SOCIAL NATURE — HOME IN-
FLUENCES — A SYMPATHIZING COLLEAGUE — LETTERS TO HIS WIFE —
LAFAYETTE — LETTER TO HIS DAUGHTER — LETTERS TO HIS WIFE — AT
HOME.

MR. BRIGGS, it will be borne in mind, was a young man when he was first intrusted with the duty of representing his district in Congress; and the twelve years he passed amid the allurements and dissipations of the National Capitol did not quench within him the fires of mature manhood. We wonder, perhaps, that he should have kept himself so absolutely as he did from all the fascinations and follies which surrounded him, preserving in all their freshness the religious scruples with which he went to Washington, and keeping his relish keen for everything pure and excellent and spiritual.

This remarkable conservation of his early tastes is not to be explained upon the supposition that he had no social inclinations, for the reverse of this is eminently true; and so fond was he of genial companionship, so gifted in what gives a zest to it, so quick and affluent in his humor, so ready and happy in conversational powers, that all this increases the marvel of his strict abstinence from the social vices which glittered everywhere around him.

Doubtless it was his strong religious principle that kept him thus "unspotted from the world;" but it is impossible to doubt that his persistent and unintermitted communion with the loved ones at home — with his wife and children — was an efficient adjunct, with the force of religious character, in giving him the complete control of his appetites and habits.

The influences of his happy home atmosphered him in imagination at Washington. In his chamber, which was described by one who visited him in it, as having " a very domestic look," he could easily surround himself with the forms and faces of the absent ones, and this spiritual companionship with them was sweeter to him than even the innocent gayeties of society.

His loving heart expended its sympathy and its strength upon those from whom he was only materially separated. This conviction is unavoidable to one who reviews his correspondence with home. This is indeed the most copious source of information concerning his unofficial life which is accessible to the biographer, and it reflects broadly, and purely also, the spirit and motive which controlled all his acts on the floor of Congress.

He had, it would seem, a colleague who sympathized with him in his domestic attachments, and the following letter presents both these worthy Congressmen in a very amiable light, and gives assurance of their stability of character.

The reader will find no difficulty in deciding that his friend, Mr. Hall, is the same to whom reference was made in an earlier chapter, and who survives his friend, to bear testimony to his excellence and nobleness, and to deplore his loss : —

WASHINGTON, 26 April, 1834.

MY DEAR WIFE:

Some time since, Mr. Hall and myself had a discussion upon the most proper and affectionate soubriquet by which we should address our wives at the commencement of our letters. I was inclined to use the christian name, he to use the term *wife*. He argued that, as the relation of husband and wife was the most dear and interesting in which human beings could stand to one another, those who are thus related ought, when they address one another by epistle, to use the term which best expresses that relation. For authority he refers to the "Sketch Book." Not having read his au thority, I could say but little about it; but, at any rate, it occurred to me that as his *author* was a bachelor, he was not exactly the *chap* to dictate to me how to address my wife. For this reason his authority did not appear to me to be entirely conclusive, and upon general reasoning, though I yield to the argument deduced from the charm of the *little wife*, especially to all such as love their wives as they ought, still I cannot get rid of the impression that I loved her who is now my wife by a name she bore before that cog- nomen was applied to her. This impression abiding, when I sit down to write, I begin my dear —— Harriet. The name of the loved maiden will always crowd into my mind before the word wife. But he accidentially let out a fact which I cannot help be- lieving has, at least, some influence in forming his strong attach- ment to the use of the connubial title, if it does not form the controlling motive. "Now," said he, "how would it look for me to begin my letters with 'my dear Dolly?'" "Ah!" said I, "my dear fellow, there's the rub,—it is that *Dolly* that creates your aversion, and not the word wife, to which you are so strongly attached." Now he would not admit, of course, that I had hit upon the very thing, but he went to thinking upon the subject, and I do not discover that he is very anxious to revive the discussion. I hold that any man who has so excellent a wife as he has, should never entertain the least prejudice against her name. On the con- trary, a man who has been so fortunate as to win a good wife is bound to believe that everything about her (except snuff-taking) is the best that possibly could be. The thing is settled. I have just read to him thus far, and he says: "It is a fact, it is the meanest name ever given to a girl." After all, there is one circumstance that cannot have escaped your notice, and which will not go very far to establish the influence which my own argument has had upon my mind, and that is, that ever since I had the conversation with him I have, I believe, commenced my letters to you with his favorite address. Still, it is one of the most common things in life for our practice to contradict our doctrine. I will not admit that my argument is unsound.

.   .   .   .

P. S. Mr. Hall wishes me to say to you, that it seems I am willing to adopt his *rule*, though I insist on my own *reasons*.

Here, as in many of his letters, the home-sickness — that malady of which no man need be ashamed — displays itself in unmistakable symptoms : —

Sunday evening.

MY DEAR WIFE:

A most beautiful day has just passed away, and the last rays of the departing sun are tinging with red the clouds which hang over the western horizon. Whilst strolling among the scattered houses of the northern part of the city, and seeing mothers and their children sitting in their doors and on their piazzas, what do you think a poor fellow, four hundred and fifty miles from the beloved of his heart, and the children of his and her affection, thought of? I imagine, now that the evening is closing in upon me, that, in the old Boro' castle, our excellent and dear mother sits with her Bible in her lap, and her aching head resting upon her hand, pondering over a life which has been full of incident. While she feels many sorrows and apprehensions of mind, her soul is solaced with hope, and she looks forward to the cheering prospect when the consolations which are promised in the blessed volume, will be hers. Her daughter sits at the south window in the dining-room, looking out as far as the twilight will permit, upon the beautiful view that spreads itself to the eye ; and while a lonely feeling steals over her, she sends a thought to the far-off south and   .   .   .

The remaining details of the home picture, sketched in this letter, so fondly drawn, may be inappropriate for the public eye ; but to those familiar with them they are dear,

and present in memory a vision of an earthly house only
less bright than that vision which faith and hope afford of
our " Father's house " and " many mansions " in the heavenly world.

The magnificent tribute of John Quincy Adams to the
memory of Lafayette, is admirably characterized in the
following letter : —

WASHINGTON, 31st December, 1834.

MY DEAR WIFE:

We have had a great day at the Capitol. At the close of the last
session, Mr. Adams was appointed by both Houses of Congress
to pronounce a eulogy upon the character of Lafayette. Some time
since, a committee was appointed to appoint a day and make arrangements for the occasion. To-day both Houses met, but no
business was done except to read the journals. At half past twelve
the Senators, accompanied by the President of the United States,
and his Cabinet Ministers, entered the Hall of Representatives.
The lobbies of the House were filled with ladies, and the galleries
with multitudes who had assembled to witness the ceremonies of
the day. Mr. Adams ascended to the Speaker's place and commenced his oration, which occupied within a few minutes of three
hours in the delivery. It was a wonderful performance. The immense multitude listened with most profound attention and stillness during the whole time. It has more than sustained the
reputation of this great man as a statesman and writer. As he
progressed with the subject, the attention of the audience increased
and the profoundest silence pervaded the great multitude which
surrounded the speaker, until the moment he ceased speaking,
when the silence was broken by the deafening applause which
broke forth in acknowledgment of the commanding powers of the
orator, and his masterly treatment of the subject. It would be
difficult to say whether, in this single performance, he erected the
most enduring monument for himself, or to the great and good
man whose eulogy he pronounced. The oration will be published,
and I will send you a copy. . . .

Thine own,

G. N. BRIGGS.

He took a great interest in his daughter's reading, and directed her choice of books, and her habits of studying them, with great assiduity : —

WASHINGTON, December 31, 1834.

MY DEAR CHILD:

I suppose you are studying hard this winter. . . . . I don't know whether you will find it profitable or not to go through in detail with the "Polynesian Researches." Though there are many things of interest in them, yet there is such minuteness of detail, of matters and things of not much consequence, I should hardly think it worth while to read them systematically. They will do better for occasional reading, as there is not such a dependence of one part upon another, as to make it necessary to read them in course. Before I left home you had commenced reading Marshall's "Life of Washington." I should prefer to have you go through with that work now with care and attention. I am reading Gibbon's " Decline and Fall of the Roman Empire." I make it my rule, in addition to my other miscellaneous reading, and my attendance in the House, and on committees, and on other public business, to dispatch a hundred pages a day. There are six volumes of more than five hundred pages each. I am through with three volumes and shall commence the fourth on Monday morning. I want you to be in the regular habit of reading every day in addition to your studies; and do it attentively and thoroughly, that it may make a lasting impression on your mind. I trust you will spend a portion of each day of your life in religious reading — reading in the Bible and other books.

The funeral of Mr. ——, of whose death I informed you last evening, took place at twelve o'clock to-day in the Capitol. Immediately after the conclusion of the services in the Representatives' Hall, a most desperate and fiend-like attempt was made to assassinate the President of the United States. The members had followed the remains of the deceased from the Hall through the great Rotunda of the Capitol out of the eastern front. When they had all passed out, just as the President, at the side of Mr. Woodbury, the Secretary of the Treasury, had passed out of the east door of the Rotunda into the Portico, a man stepped before them, and drawing a pistol, pointed it at the breast of the President, and snapped it. The percussion-cap exploded, but the pistol did not go off. They both rushed towards the desperado, and when Mr. Woodbury was about to take him by the collar, and the President to lift his arm upon him, he drew and aimed another pistol at the President, and it snapped as the other had. At this moment another gentleman knocked the assassin down, and he was instantly secured. Both pistols were heavily loaded with powder and ball. An interposing Providence prevented the dreadful tragedy. No one can give any reason for the terrible act. It is said by some that this individual has had turns of insanity, and has made a similar attempt to murder his sister's husband. On his examination, it is said, he exhibited no signs of insanity. He is an Englishman, but has been long in this country; is from twenty-five to thirty years old, — a printer by trade, and has lived in the city about three years. His name is Richard Lawrence. It is said he exhibited no anxiety or uneasiness at his examination. He told the keeper the reason of his attempt was that the General had killed his father. Of course, there was no pretence for this. His father died a natural death, as is said, many years ago. I hope, for the honor of human nature and our country, it will turn out that he is crazy. I cannot account for his rash, wicked, and desperate attempt on any other supposition.

The transaction produced a most horrifying shock in this city, as it will throughout the nation. The desperado is well secured in jail, to await his trial. The old hero conducted himself with great firmness; though, with all who were present, he was shocked and excited by the desperate deed. He soon walked down the steps to his carriage, and rode to his mansion.

Thus, I have told you all the circumstances of this most extraordinary and murderous attempt on the life of the Chief Magistrate. If anything new turns up, I will write you about it. I was not present myself. Love to all.

Affectionately thine,
Geo. N. Briggs.

The first memorial of Mr. Briggs for the year 1835, is a brief letter to his wife, in reply to her New Year's greeting, with the thoughtful tone of which it is in harmony : —

WASHINGTON, January 7, 1835.

MY DEAR WIFE:

Yours of the 2d inst. was received this morning. Your reflections on the commencement of the New Year are such as the occasion should suggest. The fleeting years, as they pass away, will soon bring us to our last, when, if we are not sensible of it before, we shall deeply feel the value of time, and realize the importance of a right improvement of it. The countless mercies we are constantly receiving from the hand of our Heavenly Father, deserve our gratitude and our obedience to His laws. We ought to render that gratitude and yield that obedience. May we be wise for the future, redeem the past, and still be the recipients of His blessings. . . . .

A few days later he writes : —

January 22, 1835.

. . . . Soon after I went to the House this morning I found that Mr. Wise, a member from Virginia, had gone over into Maryland to fight a duel with a Mr. Coke, formerly a member from the same State. About two o'clock we learned that they had exchanged shots, that Mr. Coke fell wounded, but Wise was not hit. The wound of Coke is not severe. Such an occurrence is a deep reproach to an American Congress. It is surprising that the spirit of the age does not stamp with reprobation this barbarous relic of savage nations. Until it shall cease to be honorable for men to turn murderers to vindicate their manhood, we shall not deserve the name or the blessings of a Christian people. . . . .

He thus playfully takes his excellent wife to task for indulging in needless apprehensions about his health and life in his absence from home : —

12

WASHINGTON February 1, 1835.

. . . . . . How exceedingly vain and foolish it would be in one to lie awake all night, when he was warm and comfortable, in the apprehension that to-morrow night it would be so cold that he could not sleep!

What a serious loss it would be for one to deprive himself of the pleasure of a breakfast of fine, light, nicely-fried buckwheat cakes, all garnished with yellow butter and maple molasses, from the pitiful imagining that next year the buckwheat would all be cut off, or the maple-trees would run no sap! Is it not equally unfortunate, if not as unreasonable, for a likely, sensible, blue-eyed woman, whose husband happens to be in Congress — when she is in tolerable health with three rosy children about, and as many of the comforts of life as a poor man's wife has a right to expect; and who, from three to half-a-dozen times a week, has news of the welfare of her absent husband by letters, which continue to tell her how hard he loves her and what an excellent wife she is; I say, is it not a pity that she should permit her present enjoyment to be marred by the forebodings of future evil, or the idle suggestions of fears growing out of dreams, or some other sources equally unsubstantial? . . . .

A week later he chronicles the state of the weather as being unusual, and gives us a picture of himself airing his court suit of home-made clothes : —

WASHINGTON, January 29, 1835.

MY DEAR WIFE:

The weather here for the last fortnight has been such, I think, as I have never known for that length of time in January. It is much more like an early April. I am sorry it is not colder, for such out-of-season weather is not agreeable to me. I have had no letter from you for some time; why not? I hope you are not tipping your ribbons among the beaux of Berkshire. I assure you I have been remarkably domestic this winter. Occasionally I put on my claret suit and march out, but it is merely to keep the set and hang of my clothes, and not to make an impression upon the fair of the metropolis, of whom I am about as ignorant as if I had remained in the Boro'. . . . .

The long vacation of this year was passed by the Representative at home, in diligent devotion to the business of his profession, which was not by any means set aside, beyond the necessity of the case, by his absence during the winters.

He had no idle time — not even when he was whipping the waters of the trout-brooks around his home; for even then his mind was often busy, and he was doing needful work with it, or giving it no less needful repose. Temperance speeches, attendance upon religious gatherings, and other incidental occupations, filled up all the intervals he did not devote to his business.

CHAPTER XII.

AT the opening of the first session of the Twenty-fourth Congress, Mr. Briggs was in his chair, more than ever assured of the confidence and favor of his constituents, and certainly no less resolved to be worthy of it, by a conscientious discharge of every duty of his position as their Representative.

He thus chronicles his return to the scenes and occupations with which four years' experience had made him familiar : —

WASHINGTON, December 1, 1835.

MY DEAR WIFE:

I have set myself down in my old quarters, where I have passed four years of congressional life. I have been rather solitary for the last two days. Sometimes I would half make up my mind to quit and run home; but when I remember that at home, when a fit of the blues came on, I would feel like running away from them even there, I was considerably quieted. . . . .

I should be stupid and ungrateful if I did not properly appreciate the consideration and regard which a generous people have shown me by sending me here, but I mistake myself if the *name* has much value in it, in my estimation.

I desire the good-will, respect, and esteem of my fellow-men, and I desire more to *deserve* these. This I would do by being useful to them, and by properly discharging every duty of my life. Of this, I know, I come short; but if I have ambition, it lies here. .

I called to-day at Dr. Lindsly's, and found them all well; was welcomed by them as though they were glad to see me.

The residence of Dr. Lindsly, to whom allusion is made here, was a social centre of attraction for many of the chief men in Congress, who frequently shared in its genial and generous hospitalities. Here Mr. Briggs found a home and those sympathies which served to cheer him in his unwelcome exile from his own family circle. Here, also, he formed a friendship for the estimable family of Dr. Lindsly, which is inherited and perpetuated by his children.

Under the date of December 20, 1835, he writes again to his wife, describing a preacher whom he heard that morning at the Capitol, and of whom he says, —

"I know not of what denomination he is; but in my estimation he made poor work at preaching. His aim seemed to be to convince his audience of the folly of being distressed by apprehensions of death. He seemed to take it for granted that, at death, all would enter upon a state of happiness, for he could not believe that God would send rational beings into this world to make them worse off in the next. He did not intimate that the condition of men, here or hereafter, has any connection with their conduct."

Later in the letter he continues : —

"Since meeting I have read, with great pleasure, two sermons of the late Robert Hall. He was a most extraordinary man and preacher. His mind was of the highest order. He was richly and profoundly imbued with the spirit of the gospel. His style is beautiful and forcible. He presents the great truths which relate to the salvation of the soul, in the most striking and impressive manner.

12*

"'What,' says he, 'my brethren, if we may indulge such a thought; what would be the funeral obsequies of a lost soul? Would it be possible for nature to utter a groan too deep or a cry too piercing to express the magnitude and terror of such a catastrophe?'

"How awful and momentous are such thoughts and language in contrast to the tinselled frippery of such preachers as the one I first mentioned."

The admiration of Mr. Briggs for the character and public life of Henry Clay is frequently expressed in his correspondence; but perhaps at no particular time more at length than in a letter to his wife written during this session, and upon the occasion of Mr. Clay's resumption of his seat in the Senate, after the affliction he experienced in the sudden death at Lexington, Ky., of his only and much-loved daughter : —

WASHINGTON, December 29, 1835.

MY DEAR WIFE:

This morning I went into the Senate, and soon after I got there, Mr. Clay rose to introduce a bill to distribute the avails of the public lands, and made a beautiful speech of about an hour. He has not been in the Senate for about two weeks. The melancholy news of the very sudden death of his only daughter, at Lexington, has kept him entirely secluded. When he arose he alluded to his deep domestic affliction; which, he said was the most severe that had ever visited him, and was much affected. The whole of his speech was in a mild, subdued tone. He said, in conclusion, that he looked with satisfaction to the period when he should leave public life and go into the quiet and peaceful retirement of private life. He said, when he looked back upon his past life, and remembered his humble origin, he had much reason to be satisfied with the many marks of distinction and honor that his countrymen had conferred upon him; and he was grateful for all their favors. He had the satisfaction of reflecting that he had always endeavored to do his duty, in every station to which he had been appointed. He said he was early left an orphan, that he could not recollect when the tender solicitude and care of a father had been exercised over him. He was left to the care of a widowed mother, in charge of a large family of children, without fortune and without education, or the means of obtaining it.

He alluded to his origin and history in such a sincere, simple manner, and spoke in such sweet, musical tones of voice, all under the influence of the melancholy induced by the deep affliction under which he was borne down, that the effect upon the large and listening audience surrounding him was very striking; many eyes were filled with tears, and all around the Senate Chamber, both among the Senators and spectators, many heads were bent, and many handkerchiefs were suddenly lifted to wipe away the falling tears. Never, in this country, has a man done such signal services, and met such ungrateful return, as Henry Clay. I doubt not posterity will do him ample justice, and give his great name a place high among the renowned. But bitter indeed must be the reflections of a high-souled and noble-minded patriot, who feels conscious of having devoted his life to the good of his country, when he sees that country enjoying the golden fruits of his labors and toil, turning from him, not only with cold and heartless ingratitude, but doing all in her power to cover him with obloquy and shame.

But if I don't stop you will begin to believe me a *Clay man*. It will be one of the most interesting reminiscences of my life that it has fallen to my humble lot to have mingled in the public councils with Henry Clay, and that I have listened to his warm, thrilling, and patriotic eloquence.

Thine own,
G. N. BRIGGS.

The justice and kindness of the sentiments which inspired the mind and prompted the utterances of Mr. Briggs upon all points in which the North and South were in conflict, are in striking contrast to the relentlessness and recklessness of some whose intemperate speeches " fired the Southern heart" to hatred of the North.

The following letter to his family physician is an example of his conservatism and good-will : —

WASHINGTON, 8th January, 1836.

DEAR TYLER:

As Congress adjourned over yesterday till Monday next, thus giving us lazy dogs three days of leisure, I should like to improve it by running in to see how you all *gang* in the Boro'. But four hundred and fifty miles is too long a stride for a poor short-legged fellow to take in so short a time. The sun has not looked out upon us for a week, and how much longer he will keep muffled up in thick clouds I know not. Both Houses of Congress have got deeply into the slave question, arising from petitions to abolish slavery, and the slave trade, in the District of Columbia. The Southern members are making a bold push to force the North to admit that Congress has no power over the subject of slavery in the District of Columbia. The miserable business of President-making will give them many Northern votes on many questions arising about the subject, but I trust the Representatives from the free States of the North are not yet slaves enough to give up the constitutional right of Congress to legislate in this District. But while the constitutional power is adhered to with firmness and decision, I think, both here and at home, we ought in every way in our power to manifest to our Southern brethren, our unalterable determination to respect their constitutional rights, and never attempt any interference with the institution of slavery within the limits of the States. It is altogether a subject of extreme delicacy and importance. We of the North are not fully aware, I am satisfied, of the true condition of things in many parts of the South. From the course of things in the Northern free States within the last year or two, the Southern people are fearfully apprehensive that an interference with their affairs, unauthorized by the Constitution, is intended, and that the attempt to act on the subject in the District of Columbia is meant only as an entering wedge to act upon the same thing in the States. I think, in the course which they take, they are unreasonable and indiscreet. I know not but this is the rock on which this noble Union, the work of the best patriots and the wisest Statesmen, is destined to split. But what if the Union is divided? The severest blow ever given to liberty will be struck, and not a solitary suffering slave will be liberated. This is an age of excitement, benevolence, and innovation, more remarkable for feeling and action than for deliberate and cool judgment. I hope all may be overruled for good. At present, clouds dark and boding hang over our political horizon.

Your friend,
G. N. BRIGGS.

The subjoined letter from Elder Leland[1] is so pointed and characteristic, that it cannot fail to be read with pleasure. Its sentiments of wisdom and vigor of thought, make it quite as applicable in many respects to passing events, as to those to which they were originally directed :—

CHESHIRE, January 12, 1836.

HON. SIR:

I am confident you will have the goodness to pass by any imprudence in my attempt to write to one highly elevated by his country. I aim not at high things; my head is not formed for the cap of honor; but the good of that country which has given me birth, and has nourished me more than eighty years, lies near my heart. Next to the salvation of the soul, I have advocated a scheme which would support the energy of the Government, and secure the rights of the people. The given powers of the Government (in which you are now acting as legislator) are few and defined. The powers granted and rights retained are so plainly stated in the Charter, that those who read may understand. But where honest men are agreed in the fundamental principles, they may widely differ in the agents and secondary agents, which would be the most likely to establish those principles.

1 Rev. John Leland, a distinguished Baptist minister who spent many years of a long life in Cheshire, Mass., and with whom the subject of this Memoir cherished intimate relations. The reader is referred to Dr. Sprague's "Annals of the American (Baptist) Pulpit" for a long and interesting letter from Gov. Briggs, in which he includes his personal reminiscences and impressions of his quaint clerical friend.

It seems probable that the admission of Michigan into the Union; the French question; the circulation of the writings of the abolitionists; the disposal of the surplus revenue; will occupy some of your time. The expunging of senatorial foolery will not be hammered in your shop; but in the Senate chamber it is likely the furnace will be blown seven times hotter than usual, to kill that which never did any harm; the death of which will never bequeath a pair of shoes to a child, or an ear of corn to a pig. Should the record of the resolution of censure be expunged by a line drawn across it, as black as Tophet, it would not change the mind of any man any more than the passing of the resolution did.

In the time of the revolution in England, it became a proverbial saying: "Strip a man of office and he will talk like a Whig; put him in office and he will be a Tory." It is too true that when men possess power they forget right, every man having a Pope in his belly; but true patriotism will rope the Pope, and cause the patriot to seek the good of his country (of all the world), and not his own aggrandizement.

According to our political calendar, this present year is leap year, the thirteenth bissextile of our Government. It is therefore probable that there will be some leaping in Washington this session; and pray, how could the leisure hours of the members of Congress be better spent, than in devising means for the good of the country for the four succeeding years? Whether the Committee of Ways and Means, appointed for the purpose of nominating and recommending a candidate for the next term, are likely to agree and report a bill, I do not know. My ardent desire is that there may be a fair expression of the will of the people in the choice of the eighth President; if so, who ever he be, I will acknowledge him as *my President*, whether he is the man of my choice or not; for in this case and all cases like it, "*vox populi vox Dei*" is a religious and admitted truth.

Representatives are not sent to Congress to *think* for their constituents, but to act for them (the right of *thinking* being inalienable in its nature), and he who acts contrary to the known will of the majority of his constituents is a tyrant. When a question must be acted upon, and the representative cannot in conscience

vote for that which he knows is the will of a majority of his constituents, it becomes him to tender his resignation, and let another
fill his place. Mr. Adams formerly, and Mr. Reeves recently,
acted wisely on this true principle of Republicanism, in the Senate,
and Col. Johnson did the same thing, in substance, in the Compen-
sation Bill, in the House.

I learn from the newspapers that you are on the Committee of
the Post Office and Post Roads. This institution has grown to be
a giant; and I believe that it is as much abused as any establishment of the Government. To guarantee to men their liberty by
an instrument that defends from licentiousness, and to give men
power enough to do good, and to have it so counterpoised that
they cannot abuse it, is what the friends of men have been laboring for some thousands of years; and, likely, the consummation
of all things will find men in the pursuit of it. But this perfection
is not an attribute of men; yet every march towards it is praise-
worthy.   JOHN LELAND.

Hon. GEORGE N. BRIGGS.

Social misunderstandings were always painful to Mr.
Briggs, and his gentle, placable temper disposed him to
"seek peace and pursue it," and to make sacrifices to maintain it in all relations of life. The healing of a social
breach was thus to him a matter of earnest congratula-
tion: —

WASHINGTON, Jan. 24, 1836.

MY DEAR WIFE:

It gave me great pleasure to hear of the visit of —— and ——.
I cannot bear the idea of living on any other than terms of amity
and kindness with any human being. There are ills enough in life
without having it imbittered by feuds and misunderstandings, that
often arise out of occurrences of no moment in themselves, but
which are permitted to grow into magnitude, by the omission to
have proper explanations at a proper time. It ever has been, and
hereafter shall be, my effort to be at peace with all my fellow-

beings. If there is one human being with whom I have other than
friendly personal feelings and relations, I know it not. I harbor
no hostility against any, and I know of no one to whom and for
whom it would not give me pleasure to perform an act of kindness. . . . . . I have been so fortunate thus far in life, rarely,
if ever, to have met with insults from those with whom I have
mingled. Perhaps those of more nice and sensitive feelings may
think it is because I have not been sufficiently tenacious of my
rights and watchful of my dignity. It may be so, but sure I am
that I have avoided many unpleasant predicaments, into which
those of a different view have often fallen. I am content to be
considered rather too obtuse when my *dignity* is concerned, than
to be too sensitive and high-toned. Do right and fear not, is a
maxim that will carry us safely and pleasantly through life.

The "dear domestic love" breathes out again in the
next letter to his wife, and ripples into a charming playfulness of tone : —

                              WASHINGTON, Feb. 10, 1836.

Well, my dear, the bustle of the day is again over, and I sit
down again to the pleasant duty of informing you of my welfare.
To be sure, twenty years ago, when I was teaching school in the
old town-house, and occasionally dropping in at the old castle over
the hill, neither of us exactly foresaw, that at this time I should
be here and you at the Boro', in charge of the little family we
should rear. But so it is; and although we began poor, and in
that respect hold our own as well as any couple I ever knew, yet
we have no reason to complain. We have never scratched, or put
out one another's eyes; and though I have *had* to scold you sometimes, yet I don't believe, after all, but that there *are* worse women
in the world than you are. You know I have *always* been a beau
ideal of a husband, and of course you have never had occasion to
find fault with

                              YOUR OWN.

The manners of Washington society at "feeding time"

do not seem to improve in the observation and experience of Mr. Briggs, if we may judge from what he writes : —

WASHINGTON, Feb. 12, 1836.

MY DEAR WIFE:

Last night the President had another levee, and I was fool enough to go with the multitude, no wiser than myself in this respect. I presume there were two thousand persons there. Think how much comfort there must be where two thousand men and women are huddled together, much of the time the press so great, that it was impossible for any *one* person to move in any direction, till the mass, of which he formed a part, began to stir, then, as it went, so he would go. When supper was announced, the rush for the table was terrible. I made three vigorous attempts to reach the table, but, instead of reaching it, I could not get a sight of it, and gave up the attempt, content to starve rather than squeeze to death. Supper was announced at ten-and-a-half. Some of the guests reached the tables at about two o'clock. This is a sensible proceeding in high life, truly !

Always thine,

G. N. BRIGGS.

The incident of a session of Congress protracted into the early hours of the Sabbath, is not quite so exceptional now as it was thirty years ago. It is not at all to the honor of the National Legislature that it should have grown familiar by frequent recurrence : —

WASHINGTON, March 27, 1836.

MY DEAR WIFE:

You must not look for a very spirited letter this evening. Our yesterday's session lasted till light this morning. We were together eighteen hours, during which time I did not sleep, or eat anything but a cracker and a small bit of cake; but to my fasting I ascribe my exemption from any other inconvenience save a little drowsiness. The subject before the House was a contested election from the State of North Carolina. It excited a great deal of interest, and was made by the majority a strong party question, and they resolved to put an end to it by the application of the previous question, on Saturday night. The minority thought the course unjust and oppressive, and determined to make all the resistance in their power. When the previous question is put and carried, it closes the debate, and cuts off all amendments to the proposition pending at the time. Both of these results the minority thought would be wrong in this case. The night, until twelve o'clock, was taken up by a gentleman from Kentucky, and by ineffectual motions and votes to adjourn. I suppose the yeas and nays were taken ten times. At twelve o'clock, it was objected that it was the Sabbath, and there was no public necessity for the House to sit, and they ought not to proceed with business. But party is deaf alike to the voice of justice and the commands of religion, and a dead majority voted against adjournment. Clergymen, deacons, and professed Christians determined, in obedience to the behests of party, to devote the Sabbath day to legislation of no particular urgency more than the ordinary acts of legislation. A Baptist clergyman, a Jackson man too, from Alabama, had the courage to make a motion declaring it out of order to proceed with business in the circumstances. A warm debate arose under this new question. Another motion was made to adjourn; and, on the yeas and nays being ordered, when Mr. Adams's name was called, he being first on the list, he refused to vote, on the ground that the House had no right to compel him to vote on the Sabbath, unless there was some public necessity that required it. After some delay, the call was proceeded with, and, when my name was reached, I resolved to stand by Mr. Adams, believing him to be right. I declined answering. When the last name was called, which was that of Mr. Wise, of Virginia, he refused to answer, because two gentlemen from Massachusetts had failed to answer to their names, and he was not bound to answer till they had. That carried the House back to Mr. Adams; and a motion was made to excuse him. He said he did not ask to be excused, and would not be excused. A debate now arose, of an exciting and party nature, until Mr. Wise and Mr. Bynum, of North Carolina, got into a furious quarrel, called each other all the hard

names and vile epithets they could lay hold of, and made a struggle to get at each other for violence. A scene of great disorder
ensued, which finally ended in their friends calling upon them to
say before the House, that, as they had made offensive remarks,
under great excitement, they would agree to leave the matter
where it was. They are both duellists, and it was thought necessary to interfere, to prevent a fight. The whole scene was well
calculated to show how supremely ridiculous is that miserable system, falsely called "the laws of honor."

This was a Sabbath-morning scene, in the House of Representatives of the United States. It was nothing more than what might
have been looked for, as the probable issue of blind determination
of a political party resolved at all hazards to carry their point. It
would not be just to cast all the blame for this shameful excess,
upon the majority. Both parties were excited, and both acted
unwisely, but the majority had it in their power to prevent it, by
a timely adjournment, which they refused. With the exception
of the scene I here mentioned, it was a very civil night session.
We adjourned about 5 o'clock A. M., without taking any question.
When we came into the street, the daylight shone in the east.

Thine,

G. N. BRIGGS.

The preceptive benevolence of heart and beneficence of
hand, which he enjoins in the following letter to his daughter, shine all the more effectively for the light reflected
upon them from his daily life, crowded as it was with practical illustrations of the lessons he taught : —

WASHINGTON, 3d April, 1836.

MY DAUGHTER :

.   .   .   .

You can make yourself useful by a faithful performance of these
duties of humanity. Be always willing to visit the sick and console the sorrowful. Particularly, make it your object to search
out the suffering *poor*. There is not much danger that the rich
and prosperous will be neglected. .   .   .   .   . True benevolence
makes sure that these objects shall be sought for and comforted.

The Saviour, who exemplified the benevolence of his mission on earth by preaching the gospel to the poor, and curing them of all manner of diseases, was not content to stay at home and relieve such objects of distress as came to his notice, but he "went about doing good." . . . . . I know a lady in this city, who is the pride and ornament of the highest circles of society, and who is second to no one in the Capital for the attention and respect which she receives from a host of admirers, who finds abundance of time to visit the hovels and huts of poverty and distress. She is an angel of mercy to the poor and friendless. In my estimation, her rich mind, her elegant person, and unusual accomplishments are poor things, when placed in comparison with the benevolence of her heart, exhibited in such works as I have alluded to. Two or three years since, early one evening, she received a message from a poor widow, who lived alone, in a mere shanty in the suburbs of the city, informing her that she was very sick, and wished to see her. She left her family under pretence of going to pass the night with her sister in another part of the city; and when she reached the sick woman, she found her dying, desolate and alone, save for the presence of another stranger, a woman, brought there probably by the same motives as herself. She watched over the dying, friendless widow, mitigating, as far as it was in her power, the last agony, and giving religious consolation in the trying hour. About daylight she closed the poor sufferer's eyes, and returned to her family. . . . . Instead of charities like these interfering with any of the useful or necessary pursuits of life, they will become real auxiliaries, by regulating the mind and chastening the affections. One performance of our duty always prepares us for another. Duty and happiness go hand in hand. The reward of virtuous conduct, with Him who reads the heart, depends, not so much on the amount done, as upon the motive that prompts to the doing of it.

Affectionately, your father,

G. N. BRIGGS.

"Father Taylor" is so well known, and so kindly remembered by multitudes, for his zeal in his special work, that the following letter will find many interested readers : —

WASHINGTON, 16 May, 1836.

MY DEAR WIFE:

. . . . . Yesterday, Father Taylor, of Boston, who has been several years very noted in his exertions for the sailors, preached in the Capitol. There was an immense audience. He spoke an hour and a half, with great fervor and power. He seems to be a man of deep piety, and is at times very eloquent. . . . . .

Ten or a dozen sailors came up from the navy yard, and sat around the Clerk's desk, in front of the Speaker's chair. When nearly through, he paused and said, " I was thinking of the seamen;" and, looking over upon the little cluster of sailors, with a countenance full of animation and benignity, he added, "Here they are, — I am now at home." For a few moments he spoke of the success in reclaiming the generous but dissipated sailor, and making him the humble and confiding Christian, in a manner that moved all hearts and filled many eyes with tears. He said the poor sailor, in the midst of the gloomy tempest, when the heavy thunder broke over his head and the sharp lightning disclosed the yawning gulf beneath, and the tasselled tops of the deep rising above him, had no quiet and secure retreat to retire to. He had to look the danger in the face, and could only find calmness and peace in a holy confidence in Him, who rides upon the storm and controls the sea.

In the evening he preached a very good sermon to a very crowded house, at the Methodist church. After his sermon, four or five delegates from the Cherokees took their places in the pulpit, and sung a hymn in the Cherokee language. It was full of music and devotion. Their voices were full, sweet, and harmonious. One of them spoke of the influence of the gospel among them. He said, through an interpreter, that one effect was to make the women stay at home, and cook their food. When the gospel prevails among the degraded and wretched, it improves their social condition. Instead of roving through the forest, with her little pappoose at her back, and carrying the implements of her lazy and cruel lord, the Christian squaw remains in her peaceful domestic abode, administering to the comforts of her family, cheered with the prospect of future happiness. By the influence of the

13*

gospel, he said, his people bore patiently the injuries which were heaped upon them, and, instead of seeking for vengeance upon those who brought difficulties upon them, they prayed for them. What a change this, in the breast of the savage! He closed by saying, "Brethren, I hope we shall soon meet where we can speak to one another, and praise God together, without an interpreter." One of the Indians prayed in Cherokee. The language is soft, smooth, and rich in tone. Interesting race! I was happy to see this relic of them, and hear them sing the praises of Immanuel, and pray to the Father of Mercies in their own beautiful language.

Love to all. God bless you.

G. N. BRIGGS.

CHAPTER XIII.

IT was towards the close of the long session of the
Twenty-fourth Congress, that one of the most exciting topics of that period came up for discussion. It
was the application of Arkansas for admission into
the Union. Arkansas, originally a part of Louisiana
Territory, was isolated by the admission of Louisiana as a
State, in 1812. For the next seven years Arkansas was a
part of Missouri Territory, and in 1819 was again isolated
by the admission of Missouri as a State; and now it became a Territory in its own right, which it continued to be
until June, 1836, when, at a convention held at Little Rock,
a State constitution was adopted, which was sent up to
Washington, with application for the admission of the State
into the Union. This constitution contained this memorable clause: "The General Assembly shall have no power
to pass laws for the emancipation of slaves without the
consent of their owners. They shall have no power to prevent emigrants to this State from bringing with them such
persons as are deemed slaves by the laws of any one of the
United States."

151

On the 8th of June, the bill for the admission of Arkansas came up for consideration. In the early stage of the debate, Mr. Bouldin, a member from Virginia, threw down the glove in these words : —

"If there are any serious difficulties to be raised in the House to the admission of Arkansas, upon the ground of negro slavery, I wish immediate notice of it. If my confidence is misplaced, I wish to be corrected as soon as possible, and as certainly as possible. If there really is any intention of putting any difficulty, restraint, limit — any shackle or embarrassment on the South on account of negro slavery, I wish to know it. If there are any individuals having such feelings, I wish to know them; I wish to have their names upon yeas and nays. If they are a majority, I shall act promptly, decisively, and immediately upon it, and have no doubt all the South will do the same."

What was then vaunting and boasting and menace, subsequently ripened, as all the world knows, into the most gigantic and unhappy rebellion the world ever saw.

The next day, when the consideration of the bill was resumed, the venerable John Quincy Adams rose and offered an amendment, excluding any construction upon which assent of Congress to the clause above referred to could be predicated.

Following Messrs. Adams and Cushing, of Massachusetts, and Mr. Hand, of New York, who all advocated the amendment, Mr. Briggs made a speech, also in favor of it, which is, perhaps, the best example among his Congressional efforts, of his intellectual strength, and, no less, of his forbearing spirit. For this reason it is here quoted in full : —

"My colleague (Mr. Adams) proposes to amend the eighth section of the 'Bill for the Admission of Arkansas into the Union,' by inserting the following declaration: 'And nothing in this act shall be construed as an assent by Congress to the article in the constitution.of said State in relation to slavery and the emancipation of slaves.' It must be seen, at a glance, that this simple, plain declaration contains nothing of the principle which gave rise to the Missouri controversy. In that case, a restriction was imposed on Missouri which denied to that State certain rights and powers, which under the Constitution of the United States, were possessed by other States. The advocates of the State contended that Congress had no authority to enforce that restriction or limitation upon her sovereignty. This amendment does not in the slightest degree abridge, restrain, or in any manner interfere with the prerogative of Arkansas as an independent State. If adopted, it will not postpone her admission into the Union a single day. It does not question the right of her citizens to any species of property recognized by the constitution or laws of the State. It imposes no restraint upon her political powers and sovereignty. It simply denies that by the act of admitting her into the Union, with this article incorporated into her constitution, Congress gives its assent to the principle of that article. Without this protestation, the act of admission would be at least an implied assent to this extraordinary constitutional provision. Whilst such an approbation would be of no use or benefit to that State, it would be in direct violation of the opinion of a large majority of the members of this House, and of the known sentiments of the people they represent. What good reason, then, can be urged why this amendment should not be adopted? Are gentlemen prepared to say, by their votes to reject this most reasonable proposition, that this act shall be construed as an assent by Congress to the article in the constitution of the State in relation to slavery and the emancipation of slaves? Will not such an inference be the natural and necessary result of such a vote? I ask gentlemen, whose opinions I know coincide with my own upon this subject, to consider well before they take the step which cannot be retraced.

"Mr. Chairman, the word 'slave,' or 'slavery,' is nowhere to be found in the Constitution of the United States. Whilst that instrument, by its various provisions, guarantees to the people of the

States their rights to property acknowledged by the laws of the several States, its patriotic framers most cautiously avoided the use of terms which would admit that man could be made the property of his fellow-man. If, in the course of events, the people of every State in this Union shall abolish slavery within their own limits, and the time shall come when there shall not be a bondman in all this great and free republic, generations who succeed us will find no evidence in this Constitution that such an institution as slavery ever existed. The people of Arkansas have used less caution than did the framers of the federal Constitution. Though their constitution was to be presented to a Congress, for its approval, composed of members, a majority of whom, in both branches, represent constituents opposed to slavery in every form, it contains an article, the design and effect of which is to make involuntary servitude perpetual within her limits. This is much to be regretted. If she had pursued a different course, the difficulties which now present themselves would have been avoided, without any prejudice to her rights and wishes.

" Can it be expected that the representatives from the free States of this Union will give their assent to this exceptionable article? In justice to those whom they represent, can they do less than express their dissent from it? It has been shown that this amendment can have no injurious effect upon the rights of the people of Arkansas. Will members on this floor, coming from States whose people are known to be hostile to the principle of this article in the Constitution presented for their approval, be faithful to the trust reposed in them, if they fail to declare their disapprobation of it? I call upon gentlemen from the non-slaveholding States truly to reflect the sentiments of their constituents, and to support their well-known opinions on this subject, by voting for the amendment now before us. Can they with propriety or consistency approve of a principle universally condemned by their constituents? I appeal to the candor of gentlemen from the slaveholding States, and ask them if, in their opinion, it would be just or reasonable to desire us to do this? Whilst they stand by their constituents, and manfully maintain their rights and defend their interests, shall we be recreant to our duty, and fail to avow and defend the doctrine of those who honor us with their confidence? Sir, I hope not.

"Mr. Chairman, to the utmost of my powers I will here and elsewhere support all the rights of all the States of this Union defined and secured by the Constitution of the United States. I regard them all as equally sacred and inviolable. That instrument was the result of a compromise of conflicting opinions and conflicting interests, of mutual concessions and mutual pledges. It is my duty to stand by it, and maintain it in all its parts. It is the supreme law of the land, and its provisions are alike binding upon all the citizens of all the States of this confederacy. With those rights secured by that binding charter I will never interfere. But, sir, upon this subject of slavery I cannot go the breadth of a hair beyond the obligations imposed upon me by that instrument. I never can consent, with the views which I now entertain, to give a vote, or do any other act, which shall sanction the principle or extend the existence of human slavery. In the deep conviction of my own mind and heart, I believe it to be politically and morally wrong. With all my soul I approve of and believe in the truth of that great principle, avowed and proclaimed to the world in the Declaration of Independence, 'that all men are created equal, that they are endowed by their Creator with certain inalienable rights, that among these are life, liberty, and the pursuit of happiness.' I do not look upon that declaration as the mere publication of a truth beautiful in theory only, and not capable of a practical application; on the contrary, I believe it may be, and in all free governments should be, carried out in practice. It is based upon the principles of eternal justice and truth, which will abide when all existing governments and human institutions shall decay and pass away forever.

"Holding these opinions, sir, how can I give my sanction to that highly exceptionable article in the constitution of Arkansas presented for our approval, and which by the bill before us we do approve and assent to, unless we negative that assent by some such amendment as the one under consideration? In doing so, I should violate my own sense of propriety and right, and be treacherous to the freemen who sent me here. In voting for the amendment of my colleague, I shall vindicate my own, and equally the undivided sentiments of my constituents, without impairing any of the guarantees of the Constitution, or infringing upon the rights of any State in this Union."

It may be mentioned here, as an illustration of the remarkable and habitual reticence which Mr. Briggs observed concerning his own part in public affairs, even when at home, or in his communications to his family, that in his letter to his wife, written the day after that upon which he delivered the foregoing speech, and describing some of the general aspects of the House during the pendency of the question involved in it, he makes not even the slightest allusion to his own share in the debate. The omission to do this might have been accidental, but it cannot be so regarded, in view of the constant recurrence of such omissions. It was, rather, a trait of character — a sign of the inherent modesty which always led him to leave himself in the background, even when among those who would not have construed his words into egotism. Here is an extract from the letter to which reference is made : —

"Our session yesterday was of twenty-five hours, which was the longest legislative day on record! It was like the Irishman's month of August, which was six weeks long. The House sat from ten o'clock yesterday morning until eleven this morning, without one moment's recess. At ten o'clock last night, I left in disgust. At daylight our mess, who were all at home, were summoned, by one of the officers of the House, to go to the Capitol. We went up, and found a sorry-looking set. As Wise said, some were tired, some sleepy, and some drunk. It was a scene of disorder and confusion, disgraceful to the legislature of a civilized people. This outrage upon decorum and propriety was necessary, or deemed so, to effect purposes of party. We were a committee of the whole upon the bills for the admission of the States of Mich-

igan and of Arkansas into the Union; bills of the utmost importance. Yet they were conducted amidst confusion and tumult and
disorder. I hope our session is approaching its termination."

From his quiet Lanesboro' home the enfranchised member thus writes to one of his nephews. His determination
to decline a re-election, hinted at in this letter, was not
carried out until two years later : —

LANESBORO', October, 1836.

Well, my good fellow, I suppose by this time you have lost all your
patience in waiting for a line from your uncle. But so the world
goes. With those nominal friends, who hang loosely about us at
best, we have to be very punctilious; while with our real friends,
who would cluster about us in the deep shades of adversity, we
take the the greatest liberties. It is said that husbands and wives
are more sharp with each other, and indulge in occasional bicker-
ings, because they are so conscious of the firm hold of each other's
affections, they do not fear a breach; whilst timid lovers are so full
of fears, that they do not offend in the slightest matters. Now, to
apply the doctrine, I suppose if I did not know that you loved
your Uncle George, I should be more careful to answer your letters
which you are so kind as to write me and mine. It had been my
fixed purpose to visit Cleveland during the past summer, but Congress was so long in session, and I have been so occupied since,
that I had to forego the pleasure. All who visit the West, come
home full of the praises of Cleveland. My own *interest*, and that
of my family, is that I should be in some business place, but here
I am tied down by a multitude of Lilliputian thongs, wanting resolution to snap them and be off. I have no reason to complain of
Providence in regard to my situation in life, and I have great
occasion to be grateful to the citizens of Old Berkshire for their
kindness to me. Two years ago I had not the most distant idea
of ever being a candidate for Congress again in this district. Indeed, it was my fixed purpose *not* to be. Since I came home in
July, the strong feeling of my personal and political friends in
the district, so far as I have known them, has been against my

14

retiring.   My own inclination and judgment were against being
a candidate for re-election; but under the circumstances of the
district, and with the certainty of much difficulty in fixing upon
any other person for a candidate, and the repeated solicitations
that I would not decline, I remained silent upon the subject.   The
Democrats have nominated Theodore Sedgwick.   Whether they
will elect him or not, will be seen after election.   If he is chosen,
it will only prove that the people of the district prefer him to their
old member, and their old member will not quarrel with them
about it.

Mr. Webster visited our Cattle Show and Fair last week.   He
was received with great respect by all parties, and made a good
impression upon our farmers.

Berkshire was never more prosperous than at this moment, save
and excepting its lawyers, whose condition is as cold and cheer-
less as a Siberian winter.

Keep writing on, my boy, whether I write or not.

Your friend and uncle,

G. N. BRIGGS.

To JAMES A. BRIGGS.

There are fewer traces of Mr. Briggs during the second
session of the Twenty-fourth Congress than usual.   He was
however in his place, and diligently at work; much of the
time maturing, in committees, measures for the consideration and decision of the House.   He had now been a member of the Committee on Post Offices and Post Roads
through three sessions, and his indefatigable labors in this
department of public business, his minute acquaintance
with all its details, and the deference paid to his judgment
by his colleagues, conspired to entitle him fairly to the
chairmanship of this important committee.   His connection,
however, with the minority party in the House, hindered
this official recognition of his deserts, and it came tardily
enough six years later.

From the scanty memorials in letters of this period at command, the following amusing excerpt is made, curiously sandwiched in the original manuscript, between grave religious reflections. It is not the less entertaining to those who knew him well, that they remember how emphatically he was his own physician, — and without any distrust of his faithful friend and family medical adviser, Dr. Tyler, indulged his propensity for recipes and specifics. The letter quoted from bears date of December 11, 1836 : —

"I have learned a new remedy for crazy and billious stomachs, and from the success of those who have used it, and from its simplicity, I have a mind that mother should try it, and you too, *if your stomach should ever get out of sorts!* To a quart of clear hardwood ashes and a gill of soot, add a gallon of boiling water. Let it stand a day or two. Then turn it off carefully and strain it. Take half a wineglass or more before eating. It is said to be very good also, to take it just after eating, when one's food occasions distress. I know several persons who have been essentially benefited by this simple alkali. It is cheap, and easy to try."

The first session of the Twenty-fifth Congress was made at once memorable and melancholy by the duel between Mr. Cilley, of Maine, and Mr. Graves, of Kentucky, in which the former was killed. Probably no duel occurring in this country since that between Hamilton and Burr, in 1804, excited the popular feeling to such an extent as the one here referred to. It very naturally produced a deep impression of terror and pain in the mind of Mr. Briggs, whose natural disposition recoiled, with hardly less decision than his spiritual temper, from such a method of settling differences between men of honor. He thus alludes to this sad affair in a letter to his sons, George and Henry : —

WASHINGTON, February 26, 1838.

MY DEAR BOYS:

We had a most tragical affair here last Saturday. Mr. Cilley from Maine, and Mr. Graves from Kentucky, fought a duel with rifles. On the third or fourth fire — for their seconds differ as to the number of times they fired — Mr. Cilley was shot, and died almost instantly. They fought four or five miles out of the city, in the State of Maryland. The distance they fired at, was eighty yards. Mr. Graves gave the challenge, Mr. Cilley accepted — chose the weapons, distance, and mode of fighting. The difficulty between them was of the most trifling nature. This mode of settling difficulties is said to be according to the law of *honor,* but the whole thing is founded on false notions. A thing which is contrary to the laws of the land and of God cannot be honorable. . . . .

If the wise and good of all communities would set their faces against the cruel practice of duelling, it soon would be trampled down. I am extremely sorry that one of the parties of this fatal meeting should have been from New England. His engaging in the duel was a violation of the public sentiment of the country from which he came. A New England man yielding to the code of honor, falsely so called, gives it a currency and a sanction to which it is not entitled. Even the people where it prevails say it is wrong; but public opinion makes it necessary for them to yield to it. The short and conclusive argument against it is, that it is contrary to the law of God. . . . . .

His daughter's affluent memory and pen supply the following reminiscence, in harmony with the foregoing letter:

" One of my father's friends, who had killed his man in a duel, — a Southern gentleman with whom he was on most agreeable terms, — said to him, ' If the *pillow* of the duellist could speak, the practice of duelling would soon cease.' He said one of the most amiable and genial and courteous members of the House was entirely changed in character after fighting his first duel, in which, by his unpractised hand, his opponent was killed. Ever after, he was irritable and silent and morose, — no longer a social being in his intercourse with men, or calm and good-tempered in his discussions in the House."

Here are more of his home-sick yearnings — thinly veiled by the pleasantry of his language : —

WASHINGTON, March 4, 1838.

MY DEAR WIFE:

. . . . . How I should delight to visit you at the old Boro' this evening, but as one brother said to another at sea, when he asked him if he should not like to have a dish of mother's pudding and milk for supper, "Oh, be still, Joe; that is too good to think of." Perhaps it is because I am growing old and childish, but so it is, as it seems to me, I am becoming every day more attached to my wife and children.

Ever thine,

G. N. BRIGGS.

In the following letter he pays a tribute to the memory of a clerical member of the House. Of this rare class of representatives, the South generally furnished the majority : —

WASHINGTON, May 9, 1838.

MY DEAR WIFE:

We have just performed the sad duty of laying in the tomb another of our number—Mr. Lawler, of Alabama. He died after an illness of six days. He was a Baptist preacher, and a most exemplary and excellent man. I have never known a clergyman in political life who, at all times, maintained the propriety of his character as he did. He died, as he lived, a Christian. A short time before he died, in an earnest prayer, he said his hopes had long been fixed on his Saviour, and his faith in His mercies was unshaken. In a clear and distinct voice he declared of that Saviour in whom his hopes were thus centred, that in all the trials of his life He had sustained him, and he now confided his all to Him. He bore his sickness with perfect meekness and patience, and as his fatal disease disclosed itself, he was unmoved and re-

14*

signed; said he was ready to die, and yielded himself to the king of terrors without a struggle or a sigh.

A member of Congress, who was with him, said that he died with a smile on his countenance. Who can describe the value of a religion which will enable a human being, among strangers, far from his wife and children, thus to close his life? The Chaplain who preached his funeral sermon, after stating his character and giving an account of his death, concluded his remarks by saying: "Mark the perfect man, and behold the upright, for the end of that man is peace."

I have heard his meek and humble voice at the little circle of our Congressional prayer-meetings, — it will be heard no more there, — it will be heard henceforth in high notes of praise. I would that his death might make me wiser! He was just my age, forty-two. There was no man in Congress whom I esteemed more highly for his moral worth and Christian excellence; and I regret most sincerely that I did not know of his sickness, that I might have ministered to his comfort, and witnessed his Christian spirit.

God bless you all.

Thine ever,

G. N. BRIGGS.

An excursion to Mount Vernon is the occasion of a graphic and interesting letter, which will hardly bear abridgment : —

WASHINGTON, May 13, 1838.

MY DEAR WIFE:

I told you that we were going to Mount Vernon. We had a very pleasant and interesting excursion. The mansion of Washington and the adjoining buildings are going rapidly to decay. Unless prevented, the home of the Father of his Country will soon become a scene of desolation and ruins; and nothing will remain for the curious visitor to gaze upon, but the spot upon which once stood the dwelling where he lived and died, and the lonely and dreary tomb where his remains repose. Human glory is as transitory as the monuments that are erected to their departed possessors! To-day I heard Dr. ——, of ——, who I understand is at the head of a sort of seceding Orthodox divinity-school at that place. He seems to have made some new discovery as to the free agency and moral accountability of men and their dependence upon Divine influences. It was, I suppose, to be understood (as he is a great man) that his sermon was very great; but I confess I got no idea from him, that I have not heard presented from the pulpit since the earliest days of my recollection. That man is a moral agent, and an accountable being, that he acts freely, but still that he is entirely dependent on the author of his existence for all that he is or expects to be, are truths beyond the power of contradiction; but how these things can be reconciled on the principles of human reason, is a matter that has puzzled many wise heads and good hearts. Like Elder Leland's hard word, it had better be skipped over.

No man ever feels, in view of the retributions of a future world, that his conduct here has not been entirely free and voluntary; and all who finally "*overcome*" and have an entrance among the blest, will ascribe the glory to Him who has washed us in His blood.

CHAPTER XIV.

DURING the vacation of the Twenty-fifth Congress, and under date of July 29, 1838, Mr. Briggs carried into effect his long-cherished determination to decline being a candidate for re-election. His position in Congress was in no sense a sinecure. He was too honest, too conscientious, too deeply persuaded of his responsibility both to his constituents and to God, to be less than diligent in every work of his hands. This activity, and the sense of accountability connected with it, made his Congressional life in some degree wearisome. This, however, would not of itself have induced him to think of declining its duties and its honors, had there not been a still more forcible dissuasive from its resumption to influence him. Upon this he dwells in his excellent " Address to the Electors of the Berkshire Congressional District." He says, —

" For nearly one half of the time, during the last seven years, my public duties have taken me from my family and my profession. No man can be insensible to the distinguished honor conferred upon him, in being selected by his fellow-citizens to sit in the councils of the Republic. At the same time, no one can duly understand the sacrifices which a public man thus honored has to make, until he shall have learned it in the interruption of his domestic enjoyments, the derangement of his business, and in the laborious discharge of his official obligations. In the noon-time of my life I have, by your kind indulgence, enjoyed my share of the honors, and experienced the inconveniences, which belong to public station. Now the claims of a family rising up around me, who desire my presence and need my counsel, and the propriety of making preparations for the approach of ' life's evening,' admonish me that it is time to retire from public service, and devote myself to the humbler and more quiet duties of domestic and professional life."

Soon after this "Address" was published, he was attacked by an illness, which speedily developed itself into the most malignant form of typhus fever, and from which, after several weeks, he narrowly escaped and slowly recovered.

Of this dangerous illness the faithful and loving hand of his daughter has furnished an account, which must supersede any record of it from the pen of another, and to which the biographer gladly yields the pages it fills : —

"It was wonderful, during the dreadful weeks that the fever was consuming him, how by the mere force of his will he kept his wavering mind from wild delirium. He always recognized the first indications of flightiness, and would instantly recall himself, so that through it all he seldom lost the balance of his faculties. His usual self-distrust and despondency, when ill, attended him now, though he suffered with saintly patience. He told my mother that he wished her to tell his friends 'that, though his prospects were not bright, he had no apprehensions as he approached the grave.' How unlike this to the calm radiance that rested on his soul when he *did* bow himself unto death! He used to say, during that whole sickness, that he did not taste the most simple nutriment without emotions of gratitude, not even a sip of water so refreshing always to the burning thirst.

"His faithful friend, Mr. Shaw, was a daily visitor, and sometimes ministered to him like a skilful nurse. He communicated to him, weeks after it occurred, the fact of his re-nomination for Congress, after he had positively, in a formal letter to his constituents, before his sickness, declined a re-nomination. Being present during the conversation, I well remember my father's enfeebled appearance, his surprise and agitation, and the regret he expressed. 'Oh, my dear fellow, that can't be!' said he; and Mr. Shaw, in his pleasant way, replied, telling him that *he* was entirely aside, that his friends had assumed the whole affair, and when he was well he might acquiesce with as good grace as he could.

"Our family physician, Dr. Tyler, though at that time in practice in the north part of the county, passed many consecutive days by the bedside of his friend, adding the genial influence of a life-long friendship to the skill of the physician in his attendance upon him..

"Sorrow, sickness, and death, in a place like Lanesboro', call into exercise a sympathy, and ministry of love and kindness, which can never be understood and appreciated, save by those who are bred in a purely country life. There is no neighbor that does not know in the morning what kind of a night the sick man has passed, — whether he is still 'very low,' or 'sinking,' or a 'little better,' or 'about the same,' who '*watched*,' and a thousand details which are never dreamed of in large communities, where the physicians and attendants alone know of the slow and weary hours that pass in the sick-chamber. In large communities the very multitude, in the rush of life, stifles the instinctive sympathy of our natures. There were few, far or near, who did not watch with daily anxiety, through the seven weeks of that fearful sickness, the changes little by little, until their friend and neighbor was out of danger and restored to health again. For a long time he was but the *shadow* of himself, and one could hardly recognize him. Upon one occasion, indeed, he was mistaken for an old man by a lad as familiar with him, almost, as his own children.

"He could hear no conversation or reading or music for several weeks. The first time he left his room, he came out leaning heavily on the shoulders of his two eldest children; and when, on that day, seated in the family sitting-room, *all* the household gathered to receive him, he asked to have the piano-forte opened, and to have us sing 'Golden Hill' to the hymn he always liked in that tune : —

> " I lift my heart and voice
>   To God in whom I trust;
> Oh, let me not be put to shame,
>   Nor let my hope be lost.
>
> " His mercy and his truth
>   The righteous Lord displays,
> In bringing wandering sinners home,
>   And teaching them his ways."

All choked with happy, thankful emotions, the song ceased, the hymn yet unfinished. It was one of those memorable moments when the soul finds no voice, even in music, for its utterances:"

Recovered entirely from his protracted illness, he returned to Washington and completed his fourth term in Congress, with his wonted freedom from either self-indulgence or pretension. Meanwhile, in utter disregard of his protest, his sensible and grateful constituents returned him by a generous majority of votes, at the Congressional election of that fall, for a fifth time and term.

Only a few traces of his simple but beautiful life during the winter of 1838-9 can appear in these memorials. It was natural that, with his domestic tastes and habits, and no less with his conscientious avoidance of expensive living, his Washington home should be unostentatious. He boarded, with a portion of the Massachusetts and Vermont delegations, in the quiet family of a Virginia farmer who had moved into the city. The family was composed of intelligent and agreeable persons, with whom Mr. Briggs and his colleagues formed a very pleasant acquaintance,

ripening, at length, into sincere friendship. The family,
in receiving these gentlemen, came for the first time into
contact with *Yankees*, of whom they had hitherto entertained an unqualified horror. As Mr. Briggs was the first
of this class with whom they had any communication, they
received a very favorable impression, and concluded if he
was a specimen, that they should be glad to know more of
the genus. This, the " Mary," mentioned in the following
letter, told the daughter, on their subsequent acquaintance
with each other.

After their first experiment with Yankees as boarders,
though Southerners by birth and education, they always
preferred to have a " mess" of Northern members : —

WASHINGTON, 5th Jan., 1839.

MY DEAR WIFE:

. . . . . This evening, at tea, I was speaking to Mary about
a fat hog I saw in the market; a fat porker is a rare thing here.
She said she generally "*rendered up*" the greater part of such
pork, and that they used the *cracklings* for "*pone*," which, being
interpreted, means that they try up fat pork, and put the scraps
into johnny-cakes. Since we came here, they have learned to
make minced-meat, or hash. A few mornings since, Mary told me
that they sliced up meat with a cleaver. I asked her why she did
not use a chopping-knife, and she did not know what it meant;
whereupon I went out, and found a chopping-knife and wooden
bowl, and sent it home, and, to her astonishment, she has found it
now not half the work it was before to make hash. This is a specimen of the manner in which people in this country do things.
Among the farming population, they are much farther behind
Northern ideas of conveniences than in the cities. The farmers in
Virginia have not yet learned that potatoes are worth anything to
feed hogs or cattle with. . . . . .

In proof of the unflinching adherence of Mr. Briggs to

any principle he avowed, and to any practice based upon principle, no matter how extreme might be the temptation or the inducement, to make of some occasion an exception, is the following incident, recorded in a letter to his wife, under date of Feb. 14, 1839 : —

" Several of our members expect to dine with Henry Clay to-morrow. I shall *try and keep sober.* A few days ago I dined with the President. He asked me across the table to take wine, which I, of course, declined. After dinner he came to me and asked, ' Are you, then, a teetotaller?' and I answered, ' I should say I was.' "

The admiration which Mr. Briggs cherished for Mr. Clay grew into an ardent personal regard, and even affection. The incident he refers to in the subjoined letter, addressed to his nephew, gave him as much delight as if he had been himself the object of such popular regard and applause.

When, a few months later, the ardent friends of the great Kentucky statesman were still smarting with their disappointment at the nomination of Gen. Harrison instead of Mr. Clay, he wrote to the same nephew : —

" I am glad you have reconsidered your rather hasty resolution in relation to Gen. Harrison. . . . . . His nomination has certainly been received with great unanimity by the Whig party. For this patriotic unanimity Henry Clay is entitled to the honor and credit. He led the way to it, by giving it his sanction. *None besides Henry Clay would have done it !* "

Here is the letter referred to, written while he was enjoying again the charms and cheer of his mountain-home, in the interval between the fourth and fifth of his Congressional terms of service : —

15

LANESBORO', Sept. 3, 1839.

DEAR ALFRED:

I see, in one of the Cleveland papers received from you, an allusion to the fact, that while ascending the steps of the United States Hotel in Saratoga, the young ladies dropped a wreath of flowers upon the head of Henry Clay, whereupon they talk sagely of monarchical principles! The best part of that little wreath affair is not told. At the moment Henry Clay left the multitude that was assembled around the hotel, and was ascending the steps, the fair ones dropped a wreath, unseen by him. It fell upon his shoulders. He seized it, and in an instant stretched out his long arm and threw it upon the heads of those who were crowding around him, saying, " This belongs not to me, but to the people.' In a moment, at the utterance of this sentiment of *true democracy*, the air was rent with the acclamations of the surrounding thousands.

Your affectionate uncle,

G. N. BRIGGS.

The popular voice, to such a patriotic servant of his country as Mr. Briggs, was not to be disregarded, even for personal considerations, however urgent. The opening of the Twenty-sixth Congress found him faithful to the trust committed to him at the election. He carried once more to Washington a sound judgment, a fervent zeal, a right conscience, and a toiling hand, to use in the interests of his constituents and for the broader good of his country.

During this session of Congress he reached his forty-fourth year, and gratefully commemorates the Divine goodness to him, writing thus to his wife : —

April 12, 1840.

MY BELOVED HARRIET:

This day I am forty-four years old. These are large figures when applied to the age of man. How rapidly the years have flown, and to how little account have I lived. I don't perceive that I grow wiser. One thing is true, whether I appreciate it or not, —

every year is a new memorial of the mercy and kindness of our heavenly Father. I wish I could "so number my days as to apply my heart unto wisdom." An accident has occurred this day which will probably distinguish this from all my other birthdays. After dinner, Mr. Hall and myself walked for the fresh air, out of the city, and, going in the direction of the landing-place of the Alexandria boats, which leave and return every hour, we thought we would go down in one boat and come back in the next. In the mean time, a threatening thunder-storm was rising and passing off mostly in the direction of Washington, though evidently approaching Alexandria. There being no convenient place for shelter near the dock, we were standing with several others on the steamboat dock, watching the advancing boat, the vivid lightning, and the coming rain, and speculating which would reach us first, the boat or the storm, — the former fast steaming towards the dock from the north, and the latter advancing from the west. The dock, which is about twenty feet wide, projects into the river from the east. In a slip on the north side lay a small sloop, on which was a black man, busy on deck. The boat reached the dock just as it began to sprinkle; but in the hurry of throwing the rope to make her fast, it fell short of the post, and she passed a little by, and was in the act of swinging round on the south side of the dock, when a most tremendous peal of thunder broke over our heads so suddenly that no one saw the flash that shivered the mast of the sloop only twenty or thirty feet from the spot where Mr. Hall and myself, with six or eight others, were standing. All were shocked. but none were injured except the poor black man, who was sitting at the foot of the mast. He was instantly killed. Mr. Hall saw him as he fell. The splinters from the shivered mast flew all around us. At the instant, I did not think what it was. It seemed like a large number of guns discharged back of my head. I went on deck and assisted in throwing water on the inanimate body of the poor smitten black man — but in vain; the bolt of heaven had done its office, and our poor degraded. fellow-mortal felt not the dashing water. Perhaps no sympathies will be awakened for his fate, except that felt by the white man who claimed him as his property — who will regret the loss of a thousand dollars in value.

Had the blow fallen a few feet distant, wives and children far away would have mourned the fate of those dear to them above all others. How great are His mercies in whose hands our breath is! May God have us all in His holy keeping!

In health. Love to all.

Thine ever,

G. N. BRIGGS.

None, among all the friends of Henry Clay, felt more keenly the disappointment and regret occasioned by the event that deprived the Whig party of all hope of seeing him President of the United States, than his two warm friends in Berkshire County. Mr. Shaw, from his chagrin and disgust, ceased from that period to feel an interest in political parties, — except to amuse himself in playing games with all, — and quietly withdrew from the battle.

Mr. Briggs, on the contrary, feeling intensely the ingratitude of the country towards its greatest statesman, yielded to the necessity, and with a heart devoted to the good of his country, laid aside personal regrets, and, like the leader he so much admired, adhered to the principles and policy he believed most sure to bring success and prosperity to the nation.

The following letter from Mr. Shaw, written about this time, marks the point where their paths diverge, and is such a satirical and ludicrous description of his political situation and career at this time, that it at once amuses and saddens, as did very often the words of its remarkable author.

LANESBORO', Oct., 1841.

DEAR BRIGGS: .

The time of deliverance draws near, and you doubtless feel "good." You ought to, for the country does. The nation, that is, the business part of it, regards Congress with unmixed dread.

From the position I occupy I see quite as clearly into the future as those who are more in a huddle and stand lower down. If you would or could, just for a moment, climb *up* on the fence, the prospect would fill you with amazement. You would no longer wonder why parties make mistakes, or why individuals indulge in such bitterness of feeling. Their position excludes them from a view of one another; — however, you had better not try it. The rail is filling up so fast, that those of us who got on early are full of fear that it will break, and we begin to have our little squabbles about priority of claims, and "original fence men," and the truth is, I verily believe a storm is brewing among us. Heaven preserve us! for the least agitation will bring us all down in a heap. Although we sit high and feel far above the motley crew that are reeking in the filth of the battle below, it is clear that we have our preferences. This is manifest when either of the parties make a decided move; its effects being discernible by us, we show our pleasure or fear or opposition by some sign or remark. But you will learn with sorrow, I am sure, that I am losing ground, or rather *rail*, as we say. My companions at first regarded me with great fear, and by common consent I sat pretty well *up* at one end, which was called the *head end*, or, as you would say, *taking the lead*. But it has been insinuated by some down the line that I am not entitled to the least favor, for it is said that while I was in the world below no one took my advice, and that *disappointment* rather than *patriotism* drew me on to the rail. Well, how to resist this I know not; but this I do feel, that I am losing rail every day. One fellow said the other day, while running up claims for a *hitch* forward, that all my *fenceism* was purely personal, and that if my advice at Harrisburg to put up Clay and Webster, or afterwards to put them both into the Cabinet, had been taken, I should never have shown my face among them. I felt *mad*, for the fellow had not been on a week; he had just got his quietus to a claim for a post office, and set up now for an "original fence man." However, let all this pass; you have your troubles, and don't want to be bothered with those of anybody else. This much I will say: I saw it announced the other day, that the Senators of the Whig party had met and solemnly agreed that an extra session of Congress must and

should be held. I could *sit* it no longer; I fixed my heels firmly
on the rail below, raised my body full upright, then leaning forward, and putting my hands, one before the other, on the top of
the rail, raised my right leg, and swung it round, till it struck the
head of the *patriot* right behind me, and in this position I was
arrested by the exclamation all along the line, "He is going off on
the Loco side, by heavens! He'll pitch on to —— and ——."
Either it was the noise, or the nearer view my horizontal position
gave me of the party, or the positive danger of the fall, I cannot
say, or all combined, I was poised but a moment, and with an
easy effort threw myself back again; and, looking quietly back
along the line, asked if any one could do that, taking no notice of
what had been said, lest some one might think my movement had
been a serious one. However, I let the thing pass off, and then
fell into a train of reflection, which resulted in the conclusion that
if a party having the Government by a clear voice of the people
choose to throw it away by an act of wanton folly, they will prove
that however splendid their talent, however pure their patriotism,
they are destitute of the *tact* essential to the Government of our
people.

Cordially yours,

H. Shaw.

This chapter can have no more fitting close than the
letter in which Mr. Briggs pays a beautiful tribute to the
memory and character of his much-loved and honored
friend, the able but eccentric John Leland, whose earthly
life and labors closed together at this period. He died at
Cheshire, Mass., Jan. 14, 1841, in the eighty-seventh year
of his age: —

Washington, Jan. 23, 1841.

My dear Wife:

Good old Elder Leland has gone to his rest. I don't know when
I have heard of a death that has so affected me. His venerable
and patriarchal form rises before me, as I recollect him, while in
the deep pathos of his great soul I have heard him pour forth the
truths of that gospel whose glorious triumphs I have no doubt he

is now enjoying. From my earliest recollection I have respected and admired him, but I did not know, till I heard of his death, how much I loved and revered him. I have always considered him a great man, but I did not appreciate his greatness till I saw how large a space his death has left vacant. When shall we again hear from the pulpit a man so mighty in the Scriptures as John Leland! He was not learned in the schools of divinity, though he was by no means deficient in a knowledge of polemics and theology. He drew his *knowledge* of the great truths of religion from the rich, deep, original fountain of inspiration itself. It *grieves* me to think that I shall never again see his venerable form, or hear him "speak forth the words of truth." In his intercourse with the world he was just. I never heard of a man's saying that he had wronged him. . . . . .

A great man has fallen in Israel. It will be long before we shall behold his like again. I have not time to tell the thousand recollections and emotions that rise in my mind, while I contemplate his life and death. He was the good friend of my father. He baptized my mother, and preached her funeral sermon. May we all meet him in heaven.

God bless you all.

Ever thine,
G. N. Briggs.

CHAPTER XV.

AT the opening of the Twenty-seventh Congress, Mr. Briggs received the tardy acknowledgment of his long, laborious, and eminently useful service on the Committee of the Post Office and Post Roads, by being made its chairman. It is simple justice to say that, during the two sessions of his chairmanship, he fully justified the opinion of his admiring friends, that this position was emphatically his sphere, as affording him the opportunity to complete and crown that series of postal reforms, which he had so long and successfully pressed upon Congress, by the inauguration of a movement for reducing the rates of postage to ten and five cents.

It was his last public service on the floor of the House to make this important effort, which he did with a boldness and earnestness that attested the maturity of his plans and convictions. The Senate anticipated the action of the House upon this subject, as a step imperatively demanded by the people, and their bill was sent to the House for concurrence. Mr. Briggs promptly moved to amend the bill by striking out all its provisions, and substituting those which were reported in the bill prepared in his Committee.

176

It must have been peculiarly gratifying to him to have the indorsement of the House for his plan without amendment. The bill thus passed was sent to the Senate, but that body absorbed, during the last two days of the session,[1] with executive business, did not reach it, and thus it failed of becoming a law, to the universal regret of the public, who did not however overlook, or forget, the beneficent enterprise of the Berkshire Representative in pressing it to the verge of success.

The following letter is the only memorial, at the command of the biographer, of the friendship and intercourse which existed between Mr. Briggs and General Scott. Its chief interest for the reader lies in the well-merited and ingenuous tribute the writer pays to the personal virtues and official generosity of one who had reached the highest pinnacle of military authority then instituted by the Republic : —

WASHINGTON, 31st July, 1842.

DEAR GENERAL :

I have just received your note of yesterday, accompanied by the letter of the Adjutant-General relating to the case of a private soldier, which I brought to your notice two days ago. I thank you for the promptness with which, in the midst of your multiplied cares, you have attended to that case, and for the investigation you have made of a sentence which surprised me by its severity. Allow me to say, sir, that no incident, connected with our military affairs has given me more pleasure, than to witness the readiness and alacrity with which the head of our army has given attention to the case of a humble private soldier. I trust when there shall have been time for the spirit and feeling of the ' General-in-Chief to be diffused through the army, there will be no

---

1 The bill was passed by the House March 2d, and Congress adjourned on March 4th, — when Mr. Briggs closed his Congressional career.

more such cases calling for his interference. The union of the
enlightened and elevated soldier, and the man interested in all
the concerns of humanity, in the person of the General-in-Chief,
cannot but exalt our military character, and reflect a lustre on our
country. Believe me, sir, I should be ashamed to say thus much
to you as a mere compliment. I do it as a slight, but sincere, tribute to an officer who is entitled to it by the ready and prompt manner in which he has given his official attention to the interest of
one of the humblest soldiers under his command.

With sincere respect, I am yours,

GEO. N. BRIGGS.

The stainless purity of the public and private character
of John Quincy Adams, and no less his great attainments
and eventful life, won the veneration, as well as the admiration and affection, of Mr. Briggs. His inflexible and fearless adherence to principle, irrespective of party, made him
a model in the estimation of one who, in these qualities,
emulated his noble example; qualities which distinguished
the true patriot and the incorruptible statesman from the
scheming and managing politician.

"I remember," — says the daughter, to whose pen this Memoir
is chiefly indebted for its *vraisemblance*, — " I remember hearing
my father tell an instance of his trying to avoid giving a vote
upon some not very important question, which came up in Congress; upon which he disagreed with Mr. Adams, and did not
wish to vote against him. He left the Hall to evade the vote,
quite at variance with his uniform custom. The movement did
not escape his argus-eyed colleague. The next time Mr. Adams
met him, he instantly charged him with it — ' You dodged the vote,
my friend; ' to which my father pleaded guilty."

Further reminiscences of the remarkable patriot, in connection with her father, are from Mrs. Bigelow's affluent
store : —

"When, in 1847, the requisition was made by the United States upon the State of Massachusetts for volunteers for the Mexican War, a war from which all the feelings of his nature recoiled, after deciding upon his course, and acting upon it in that most delicate exigency, he said to me once, that he felt more anxiety for the judgment of Mr. Adams upon the transaction than that of any other public man, and, to his gratification, the venerable man called upon him in Boston, soon after the adjournment of Congress, and when alone with him, with the cordiality of a father, assured him of his entire approval of the measure, introducing the subject himself by remarking: 'I watched you with much interest,' and ended by saying: ' *You did right; I thought you would.*'

"He was always most genial towards my father, and they interchanged frequent acts of kindness and courtesy. While in Washington, during a bilious fever which shut up my father there, after the adjournment of Congress, Mr. Adams came frequently to visit him, and taking his seat familiarly upon a trunk at the foot of the bed, talked in a most agreeable and paternal manner, encouraging him, and cheering the weary lapsing of those hours of his imprisonment as an invalid. The note which is here transmitted, and a letter on an earlier page in this volume, are brief memorials of a friendship which it will ever be a pleasure to remember.

"Another anecdote of the two is worthy of record. My father said to him one day in the House: 'I have been reading your mother's letters, Mr. Adams, and I see what made you a man.' Mr. Adams laid aside what he was doing, and began to talk with much interest about his mother, and said: 'Whatever there is good or bad in me — no, not *bad*, but whatever there is *good* in me, I owe it to my mother.'

"During Mr. Adams's last journey through Massachusetts, on his return from a Western tour, he passed a few hours in Pittsfield, meeting the citizens at a public reception, at which my father addressed him in behalf of the people."

Here is the letter to which reference is made in the above pleasing reminiscences: —

QUINCY, Sept. 24, 1842.

My dear Sir:

Nothing could give me warmer gratification than to comply with your kind invitation, repeated in your letter of the 21st inst.. to attend your Cattle Show and Fair in the first week of next month.

But independently of the admonitions of age, and its infirmities which daily thicken upon me, to withhold myself from all public or mass meetings, and especially from all at which I should myself be an object of notice, even the most flattering; my late constituents and neighbors have taken such possession of me, since my return home, that I am disabled from any excursion, more than ten miles distant, for weeks to come. I have two engagements for Boston for the 6th of October, which is the second day of your exhibition, which render my attendance there impracticable. For the solicitude of my fellow-citizens in your quarter to see me, and to honor me with personal testimonials of their approbation and esteem, I pray you assure them of my heart-felt gratitude. Had they no other title to my respect and esteem, than the continued confidence and the oft-renewed commission of trust to their Representative in Congress,—my colleague of twelve years' standing in the House,—that steadfastness alone would be worth more in my estimation than a hundred diplomas. I infer with much pleasure, from the firmness of your handwriting and from the date of your letter at Pittsfield, that you have entirely recovered from your indisposition, and hope to meet you again in Washington the first Monday in December, under better auspices than those which have overshadowed us since Sir Christopher Sly was installed in the White House.

I am, dear sir, ever faithfully your friend,

JOHN QUINCY ADAMS.

It will be seen that the next letter, written while Mr. Briggs was passing, *at home*, his last Congressional recess, is not dated, as usual, at Lanesboro'. While he was yet at his post in the Capitol, his family forsook their long-loved home in the Boro', for a more commodious and convenient dwelling in Pittsfield. The breaking up of old associations was not the only painful aspect of this domestic revolution. The honored father came to his new abode, enfeebled by the illness which had detained him in Washington. His daughter says, —

" He was miserably low in health, strength, and spirits ; and was as homesick as boy ever was when pining under the first banishment from the paternal roof in the exile of a boarding-school. The kind hospitalities and devoted attentions and social virtues of our new neighbors and friends, greatly cheered him however, and conduced directly to the restoration of his health and spirits. From this time there sprung up a peculiar and intimate friendship and intercourse with Mr. and Mrs. Lemuel Pomeroy, which continued unabated till death." [1]

His nephew Alfred, who left his hospitable, and to him truly paternal home, in 1832, had now after ten years made his abode, and was making a name, in Cleveland. His uncle cordially congratulates him upon the prospect opening before him : —

PITTSFIELD, 24th Sept., 1842.

DEAR ALFRED :

Your letter was received yesterday. As ever, I was glad to hear from you. I had seen in the public prints complimentary notices of your speaking at a large public meeting where Gov. Corwin and Mr. Ewing were present. Ever since you left me, in 1832, I have felt a deep interest in your destiny. I have been happy always to learn that you have maintained, untarnished, your good character. A reputation not growing out of a well-regulated moral character may, indeed, for a while attract the public gaze, and give its possessor a currency ; but the time will come when, like bank-bills that have no specie basis to rest upon, payment being demanded, it

---

" 1 The memory," says the daughter, " of the generous and courtly old gentleman and his noble and excellent wife, whose lives were so filled with good deeds, will long linger at the still hospitable old homestead."

will be protested and found to be fictitious and worthless. I am glad, always, to hear of you that your *aim* is to be right. I always hear with parental pleasure of anything to your honor, and, if possible, feel a greater pleasure that I hear nothing to your dishonor. You should be careful that you set not too great value on public applause. Though very agreeable, it is not a pillar to be relied on for support in cases of trial and difficulty. When consistent with a conscientious self-approval, it is an agreeable breeze that bears the bark smoothly on, but is not often to be relied on in the storm. Often the evil spirit of the deep will cause the true man's bark to be tossed high, and plunged deep into the troubled waters. In these matters I have nothing to complain of. I have had now almost a twelve years' voyage upon the political sea. I have however been so inconsiderable a voyager, that I was not worth raising a storm about. I am now nearly into port, and hope to meet with no breakers during the short residue of the voyage. I do not intend to be a candidate for re-election; I sigh for the quiet and repose of private life; and hope to be able to regain as much professional patronage, as to enable me to live comfortably with my family the remainder of my days. I would fain do good, and be useful in the humble sphere where Providence may place me. To make much figure in the world, I never have expected, and never expect to. If I can, by the right improvement of my life, be prepared to surrender it when its Author shall call for it, I shall, I hope, not have lived in vain.

The frequent and always familiar correspondence which marked the long friendship of Henry Shaw and the subject of this Memoir, suffered an interruption of some years, across which interval the shadow of political differences was projected. But it was, on both sides, too sincere a friendship to remain in permanent eclipse. Mr. Shaw yearned for the renewed companionship of one whose early life he had greatly influenced and often stimulated. The following playful letter, which has a chronological fitness for insertion here, will serve to illustrate this happy resumption

of their intercourse through the post, which was however
almost the only medium of their communion, for soon after
the date of‚ this letter Mr. Shaw removed from Lanesboro'
to New York — foiled and disappointed, it may be, in his
scheme for making " a happy valley" by transplanting his
beloved friends into the pastoral haunts he loved so well :

LANESBORO,' Jan. 16, 1843.

DEAR BRIGGS :

You will feel a little surprised probably at reading this, for you
may well wonder at my impudence in meddling with affairs that
are personally your own. But I think there remain some *rights*, to
be sure quite qualified ones, of mine in you. For a quarter of a
century you have had my confidence, and been more or less the
object of my reflections. Of this, however, we will say no more.
You have reached a period of life when prudence requires of you
a deliberate review of the past and a sober judgment of the future.
You are now, to a certain extent, unsettled. You have an encamp-
ment, but not a home. Your public, not more than your private
character and domestic peace, require that you should have a *home*.
You have good agricultural tastes and frugal habits — now let me
obtrude my advice. Come back to the Boro' and buy a farm ! You
cannot again renew your profession except as a counsellor, and
this position would be just as favorable to that part of your profession as a village. Now this is briefly my advice, and I am
somewhat moved in this matter by the fact that you could now
get a choice of farms among us at most reasonable rates, and
moreover by a strong desire to renew this beautiful valley. There
is another distinguished man, dear to me, who, I have some hopes,
may come among us. Why not enlarge the number, and make a
noble exile of worthies, who could meet and mourn together over
the lost state of public morals.

Now compare an independent agricultural life with constant, but
easy and healthful employment, with life in a laboring, heartless,
catch-penny village, with the fulness that makes the heart glad,
instead of milk bought by the pint. Look at it all over, and weigh

it well, and may wisdom preside over your deliberations. A good farm with plenty of fine stock, a good pair of nags, and a decent carriage, and your time *all your own*, with the silver brooks running through your *own* meadow, and speckled trout lying in wait for you. This is the condition for ripe manhood, and a cheerful and quiet preparation for that old age that is coming along — well — now — think of it. Anything I can do to forward a plan so rational, so full of philosophic ease, not unmingled with a reasonable profit, you can command.

Allow me to add that my family have been consulted on this subject, and this suggestion has received their unanimous approbation. All well but Cliff., who has been ill all winter; he is some better now.

Cordially yours,

H. Shaw.

As this is the last letter from the genial writer which is preserved among the materials for this biography, and the name of Henry Shaw lapses here from its pages, as it did only a few years after its date from the roll of the living, an anticipative allusion to his death will hardly be regarded as out of place. He died in Peekskill, N. Y., in the month of October, 1857, in the sixty-eighth year of his age. His remains were conveyed to his old and beloved home in Lanesboro', and Mr. Briggs was absent when they passed through Pittsfield. This fact added to the keen sorrow which he felt for the loss of so dear and faithful a friend, for he often deplored it, saying: "It would have been a mournful, but nevertheless real, satisfaction to have had his cherished form rest under my roof on its silent passage to the grave."

With this allusion to the earthly termination of a friendship persistent in its nature, pure in its motives, and rich in its mutual sympathies and solaces, this chapter finds an appropriate close.

CHAPTER XVI.

THE retired statesman was not long permitted to hide himself in the grateful obscurity of his quiet village home. His worth in public life was too vividly realized by the people of his native State, to give him that respite from its obligations for which he really longed, when he turned his back upon Washington at the close of the Twenty-seventh Congress. If he needed rest, he must find it in a change of scene and service, which to many men is quite as effectual for the recuperation of their energies, physical and intellectual, as absolute repose. Thus thought the people of the Commonwealth, whose interests he had watched over in the councils of the nation, and accordingly, with the earliest movement of the political parties in Massachusetts for the choice of the next Governor, he was put in cordial and eager nomination by the Whigs, the then dominant party.

It is unquestionably true that no name could possibly have kindled more enthusiasm throughout the Commonwealth than that of George N. Briggs. It was greeted with approval from its seaboard to its western-most hills. It

16*   185 carried with it, to the quick recognition of the intelligent and virtuous population, a pledge of fidelity, economy, and discretion in the administration of the Government; and beyond this it stirred the hearts of Christian men with the presage and promise of a strong infusion, into the executive influence, of that "righteousness which exalteth a people."

With these elements of hope and confidence, working in the minds and hearts of a multitude of the great party he represented, the result of the canvass was felt everywhere to be " a foregone conclusion." He was triumphantly elected. The State was filled with rejoicing at a result justly deemed so auspicious to all its highest interests — civil, social, and moral. There is a ring in the tone, and a relish in the taste, of the general congratulations of the newspapers and speeches of that period, which clearly individualize and crown his election as a speciality of public good. There is, to be sure, always an exultation of party organs and orators over a successful campaign and a fortunate candidate; but all this is clearly distinguishable from the intense and pleasurable and proud satisfaction with which the people of Massachusetts — the thrifty farmers, the enterprising manufacturers, the honest artisans, the professional classes, and peculiarly the religious community — combined to hail the accession, to the position of chief authority in the good old Commonwealth, of one who had been among her Representatives in Congress, — for twelve years, — like Bayard in character, *sans peur et sans reproche*, and like himself chiefly, in legislative fidelity and efficiency, unsurpassed and indeed almost unique.

A demonstration of the popular favor and approval so decided as that which quietly watched him voluntarily doffing the robes of Representative rank, that it might instantly thereafter invest him with the purple of its own highest honor — could not be effectually antagonized by any measure of resoluteness in a bosom that throbbed like his with unselfish pulsations. He yielded his wishes for home-life and home-employments, for the already long surrendered happiness of his family and fireside ; and prepared himself for his new toils and responsibilities — thinking more of these than of the honors with which they were linked in the bonds of duty thus thrown around him by the superior will of the people.

Never went a citizen of a free and prosperous and influential and virtuous Commonwealth, up from his coveted retirement, to an uncoveted seat of authority and proud distinction, with less ambition for self-aggrandizement, and larger aspirations for the popular weal, than did he in obeying the voice of Massachusetts, bidding him administer her laws and preside over her material and moral interests.

He was not looked up to with the almost blind admiration which splendid genius inspires in the multitude. He was no demi-god among his fellow-mortals. They knew him for a man like themselves, and the more like them that he was not extraordinary in intellectual faculties, or marvellous in the wealth of suddenly-revealed resources for any emergency. They knew him to have sprung from an almost obscure poverty, and by the persistence of his courageous mind · and honest heart to have left that estate so far behind him, that he was then and there a peer of the best and noblest citizens. They knew him to be true and steadfast in his adherence to an intelligent and deliberate judgment of the right and the wise and the good, in the great economies of a self-governing people. They could heartily trust him without misgiving, without jealousies, and they put the helm of the good ship of State into his hands, sure that the compass and the chart and the abiding stars, would never be superseded in his estimation by fickle theories and flashing meteors.

This is not the place where his successes as the Chief Magistrate of a great and growing Commonwealth are to be summed up ; but rather the place whence we follow those successes in an impartial review to the end of the seven years of his service, to be then rewarded, not with the Leah of a grudged and unloving approval, but with the Rachel of a true and heart-felt applause.

Very soon after the year 1844 was ushered in, George N. Briggs went to Boston to assume the functions with which the State of Massachusetts had invested him, and henceforward he will bear in these memorials the name by which he is now universally known — that of Governor Briggs. He reached the city on the sixth of January, and it may be chronicled as characteristic of the man that he took up his quarters at the Marlboro' Hotel — then distinguished from the fashionable hotels by its strict adherence to temperance principles, and by the social and religious habits of its guests.

One of the prominent religious journals of the city thus alluded to this act of the new Chief Magistrate : —

" If the Governor discovers as much love of quiet and order, and as high a regard for temperance, religion, and the social virtues in his official acts as he has done in the choice of a home in Boston, the public may well confide in the wisdom of his measures. His deportment also at the hotel answers to the description we have so often had of him. He is easy and affable in his manners, takes his meals at the public table, is present at the altar of worship morning and evening, in the public parlors, and does not affect to be anything more than an honest man and a Christian citizen."

Doubtless the simplicity and homeliness of the Governor's taste " in the choice of a home in Boston," so heartily commended by the religious press, did not equally commend him to all classes of citizens. Some may have set him down at once as not up to the times, and decidedly fogyish in his manners, especially in view of the morning and evening prayers. But even to this class these things, at which they affected to smile or to laugh, must have been the tokens of that sobriety of temper, that solidity of character and that sturdiness of principle which they knew well were the safeguards of public as well as of private virtue. It is a small item for a biographer to chronicle where a man chooses his lodgings; but there is a deep meaning in the old adage, " A man is known by the company he keeps." The new Governor of Massachusetts kept the company of those who respected themselves and reverenced God.

The " reporters " made him the object of most minute delineation,—from his beard to his bootees,—and especially remarked his habit of wearing a black stock without a collar. As he persisted in this practice all his life, and many unfounded rumors and fancies are afloat with reference to the origin of the habit, it may not be amiss to set them at rest. There is a slight suspicion of truth in the common anecdote, that he exchanged pledges with a friend, " to wear no collar while he should drink no gin." The little truth here is quite inverted, however. Bantered by a friend one day about his total abstinence notions and his no-collar habit, he playfully rejoined, that if his friend would sign the pledge and cut off his queue, he would wear a collar.

He did not wear one, simply from preference and for convenience.

As in the course of his Congressional life, so in that of
his Gubernatorial career, his letters will best reveal the
man — always characterized by an agreeable simplicity,
and often by a charming *naiveté*.

The following letter to his wife claims precedence of
others, not only by its chronological order, but because it
contains a reference to the worthy old gentleman (a warm
friend of the Governor) who is referred to in the explanation just given of the no-collar legend : —

Boston, 2d Feb., 1844.

My dear Wife:

My performances to-day have been to attend the Council, receive
ten Indians as visitors, dressed out in the most Indian style you
can imagine. At four o'clock, went to a dinner at Abbott Lawrence's. At half past seven, went to hear Dr. Hopkins's lecture,
which was indeed a rich treat. At nine, went to a party at Deacon
Grant's. Isn't this a pretty good day's work? To-morrow I am
going to Cambridge, to dine with President Quincy. Tell Mr.
Pomeroy I go it without collar or wine. Wine is going out of
fashion. Tell him unless he comes in soon, he will be more out of
fashion than I am without a collar! As for anything stronger
than wine, I have not heard of any human being drinking it since
I have been in Boston. Such a thing, among well-bred people,
belongs to a time far back. . . . . .

The right-mindedness of the man whose life is passing
in review, is signally and attractively displayed in his
letter to a personal and political friend, whose creed in
politics was much like that of the bold Robin Hood : —

. . . . . "the simple plan,
That he should take who has the power,
And he should keep who can."

The morality of the letter is lofty and exemplary, and, illustrated in practice, it is as refreshing as it is rare : —

BOSTON, Mar. 2, 1844.

DEAR —— :

I presume by the tenor of your letter, that you think that this administration should turn out the officers appointed by Gov. Morton, and fill their places with Whigs. This I understand to be the interpretation of your letter. I must say, frankly, I am sorry to learn that this is your view, because I regret exceedingly to find myself differing from one with whom, on such subjects, I have long, usually concurred, and whose judgment I so highly prize.

I believe, in the first place, that to turn out a single man appointed by our opponents, merely because he is not on our side in politics, when he is faithfully discharging his duties, would be wrong; and in the second place, that it would be impolitic. When Gov. Morton came into power, he found nearly all the offices filled with Whigs, who were appointed to the places they held because they were Whigs. He did not displace or turn out a single man of all those he had the power to remove; but when vacancies occurred, he filled them with his own political friends, precisely as our own party had always done. Upon what principle could I, as the Chief Magistrate of Massachusetts, now turn out men whom he appointed to offices that had become vacant merely because they belonged to another party, and *their* Governor saw fit to appoint them instead of Whigs? The one thing for which we, as a party, have censured the opposition most, is for the practice of that odious principle, "to the victors belong the spoils," and for turning men out of office on account of their political principles. Since 1811, I believe there has not been a single instance in this State, of a man being turned out of office for such a reason. In 1811, the Republican party did make a general sweep — the next year the people swept them! Though I should have filled many, perhaps all of the places to which Governor Morton made appointments, with different men from those whom he appointed, still, as he did appoint them, so long as they do their duty well, I cannot remove them from office because they differ from me in politics. Of the correctness of this course I have no doubt; and I cannot depart from it without violating my own sense of right and justice. If my friends should approve this course, I shall be glad; if not, and they prefer to put one in my place who would act differently, I should retain the consciousness of having acted according to the dictates of my own judgment, and that consciousness, I need not say to you, would be of more value to me when I must render a final account of my steward-ship than everything else.

I have thus frankly given my views of the subject, upon which I am glad to have you express yours with equal frankness. This is the principle upon which I feel bound to act. . . . . .

With much esteem, I am your friend,

G. N. BRIGGS.

In further illustration of his political morality, a sort of ethics which some men account mythical, but which with him was a vital principle of conduct, is his answer to an invitation to attend a political meeting, deemed of great importance : —

"Agreeable as it would be to me as a private citizen, to attend your meeting; as the Chief Magistrate of the Commonwealth, I cannot, with my own views of propriety, do so. During the last twenty years no one cause, in my opinion, has contributed so much to demoralize the politics of this country, both in the Federal and State Governments, as the prostitution of official power and influence to electioneering purposes.

"Against this injurious perversion of power, delegated for higher and nobler purposes, the Whigs, as a party, have protested. And so far as I know, the Whigs of Massachusetts, when in office, have endeavored to avoid an error which they have censured in others. How can a public officer so effectually promote the honor and suc-cess of the party which clothes him with authority, as by a quiet, diligent, and faithful attention to the duties of his station? Be-lieving these to be the views of that portion of my fellow-citizens whose favor placed me in the responsible office which I now hold,

I entered upon its duties with a firm determination to carry out, so far as lies in my power, in this and all other respects, the principles which they professed. I cannot doubt, moreover, that such a course will be viewed with favor by the spirited, intelligent, and true-hearted Whig young men of the city of Boston." . . . .

Of his official messages and acts, during his first term, there are none requiring special note. The impression he made upon the Legislature, and upon the Capital of the Commonwealth, unquestionably justified the many kind things said of him in advance of his official appearance there. He returned to Pittsfield and his home, having won "golden opinions."

The "Berkshire Jubilee" was celebrated in August of this year (1844), and Governor Briggs presided at this most beautiful and unique commemorative festival. It was a reunion of the sons and daughters of that most lovely region, not inaptly called "the Piedmont of America" — a region where hill and valley, lake and streamlet, alternate their charms with endless succession and scarcely less variety. Through much of its extent winds the lovely Housatonic, its banks skirted with graceful elms and dainty maples, and adorned in the flush of summer days with the delicate clusters of the clematis. But that the chief records of the "Jubilee" are to enrich this volume,[1] the biographer would linger a while, indulging reminiscences of its memorable delights.

It was celebrated with song and speech and sermon; with feasting and music; with wisdom and wit. Poets and philosophers and divines and merchant princes, brought their tribute to their Alma Mater, and all the village held high holiday.

[1] See Appendix, I.

17

The literary performances were conducted at a stand erected upon an eminence on the edge of the village, now included within it, and bearing the memorial name of " Jubilee Hill." Its prospects are as beautiful to-day as they were when the vast throng of that occasion gazed thence upon their fair enchantments — or, as when fifty years before that happy day, bright-eyed boys and girls looked out upon the scenes, little dreaming of the " Jubilee " they would keep, half a hundred years beyond their vision.

With happy tact, Governor Briggs presided at the festival, and made a very felicitous address, which was by no means the least attraction of the day. He always recalled the' occasion with great delight, and his name is inseparably woven with its bright and beautiful associations.

The successive winters from 1844 to 1851, found Governor Briggs in Boston, as surely as the sweet summer intervals of all those years allured him to rural, beautiful Berkshire, and gave scope to his trouting and rambling propensities, and no less to his benevolent ministries among the sick and the poor, whose homes were less dreary, and whose hearts were less comfortless, for his words of blessing and his acts of bounty.

Glimpses of him in the Chair of State, or, rather, when he had exchanged that for the easier chair in his chamber, or when he was participating in the social, philanthropic and sacred enjoyments of the tri-mountain city, are afforded in his unintermitted correspondence, never remarkable perhaps for the brilliance that is often meretricious only, but equally never dull with oppressive dignity, or vapid with mere frivolities.

Among the many memorials of personal regard and remembrance which Governor Briggs received from time to time, few, if any, were more prized than a simple black-thorn stick sent to him from Greece, by an American missionary in that storied land. To the friend, who was the medium of communication between him and the donor, he thus writes : —

PITTSFIELD, 3 Oct., 1844.

MY DEAR SIR:

I have your kind favor of the first inst., accompanied by a beautiful black-thorn cane, which you say is sent me as a present from the Rev. Nathan Benjamin, a missionary in Greece. In his note, a copy of which you forward, he says, " This stick is wrought from a shepherd's crook, procured by me at Delphi. It grew upon Mt. Parnassus." I have no words to express to you how highly I prize this beautiful token of remembrance from an absent friend. A cane cut on Mt. Parnassus would, from the place of its origin, be a valuable present; but, when as in this case, it comes from one of the Christian sons of Berkshire, who has left his home and friends to carry the story of *Calvary* to the people of that distant and classic land, it is inexpressibly precious. Mr. Benjamin is mistaken in supposing I had forgotten him. I well remember him when a modest, serious, persevering youth, by industry and studiousness preparing himself for the great and good work upon which he has since entered. May the Divine Author of that religion he has gone to promulgate, have him in His care, and give him success in his labors. Most sincerely I thank him for this memorial of his regard, and beg you to accept for yourself my grateful acknowledgment for the obliging and friendly manner in which you have communicated it.

Truly your friend,
G. N. BRIGGS.

His strong domestic attachments and affections increased with his years ; and his winter absences, in the discharge of his official duties, served to endear more and more his happy home to his heart. During his second term, in Boston, he writes : —

BOSTON, 4th Feb., 1845.

MY DEAR WIFE:

In George's letter, received to-day, he says you begin to complain because I write less often than formerly. I thought I had written within a day or two, but I fear I have not. Quite sure I am that I have never been from home when you were so constantly in my thoughts as you have been this winter. Every year adds to those ties formed now *many* years ago; and as each passing year brings with it the certainty that that dear union is drawing to its close, makes every day's separation to me more keenly felt. Our grown-up children, the whitened hairs that are stealing over my head, the *departing*, one after another, of those loved ones with whom we mingled in sunny youth, — all remind me that we are approaching the evening of life. We began the world poor and humble; and though riches have not filled our coffers, and though we have been by no means exempt from the ills of life, yet we have cause for everlasting gratitude to that great and good Benefactor and Parent who has watched over and cared for us. Though many of our dear friends have gone down to the peaceful grave, many yet remain to cheer us by their kindness. Of the four children God has given us, three remain; while He has taken away one, to loosen the ties that too strongly bind us to the world, and to add one more motive to stimulate our zeal and hope to reach that bright world where she now worships Him who, while on earth, put his hands upon and blessed little children. Could I feel a well-founded assurance that in God's own good time we, her parents, with the three dear children, should meet her angel spirit and " worship the Lamb and Him that sitteth on the throne " with her, everything else in this life would be comparatively of little moment. I know this feeling may too nearly resemble that selfish spirit that made the two brothers ask that they might sit, the one on the right hand the other on the left hand, in the Saviour's kingdom. Still it is but natural that we should feel more deeply for the spiritual welfare of those nearest us on earth, as we do for their temporal interest. I have as ardent wishes to see my children honored and prosperous as any parent ought to have; but to have their names written in the "Lamb's book of life" would be an immortal honor, — a rich inheritance as far transcending all the riches and promotions of earth as the interests of eternity transcend the transient things of time. May we all "keep our hearts with all diligence,"knowing that "out of them are the issues of life." . . . . .

In the subjoined letter to his faithful friend and physician, he indulges in retrospective glances, and in such personal reflections as were characteristic of his mind and heart : —

BOSTON, Feb. 23, 1845.

DEAR DOCTOR :

I was concerned to learn a few days since of the illness of my sister, W. I am glad to know that she is under your care, as I am sure that everything will be done for her that can be. Will you let me know how she is? I shall be anxious till I hear. I am very anxious indeed to get home, and have a few days at least of repose and quiet. Perhaps I have as much ease as any man in such a station as I occupy, or as any one has a right to expect in such a place ; yet its cares and responsibilities are very far from making it a bed of roses for me. The responsibility of a public servant to his constituents is well calculated to make him deeply solicitous to look well to his steps, but a proper sense of his accountability to the Judge of all the earth, for such a stewardship, is much more fearful to one who feels the want of the requisite qualifications for such a trust. Though constituents may not always appreciate the motives of their agent, when his public acts do not conform to their wishes, yet he is certain, if honest, good intentions govern his course, that He who weighs conduct by motives will judge him in mercy, if he errs in the details, or mistakes the best means of accomplishing the end. When I look around me, and see and feel what is upon me here, I can hardly realize that I am the same individual who nearly thirty years ago spent such pleasant days and weeks in your peaceful and happy family, in the quiet old Boro'. How those scenes and the actors in them have passed away! Still memory lingers around them with mournful pleasure, and loves to

17*

call up one after another of those friends who have departed forever from the earth. How often my mind, before I am conscious of what I am doing, is found passing from house to house in that beautiful town, in pursuit of those I loved, and scarce a dwelling is visited in which death has not made a conquest. Soon, and but *One* knows how soon, some friend, in looking over the list of those with whom he is now familiar, will find your name and mine stricken from among the living. My highest ambition is, that when my poor name shall be thus recalled to some surviving, absent friend, he may be able to connect it with some humble act by which any of my fellow-beings have in some respect been made happier or better by my being upon the earth. To me the reflection is sad enough, that I have lived so long, and yet have so little, if anything, to entitle me to such a recollection. How infinitely more important it is, however, that we do something that shall lead "the Friend that sticketh closer than a brother" to say to us in the great day of decision, "Inasmuch as ye have done it unto one of the least of these little ones, ye have done it unto me." . . .

I am sincerely as ever yours,

GEO. N. BRIGGS.

To Dr. W. H. TYLER.

Here follow, in quick succession, two letters to that nephew in whom he took an almost parental interest, — the one a letter of condolence with him upon the death of his young wife, and the other a letter of counsel with regard to his entering into public life, of which some tidings reached him soon after he arrived at home in the spring of 1845 : —

PITTSFIELD, 28 April, 1845.

MY DEAR ALFRED :

That which we have feared has come upon us. Margaretta has been called home. When she became yours, we esteemed and respected her on your account; but when we knew her, we loved her for what she was. We can hardly be reconciled to the thought that we shall never more be cheered by her amiable and social qualities. Deeply the arrow pierced your heart, but it was directed by the hand of a Friend. Your loved one, who yesterday was a

Christian in a sorrowing and imperfect state, to-day is a saint in heaven. Oh, what a change! to her an infinite gain. Perhaps the thought is prompted by disappointed affection, since we have never seen Margaretta, but I do indulge it, — that I may yet meet your dear one in that happy world where friends will never separate, and friendship be perpetual. I hope to meet and know her. Next to the presence of God and the Lamb, nothing would so much promote the felicity of those in heaven, as to meet and recognize their friends on earth.

I doubt not, my dear Alfred, that in the depths of your bereavement, you find consolation in that religion which sustained your wife in her long illness, and sustained her in death. Her beauty, her refined and accomplished manners, and her kind and benevolent heart, will live in your memory until, with her, you sink into the grave. Then you will meet her redeemed spirit and love her forever. How blessed is that religion which holds out to the afflicted ones of earth such a hope as this! This world has no such treasure.

Your affectionate uncle,

GEO. N. BRIGGS.

PITTSFIELD, 5th May, 1846.

DEAR ALFRED:

. . . . . . I have understood in some way that there is a prospect of your becoming a candidate for Congress this fall. If it come, let it come of *itself*. I have no fear, my dear Alfred, of your doing anything improper to get a nomination, or an election. Let any political place or promotion be regarded as an incident, and not relied upon. Do nothing in getting it, or *in* it after it is attained, which cannot be looked back upon with complacency, or in doing which you may not expect the approbation of Him whose friendship is life, and whose loving kindness is better than life. In the vicissitudes of your checkered life, my dear boy, I have no fear that you will cut loose from the anchor of principle, to which you have held so far in life, and to which you will hold fast and be safe amid all the storms that may toss you on the ocean of life.

May you have many years of prosperity and happiness.

Affectionately your friend and uncle,

G. N. BRIGGS.

CHAPTER XVII.

THE chief incident in the experience of Gov. Briggs
during his second year of office was the marriage
of his daughter Harriet. She was his *only* daughter, and so much the light of his home that not all
the happy circumstances in which she was about to
leave it, availed to hide from him the shadows which her
departure would cast over it. In September of 1845 she
was married to Capt. Charles H. Bigelow, of the United
States Engineers; and although the son-in-law was welcomed by the father with all the sincerity of regard due to
his personal attractions, his moral worth, and his now intimate connection with his family,—there was a pang at the
father's heart while he felt in advance the separation to
come, and knew that henceforward there was to be some
one nearer to his beloved daughter's heart than himself.

Captain Bigelow was, indeed, a man to win the confidence
and admiration and love of a heart so ingenuous and child-
like in its outgoings as that of his father-in-law. He was
of most prepossessing appearance, and of manners not less

fascinating. His intellectual powers were large and brilliant. He excelled in conversation, and displayed, without
ostentation, the richness of those stores of knowledge which
he had laid up. When to this it is added that his character
was as charming as his personal graces, — elevated by true
piety and disciplined by self-control, — it will not be questioned that he was made lovingly welcome to his happy
fortune, even by the father, who said to an old friend, a
day or two after the wedding and the departure, while the
quick tears stood in his eyes, "It makes a baby of me."

The tender intimacy and affection which grew up between
the father-in-law and the son-in-law, is to this hour one
of the most cherished and sacred memories in the two
homes, which in less than a short score of years were so
deeply overshadowed, in quick and sad succession, by the
death first of the one and then of the other.

The hand of the one who felt this double bereavement
most keenly of all those whom it afflicted, has traced for
these pages a memorial of that affection most touching and
beautiful; and although it carries the reader many years
forward in this life-history, the volume can afford no more
appropriate place for its insertion than this, which brings
it into juxtaposition with the biographer's words concerning the noble subject of its loving tribute: —

"The deep and fond affection which years ripened between my
father and his son-in-law, Capt. Charles H. Bigelow, was of an
extraordinary type, and had in it the tenderness and fervor of a
woman's love, combined with the manliness of their own. Capt.
Bigelow won the faith and affection and admiration of all who
knew him intimately. He was so true to all that elevates and
ennobles man, that wherever he took his place, all felt his power.
Not alone his brilliant intellect or his learning, or his strength of
character and intensely active energies, or his conversational

talents, — but the transparent truth and honesty of his nature, his whole-heartedness in whatever he undertook, his kindness and gentleness, and his piety towards God, rendered him to my father beloved and respected. Hours after hours of the days of their delightful friendship they passed in talking, sitting in the quiet of their own homes, walking over the fields, or driving through the valleys of the Merrimack or over the hills of Berkshire. These conversations were among the chief joys of both. Acting and reacting on each other, so unlike in many respects, and yet so sympathetic and so assimilated in opinions and tastes, — Capt. B., proud yet so humble, self-reliant yet so self-depreciating, generous, impulsive, passionate, fearless, frank, imaginative, — literally frolicsome as a boy and loving as a child; my father loved and moulded him after *his own sweet nature*, so that they had *one heart*. My father gave him, as he himself acknowledged, his first impulse towards true benevolence. He said that until he came to know intimately my father's *life*, the duty of benevolence had been with him very much an intellectual conviction only. As in the Saviour, he saw and felt the beauty and power of a life of love, and was himself transformed into the same image.

"No occurrence during my father's last hours so overcame and unmanned him as meeting this son. He folded him to his breast as a mother folds to hers the child of her love. Those who saw his head bowed upon the bosom heaving with a strong man's emotion, felt how 'they loved one another.' They had often talked of death, and Capt. Bigelow had twice been saved from what seemed to be inevitable destruction. I am sure that none of his children were nearer to my father's heart than ' *Charles*.'

" Standing by the silent form of one he loved so well, the vision of his new life opening through the veiled white presence and closed eyes before us, the triumph of death achieved, that son still in his strength and amid the earnest strife of human events, exclaimed, with strong emotion, ' He is to be envied ! ' Six short months after, the two were laid side by side. ' They sleep well.' Very lovely and pleasant were they in their lives, and in death they are not divided."

The following letter was the first the glad, yet grieving, father addressed to his daughter in her new home. Of the poor girl, who is mentioned in it, these memorials will hereafter afford a more extended notice : —

PITTSFIELD, 12 Oct., 1845.

MY DEAR DAUGHTER:

Here we are ("but we are not *all* here"), quiet and peaceful within, while the storm beats without. All pretty well except Henry, who has ague in the face. He has suffered extremely; but we hope the worst is over. Things go on much as usual; neighbors all well. This morning I called to see *Jane*. Poor girl! it seems as if she were going soon. She has had a bad week. All the family, or rather both families, have been sick, except the old lady. I said to her, " Jane, our prospect would be a gloomy one, if we could not look forward to a better world than this." She raised those beautiful, clear blue eyes, and with a smile that seemed not of earth, said "Yes." I asked her what she thought of her recovery. She said the doctor told her last Sunday there was no hope for her. I inquired if she wished to get well. She said, " I should be glad to get well, but I hope I am resigned to the will of God." In answer to another question, which she understood to be an inquiry about her future, she said, in a tone and manner deeply affecting, "I think I shall be at rest." Oh, I thought, could the man absorbed in the pursuit of wealth, the man insane with ambition, hear the response of this lovely child, like the opening rose-bud, fading and drooping before its freshness and fragrance were fully known, — what a lesson it would be to him! I desired that it might be a useful one to me. She *may* live some time; but the seal of the destroyer is upon her marble forehead. When her frail, symmetrical form and sweet face shall fall and fade beneath his power, how soon she, whom we now speak of as " Poor Jane," will be a radiant angel. Queens and princesses and courtly ladies, who have never looked into so humble an abode as hers is now, would be amazed to see her shining robes and happy spirit in the home of the blessed.

I intended to tell you, when I began, how lonely we are to-day, and how much we have missed one who has been with us since the day I looked upon her in her "swaddling clothes," in the upper room in the old homestead in Lanesboro', down to three weeks since. But the thoughts of Jane rose up and rebuked me, and, sad though it is to believe that our home is no longer to be cheered and shared by one so loved, still we would not have it otherwise. You have known full well before this that I was entirely satisfied with the connection you have formed. It is all I could ask for one so dear to me. Everything about Charles is as I would have it. But the consideration that crowns all is, that he has chosen that which the young man who came to Jesus lacked, and, lacking, went away sorrowful.

I want to see all my children prospering in this world, but to see them *Christians* is my first great wish.

All send love. Love to Charles and George and all friends.

Affectionately, your father,

G. N. BRIGGS.

At this time George was absent, but not forgotten. That heart is to be pitied which is not child-like enough to be delighted with the picture of frolicsome "Tray" : —

PITTSFIELD, Oct. 30, 1845.

MY DEAR SON:

Your mother wonders what has become of George. She says you have not written. All things move on here in the old track. We are having a Teachers' Institute. It has been in session more than a week. About a hundred young men and girls are in attendance. The lessons and lectures are full of interest, and the scholars are full of zeal. It will do much good. I attend regularly. One of the young men asked me the other day where I expected to teach this winter. Rather an ominous question!

We expect you home a week from to-morrow. If you do not come your mother will be after you. All well. *Tray* is in fine spirits. He has done two things lately which have distinguished him. In the first place, he chased a cow out of the yard with great vigor and loud barking, but, unluckily, just as she got into the street she stepped on his foot, when he came back with a new tune, which he played long and loud. In the next place, while eating off his plate a little chicken thought it might take a crumb, when Tray, in a pet, bit off its head.

Nothing else remarkable. All well.

Affectionately, your father,
G. N. BRIGGS.

His daughter's hand has traced for these pages a short and simple annal of poor Tray. It reveals the tender heart of the man who had not only compassion, but affection, for the humblest creature dependent upon his care and bounty. His ingenuous half apology, half confession, at the breakfast-table, might have served for an epitaph in stone over Tray's grave. It will endure as long, though written upon "fleshly tablets" only : —

"Few visitors at the house," says his daughter, "during the life-time of this favorite of my father's, — the faithful Tray, — will not recall the playful, brilliant creature. Seldom useful or unamiable, he entertained himself and others with such a development of brains and heart and fun, as is rarely seen among those less gifted of his race. He was a medium-sized spaniel, with glossy chestnut curls and hazel eyes — eyes so human and tender in their expression, that one fell to moralizing with Jacques, when ' returning their strange gaze.' He was my father's *inseparable* at home and about the village, and attended him to Boston with other members of the family, and sat with them to Whipple for a family group; and afterwards he was sent, as a great favor (to Tray and his friends!), to reside out of town with us at Lawrence, in order that he might recover the health and vigor which the feeding and con-finement of a Boston hotel had impaired. The quickness with which the instinct of the dog discovered my father's approach to our house in Lawrence, on his occasional visits there, was truly *amazing*. He announced him always with a quick, sharp cry, and with the greatest demonstrations of welcome at the door or win-dow, and often gave us the first intimation of a visit from him.

"Tray, alas! was *mortal*, and we buried him in a sunny nook

18

under the elm, in the corner of the yard, with fitting tributes to one like him, — 'beautiful, faithful, lamented.' He died the day previous to one of my father's visits; and the morning after he said, at breakfast, 'I don't know but I am a *fool;* but I have not slept a wink this night for thinking of *that dog.*' "

Immediately after the close of the session of the Teachers' Institute, alluded to in his letter of Oct. 30th to his son, he wrote thus to the gentleman at whose expense this truly valuable adjunct to the educational interests of the State was established and maintained: It has since diffused itself and its beneficent influences throughout this Commonwealth and widely over the land, vastly promoting the work of popular education, and helping hundreds of young men and women in their honest endeavors to qualify themselves for the work of instruction : —

PITTSFIELD, 1st Nov., 1845.

MY DEAR SIR :

The first experiment of a teachers' institute in this Commonwealth, under your munificent patronage, has been a successful one. The ten days' session of the institute held in this village closed last evening. I am sure, if you had witnessed its progress and termination, you would have felt that the money which you have expended upon it had already returned a hundred-fold. A hundred young men and women from the various towns in the county, ardent in the cause of education, separated after the session with the delightful consciousness that they had been essentially benefited by the instructions which they had received from the excellent teachers who had given them lectures and lessons. Every heart felt the warmest gratitude to the benefactor who had kindly furnished them this agreeable means of improvement. All praise is due to Mr. Mann, Mr. Fowle, and Miss Tilden, for their valuable services. Mr. Rowe, of the grammar school in this town, also aided them. The whole public watched its progress, and is deeply impressed with the utility of the movement. Judging from the effect of the experiment here, I am confident these meetings of teachers in different parts of the State, the present autumn, will be regarded as an important era in the history of our common schools.

I sincerely congratulate you upon the result of this new effort by you to benefit the rising generation.

Truly yours,

G. N. Briggs.

Hon. E. Dwight, Boston.

Political strife in Massachusetts mounted high in the autumn of 1845, and, notwithstanding the wide popularity of Governor Briggs, extending to not a few of the opposite party, who estimated his sterling virtues and inflexible adherence to principle as above mere partisan qualifications, the issue of the election hung in doubt. When it was over, and the incumbent triumphantly returned by the people to his chair, he wrote to his son-in-law a letter remarkable for its allusions to his personal interest in the result, and which indeed must be construed as involving chiefly the success of the principles represented in him : —

PITTSFIELD, Nov. 13, 1845.

DEAR CHARLES:

. . . . . The election is over, and, for the old Bay State, well over.[1] Boston has outdone herself. With the difficulties she had to encounter, I think she has achieved a more remarkable victory than ever before. All eyes were turned towards her, from Texas to the St. Johns. She is Boston still, and Massachusetts is Massachusetts still. The result shows a triumph of principle. In this she has covered herself with honor. Let justice, stability,

---

[1] After the election, when Father Taylor, of the Sailors' Bethel, read the Governor's Proclamation of Thanksgiving, after fervently and devoutly uttering the usual formula, "God save the Commonwealth of Massachusetts," he lifted up his flashing eyes, and added, with fervor, "That HE *did* last Monday!"

and truth be her motto, and no matter how humble those she puts forward, she will prevail.

Yours ever,

G. N. BRIGGS.

Among the numerous gifts which were tendered for the acceptance of Governor Briggs, and happily involving him, from its very nature, in no embarrassment, and in no question as to his duty with regard to its reception, was a pair of spectacles mounted in silver, the work of a lad in South-bridge, who accompanied his simple offering with the following letter : —

SOUTHBRIDGE, Dec. 1, 1845.

GOVERNOR BRIGGS :

Will your Excellency please accept the accompanying present, as a small tribute of respect for your principles in favor of mechanics. Though not a voter, should I live to the age of manhood I hope to be correct in principle, and be governed by those for which you have so ably contended. My present is small, but I have exercised my best ingenuity in workmanship, the whole being done by my own hands. Hoping that you will find the spectacles useful, and that you will live a long and happy life, is the sincere wish of

Yours, truly,

WM. E. FOSTER.

The Governor's reply to this letter is worthy of a place among the choicest of the productions of his mind and pen : —

PITTSFIELD, 12th Dec., 1845.

MY YOUNG FRIEND :

When in Boston last week I received through my friend, Hon. Linus Child, your letter of the 1st inst., and a beautiful pair of silver-mounted spectacles which you were so kind as to present to me as a tribute of respect to my "principles in favor of mechanics." You say "the whole was done by your own hands." As a specimen of finished workmanship, they would do credit to a mechanic of any age. If you are "not old enough to vote," the beautiful present which you send me exhibits a mastery of mechanical skill that is acquired but by few *men*, after the practice and experience of their whole lives.

The glasses fit my eyes exactly. I shall long keep them as an interesting and remarkable specimen of the ingenuity and skill of a young mechanic of my own native State. They could not have come from any donor that would have given me more sincere gratification. My ever-venerated father was a laborious, honest mechanic. Several years of my early youth were spent in a hatter's shop. The dearest recollections of my life must be blotted from my memory before I shall cease to regard all worthy mechanics with kindness and respect.

My young friend, I beg you to accept my best thanks for this valued present. May you live not only to become an intelligent voter, but to give your countrymen the benefit of your experience and ingenuity as a mechanic. By a life of industry, temperance, and virtue, may you win the respect of the wise and good, and be rewarded with honor and prosperity, and may you "keep your *heart* with all diligence, for out of it are the issues of life."

Your obliged and grateful friend,

GEORGE N. BRIGGS.

At the celebration of the fifteenth anniversary of the Massachusetts Charitable Association, held in Boston, he gave a broader expression of his interest in mechanics and mechanical pursuits; a part of it is given here, as imperfectly reported for one of the newspapers of the day. The speech was made in response to one of the regular toasts:

" *The good old Commonwealth of Massachusetts* — as she stands — with all her institutions. May God forever bless her."

After the music ceased his Excellency, Governor Briggs, amidst the enthusiastic applause of the whole assembly, rose to reply: —

18*

"He said that since it was expected he should speak for the 'good old Commonwealth of Massachusetts,' he was sure he could say she was grateful for this notice which her children took of her, and that she regarded this Association as among the best and most worthy of her children. But as to anything further he hardly knew whither to direct his thoughts, in the few remarks which might be expected from him. If he thought of the character of the Association and its members, the sea of mechanics' faces before him told what that was; if of its objects, they had been presented to-day in the most beautiful language and mathemetical manner (if he might be allowed so to say); if of the venerable and honored men who had numbered themselves within its ranks, their names were emblazoned upon the walls, and nothing he could say would call them more vividly to mind. He experienced emotions upon this occasion which he wanted terms fully to express. But he should not be misunderstood in saying that he reverted, in thought, to the time when he too was an actual mechanic, and that, within the last hour or two, he had felt more regret than ever at having ceased to be one. (Applause.)

"But yet he could not bring himself to follow the course seemingly prescribed by the theory, if not by the practice of some, to unjustly elevate the mechanic at the expense of his brethren in the community. To talk of mechanics as a class and to undertake to give them the preference to, and set them above, all other classes, he knew his intelligent hearers would regard as an insult. They were too manly, too noble-hearted, to desire any such thing. There was no test class in our community. It was false to pretend that one existed. And as among individuals he only was best who bore the best character; so among classes, only the one was best which did most for our common country. . . . . .

"Who was there, amongst all his hearers, that did not feel a glow of honest pride as he cast his eyes upon yonder honored name (Franklin)? (Cheers.) What was he who bore it but a mechanic? A Boston mechanic, too! (Great applause.) Born almost within a stone's throw of this very spot, and brought up in the midst of the localities, around which cluster so many associations, it was his fortune nobly to sustain the dignity of his calling

and the honor of his home. It was related of the family, that
Franklin's father was in the habit of reading to his children a
chapter in Proverbs, wherein was the following verse, — 'Seest
thou a man diligent in his business? he shall stand before kings;
he shall not stand before mean men.' The children heard, remembered, and pondered upon the sacred truths of revelation. By and
by, the old puritanical father was laid in the grave, but the effect
of his teaching remained. And finally, during the war of the Revolution, when the American nation sent their first minister to
France, it was Benjamin Franklin, the Boston mechanic, who
represented the republic, and 'stood before kings' at the magnificent Court of St. Cloud. (Much applause.)"

During his third official term of residence in Boston, he
writes, from his old quarters, it will be seen, to his daughter
at Lawrence, —

MARLBORO' HOTEL, Sunday evening.

MY DEAR DAUGHTER:

I intend to go home a week from to-morrow, but the Legislature
may keep me longer. Mrs. C. and I went up the Mississippi last
evening, and had a pleasant voyage.[1] She was much pleased with
the picture. I have attended church twice at Mr. Hague's to-day;
preached once myself to the Sabbath school. I can't say that I
talked like a child to them, but feel more as if I had talked like a
fool to them. I believe I am getting too old to talk, as it seems to
me that I make worse work of it every attempt I make. As I
intend to come to Lawrence (for it is Lawrence now according to
law) before I go to Berkshire, I will, Providence permitting, come
on Tuesday evening. . . . . .

After an address in Boston in one of the schools, Mr.
Amos Lawrence, in a letter to his son, says, "Your
father *never* made two speeches that will tell on the welfare

[1] In a visit to Banvard's panorama of that river, which was then upon its first
exhibition in Boston.

of his hearers more effectively than his addresses of ten or fifteen minutes, in each room for the two hundred and fifty boys and the two hundred and fifty girls of the ' *Mather School.* ' "

In a playful, characteristic note, of nearly the same date, to Governor Briggs, he writes to him, —

DEAR GOVERNOR:

You see your *medicine works.* Those five hundred children will be likely to remember your last Saturday's discourse, and the events of *this week.* Do you need my help to *pick flowers ?* — If so, I am at your service to-day. I have been to ride, gloomy as it is. Charles will come towards evening, if you say so.

Your friend,
AMOS LAWRENCE.

The following informal note from Col. Perkins, was inclosed in a letter to his daughter by Governor Briggs, and on the inside he made the memoranda concerning its writer, which are subjoined. They possessed great interest at the time, and have by no means less now, that every one named in it has passed from this life : —

TEMPLE PLACE, April 19, 1847.

DEAR SIR:

Please to remember that you promised to patronize our Domestic Theatre, which closes to-morrow evening. The curtain rises at seven o'clock, I hope it will suit your convenience to be with us at half past six.

Respectfully, your obedient servant,
T. H. PERKINS.

" TO HIS EXCELLENCY, GOV. BRIGGS:

" Col. Perkins is eighty-four years old. When at a dinner on the 22d of December last, at Plymouth, he stated that forty years ago he called to see a very old man by the name of Cobb, who was one hundred and thirteen years old, and that Cobb told him he remembered Perigreen White, who was born at Plymouth, and was the first person born in New England.

" A few days before the date of this note, Mr. Abbott Lawrence and myself called on Col. Perkins, and passed a half-hour with him. He was in fine health and spirits. He said on the morning of the Boston massacre, which was on the 5th of March, 1770, a man who lived with his mother took him in his arms, and he well remembered the blood which was frozen in the gutter. The man took him to three different places, and he saw the dead bodies of the persons who had been killed the night before by the British soldiers.

" He said he spent some time in France during the French revolution. He arrived there a few days after the fall of Robespierre, and was present and saw the whole Revolutionary Tribunal executed. There were sixteen of them. They were brought to the place of execution in three carts, and from the time that the carts stopped to the time that the heads of the sixteen persons were thrown into a basket, it was only fourteen minutes, of which space two minutes were occupied in removing and bringing up the carts. He also saw several members of the convention beheaded. Col. Perkins is a native of Boston. For success, character, and princely munificence, he stands very high in the first rank in a long and honored line of Boston merchants. He is now one of the most agreeable, instructive, and interesting men of this city. After alluding to many interesting occurrences and incidents, which he had witnessed in early life, he patted me on the shoulder, and said, in the most cheery and pleasant manner : ' Governor, you see that there is some pleasure in being old.' The half hour spent with him will be remembered with pleasure to the latest period of my life. The same afternoon Mr. Lawrence and I called upon and had a visit with Mr. Loring, another of the merchant princes of Boston, who is eighty-four years old.

" BOSTON, April 24, 1847."

The relations between the Governor and Amos Lawrence were of an intimate nature. His old friend sent to him the album of his twin granddaughters, whose mother was dead, begging him to inscribe a memorial within it. He wrote the following under the date of September 28, 1847 : —

"My dear Children:

"This little book has been sent to me by your grandfather, with the request that I would write in it. I should be glad indeed to say a word to gratify him, or that would be interesting or useful to you. You are to him the dearest jewels on earth, because you are the precious memorials of that loved daughter of his, your mother, who is now a saint in heaven. To see you grow up lovely and virtuous as your mother was, would make him happy. May our Father in heaven preserve your lives — may you early learn wisdom, walk in her peaceful ways, and love the Saviour, so that when your grandfather shall reach the close of his useful life, his care and anxiety for you shall cease, and his body shall sleep beneath that old peaceful oak now spreading its protecting arms over your mother's grave, the virtues that adorned them shall live in you."

In October of this year, while the great stone dam built by the Essex Company, in Lawrence, Mass., across the Merrimack River, was in progress, a section of the coffer dam was carried away, and Captain Bigelow, with several other persons, were thrown with the wreck into the river. He was dangerously hurt, and indeed received injuries which, though not until many years after, resulted in his death. Tidings of this disaster called forth the following letter of sympathy and comfort : —

PITTSFIELD, October 15, 1847.

My dear Daughter:

We looked with great solicitude for the mails of yesterday and to-day to bring us tidings of Charles, and we have great reason for gratitude to God, that, thus far, they have been better than we feared. What a wonder it is that Charles was saved from instant death! Surely, it is to the Lord "that maketh a way in the sea and a path in the mighty waters" that we owe the deliverance of him we so much love, from instant destruction. I hope you will not, in your anxiety, forget how much you and all of us owe to Him who watches the falling sparrow, for that almost miraculous deliverance. Let your mind be stayed on Him, and trust in His wisdom and goodness for the future. Now, everything is as favorable as could be expected. For the future, we have no right to be anxious. It will all be ordered in wisdom and goodness. Well may Charles say : "The waters compassed me about, the depths closed me roundabout; yet hast thou brought up my life from the pit, oh, Lord, my God!" I should have been with you before this, but for your mother's feeble state.

Tell Charles my heart is with him, and I hope, in his sufferings, he will be sustained by a power far more stable than earthly friends can exert. I did not know till now, for it had not been proved, he was in my affections so *fully* a *son.* He is indeed a golden link in that family chain which binds us together, and I hope and trust that chain is not *now* to be severed. You have our hearts' desire for speedy deliverance from the affliction that now presses upon you. Be assured, my child, while your mother and I live, any suffering which you or your dear husband shall feel, will be our suffering; your joys will be our joys. Be of good courage, and trust that soon all will be well. Our friends in Pittsfield have taken a deep interest in Charles's case, and show great solicitude for his recovery.

Affectionately, your father,

G. N. BRIGGS.

CHAPTER XVIII.

IN no single aspect of his life, perhaps, does Governor Briggs appear to greater advantage, or at least more to the general surprise, than in his relation to the great educational interests of the Commonwealth — from the lowest to the highest of their exponents. It is not indeed surprising to any, or especially creditable to himself, that he valued education immeasurably — estimating wisdom above rubies; and yet even here, he was an exception to perhaps the majority of those who, rising to eminence without its aid, are apt to be puffed up with the proud but miserable conceit that it is but a dainty crutch, which may be depreciated by him who has dispensed with it. None had a truer, a loftier conception of the beneficence and beauty of education than himself, and he would doubtless have repined more at his deficiencies in intellectual cultivation, if he had not been happily hindered from doing so by the incessant activities of his mind and hands, in the use and improvement of all he did know and daily acquired.

What is remarkable in his relations to education, is the character, the breadth, the seemingly intuitive perceptions he had of the sources and methods and values and correlations of all departments of this great instrument of mental development and growth. Had he been an "admirable Crichton" for varied and erudite acquirements, or a Bacon for grand philosophical comprehensions and inductions, or a Macaulay for historical lore, or a Story for legal profundity, he would scarcely have displayed, in any of the diverse spheres of his practical applications of his limited acquirements from books, a juster appreciation of the relations of those he grasped, to the occasion and to the public good. He was not a theorist, for necessity made him practical ; while his sterling sense, his active benevolence, his natural intellectuality, and above all, his conscientious piety, kept him far removed from the impracticable.

The schools, the seminaries, the colleges of the Commonwealth had among their most distinguished and Doctored alumni, no truer friend, no more discriminating advocate than he was, in public and in private. His educational speeches, whether in the public school-rooms, or on festival occasions, or at College Commencements, were wisely thought and fitly spoken.

He was the orator on the interesting occasion of the Inauguration of the State Normal School at Westfield, Massachusetts, and in the course of his address, he made the following happy allusion to himself, greatly to the delight of his auditors : —

" I can recall the case of a poor boy who once sat upon the hard plank seat in one of these schools, in one of the poorest districts in this State, while his father was toiling at the anvil for his daily bread; who, under the smiles of a kind Providence, has been honored by his fellow-citizens infinitely beyond his deserts, and who, as Chief Magistrate of this Commonwealth, deems it his highest honor to plead for the cause of common-school education."

19

His educational position was remarkable also in its great advancement beyond the point where most self-made men are apt to rest, — that of a warm advocacy and support of common and high schools, — as independent of and apart from the great collegiate fountains. Governor Briggs was never shackled by this misapprehension of the true force in public education of the College. His catholic mind grasped the great theory of education from the lowest to the highest arenas, and no less surely and clearly the controlling value of the mainspring of all its workings, the College system.

The able and excellent President of Williams College, of which Governor Briggs was an efficient trustee, and often a deeply-interested visitor, has so admirably delineated this educational feature of his career, both in his official and in his private life, — that it may well stand here as his record, — making any further biographical labor on this point needless. The reader will unite with the biographer in thanking the author for this tribute to his friend : —

"Governor Briggs was officially connected with education during seven years as Governor of the Commonwealth of Massachusetts, and during sixteen years as a Trustee of Williams College.

"As Governor, he was more particularly interested in the condition of the common schools of the State. This was partly from their intrinsic importance, and partly because public attention was at that time strongly concentrated upon them. Her common schools had been the pride of New England, but through neglect and consequent mismanagement, — neglect probably from the impression that what was so universally praised would take care of itself, — the system had fallen behind the demands of the age, and was fast losing its efficiency. School-houses were unsightly and uncomfortable, teachers were poorly qualified, their methods of teaching were false, and private schools were multiplying. This had led to alarm, to investigation, and to the creation — eight years before the election of Governor Briggs — of the Board of Education. In connection with this Board, there was inaugurated for the State a new system, especially in relation to the education of teachers, requiring increased expenditure, and creating much discussion. It was in the midst of this unsettled state of things that Governor Briggs entered upon his office, and he became at once the prompt and enlightened supporter of all measures tending to the renovation of the system, and as chairman *ex officio* of the Board of Education, during those critical years, his influence was great.

"Of the principle itself, which underlies the whole system of common-school education, Governor Briggs was always an earnest advocate. In the first report of the Board of Education to the Legislature, which he signed as chairman, that principle was thus stated :

"'The cardinal principle which lies at the foundation of our educational system is, that all the children of the State shall be educated by the State. As our Republican Government was founded upon the virtue and intelligence of the people, it was rightly concluded by its framers, that, without a wise educational system, the Government itself could not exist, and in ordaining that the expenses of educating the people should be defrayed by the people at large, without reference to the particular benefit to individuals, it was considered that those who, perhaps without children of their own, nevertheless would be compelled to pay a large tax, would receive an ample equivalent in the protection of their persons, and the security of their property.'

"This principle was clearly seen by Governor Briggs from the first, and was efficiently carried out during the whole course of his administration. How fully it was incorporated into his modes of thought, and became axiomatic with him as a statesman and a social reformer, appears from the mode of its recognition in a speech near the close of his life. 'There,' says he, 'you have it, a principle, which, as a law, has been in force in Massachusetts for more than two hundred years, and in few words this is it, that

every child in the State should be educated, and educated by the
money of the State. That is the principle proclaimed by these
early adventurers with great earnestness, when there was an unbroken wilderness from the little circle around Boston and Plymouth, to the dark waves of the Pacific. Three thousand miles
of ocean rolled between them and civilization and home. Before
them was a dark, untrodden wilderness, save by the moccasined
foot of the savage native, and they numbering a population of less
than twenty thousand. Thus circumstanced, thus surrounded,
they, for the first time within the history of human society enacted
into law the principle that the State should be educated by the
money of the State. . . . . . My assertion is, that there is
no possible object belonging to community or government, that
has higher claims on the property of the community than the universal education of children.'

"In carrying out the above principle, by giving a new impulse to
common schools, the Board of Education relied chiefly upon the
labors of their Secretary, and upon Normal Schools. To these,
however, were added Teachers' Institutes, with lectures and
specific subjects employed by the State, and also assistants to the
Secretary, both permanent and temporary, in awakening an interest in the schools throughout the State. All these were new, the
experiment of Normal Schools in this country having been first
tried in Massachusetts; some of them were commenced during
the administration of Governor Briggs, and questions of much
interest respecting them all were to be settled.

"Having been associated with Governor Briggs two years on the
Board of Education, the writer of this knows that the Normal
Schools were regarded by him with great favor, and that he sought
and favored the most liberal provision not only in their behalf,
but also in behalf of every collateral means by which the cause of
common-school education could be advanced.

"But not only did Governor Briggs thus appreciate and carry out
the great principle of common-school education, he also appreciated fully, and sought to foster education in its higher forms. Of
a liberal education, as furnished by our colleges, he was a staunch
and earnest advocate. In his speech at an Agricultural Fair, he

said 'He wanted to see the time when there should be none more intelligent than farmers, when the farmers' boys should go to Amherst or Cambridge, or Williams, and return to their homes prepared to settle down as intelligent, useful, and happy farmers.'

"In this he showed the largeness of his nature, and a comprehensiveness and liberality characteristic of his whole course. Himself self-educated, and well understanding that a considerable party would have been conciliated by his ignoring, if not opposing liberal education, he yet had no hesitation in preferring the part of the statesman to that of the demagogue, and in laboring on the broadest principles for the good of the whole.

"'I go,' said he, subsequently, 'for democracy; not that of party, but that democracy which elevates man. And, depend upon it, that is the system; nothing else will do.'

"He not only saw the inseparable connection of education in the common schools with a high state of liberal education, but also that the possible extent and value of self-education must depend on the same thing. A self-educated man is one who avails himself of the advantages furnished by the community in which he lives for knowledge and discipline, without going through with prescribed courses under the guidance of teachers. But those advantages will be in proportion to the diffusion among the people of the fruits of a liberal education. The knowledge that in one age is originated by the learned and scientific, within the walls of colleges and universities, becomes after a time incorporated with the elementary forms of thought among the common people. Accordingly, the common mind is now unconsciously educated by Sir Isaac Newton and La Place in Astronomy, by Davy in Chemistry, by Linnæus and Jussieu in Botany, and by every great thinker and master of method in the science of politics, of morals, or of mind. The rapidity of this process for the masses, is modified by various considerations, but under free institutions, with a free press, the whole community becomes like one great university, and it becomes possible for individuals happily born to work themselves up, without the usual helps, to a high point of culture and enlargement. Such persons may have access through conversation, books, popular lectures, to all that is known; but the point of elevation possible for them will depend upon what has been done by those liberally educated who have gone before them.

" The organic relation of the different degrees and forms of education just referred to, was well understood by Governor Briggs, and accordingly, when in 1845, he was elected a trustee of Williams College, he at once entered heartily upon the duties of that office, and it may be added that he became more and more interested in them till the close of his life. It was in connection with the meetings of this Board, that some of the finer social and moral traits of Governor Briggs were conspicuous.

" It was not merely his sound judgment and good business capacity that made him so welcome at the meetings of the Board, but the happy combination in him of dignity with urbanity, and the utmost freedom of social intercourse. He watched carefully the course of the business, and at all its turning-points gave his full attention, but when the stress was off there was a playfulness and an exuberance of the social nature, a genial humor and an exhaustless fund of anecdote, that gave a charm to his presence and a social aspect to meetings, that, without such qualities, became merely those for the dry details of business.. It was these qualities, joined to his warm and increasing attachment to the college, that caused its friends, and especially the members of the Board of Trustees, to feel that his death was a personal bereavement.

" It is also to be added in this connection, that Governor Briggs was peculiarly happy in those impromptu addresses so often called for at Commencement, during the progress of its various meetings and literary festivities. As impromptu, they were the more enjoyed; but for humor, pathos, and high intellectual power, they must have been among his finest efforts.

" Having thus seen the attitude of Governor Briggs towards common schools and the higher seminaries, it remains to give his view of the proper relations to each other of intellectual and of moral and religious education. This is a radical question in education, and one on which there has been much diversity of opinion. That the two should be associated Governor Briggs had no doubt, and he expressed himself strongly on this point. ' The Pilgrims,' says he, 'brought with them right ideas on this subject. The meeting-house and the school-house were the two first and great ideas that existed in their minds and controlled their conduct. First, they erected a humble and convenient house in which to assemble and worship their Creator. Next, they built the school-house. Their good sense, reason, and religion taught them that these two go together. They knew that the mind of man was naturally inclined to superstition, and that religion, which would regulate and control the heart, would not enlighten the mind, but that it wanted educating, — that the intellect and the heart were to be attended to. They knew that the intellect, however highly cultivated, might leave the heart all wrong. Therefore the meeting-house and the school-house were provided to aid each other, to overlook each other, to check each other, if you please. In the beautiful language of one of our New England poets, we could say of them, —

> ' "Nor heeds the puny skeptic's hand,
> While near the school the church-spire stands;
> Nor fears the gloomy bigot's rule,
> While near the church-spire stands the school."

"He desired the introduction into the common schools of nothing that could be fairly objected to by any religious denomination who receive the Scriptures, and wish to have them read by the whole people. But the Scriptures themselves he would have read. They were the subject of his frequent and almost impassioned eulogy, and on the knowledge of them by the people he rested his hopes of the permanency of our institutions.

"'We labor,' says he, 'under a great mistake about the Bible in relation to education. What an idea, that the Bible should only be read at stated times and in a very grave and staid manner, and to draw from it religious instruction! The Bible, as a reading-book, is the most interesting book in the world. Literary men give it this credit. It is the most perfect literary production on earth.' Regarding the Bible thus, and, also, because 'it affords,' as he said, 'the only perfect rule of moral conduct and religious instruction,' he favored the reading of it in the common schools. The recognition of the Bible, and the infusion of its principles into the common mind, he regarded as essential to the results contemplated by our whole system of public education.

"From the training and position of Governor Briggs, his opinions on the subject of education deserve great weight. Being the outgrowth and representative of free institutions, having their impress upon him in every lineament, and feeling their spirit in every fibre, no man was more thoroughly identified with the people, or more honestly and intelligently sought their good. Without the advantage of a liberal education, he rose to the highest offices in the gift of the people of his State, and filled them for an unusual period with great acceptance and public benefit. No man, therefore, knew better than he the necessities of the people, or the difficulties and disadvantages of young men left to make their own way in the world. And not only had he gained high position through difficulties, but also high culture, and thus stood on an eminence from which he could survey the whole ground. As the result, we have, as has been seen, his position and views on the three great points on which the interests of our educational system turn.

"1. Governor Briggs comprehended most fully, and sustained most earnestly, the fundamental principle of free education, and, it may be added, of republican freedom — that the children of the State shall be so far educated by the property of the State as to be qualified for the duties of citizenship.

"2. He favored a liberal education, both for its intrinsic excellence, as giving dignity to man, and for its indispensable agency in sustaining and elevating the tone and standard of the common schools.

"3. He insisted that the education of the heart should be attended to in connection with that of the intellect; and for this he regarded the Bible as the main instrument.

"These are the essential principles of our American system of education. Upon the adoption and intelligent application of these principles, the permanence of our institutions depends; and it was not among the least benefits conferred upon his country by the great and good man whom we now commemorate, that he expressed them so strongly, and acted upon them so faithfully."

In 1846, the then somewhat rare occasion arose for the public inauguration of a new President of Harvard College. Edward Everett had been chosen to fill the vacancy occasioned by the retirement of Mr. Quincy.

The Governor of the Commonwealth had been immemorially Chairman of its Board of Overseers, and it was his province to induct a newly-elected President into his office, and to invest him with the administrative functions of the college. To this duty, Governor Briggs addressed himself with that happy tact which made all occasions alike to him, whatever the degree of their importance, occasions of successful performance of duty.

His address to Mr. Everett is a model of simplicity and appropriate brevity, chaste in language, felicitous in its allusions, and honorable to its author for its broad and just appreciation of that learning — without the aid of which, but not without deep regret at his disadvantage in not having enjoyed it — he had achieved distinctions and honors which any graduate of Harvard might envy. The address is quoted in full : —

EDWARD EVERETT:

SIR, — You having been duly elected President of Harvard College, in compliance with ancient custom, and in the name of the Overseers, I do now invest you with the government and authority of that institution, to be exercised in the same manner and to the same extent as has been heretofore done by your predecessors in office. I deliver to you these keys, with these books and papers, as badges of your authority, confident that you will exercise and administer the same according to the usages of the institution, and in obedience to the laws and constitution of the Commonwealth.

Allow me, sir, to congratulate you and the officers and friends of this venerable University upon the auspicious circumstances in which you enter into office.

Having filled the most important civil stations in your own State, and under the Government of the republic, with credit to yourself and with honor to your country, you have now come up to this literary eminence, at the bidding of its authority, to take charge of the parent University of the New World.

The entire unanimity with which you were chosen to this responsible trust, bears testimony to the estimate in which your qualifications were held by those whose duty it was to fill the vacancy occasioned by the retirement of your distinguished predecessor. A long line of learned and good men have, by their example, illuminated the path in which you are to walk. It does not become me to speak of the duties you are to perform. They are before you, and in anticipation you know them by heart.

To influence the young men of this country, to enlighten their minds, make right impressions upon their yielding hearts, to fashion their manners, mould their characters, and send them forth into the world qualified to act their part in society, and fulfil their destiny on earth, is, in my estimation, the highest and noblest object to which genius and learning and patriotism and piety can be devoted.

In early youth, your Alma Mater adorned you with her brightest honors, and bade you go forth into the world. Like a dutiful son, you have returned to render her the services of ripened manhood, and to aid her in raising up and sending out still other happy and promising sons.

More than half a century ago, Edmund Burke, in speaking of the English and French nobility, said, "The latter had the advantage of the former, in being surrounded by the powerful outguard of a military education." History has shown how powerless that outguard was in protecting the nobility of France, and France herself, against the attacks of an internal foe. It will be your higher purpose, and the purpose of those who co-operate with you in this ancient seat of learning, to protect the youth committed to your care by planting in the citadel of their hearts the more powerful *internal* guard of a Christian Education.

While pouring upon their opening minds the light of Literature and Science, there will be presented to them the beauties of practical Christianity, and strongly inculcated upon their moral nature the sublime doctrines and holy precepts of "Him who spake as never *man* spake." Here let young men learn that true heroism consists in doing good; that the highest attainment of personal honor is the forgiveness of injuries, and that God has made greatness and goodness inseparable.

It only remains for me to express the great satisfaction which I feel in being made the organ of the Board of Overseers for inducting you into office; and I am sure, sir, that I may say for the people of the whole Commonwealth, you have their confidence in advance, that by a liberal and just administration of the affairs of the college, you will, so far as in you lies, maintain its high reputation, make its benefits accessible to the aspirants after knowledge among all classes of our young men, and strengthen the public attachment for this institution of the State, which was founded by the liberality, the wisdom, and the prayers of our Puritan Fathers.

CHAPTER XIX.

FEW special memorials of Governor Briggs during the year 1848, are found in his correspondence, and this period was unmarked by anything striking in his public life.

One letter, and a fragment of another, must suffice to represent the year in these pages.

The date of the letter is suggestive of tricks, and tricks were evidently in the mind of the writer when he penned it. He glides, however unconsciously, from gay to grave; though not—to complete the thought—"from lively to severe." It is only a transcript of a gentle, generous, and graceful heart. How strange, in the light of the truth, seems the presentiment expressed in this letter, that his wife "would be clad in the garments of widowhood." She sits to-day in those garments, pondering "the ways of God to man," and thanking Him for precious memories of her sainted husband:—

BOSTON, April 1, 1848.

MY DEAR DAUGHTER:

It is thirty-one years to-day since I put into the post-office in Lanesboro' the well-remembered April-fool letter to your mother, which she received, believing it to be from a distant lover. It seems but a day since this boyish freak was performed with such amusement to the author, and such momentary chagrin to the

228

young girl who received it. But now I am writing to the daughter of that April-fooled girl, who is six or seven years older than her mother was at that time. Neither the *fooler* nor the *fooled* knew at that time that their destinies were to be one in this world, though I presume in both their hearts the seeds of an affection were planted which soon began to spring up, and which I hope will bloom and last forever. Happy union has that been to me. As the scenes of youth and the friends of other years pass more and more away, the tender and delicate ties that then bound our young hearts together, are growing now into bands of iron, which time with its vicissitudes makes stronger and stronger. Your mother was dear to me when a thoughtless boy, and when all around me was bright and gay; but now when the frosts of age begin to chill the outer world and whiten the locks which were then glossy with youth, she is a thousand times more so. Having lived so long and to so little good effect, and feeling the painful consciousness that I am of so little consequence to any in the world except her, she seems to me the only object that strongly binds me to the earth. She gave me her heart and hand when a penniless stranger; never since that day has that heart beat, save for me and her family. Though I have always been strong, and she feeble, I have long been impressed with the idea that the day would come when she would be clad in the garments of widow-hood. Of that, however, it becomes not me to speak. It will be, as it seems, good to Him who orders all things well. This you will think a singular letter for all-fools day, but after I sat down to write, my thoughts led off in this direction, and I have followed them.

Love to Charles.

Affectionately your father,

G. N. BRIGGS.

His extra-official labors were continually numerous, and as continually of a philanthropic or religious nature. Witness this record — an extract from a letter to his wife: —

"Yesterday, I kept fast by going out in the morning to Somerville, and in the afternoon to Charlestown, and making speeches

20

at two Sabbath-school celebrations. I thought it would be a
pleasant way to keep the day. Wednesday evening I went to
West Newton, and made a temperance speech. So you see thus
far this week I have made four speeches, such as they were.
They were the best I could make any how. I have one consolation; I made them with the hope of doing good. Whether they
will or not, depends upon Him, without whose blessing all the
efforts of men are vain. Be of good cheer. I hope before long to
be with you. Love to Henry, grandma, to the girls and to John,
and all the neighbors who think it worth receiving.

Ever thine,
G. N. BRIGGS.

A year later he addressed the following communication
to Zachary Taylor, then just inaugurated President of the
United States : —

"It is," says one who knew the writer intimately, "such an expression of the true patriotism of his character, and of the principles on which it is based, that at this hour it has great force;
and shows how firmly and steadily, in this exigency of our
country, he would maintain his confidence in public men of honest
intentions and fair ability, as believing them adequate to achieve
success in the management of public affairs. Another trait appears worthy of mark; the cordiality with which he sustained for
office a candidate who was not his choice, because fairly presented
for the suffrages of the people by their representatives in convention. He gave his support to General Taylor, because he believed
him to be an honest man, just as in another instance he withheld
it from a man he believed to be dishonest, because, he declared, he
never had, and he never would, give his vote for a man he believed
to be untrue."

BOSTON, 20th March, 1849.

DEAR SIR:

As the public now claim you, I trust that a communication from
an entire stranger will be excused.

Perhaps in frankness, I ought to say, that until your name was presented as a candidate for the Presidency by the Whig convention at Philadelphia, there was no man in Massachusetts, more opposed to your nomination than I was. From the time of that nomination, which I believed to be fair, no one felt a deeper interest in your success. I believed the great interests of the country demanded it. Your letters, especially the Allison letter,[1] laid down principles of action for a Chief Magistrate, which, if followed out, would restore this glorious, free constitutional government of ours to its original intent and purity, leaving its various departments to their own appropriate and legitimate action. You said you were a Whig, and, if elected, you would be the President of the people, and not of a party. The people believed you honest, and have taken you at your word. They knew you were without experience in the practical affairs of the Government, but that great word *honest* had a *charm* for the masses which politicians knew not of. They have invested you with power in the full confidence that that power would be wisely and constitutionally used. Thus far your words and deeds in power have justified the confidence inspired by your words and conduct before you were placed in authority.

Allow me to say, sir, that nothing you have said or done has given so much pleasure to the great body of the people of the United States, and inspired them with such confident hopes of the success of your administration, as the declaration from your lips and your pen, that you would make honesty, ability, and fidelity, and a good private character, indispensable qualifications for office. I do not use your precise words, but I am sure I have not mistaken your sentiment, — a sentiment which, announced by the Chief Magistrate of the Union, made the heart of this whole people glad. When you said it, they believed you meant what you said. I know, the rule will exclude many *open-mouthed patriots* from office, but I hope you will stand to it if the heavens fall.

Edmund Burke once said that "honest, good intention, which is as sure of being seen at first, as fraud is of being detected at last, is of no mean force in the government of mankind." The

---

[1] Letter to Capt. J. S. Allison, of April 22, 1848.

remark is as philosophical as it is beautiful. *Honesty*, in too many of the affairs of this country, has been more rare than ability. The last without the first is full of dangers. The *first*, with a respectable share of the last, will serve the public with success. I trust that licentiousness, intemperance, and dishonesty will not be permitted hereafter to revel in the public offices of this nation.

No President, since Washington, has had more of the nation's confidence in advance, than you enjoy. The people all wish you success. I have no fear that their confidence will be disappointed.

May your administration deserve the title of *wise* and *good*. Such a title will be a glory when the names of your remarkable battles will be forgotten. May the good Providence that has shielded you in the midst of ten thousand dangers, now aid, protect, and bless you.

With my best wishes for your health and happiness and that of your family, I am

Respectfully and truly yours,

G. N. BRIGGS.

To Z. TAYLOR, President of the United States.

The next letter presents him to us again in Berkshire, but as he, with a somewhat facetious sadness, expresses it, without a home. It was addressed to Mr. and Mrs. Bigelow : —

PITTSFIELD, 7th May, 1849.

DEAR CHILDREN:

On reaching the station in this place on Thursday, and delivering over six pieces of baggage to Burlingham, he, as in duty bound, asked me if he should deliver it at the Berkshire. I said, "No, at my house." Whereupon he said, "Your folks have moved, and Mrs. B. is at the Berkshire." This was indeed refreshing to a weary pilgrim, who had been pining for home for many a long week. But the fact was apparent that I had no home, so I trudged down to the Berkshire, and found my way to No. 13, and met a woman I had been in the habit of seeing in other places. The disappointment in not finding a home was more than compen-

sated in seeing the woman aforesaid in very good health, albeit
a little tired—having in the morning walked before breakfast up to
the house that is to be, and then walked back again after breakfast. I wonder I did not find her down with nervous headache.
The girls and John are at the little long house on the place;
Grandma at B——'s; your mother and I at the Berkshire, and
A. in parts unknown. The family seem to be *dispersed*. Matters
and things, under the administration of Burbank and Stoddard,
with six or eight masons and carpenters and joiners, are progress-
ing rapidly; so that I hope before long we shall begin to re-assem-
ble around a common hearth.

To-day I harnessed Billy into the horse-cart. It was so heavy
and stiff and clumsy, and the fixtures were so different from those
he had been wont to be surrounded with, that for some little time
he hardly knew what to make of it. But I spoke to him kindly on
the subject, and explained matters to him, so that he at once
became reconciled, and made the most respectable appearance of
any horse and cart that ever passed through the streets of our
renowned village, to say nothing of his driver. It is time to close
this important epistle. *I* and your mother send love to all.

Affectionately your father,

G. N. BRIGGS.

With his entrance into his new abode, he began what was
to him really a new and fascinating life. A picture of
that life, from the hand of his daughter, leaves the biographer nothing to do, and the reader nothing to desire, in its
delineation : —

"During the month of May, 1849, the family re-assembled in
their new home, and my father began the agricultural life so pleasing to his tastes, and so refreshing in the intervals of repose from
his public services. His Berkshire farm, consisting of a few acres
of land, is a few minutes' walk west of the village of Pittsfield, on
the sunny side of one of its hills. He soon placed it under the best
cultivation, and it really became to him an object of thoughtful
attention. Applying his practical good sense to the details of

20*

agriculture, he proved himself a skilful, *successful* farmer. Without any attempt at elaborate embellishment, or the least showiness, everything was arranged in keeping with his moderate means
and simple tastes. Nowhere was the grass more abundant or
sweeter than in his meadows or in the rock pasture, — sweetened
by the sunshine and its own dews and springs, — where the milch
cows throve, cows whose descent he traced with peculiar satisfaction back to the fawn-faced heifer, sent to him in 1819 from a
farm in South Adams by Thom Farnham, a man of great natural
talent, of remarkable common sense, and 'of infinite humor.'

"My father was one for whom 'the apple-tree has sentiment.'
The fragrance and beauty and promise of spring, and the wealth
of autumn, made the orchard a *joy* to him. The pear-tree at the
corner of the house, a standard of the old stock, he regarded as a
venerable almoner of most luscious bounties. Some of his friends
will remember how, when the fruit was gathered from year to
year, and almost always with his own hand, he was wont to appear
at their doors with basket on his arm, to share with them these
autumn riches, expecting them to admire with him the russet pears
set off by the ruddy crab-apples that gleamed around them.

"The patches of wheat, or oats, or corn, or potatoes, were
watched with unceasing care, which was sometimes greatly exercised by summer tempests, or parching drought, premature frosts,
and depredating enemies. One summer a beautiful field of oats
had been his peculiar solicitude and *satisfaction* among the crops.
He was absent, attending Commencement at Williams College,
when these were harvested. The day had been showery. Seated
among the trustees on the stage in the church, the second day of
Commencement, he very much amused one of his sons by beckoning to him during a pause in the exercises, and briefly asking him,
'Did the oats get wet?' The reply satisfied him, no doubt: 'No,
sir; they were all in before I left.'

"He entered the hay-field with the zest of a boy, which was by
no means abated in the burden and heat of the day. He made a
point of always carrying into the field the well-filled luncheon-
basket, arranging, dispensing, and sharing the contents with the
social pleasure that the appetizing occupation of haying inspires.

THE HOMESTEAD AT PITTSFIELD.

Under the shadows of the trees, amid the incense of the new-mown grass, these moments of rest were refreshing, not more to his body than to his soul, so sensitive to all sweet influences. He had true sympathy with the laborer whose toil he lightened by sharing it, but more really by his pleasant words and a sight of his genial face. Among the incidents of the hay-field, he enjoyed the horse Billy's demonstrations of spirit and strength when taking in the loads.

"During one of the summer days of 1860, while in the field, he had a partial sunstroke, and came near dying. Afterwards, he exposed himself to the heat with a good deal of caution, though during the last season he mowed.

"He seemed to us the happiest man in the world when busy with the occupations of the farm, no matter how complicated or oppressive were his public affairs. He made us think of 'contentment with godliness;' though, after the clouds rested so darkly on his country, few saw him who did not mark the changed tone of the man; and we, who loved him most, knew why the form was bowed as with the weight of a great burden, and why he was so weary and silent, and his heart so troubled.

"The *birds* he was always first to discover and welcome with the early spring. 'Our robin' was his favorite. He never tired of his plaintive musical note. A pair of robins came year after year and built their nest undisturbed in the piazza. There seemed to be an understanding between him and the birds.

"The doves used to fly from their cotes and alight on his head and shoulders, and the chickens to fly upon his arms and follow him all about, when he went into their yard. This they did to no others who fed them. He never moved or spoke roughly when dealing with his animals. He seemed on confidential terms with them, and had great control over them. He could call the cows from the most distant part of the pasture, and Billy, his pet horse for nearly twenty years (that drew the hearse when the dear form was borne to the grave), at a signal from his master would lay his head caressingly on his shoulder, with such intelligence and kindness that both parties were always highly gratified."

CHAPTER XX.

OWARDS the close of the year 1849 — the last year but one of the official life of Governor Briggs — there transpired an event, memorable in the annals of crime, followed by a trial and a vindication of the majesty of law, which deserve, and will find, a place in all subsequent records of the most remarkable criminal causes in history.

This crime was a murder, —

> "Murder most foul, as in the best it is,
> But this most foul, strange and unnatural."

It was the murder of a well-known professional man in Boston, Dr. George Parkman, by one of the Faculty of Harvard University — John W. Webster, the Professor of Chemistry. The character and connections of the murderer and of his victim; the atrocious circumstances of the crime; the extraordinary developments in the process of its discovery and accusation of the supposed criminal, excited the public mind from one end of the country to another, to an almost unparalleled degree.

The trial of this extraordinary case served, naturally, to intensify this excitement. The fame of it spread beyond the sea, and the Crown Advocate of England is reported

238

to have said of it that " the decision of the case would advance or retard the cause of justice throughout Europe for a century."

The relation of Governor Briggs to this memorable cause began when the law had completed its stern processes, fastening upon the wretched prisoner indisputable proofs of his guilt, and when justice, taking these evidences in her hand, pronounced upon him the sentence of condemnation to death.

Now began for such a man as he, whose life is here written, a consciousness of dread but unavoidable responsibility, and a conflict between his tender nature and his unwavering, unobscured sense of duty, of which no language can convey any adequate impression.

The sentence of death, so terrible in the case of the humblest and most obscure criminal, was in the case of a distinguished professional man, connected with the oldest college in the land, invested to the public apprehension with peculiar, and, as some insisted, with insufferable horror. It must be set aside by pardon or commutation, if such a result should require incredible exertions and innumerable measures for its accomplishment.

As a part of the vast endeavor made to mollify the stern verdict of justice in this case, the Governor was subjected to solicitations, entreaties, pleas, threatenings, and — most unlikely of all arguments with such a man — to offered bribes, if haply he might be prevailed upon to commute the sentence pronounced against the criminal.

To contemplate him standing unmoved before this storm of pride and passion and pity, — all working in strange and eager combination, to stir him from his official integrity, is to be filled with the profoundest admiration of that greatness of soul, which alone kept him from the weakness of misguided mercy at that solemn hour. He stood firm. The nation held its breath with a deep applause, suppressed only by the awful tragedy and terror, yet to be consummated in the public execution of the criminal. The public voice of this great continent, and echoes of it from the shores of the Old World, at length declared the sublimity of his more than Roman — his Christian — firmness in withholding his hand from altering, by one whit, the sentence of the Court against the murderer.

The cause itself will pass into history, and a life of Governor Briggs would be strangely incomplete without more than this brief notice of it. Gladly, therefore, does the biographer give place here to a chronicle of the circumstances connecting Governor Briggs with the case, and his decision on the appeal for the executive clemency, prepared by request by Mr. Clifford, who was then Attorney-General of the Commonwealth, and conducted the case on its trial, with an ability which won universal acknowledgment. To his paper, the rest of this chapter is devoted, and its interest will doubtless leave the reader in no regret at the length of it: —

"Among the perplexing and responsible duties imposed on a Governor of Massachusetts by the obligations of his office, there is no one, the performance of which is more decisive of the quality of the man and the character of the Magistrate than his exercise of the pardoning power, which by the Constitution of the Commonwealth is confided to the Executive.

"The firmness that cannot only resist the agonizing entreaties of friends, the ingenious pleadings of counsel, and the popular appeals, that are so easily evoked on behalf of the convicted criminal, but can also repress the natural desires which most men feel to exercise the prerogative of mercy, even at the expense of justice, is a quality that finds its support in a conscientious fidelity to duty alone. In Governor Briggs this characteristic was eminently conspicuous, for it was exhibited under the strong contrast of a singularly gracious and sympathetic nature. During his long and honorable service in the chair of State, it was often put to a severe and trying test, but in no instance was he betrayed into a conscious departure from the obligation imposed upon him by his official oath.

"Grateful as it might be to his feelings to yield to the solicitations of those who besought him to interpose between the claims of justice and the appeals to executive clemency, he never forgot the great truth, that a mistaken lenity to the individual inevitably tends to weaken the authority of the law, and is in itself a dangerous provocative to crime.

"One of the most attractive incidents in the history of a monarch, whose equitable reign over the people of France had earned for him a better fate than to be driven forth from her soil as a fugitive and an exile, is narrated of Louis Philippe by his principal Minister, Guizot, the accomplished author of the 'History of Civilization.' Calling at the palace at a late hour of the night with an important dispatch upon urgent public business, to receive which he supposed the king would have to be roused from his bed, he found him, to his surprise, hard at work in his cabinet adjoining his bed-chamber, with a large manuscript volume before him. His curiosity prompted him to ask his Majesty what was the nature of his unusual toil; when he found that the volume on which the king was engaged contained a *resume* of the cases in which he was required to exercise the royal prerogative of determining the question of capital punishment. He learned that in every case of a capital conviction, when the papers were laid before his Majesty by the Minister of Justice, for his signature to the warrant of execution, it was the practice of Louis Philippe to make an analysis of the case, presenting all the considerations for and against the remission of the dread penalty, before affixing the royal authority to a warrant for the execution of the humblest citizen of France, and that the hours for this self-imposed and self-denying labor were wrested from the ordinary periods of repose and sleep.

21*

"No higher testimonial of fidelity to his great trust than this, can be found in the history of a crowned king of any country or age. But it finds its parallel in the conscientious diligence with which our republican ruler, Governor Briggs, examined all similar cases while the same prerogative was confided to him. He spared no labor in the investigation of every case in which an appeal was made to the executive clemency; and, having fully satisfied his own conscience what his duty as a magistrate required, he was inflexible in repelling every lower motive as a controlling influence over his official action.

"The most signal instance of this is to be found in the celebrated case of Dr. Webster, which occurred during his administration. The reputation of the prisoner, the character and standing of the deceased, the circumstances of the homicide, the manner in which its perpetration was for a time successfully concealed by the barbarous murderer's revolting mutilation and almost entire destruction of the body of his victim, and the wonderful chain of circumstantial proof which led to his detection and conviction,—all combined to invest the case with a degree of interest, both at home and abroad, that has never been equalled by any criminal trial in this country.

"Dr. John W. Webster was the son of a highly respectable druggist in Boston, was educated at Harvard College, and graduated in the Class of 1811, one of the most distinguished, by the subsequent career of its members, to be found upon the rolls of that ancient University. A portion of his preparatory term of study for entering upon his profession, was spent in the medical schools of London; and on his return to his native city he was appointed the Professor of Chemistry in the medical department of the University. He married a lady of rare excellence and worth, who was connected with some of the most cultivated and respected families of Boston; and at the time of his arrest and trial, was the father of three interesting and accomplished daughters. Such a man, surrounded and shielded by the highest social and moral influences, would seem to have pledged such hostages to fortune as to have placed him far above the temptation to crime.

"His victim was Dr. George Parkman, the head of one of the

leading families of the same city, a graduate of the same university, and a distinguished member of the same profession, who had devoted a portion of his large possessions to the munificent endowment of the institution in which Dr. Webster held his professorship, and to the erection of the very building in which he met a violent death at Professor Webster's hands.

"A case involving such elements as these could not fail to excite an extraordinary interest throughout the country. From the time of the prisoner's arrest, in November, 1849, to the day of his execution, August 30, 1850, it was the topic of unceasing comment by the press, and of much ignorant and misinformed criticism of all who were in any way connected with the trial. During all this period Governor Briggs was constantly receiving communications of every conceivable variety of tone and character, and, with very few exceptions, all of them addressed to his compassion and his sympathies, in behalf of the prisoner and his heart-broken family. After the trial and sentence, a petition of the convict for a pardon was presented to the Governor and Council. This petition, every word of which was in the handwriting of Dr. Webster himself, carefully prepared by him while under the awful sentence of death, was, in view of his subsequent confession, that its essential statements were deliberate falsehoods, a most extraordinary document. Its character may be inferred from the following extracts : —

"'Having been convicted,' he says, 'before the Supreme Judicial Court, of the murder of Dr. George Parkman, I would most respectfully petition your Excellency and the Honorable Council, to be permitted to declare, in the most solemn manner, that I am entirely innocent of this awful crime; that I never entertained any other than the kindest feelings towards him; and that I never had any inducement to injure, in any way, him whom I have long numbered among my best friends.

"'To Him who seeth in secret, and before whom I may ere long be called to appear, would I appeal for the truth of what I now declare, as also for the truth of the solemn declaration, that I had no agency in placing the remains of a human body in or under my rooms in the Medical College in Boston, nor do I know by whom they were so placed. I am the victim of circumstances, or

of a foul conspiracy, or of the attempt of some individual to
cause suspicion to fall upon me, influenced perhaps by the prospect of obtaining a large reward. . . . . .

" ' Repeating in the most positive and solemn manner, and under
the fullest sense of my responsibility, as a man and as a Christian,
that I am wholly innocent of this charge, to the truth of which
the Searcher of all hearts is a witness, I would humbly and respectfully pray that the privilege I have asked may be granted.'

" The effect of such solemn asseverations and imprecations as
these upon the mind of such a man as Governor Briggs, to whom
the ' Searcher of all hearts ' was a constant presence, and not a
mere conventional phrase, or a figure of rhetoric, could not be
otherwise than decisive of an entire want of trust in any subsequent
statements which conflicted with them, however strongly pressed
upon them by the prisoner's protestations of penitence and remorse.

" On the other hand, he was not moved by them to any relaxation
of diligence in his investigation of the grounds upon which the
appeal to his clemency was finally placed by the spiritual adviser
of the convict,— the Rev. Dr. Putnam,— by whom this petition was
withdrawn, when he subsequently presented to the Governor the
confessional statement of Dr. Webster, in which the homicide was
admitted.   He attended the meeting of the Committee of the
Council before whom the hearings upon the petition were had; he
received deputations from religious societies and anti-capital
punishment associations from all parts of the country, and patiently heard their arguments and appeals for a commutation of the
sentence; and what was more painful to his kindly nature than
everything else, he listened, with an earnest sympathy, to the
pleadings for mercy that were pressed upon him by the immediate
family and personal friends of the prisoner.

" But he knew, that to justify his official interposition in a case
like this, something beside all these influences' must be brought to
bear upon a magistrate who had solemnly pledged himself to see
that the ' laws were faithfully executed.'   He knew that no person
charged with crime in any Christian commonwealth, had ever
received more humane treatment from all the officers of the law
concerned in his prosecution than had been extended to this pris-

oner, and that no one had ever stood condemned by the verdict of a jury after a fairer and more impartial trial. He knew that the sentence. which he was so pressingly urged to set aside, was not his sentence upon the unhappy criminal, but the sentence of the laws which he was sworn to maintain, and that to warrant his interference with it, his reason and judgment must be convinced that the public interest would be subserved, and the sacred inviolability of the law lose none of its sanctions by his official action.

"Faithful to these convictions of duty, after the action of his Council had been submitted to him, he drew up the following admirable paper, announcing the conclusions to which he had been led by the review of the case before him. It is due to his memory that it should be published entire; for while, in justice to the motives by which he was actuated in this exigent and trying moment of his official career, it could not well be abbreviated, it contains a clear and interesting outline of the history of one of the most remarkable cases of crime that has ever darkened the pages of legal or human annals : —

" 'To the Honorable Council:

" 'The Council having considered and acted upon the case of John W. Webster, a convict under the sentence of death, it now becomes my duty as the Chief Executive Magistrate of the Commonwealth, to make a final decision on a question involving the life of the prisoner. I feel the weight of the responsibility. But it is a responsibility found in the path of official duty, and I am not disposed to evade it or to shrink from it. For eight months past this extraordinary case has created a deep and painful interest among the people of Massachusetts and of the whole Union. Its history is as brief as it is terrible and instructive. Every new development in its progress has been more strange, and has increased that interest.

" 'On the 23d of November, 1849, Dr. George Parkman, a well-known and highly respectable citizen of Boston, left his house and family on business, as was usual for him, and never returned to them. His unexpected absence alarmed his family, and excited the attention of the people in and around Boston. In the course of a day or two, it was understood that the prisoner had said that Dr.

21*

Parkman met him at his rooms in the Medical College, in the west part of the city, not far from half-past one o'clock on the day of his disappearance, and that he then and there paid him a sum of money, which he, Dr. Parkman, took into his hands, and thereupon hastily rushed from the room towards the outer door. Dr. Parkman was also seen by other persons, about the same time of day, within forty feet of the Medical College, and walking quickly towards it. These, with other circumstances, directed the public mind towards the college buildings. The next Friday, one week after the disappearance of Dr. Parkman, the dismembered parts of a human body were found, in different places, in and under the rooms occupied by the prisoner in that college, — some of them in a furnace, nearly destroyed by fire; some of them packed in a tea-chest; and other parts in a vault of a privy attached to his laboratory. Suspicions were strongly fixed upon him, and he was arrested and committed to Leverett Street jail. A coroner's inquest was called, and, after a long investigation of the facts of the case conducted in secret, the jury reported that the remains found were parts of the body of the late Dr. George Parkman; that he came to his death by violence, in the Medical College in Boston, on Friday the 23d day of November, and that he was killed by John W. Webster.

" ' In January, 1850, the case was laid before the Grand Jury for the County of Suffolk, and the investigation before that body resulted in finding a bill of indictment against the prisoner for the wilful murder of Dr. Parkman. He was arraigned on the indictment, and pleaded not guilty. Two of the most able and distinguished lawyers of the Commonwealth were upon his own selection assigned to him for counsel by the Supreme Court, and the time for his trial before the full bench fixed for the nineteenth day of March. Some time before the day of trial, the Attorney-General furnished the counsel for the prisoner not only the names of the witnesses examined by the Grand Jury, which is required in all capital cases in this Commonwealth, but also a copy of the testimony which had been produced against him before that body. The time appointed for the trial arrived, when four judges of the Supreme Court were present, and sat during the trial. In pursuance of the provisions of the law, sixty jurors had been drawn from the jury-box in the County of Suffolk. By the law the prisoner had a right peremptorily, without assigning any reason, to challenge twenty jurors, and, for sufficient reasons, to object to any others whose names might be called. In the impanelling of the jury who tried him, the prisoner exercised his right of peremptory challenge in only fourteen instances. The trial was one of surpassing interest and solemnity, and lasted eleven days. On the part of the prisoner the case was argued with great earnestness, candor, and ability, by the Hon. Pliny Merrick, his senior counsel, and the case was closed by the Attorney-General, the Hon. John H. Clifford, in an address of singular power and effect.

" 'After the Attorney-General had finished his argument, the Court informed the prisoner that he had the right, which he might exercise or not as he pleased, to make such remarks to the jury as he saw fit. The prisoner arose, and for some time addressed the jury in his own behalf.

" 'An elaborate, clear, and comprehensive charge was given by the Chief Justice, after consultation with the other members of the court who sat with him at the trial. The Jury retired to their room; and, after an absence of three hours, late on Saturday evening, returned into court with a verdict of guilty. The next Monday morning the prisoner was again brought into court, and received from the Chief Justice the sentence of the law, which doomed him to suffer death by hanging, at such time as the Executive of the Commonwealth should appoint. In a few days a copy of the record of his conviction was transmitted to the Governor and Council, agreeably to the provisions of law, by the sheriff of the county of Suffolk. On the 24th of April the prisoner sent by the hand of his friend to the Governor and Council a petition for a pardon under his own hand, on the ground of his entire innocence of the crime of which he had been convicted, and for which he was under sentence of death. All proceedings upon this petition before the Executive were suspended, in consequence of having received notice from the counsel of the prisoner that they were about to make application to the Supreme Court for a writ of error to issue in his case, on account of certain alleged irregularities said to have been discovered in the course of the proceedings against him. That application was heard before the full court, all the five judges being present, and overruled. In the opinion of the court, pronounced by the Chief Justice, all the proceedings in the case were declared to be according to established judicial forms and the laws of the Commonwealth.

"'On the fourth day of June, and before, the question on the writ of error had been settled by the Court, the Rev. Dr. Putnam, for the prisoner, asked to be permitted to withdraw the petition for a pardon above named, from further consideration. The Governor and Council permitted him to do so, and the petition was placed in his hands.

"'On the first day of July, Dr. Putnam placed in the hands of the Governor another petition, signed by the prisoner, asking for a commutation of his sentence. On the 2d day of July this petition was referred to the Committee on Pardons, and on the same day Dr. Putnam appeared before them and made a statement, which he said was authorized by the prisoner, in which the prisoner admitted that he killed Dr. Parkman, at the time and in the place charged against him, but denied that the act was premeditated. He narrated what the prisoner declared to be the manner of killing, and described minutely the mode and process by which the body of Dr. Parkman was disposed of after death. The prisoner alleged that "the single blow with a stick of wood," by which Dr. Parkman was killed, was given by him in a moment of uncontrolled passion, excited by the insulting language heaped upon him by Dr. Parkman, and "by thrusting a letter which he held in his hand, and his fist in his face," and that "he did not know, nor think, nor care where he should hit him, or how hard, nor what the effect would be." Upon the statement of the prisoner, and the other facts proved at the trial, Dr. Putnam addressed the committee at length in an able and impressive argument in favor of a commutation of the sentence of the Court. A petition from the family of the prisoner, and a large number of other petitions received before and after the confession, and from people, men and women, in other States, were before the committee. The committee gave three other hearings to those who wished to be heard in aid of the prisoner's petition, and in support of the views of Dr. Putnam.

" 'The Committee on Pardons, consisting of the Lieutenant-Governor and four other Councillors, after a full, careful, and patient hearing, came to a unanimous conclusion that there were no sufficient reasons to justify them in recommending the interposition of Executive clemency. They recommended that the Governor be advised to have the sentence of the law, as pronounced by the Court, carried into effect on the 30th day of August next. The Council, with but one exception, concurred in the report of the committee, and advised the Governor to carry out the sentence of the law as recommended by them.

" 'In carefully and anxiously examining and considering the case, I do not feel authorized, by any considerations which have been presented to my mind, to set aside the verdict of the Jury, arrest the solemn decree of the law, as pronounced by the highest judicial tribunal of the Commonwealth, and disregard the deliberate opinion and advice of the Council. If the circumstances of the killing, as stated by the prisoner, are taken to be true, it may well be questioned whether the Executive could interfere without doing violence to the settled laws of the Commonwealth. It will hardly be pretended by any one that the declaration of a prisoner under sentence of death should be permitted to outweigh the doings of the Court and Jury, and rescue him from the consequences that are to follow those proceedings. In this case, it is candidly stated by Dr. Putnam, in his able argument for the prisoner, and in several petitions presented in favor of commutation received since his confession, that, standing as he does, the word of the prisoner is entitled to no credit. If the circumstances disclosed on the trial are relied upon to support this statement, the reply is that those circumstances were urged in his favor before the Jury, and they have decided against him.

" 'The facts of this appalling case are before the world. They will forever fill one of the gloomiest pages in the record of crime among civilized men. It is undisputed that on the 23d day of November, 1849, John W. Webster, a Professor in Harvard University, and in the Medical College in Boston, did, at mid-day, in

his room in that College, within a few feet of the place where he
daily stood to deliver scientific lectures to a large class of young
men, with unlawful violence take the life of Dr. George Parkman,
a respectable citizen of Boston, who had come to that room at
the request of the prisoner; that after taking his life, he eviscer-
ated the body of his victim, burning parts of it in a furnace, and
depositing other portions of it in different parts of the building,
where they were found by persons who were seeking after Dr.
Parkman; that, after killing him, he robbed his lifeless creditor by
taking from him two notes of hand signed by himself, to which he
had no right, and committed still another crime by making false
marks upon those notes; and that a jury of his country, impan-
elled according to law under the direction of four of the five eminent judges constituting the Supreme Judicial Court of Massachusetts, after a long, patient, and impartial trial, and after hearing
in his defence the arguments of learned and eloquent counsel,
upon their oaths found him guilty of wilful murder. Upon that
verdict the Court pronounced the awful sentence of death. In
such a case, there should be obvious and controlling reasons to
sustain the pardoning power in interfering to arrest the sword of
justice. I do not see these reasons. All the circumstances of
this most lamentable case force me to the conclusion, that the
safety of the community, the inviolability of the law, and the principles of impartial justice demand the execution of the sentence.

"'I hope it is not necessary for me to say that it would have given
me unspeakable pleasure to come to a different result, and that I
would do anything on earth in my power, short of violating duty,
to alleviate the sufferings of a crushed and broken-hearted family.

"'G. N. BRIGGS.'

"'COUNCIL CHAMBER, July 19, 1850.'

"The conclusions thus reached by Governor Briggs, found their
complete justification in the most impartial criticisms of this case
by professional writers, both at home and abroad; among these
may be mentioned those of Professor Mittermaier, of the University of Heidelberg, one of the most learned and accomplished
jurisprudents of continental Europe, and of Samuel Warren, a
leading English barrister, well known by his writings both in

literature and the law. In concluding a series of articles in *Black-wood's Magazine*, entitled 'Modern Criminal Trials,' this author says, —

. " ' It was our intention to have included in this paper a sketch of a great American trial for murder, — that of the late Professor Webster, for the murder of Dr. Parkman; a fearful occurrence, — a black and dismal tragedy from beginning to end, exhibiting most remarkable indications, as it appears to us, of that overruling Providence which sometimes sees fit to allow its awful agency in human affairs to become visible to us.

" ' The circumstances attending the murder were invested with enthralling interest, and it has to the eye of the moralist some very hideous features. . The efforts made by the prisoner — a man of intellect, learning, and high professional station — to avert sus- picion and escape from the awful consequences of crime, are sickening to read of. His idiosyncrasy, also, is a psychological study; and the network of circumstantial evidence in which he became inextricably enmeshed, will be regarded with watchful interest alike by lay and professional readers.' [1]

" But the most decisive testimony on this point, and that which most completely sustained the course taken by Governor Briggs in the discharge of his responsible trust, came from Dr. Webster himself. It is interesting as evidence of the irrepressible nature of truth when all motives for concealing or distorting it are re- moved from the mind of the most hardened criminal, and furnishes a fit conclusion to this review of Governor Briggs in connection with this memorable chapter in the history of crime. After all hope of a pardon or a commutation of his sentence had been extin- guished, and when he had seriously and with singleness of purpose addressed himself to the great work of making his peace with his Maker, in which, under the guidance and with the inestimable aid of his spiritual adviser, the Rev. Dr. Putnam, it is hoped he was successful; on the 25th of August, the Sunday preceding his execu-

---

[1] The following well-deserved compliment is contained in the article referred to above: " The argument of Mr. Clifford for the prosecution cannot be excelled in clear and conclusive reasoning, conveyed in language equally elegant and forci- ble. Its effect as a demonstration of the guilt of the accused is fearful."

tion, Dr. Webster sought an interview with the jailer, Mr. Gustavus Andrews. After some conversation relative to the approaching event of his execution, and his sense of Mr. Andrews's kindness to him, he requested of Mr. Andrews, as a favor, that he would pre-. pare his person for the scaffold. Mr. Andrews replied that he was under the direction of the sheriff, but if it was of any consequence to him he would endeavor to comply with his request. This subject disposed of, Professor Webster then went on to say: ' *Mr. Andrews, I consider this whole thing perfect justice! The officers of the law are right! Everybody is right; and I am wrong! And I feel that if the yielding up of my life to the injured law will atone, even in part, for the crime I have committed, that is a consolation!* '

" Subsequently to the above interview, and two days before the execution, Sheriff Eveleth called on the prisoner to prepare him for the final discharge of his official duty, when in the course of conversation, in allusion to a suggestion that had been made of the possibility of suicide, the sheriff remarked that he inferred from the prisoner's statement he entertained no idea of attempting to avoid the execution by any act of his own.

" ' *Why should I?* ' replied Professor Webster. ' *All the proceedings in my case have been just. The Court discharged their duty. The law officers of the Commonwealth did their duty and no more! The verdict of the Jury was just! The sentence of the Court was just; and it is just that I should die on the scaffold, in accordance with that sentence.* ' "

CHAPTER XXI.

CLOSE OF HIS GUBERNATORIAL LIFE — HIS ADDRESS DECLINING A RE-
NOMINATION — ANNIVERSARY ORATION AT CONCORD, MASS. — A CANDI-
DATE IN SPITE OF HIMSELF — DEFEATED IN THE LEGISLATURE — LETTERS
TO HIS DAUGHTER — HIS RETIREMENT FROM OFFICE — HIS OWN REVIEW
OF HIS PUBLIC LIFE — TRIBUTE FROM ANOTHER.

THE year 1850 was the last of that term of seven years during which Governor Briggs administered the affairs of the Commonwealth of Massachusetts, — with the single exception of that of Caleb Strong,[1] the longest term of such service in the history of the State.

In the spring of this year the cares of state oppressed him with so much force, that the desire to lay them aside prevailed with him to decline a re-nomination. The dreadful responsibilities from which he did not shrink in the case reported in the preceding chapter, were still vivid in his remembrance, and no doubt quickened his purpose of retiring from a position which involved him in the hazard of meeting other terrible emergencies.

The following address bears date of April 27, 1850 : —

To the Electors of Massachusetts:

Fellow-Citizens, — By your favor I have been seven times chosen Governor of the Commonwealth, — three times by a majority of the popular vote, and four times, after having received a

---

1 Caleb Strong was Governor of Massachusetts from 1800 to 1807, a period just as long as that of Governor Briggs's service. He was, however, Governor a second time, from 1812 to 1816, making his whole period of service eleven years.

large plurality of that vote, I have been chosen by a majority of both branches of the Legislature.

Deeming it not improbable that my name, amongst others, might be thought of for the same place at the approaching election, I take this occasion to announce my purpose of not again being a candidate for the high office.

In respectfully declining to be any longer a candidate for the suffrages of my fellow-citizens, I have no language by which to express to them the gratitude I feel for the honors conferred upon me by the repeated testimonials of their confidence. While I express my obligations to these generous and constant friends by whose votes I have been elevated to office, it is but justice to my political opponents to say that I have received kind and considerate treatment from them.

Previous to being chosen Governor, I had been six times elected to Congress by the freemen of the Seventh Congressional District. I take great pleasure in declaring that it has rarely been the fortune of one who has been nineteen years in public life, and who has thirteen times passed the ordeal of popular election, to have had so little cause to complain of the treatment of political opponents as I have had.

I shall carry with me into retirement no unkind or hostile feelings toward any fellow-being. If I have given just occasion for others to entertain such feelings towards me, I should be most happy to be informed of it, and to have the opportunity of doing them justice. Upon his native Commonwealth, under whose free and fostering constitution one of the humblest of her people has been raised by the suffrages of her voters to the chair of her chief magistracy, a grateful son will never cease to implore the blessing of Heaven. Long may her people be prosperous and happy; may intelligence and virtue be the stability of their times. In their politics, may they be enlightened, consistent, and honest; in their religion, sincere and charitable and blameless; in their dealings and intercourse with each other, and in their transactions with, and their conduct towards their sister States, may they be just, fearing God.

With heart-felt and lasting respect, I am your friend and fellow-citizen,

G. N. BRIGGS.

Of the numerous public services in which Governor Briggs formed a conspicuous official part, few were more interesting than the seventy-fifth anniversary of the nineteenth of April, 1775, in Concord, Mass. Upon this occasion he delivered the following oration, which is worthy to be preserved with the best memorials of his public life : —

"MR. PRESIDENT, — The sentiment in honor of our ancient Commonwealth which you have just announced speaks for itself. It requires no response from me. As children, we all love and honor her; and I trust it will not be deemed improper on this occasion for me to say that her character and history from the time of provincial dependence to the present time, and her standing among her sister States, entitles her to the love and reverence of her children. But, sir, if upon the great theme which this day fills all hearts, I had anything to say when I came here, let me tell you the all-grasping reapers who have preceded me have taken it all away.

"Far back in distant ages, when a Moabitish stranger went into the field of one of the magnates of the land of Canaan 'to glean and gather after the reapers among the sheaves,' the lord of the harvest commanded his reapers to let the damsel 'glean even among the sheaves, and reproach her not.' I wish that these gentlemen had shown a little of the humanity and kindness of that Oriental landholder. Why, sir, in my solicitude I have been searching the field, and can find scarcely a head of wheat left. There is, however, one thing that they have not said in connection with the nineteenth of April, 1775. They did not state the historic fact that the incursion of the British army on that day was the first and the last time, since Massachusetts has had a political existence, when a foreign enemy has penetrated so far into her territory. This is a truth which her people may regard with pride and with gratitude. Few States nearly two hundred and fifty years old can say as much. I trust the result of that experiment will admonish her enemies, if enemies she shall ever have, that the experiment had better not be repeated. That proved legion of

loyalists expected as they advanced to see the pale and trembling
rebels sh ink and flee before them. Great was their disappointment! Sir, what a day was that for Massachusetts! Well did
Samuel Adams exclaim, when he heard the volley at Lexington:
' *Oh, what a glorious morning is this!* ' Words of prophecy and
patriotism! They will be repeated with enthusiastic awe, and
inspire the lovers of freedom to the latest generation.

   " Mr. President, I wish that venerable old man, who but this
moment stood before these assembled thousands, could rehearse
in our hearing the thrilling incidents of that auspicious morning.
When on a visit to Lexington last winter, one who participated in
those incidents told me that on the bright moonlight evening that
preceded the morning of the nineteenth of April, while returning
to his father's house, for he had been out fifing for a company of
boys, he met several British officers on horseback, who preceded
the army which came before the rising sun. After reaching home
and retiring to bed, about one o'clock his mother, calling to him
from the chamber door, said, ' *Jonathan, you must get up; the regulars are coming, and something must be done!* ' The hoary-headed
patriarch who has just retired from your sight was the boy, who by
his more than Spartan mother seventy-five years ago was summoned
to get up in the middle of the night, and ' to do something,' for ' the
regulars were coming.' Jonathan got up; and what do you think
he did? What could a boy sixteen years old do in such an emergency? I'll tell you what he did. He went out and blew that shrill
little fife, to alarm the neighbors, rally the minute men, and call the
patriots together. Mothers of Massachusetts, do you hear that?
Young men of Massachusetts, do you hear that? ' The regulars are
coming !' And who were the regulars? They were the embodied
power of the British kingdom, the armed representatives of the
British king, — disciplined, brave, and obedient soldiers, commanded by gallant and choice officers, — advancing in the stillness
of the night to drive back the rebels and seize upon their military
stores in a neighboring town. At the approach of such an army
at that awful hour, we hear the voice of an American mother, calling her boy to leave his bed, ' to get up,' and do something. Before
he saw the sun on that bright and ominous morning, he stood by

the side of the stout-hearted Parker at the head of his company on Lexington green, and raised the martial blood of his country-men by the piercing notes of his spirit-stirring fife. There he stood with that little band of armed freemen hastily called together in the very presence of British legions. He saw the dauntless Pit-cairn at their head. He heard the order given to load with powder and ball, and saw it executed. He saw them march up with an imperious and threatening air. He heard the word, 'Rebels, dis-perse!' 'Rebels, lay down your arms!' He saw the flash and the smoke, and heard the sharp report of the guns which broke the stillness of that first morning of the American Revolution. Yes, sir; he was in the midst of that great scene! Those eyes, now dimmed with the visions of a hundred years, saw it, — that heart, now feebly beating in that aged breast, felt it!

"The first martyrs in the great cause of their country fell at Lexington; and the fratricidal host marched on to Concord. Faithful couriers and deep-toned bells aroused the patriots of Concord and the adjoining towns, who had heard of the massacre of their neighbors, and they were prepared to meet the approach-ing foe. At the old North Bridge that foe again fired upon the peaceful yeomanry of Massachusetts, still firmly standing in de-fence of their rights. The blood of other victims gushed and flowed upon the soil. The fire was returned, and two British sol-diers fell. The enemy hastily retreated. Here sits Amos Baker, the sole survivor of that memorable fight. That arm now enfee-bled with age, then youthful and strong, helped to drive back the enemies of his country. Thank God that these two only remain-ing actors in the scenes of that day — the one at Lexington, the other at Concord — are here to heighten the interest of this seventy-fifth anniversary. They are here for the last time; and the youth who now look upon them will in their old age relate with patriotic emotion, to the children of a generation not yet born, the wonder-ful fact that they saw, in 1850, two soldiers who fought at Lexing-ton and Concord. When, in the neighborhood of Lexington, Samuel Adams heard the guns, he exclaimed, '*Oh, what a glorious morning is this!*' Early on the same morning, as General Warren landed at Charlestown from the ferry-boat which had brought him

22*

over from Boston, on being asked what he thought of the political prospect of the times, replied, ' *Keep up a brave heart; they have begun it, — that either party could do; — we'll end it, — that only one can do.*' A soldier at Concord said: ' *The war is now begun; the Lord only knows where it will end.*'

"This remarkable sentiment, uttered by noble patriots on the same day in different places, shows how the spirit of freedom pervaded the hearts of the people of Massachusetts. It was a glorious day for Lexington and Concord and Middlesex, for Massachusetts and the thirteen British colonies. It was a glorious day for liberty, for patriotism, for humanity. Every blow struck for liberty amongst men, since the nineteenth of April, 1775, has but echoed the guns of that eventful morning.

"Mr. President, I give you this sentiment: The nineteenth of April, 1775, — with the patriotic and prophetic exclamation of Samuel Adams, when he heard the guns at Lexington, ' Oh, what a glorious morning is this!' "

The sturdy and independent "electors," to whom Governor Briggs declared his intention of retiring from their service, exercised their "independence" in paying no heed to his address. He was again nominated, and at the election, for the first time in his life, he was defeated. His defeat, however, was not directly from the people, of whose votes he received a very large plurality. It was in the Legislature, into which the election was thrown, that the hitherto invariable fortune of his political ventures deserted him. He had the satisfaction of knowing, however, that he himself had taken the initiative in the matter of his retirement. He thus writes to his daughter after the result was declared : —

PITTSFIELD, Nov., 1850.

MY DEAR DAUGHTER:

The result of the election you have learned ere this. It was not unexpected to me. I have no cause to complain of anybody,

for I have already had more political success than I had any claim
to. I hope I have not been instrumental in the defeat of the *Whig
cause,* for I believe it a *just* and *patriotic one;* but I would not have
done, or *consented to the doing* of an unjust or improper thing to
have saved it from defeat.

Your mother thinks she shall have company this winter.

Affectionately, your father,

G. N. BRIGGS.

What hand could so fitly record the close of his long public service as his own, and it is so humbly and yet so
nobly done in the following letter to his daughter, that the
letter itself ought to be a part of his public portraiture,
and is therefore included therein : —

BOSTON, 9th Jan., 1851.

MY DEAR DAUGHTER:

. . . . . I felt sad enough, to read in Henry's letter of the
ruin of the old church in Pittsfield. It seemed melancholy to feel
that those venerable walls, hallowed by so many sacred and endearing recollections and associations, were smouldering and
fallen. How many prayers and songs of praise have been heard
within their inclosure. And then the truth-telling clock, true to
its trust, struck the hour on the old bell when enveloped in smoke
and fire, as if it were resolved to be true and faithful to the end.

To-morrow or next day I expect to close my public life.

In looking back upon the seven years that I have been Governor,
I am not conscious of doing any public act that I did not believe
to be right, and for the best good of the State. If the Judge of
all the Earth approves my intentions, I know He will pardon my
imperfections. That approval, I shall now esteem above all the
applause of men, and hereafter it will be worth more than all the
world. For the future, my unimportant life will be retirement. I
know I desire to have it useful. What my opinions 'and feelings
are I know, and I am sure that the political world have but little
sympathy with those views and feelings. I hope my honest efforts
are not entirely overlooked and disregarded by the wise and good,

and I hope for a little while the poor and needy ones will remember me with pleasure, and feel that I am their friend; and oh, if I shall be so happy as to be remembered by the *Saviour* in the day when he makes up his jewels, it will be enough.

Affectionately, your father,

G. N. BRIGGS.

Governor Briggs went to Boston at the opening of the Legislative session in 1851, to resign his office and authority to his successor.

Before this was done, he received from the honorable Board of Councillors, with whom he had been associated, the following letter, conveying to him the expression of their official and personal regard and esteem: —

COUNCIL CHAMBER, Jan. 11, 1851.

TO HIS EXCELLENCY, GEO. N. BRIGGS:

DEAR SIR, — As the time is at hand when our term of service will expire, and we shall each return to his home, no more to be summoned to meet you in Council, we deem it proper at parting, to present to you some of the impressions made upon our minds arising from our connection with you, in the public service, the year past.

That our duties always responsible, and in many instances peculiarly trying, have been made easy, and for the most part agreeable, is owing in no small measure to the kindness with which you have, on all occasions, imparted to each of us, from your large stores of wisdom and experience. That our action has always been so harmonious is likewise due, in no small degree, to the frankness with which you have expressed your opinions when solicited to do so, to your desire to hear the opinion of others, and to the kind and uniform deference which you have, in all cases, paid to those opinions. If the Executive administration of the Government has been satisfactory to the people, and we firmly believe it has been, it may be ascribed mainly to the fact, that our Chief Magistrate has been governed by one single motive, -- an ardent desire to promote the public welfare, uninfluenced by fear, favor, or affection, and guided by strong discriminating judgment. We were sent to you by the people of Massachusetts to be your Councillors. Some of us met you as strangers, with no common tie, except that of being members of the same political party, engaged in the same cause as servants of the Commonwealth. But not thus do we part. Our connection with you, which is now to be severed, has led us to look from the magistrate to the man; and in him we have found one whom we shall ever be pleased and proud to call our friend, and to whom, in private life, it will be a greater satisfaction to render a personal service, whenever it may be in the power of either of us to do so, than it has been to aid the magistrate in the affairs of Government, however cheerfully and freely that aid may at any time have been rendered.

With the warmest wishes that prosperity may attend your future course in life, and that you may realize the full share of happiness which falls to the lot of the most favored among men, we now bid you an affectionate farewell.

Your friends,

SAMUEL WOOD,	SOLOMON DAVIS,
TIMOTHY GRIDLEY,	THOMAS TOLMAN,
JOHN TENNEY,	P. S. COPELAND,
CHAS. M. OWEN,	SAM'L L. CROCKER,

LUTHER V. BELL.

His last official act as Governor, was to make the address of Inauguration and greeting to the newly-elected incumbent of that Chair of State, from which he was retiring with enviable fame. He thus addressed Governor Boutwell: —

"MAY IT PLEASE YOUR EXCELLENCY:

"Seven years ago, I was introduced into that chair by a distinguished citizen who had been chosen Governor by that one of the political parties which has placed you in power. In obedience to the command of the majority of the Legislature, uttered according to the forms of the Constitution, I now surrender it to you and retire. Sir, no human institutions are perfect, but I believe the sun does not shine upon any political community numbering a million of people, which enjoys greater physical, civil, educational, and moral blessings, than the people of Massachusetts enjoy.

"Allow me, sir, to say, that whoever may administer her government, as long as I live, I shall rejoice in her prosperity and renown."

To which Governor Boutwell replied : —

"GOVERNOR BRIGGS, — I have accepted the office to which I have been called, agreeably to the Constitution, with great distrust of myself, and with the deepest solicitude; but the entrance to its duties has been rendered pleasant by the kindness you have extended to me on this occasion.

"It is your satisfaction, sir, that you retire from a position which you have so ably and honorably occupied, with a degree of popular support which neither was, nor could have been accorded to any other man."

"And however honorable may be the position of the public servant who enters upon the discharge of important duties, the position of that public servant who retires with the consciousness of having justly performed them, is much more enviable. If at the close of my term of office such shall be my fortune, as it is now yours, that occasion will be more agreeable to me than the present."

Before this chapter of his life is brought to a close, it is fitting that his own review of all the period he had now spent in the public service, should be included with the testimonies and reminiscences of others.

He left among his papers such a review in his own hand — brief but comprehensive, and not more remarkable for its terseness than for its modesty and simplicity.

It is impossible to read it without obtaining from it an impression of the simple dignity, the sterling integrity, and the true but unobtrusive greatness of his character, which all that others have said of these qualities may yet have failed so happily and convincingly to express.

It is needless to detain the reader longer from this self-recorded abstract of his popular services : —

"I was six times elected to Congress from the Berkshire District, and seven times chosen Governor of Massachusetts. I never asked a man to vote for me for either of these offices, or asked a man to attend a political convention where I was nominated, or to use any influence in any way to promote my election to either of these offices.

"During the seven years I was Governor of Massachusetts, I nominated four Judges of the Supreme Court and fourteen of the Court of Common Pleas. Seventeen of them were appointed and confirmed — one who was nominated Judge of the Supreme Court — Charles Allen, of Worcester — declined after he was nominated, and his nomination was withdrawn. The nomination of Judge of the Supreme Court was once offered to Rufus Choate, but he declined it. I do not now remember, in all the appointments, that there was a personal request from a single one of the persons appointed, or anything like a personal solicitation on the part of their friends. When there was no personal acquaintance on the part of the Executive of persons named or thought of, inquiries were made as to qualifications of individuals, of men of high professional standing, but not of politicians.

"The persons appointed to the Supreme Court were Theron Metcalf of Dedham, Richard Fletcher and George T. Bigelow of Boston, and Charles E. Forbes of Northampton. Those appointed to the Bench of the Court of Common Pleas, were Daniel Wells, Chief Justice, of Greenfield, Charles E. Forbes of Northampton, Horatio Byington of Stockbridge, Emory Washburn and Pliny Merrick of Worcester, Thomas Hopkinson of Lowell, Edward Mellen of Wayland, E. Rockwood Hoar of Concord, Luther S. Cushing and George T. Bigelow of Boston, Joshua H. Ward and Jonathan C. Perkins of Salem, and H. G. O. Colby of New Bedford. The office of Judge of the Supreme Court was indirectly offered to two other distinguished lawyers of Boston, both of whom declined it.

"In looking back upon the official acts of my life I do not, at this time, see any reason to regret the selections that were made for these important and responsible situations.

"I wrote seven annual messages to the Legislature. Being unacquainted practically with the Government of Massachusetts, I read the first message to a friend who was well acquainted with the affairs of the Commonwealth. With that exception, no man, during the seven years, ever saw or heard a message, knew or asked what was in it, or requested me to put in or leave out anything of any message which I wrote. The only exception is the one named above, and my two sons, who made copies of the messages; with these exceptions, no man saw anything about any one of them until they went into the hands of the public printers.

"No man ever said to me that the interest of the Whig party required, or would be promoted or injured by my doing or omitting to do anything. The most entire harmony prevailed in the Council Chamber during the whole time. There never was a rejection of a nomination, or any discussion that might not as well have been public as in the Council Chamber. I never heard a discourteous word or remark at the Council Board during the seven years I was there."

The following pleasing incident illustrates his independence of character, presenting him to us as uninfluenced by the prejudices and equally by the preferences of others, in all circumstances where his conscience approved his conduct.

While he was Governor of the Commonwealth, a gentleman from Boston, whom he knew well, visited him at his house, to confer with him upon certain political matters. In the course of the conversation, or rather in a pause of it, the visitor remarked, as if incidentally:

"Governor, a few evenings since, among our friends, a

matter came up in which you were mentioned; but as it was personal, I am not sure that I do right to speak of it."

" Oh, speak out, speak out," said the Governor.

" Well, then, our friends agreed that for one who occupies so honorable and dignified a position as Governor of the State, you attend too many temperance conventions and make too many temperance speeches. They think it is not exactly the thing for a Governor."

To which, with his usual sauvity, he replied : " When you see those friends on your return, give them my best respects, and say to them, that in my opinion, to attend temperance meetings and conventions, and make temperance speeches, is not only the most dignified, but the most *honorable*, as well as most *useful* employment the people of Massachusetts can put their Governor to, and that while I am Governor I shall continue at this business."

One who knew him well, adds to these interesting reflections of the honesty of his official life, this pleasing reminiscence : —

" I have also heard my friend say that he never spent a penny to promote his election to any office he ever held."

Unquestionably the public life of Governor Briggs was cast in a rare mould. Without the severe assumption that venality is a general characteristic of men in office — it is certainly true, that multitudes of them are not controlled by such principles of honor and rectitude as those which fashioned and adorned the whole public career of the man, upon whose life we are looking. He was an exception to most men in Congress and in the chair of the Chief Magistrate, if not in the creed of political ethics — yet certainly in the practice of them.

His character commends itself impressively to the young

23

men of the nation, who are aspiring, as he did *not*, perhaps, to its honors and trusts. They may indeed seize
them without his virtue, but without that they certainly
will not wear them to the lasting honor of their names, or
to the true benefit of their generation. There was throughout his public service no hour and no act in which he
could not have been truly described in the well-known
words : " *Justum et tenacem propositi virum.*" [1]

1 A man just and steady of purpose.

CHAPTER XXII.

THREE quiet, happy and prosperous years of private life, unburdened with any official rank or requirements, and free from all solicitudes, except
those which were inseparable from his domestic,
social, and spiritual relationships, followed the retirement of Governor Briggs from the chair of state.

He resumed his profession of the law, and busily brushed
away the dust which had settled upon his books, and, not
unlikely, upon his brain also; for his mind had been too
full of the important public interests committed to his keeping to maintain a very strong hold upon either principles
or precedents in that subtile realm which is called the law.

His innate sense and his uncompromising reverence of
justice kept him, indeed, in some important manner alive
to the law as an exponent of right; but its technicalities
and formalities had to be renewed in his memory.

He could not, however, consent to do anything by halves,
and he carried into every case committed to his hands, a
conscientiousness which was a better (though it may have
been an unrecognized) warrant to his clients for its faithful
management, than any professional pledges they might have
exacted from their advocate.

His farm and his broader forensic sphere now agreeably divided his services.   He found in the former that healthful delight which gave a zest to all professional labor, and proved the happy succedaneum of every exhausting mental occupation.

Early in the first year of this grateful retirement, and while yet the snows of a Berkshire winter were relentless in their usurpation of hillside and meadow, he indulged himself in correspondence with his friends, to more than his customary extent.

Among his correspondence of that period there stands out prominently a triad of related letters, bearing three different names, — one his own, another that of his friend Amos Lawrence, and the third that of James Hamilton, the well-known English preacher and writer, whose "Life in Earnest" has served to quicken and freshen so many hearts both sides of the sea.   These letters are interesting. especially as reflexes of the characters they represent. They possess a striking individuality.   Two of them — the Governor and the preacher — had never met, and their slight acquaintance with each other was derived through their mutual friend, the merchant prince.

As a hearty admirer of the writings of his English friend, Mr. Lawrence had wisely expended considerable sums of money in reprinting and circulating some of his essays and tracts.   For this favor, which Mr. Hamilton counted an honor, and for other kindnesses, he thanks his American friend, in the first of this triad of letters.

It is to be regretted, perhaps, that no copy of the letter from Governor Briggs to Mr. Lawrence, which the latter transmitted to England, and which so gratified his distinguished correspondent there, is at command for use in these memorials : —

[I. — Rev. Dr. Hamilton to Amos Lawrence.]

42 GOWER STREET, LONDON, Feb. 15, 1851.

MY DEAR SIR :

No letters which authorship has brought to me ever gave me such pleasure as I received from yours of July 18, 1849, inclosing. one which Governor Briggs had written to you. That strangers so distinguished should take such interest in my writings and should express themselves so kindly towards myself, overwhelmed me with a pleasing surprise and with thankfulness to God who had given me such favor. I confess, too, it helped to make me *love more* the country which has always been to me the dearest next my own. In conjunction with some much-prized friendships which I have formed among your ministers, it would *almost* tempt me to cross the Atlantic. But I am so bad a sailor that I fear I must postpone personal intercourse with those American friends who do not come to England, until we reach the land where there is *no more sea.*

To you also I am indebted for the friendship of Mr. and Mrs. Abbott Lawrence. Mrs. Hamilton and I feel ashamed of the kindness which they have shown to us, and yet we are greatly delighted with it. No foreign minister is such a favorite with the British public, and we feel it no small honor and privilege to have been so cordially received at the American embassy. And yet you will think it does not look very grateful to delay writing so long. But I am very conscious that it is because your letter gave me such unusual pleasure, that I have found it more difficult to send an answer. I could not help feeling that anything I might say would, in importance and in the power of affording gratification, be no equivalent to what you had written to me. However feebly expressed, be pleased to accept my heart-felt thanks for all the cost and trouble you have incurred in circulating my publications. It is pleasant to me to think that your motive in distributing them could not, in the first instance, be friendship for the author; and to both of us it will be the most welcome result, if they promote,

23*

in any measure, the cause of practical Christianity. Owing to weakness in the throat and chest, I cannot preach so much as many of my neighbors; and therefore I feel the more anxious that my tracts should do something for the honor of the Saviour and the welfare of mankind.

Accept, too, my best thanks for the huge parcel of reports and sermons. They have been a source of much instruction. Your benevolent institutions seem to me to be more purpose-like and efficient than ours. The account of the Perkins' Blind Asylum is especially striking.

You were kind enough to reprint my last year's lecture to young men. I could hardly wish the same distinction bestowed on its successor, because it is a fragment. I have some thought of extending it into a short exposition of Ecclesiastes, which is a book well suited to the times, but little understood.

Believe me, my dear and kind friend, with the greatest esteem and affection,

Yours, most truly,

JAMES HAMILTON.

[II.—Amos Lawrence to Hon. G. N. Briggs.]

BOSTON, Mar. 18, 1851.

MY DEAR FRIEND:

You will see by the foregoing letter from Dr. Hamilton, that a part of it belongs to you, and I accordingly give a copy of the whole.

He is an extraordinary man, and acting with mighty power upon his own country, and, I hope, with considerable power on this. The Lecture to Young Men, delivered the present year, I send for your examination, and, notwithstanding the Doctor's modesty about its publication, if you think it such an one as you would like to scatter with its predecessor, and will write a brief notice commending it, to be published with it, and will allow me to publish it *for you*, at my expense, for gratuitous distribution, I will do it, and will write to the good Doctor, acknowledging the tract and asking him to send forward his further exposition. Pray, let me send your note to him if you like this tract (and some of our friends pronounce it his *best*); and do come and see me very soon, — I

, love old friends better than new ones. So do find an excuse for
coming. Our Minister in England is spending his money for the
honor of his country and the comfort of himself. No man can do
the work better. Have you written to him yet?

Love to Mrs. B. and Harriet, in which wife joins me.

Your friend,

AMOS LAWRENCE.

P. S. — Please say to Dr. Todd that I sent his Pilgrim Address
to the original Pilgrim Church in Southwark, formed in 1616, and I
shall feel obliged for another copy. A. L.

[III. — Governor Briggs to Amos Lawrence.]

PITTSFIELD, March 31st, 1851.

MY DEAR FRIEND:

Your kind note of the 18th inst. came duly to hand in a package
of other good things, — Dr. Hamilton's lecture to the Young Men's
Christian Association in London on the 4th of February last, entitled "Solomon the Prince and Solomon the Preacher," — which
was one of the best of all, being among them.

Absence from home and various other hindrances have prevented an earlier reply. I cannot tell you how much I have been
charmed, delighted, and instructed by the reading of this rich and
beautiful lecture. As a fellow-man and a fellow-Christian, I feel
under great obligations to the eloquent author of this production
for his efforts to impress upon the minds of the young men of his
generation correct views of the sacred Scriptures, and the great
truths which they inculcate. His remarkable lecture before the
same association last year, upon "The Literary Attractions of the
Bible," is eminently calculated to produce that most desirable
result. Thousands of young men in this country have read with
thrilling interest that beautiful address. Its effects upon them,
and upon those who feel their influence, will be manifest after its
worthy author shall have entered upon his reward in another and
happier state of existence. I am highly gratified with the suggestion which you make in your note, of presenting to the young men
of our country "Solomon the Prince and Solomon the Preacher."
By doing so you will increase the obligation which your country-

men and humanity are already under to you for your numerous and continued acts of munificence. I should be most happy in any way to be instrumental in laying before our young men this intellectual and moral treasure.

How the destiny of our country would brighten, if the noble and truly Christian sentiment uttered by Dr. Hamilton in his last lecture, that "the *saint is greater than the sage, and discipleship to Jesus is the pinnacle of human dignity*," could be made to sink deep into the hearts of the young men of these United States. . . . . .

Sincerely and truly your friend,

GEO. N. BRIGGS.

One of the curious and somewhat unique cases which Governor Briggs conducted before the Berkshire bar, was the *Elephant* suit. It created much interest at the time. In the letter to his daughter, which follows, he gives the outlines of this case, and makes further details unnecessary : —

PITTSFIELD, Nov. —, 1851.

MY DEAR DAUGHTER:

We have no new or startling events in our family or neighborhood since my last epistle to be recorded in this, saving and excepting an occurrence of some consequence to me in a professional point of view. You have probably seen in the papers that the elephant Columbus fell through the bridge in South Adams, and was so injured that he died a week afterwards in Lenox. His owner, thinking the town of Adams might be liable to him for damages, did me the favor to retain me and place the case in my hands, with a pretty handsome retainer. What the town will do about it remains to be seen. It will be quite an important matter to the town and owner. The animal was valued at fifteen thousand dollars ($15,000). The owner said he would not have taken that for him, and that he cannot be replaced for that sum. He was, I believe, the largest in America. Tell the junior branch of the firm on Bank corner, if he will look up the law and settle the question, whether the town is liable for not having a bridge strong enough to hold up an elephant weighing five tons, he may see the elephant for nothing a'most! . . . . .

Your affectionate father,

GEORGE N. BRIGGS.

This suit was as tedious, almost, as a case in chancery. It came in successive aspects to the jury; and although in every instance the judge charged the jurors that, according to law, the town of Adams was responsible for the loss, the juries could never agree; and eventually, after the case was argued before the Supreme Court in Boston,[1] it was settled by compromise between the parties.

With the confinement of severe indisposition, there came to the father's heart pleasant reminiscences of his early married life, and he writes to his daughter : —

PITTSFIELD, Mar. 4, 1852.

MY DEAR CHILD:

You see I am able to report to you to-day. Except the rheumatic trouble in my legs, I am very comfortable. While the family were at dinner, I bundled up and took a little walk on the piazza. The fresh air was sweet. I hope the next fair day to ride out. . . . .

Thirty years ago to-day, your mother and I, and a *little* daughter, and only child, lived in a *little* green house in South Adams. It had three rooms, including the chamber; no cellar, no woodhouse. I paid thirty dollars rent for it. Our means were limited, and our wants very few. We were as happy, probably, as we have ever been. About four o'clock in the afternoon we were delighted to have come to live with us a nice little baby *boy* — we hope he will live with us forever. Living in such a house on very small means, in regard to property, several hundred dollars worse than nothing, yet with life before us, with a daughter and a son, the *present* was happy, and the future bright. A good Providence has

---

1 This was in April, 1861. Henry S. Briggs, Esq., the youngest son of Governor Briggs, was conducting the case, and withdrew from the court, under orders to take command of the Allen Guard, in the Massachusetts Eighth Regiment.

made that future better and brighter than we ever hoped. Since
then he has added two to our number of children. One of them,
I doubt not, is among the angels in Heaven. I hope, if it please
God, they will live to see their parents gathered to their fathers in
a ripe old age, and in the triumphs of Christian faith.

Your affectionate father,

GEO. N. BRIGGS.

The summer with its farm duties and its perpetual out-
of-door delights, and then the Fall term of the Courts, be-
guiled so much of his time that letters are few again, until
the eager and the nipping air of November made the library
more comfortable than the meadow or the orchard, when he
writes thus : —

PITTSFIELD, 7th Nov., 1852.

MY DEAR DAUGHTER:

I suppose by this time, you at Lawrence begin to think that we
in Pittsfield have forsaken you. I have been most of the time at
court, except the time which was spent at the election that has
resulted so beautifully. In what is to come, the people as in times
past, are to share in common the fruits of Government. If the
election has resulted beneficially to the country, we shall all be
blessed; if for evil, *all* will have to help bear the evils. It is about
eight o'clock. Your mother and I are here in the library, — she
with Georgie in her lap. We have been talking about the time
when we lived with a *little girl* in the little green house, and contrasting our situation then with that of our children now. The
presence of this little boy shows that we have glided very far
down the current since the days referred to.

It is a most unwelcome reflection, that I am no wiser or better,
and what is more strange, no *graver* than in those by-gone days.
No better prepared to live, no fitter to die, than I was. This with
the certainty that I am much nearer death and retribution, is a
painful consciousness. A thousand broken resolutions render it
more than probable that I shall not improve. A trembling hope
in the merits and pardoning mercy of the crucified and Almighty

Saviour is my only consolation for the future. 'Happy, if when I pass through the valley and the shadow of death, I can declare with entire confidence, as did our lovely friend Jane, "I will fear no evil. Thy rod and thy staff they comfort me." That rod and that staff the dying statesman, at Marshfield, said he wanted. I hope he found it and relied on it. How beautiful is that religion that stoops from its own bright Heaven, and offers the same support and consolation in the hour of need and extremity to the timid maiden and the man of giant mind. Without that rod and staff, the one is just as helpless and lost as the other; with it, they both are *safe*, and will go securely through the dark valley, and reach in triumph the celestial city beyond. .

All send love to Charles and George. Thanksgiving is coming!

Affectionately, your father,

G. N. BRIGGS.

The following letter describes a dream, of which he always cherished particular and vivid recollection, appealing so directly and so powerfully as it did to his religious nature, and to the most sacred emotions of his being : —   .

PITTSFIELD, Dec. 5, 1852.

MY DEAR DAUGHTER :

After leaving Lawrence on Tuesday, I dined with Mr. Winthrop. The dinner was a pleasant affair. Twenty-four dined, I believe, including Mrs. Winthrop, whom I saw for the first time. Mr. Quincy, senior, was there. Mr. Winthrop said I was to sit between Mr. Quincy and Abbott Lawrence, and he thought if I was not satisfied with my position, I must be an unreasonable fellow. I was very much delighted to meet Abbott,[1] and he "*let on*" that he was glad to meet me. His *greeting* was *hearty* as ever, and it seemed as if it had not been long since we met. There was nothing *strange* in his appearance or manner that needed to become acquainted with. As we were both going to the Mercantile Association to hear Choate, he insisted that I should go home with him

---

[1] Hon. Abbott Lawrence.

to see Mrs. L. and K. I did so, and was very happy at meeting both them and B. Next to my own children, I know no young man in whose destiny I have felt so much interest as in B.'s. He goes back an *attaché* to the minister at St. James.

Came home on Thursday. All well as usual. Nothing new, except my dream last night:—I thought I set off for the village, and when I entered the road at the east end of our avenue, I found myself standing in the air, just above the tops of the trees, with my face towards the village. It was night; but a few rays of light shot forth from the east, of inconceivable brightness. They struck the steeple and cross of the Baptist meeting-house, and made them perfectly transparent. Retaining their shape, they looked as though they were composed of millions of diamonds. A low tower at the right of that, had very much the same appearance. While I was thus standing with perfect ease and composure in the air, a wagon-load of people in the street below me, and a little to the left, stopped and looked up at me with seeming surprise. They saw me distinctly, as the light from the east shone in my face; but they did not turn around to see the wonderful and beautiful spectacle which I saw. Soon the light quietly faded away, and darkness came over the scene. With perfect quietness and peace of mind I came down to the earth. Something said to me, "This is a specimen of the brightness of '*His coming.*'" If those few rays of light shooting from the east were a specimen of the brightness of His coming, no created being can conceive of the flood of glory that will fill the world when the Son of God shall appear in the east in the sight of an astonished universe.

Affectionately, your father,

GEORGE N. BRIGGS.

Among copies of letters from his own pen, the following is without date or address, but from its tone, and from the frank and confidential character of the friendship the two had for each other, it is quite certain it was addressed to Mr. Abbott Lawrence:—

" DEAR L.:

" For some time past you have been much in my mind. So you shall have my thoughts on paper. *You* may think that I had better keep them to myself; but I know that there is not a particle of selfishness in what I propose to say; and as I am sure you will properly appreciate the motives which lead me to say it, I proceed. The world knows what you know — that you are very rich, that wealth is flowing into your coffers rapidly. What you will do with that wealth is to *you* and to the world a question of great consequence. To no human being are you accountable for what you will do with it; but to *Him* whose steward you are, like all the rest of us, you will *have an account* to give. Your reputation and fame are involved in the decision of this question. You have given evidence incontestable that you have no narrow or miserly heart. Should you go on as you have begun, and practice the same liberality that has hitherto marked your conduct, and at the close of your life leave your large estate to your family, the world will think well of you and your children will thank you. There is another course. You may leave to your children all that will be useful or safe to them, — and by no means need you deal narrowly with them, for you have an *excellent family;* but, after doing that, you can with the balance make yourself a *public benefactor,* to an extent that no man in this country or in any other has ever done. Suppose that in every county in your own Commonwealth, you establish and endow a permanent free school for the benefit of the indigent and orphans, to last forever, or found and endow other charitable or moral institutions in or out of your own Commonwealth, — what would be the effect of such a distribution of your *surplus* wealth, after reserving a munificent provision for your family? — I mean the effect upon your happiness, your fame, your descendants, and the world. To see such things done under *your own eye, while living,* would make you the *happiest* man on earth. It would make out your title as benefactor of mankind, erect monuments upon which your descendants, to the latest generations, would look with pride and gratitude. Who can *conceive* the perennial benefits flowing to the beneficiaries of such bounty? Why, my dear sir, generation after

24

generation would rise up and call you blessed, and their benedictions would come from the hearts of thousands who will be rescued from ignorance and its baleful consequences by your magnificent liberality. You would live forever fresh in the gratitude and admiration of your fellow-men. Contrast such fame with that of dying the richest man in New England, possessing a liberality such as I am proud to say belongs to many men in your city, and leaving the balance to be enjoyed or wasted by your descendants, as they shall be wise or foolish.

"I have, my dear L., described a course which would prove you to be the best and wisest man of your age, because the greatest benefactor of your age. These monuments of your munificence should be erected under your own direction while living, and not be left to be done by others with your money after you *can use it no longer.* Look at the folly of Stephen Girard in this respect. He *worshipped* his *mammon* while he lived, and folly and madness have rioted in his treasures since his death.

"These may seem to you strange suggestions, and it may seem more strange that they should be made in this manner. There is not another rich man on earth to whom they would be made by me. I know they will be received in the spirit in which they are made. I should rather have the *fame* which you have the power of giving yourself, than to be the desolator of Europe in the person of Napoleon Bonaparte, or to sit on the throne of the Cæsars.

"Sincerely your friend,

"GEO. N. BRIGGS."

CHAPTER XXIII.

IN the month of August, 1853, he was appointed by Governor Clifford, Judge of the Court of Common Pleas, — an honor which gratified both its recipient and the public. Of this appointment his daughter says : —

"The position was very agreeable, and seemed well. suited to the closing years of a life whose youth and early manhood had been spent amid exciting and important public events, and in the anxieties and toils of his profession.

"He entered upon these new responsibilities in a ripened maturity' of character and experience. During the term of six years, that he held the office of judge, there was little opportunity for distinction, but that his ability was quite an average is seen, as I am informed, from the proportion of his decisions that were sustained by the Supreme Court, as compared with those of his associates.

"In pronouncing sentence upon the convicted, it was remarkable how paternal and kind he invariably was, especially to the *young*, mingling admonition with encouragement to reformation, at the same time not abating, in the least, the severity and justice of the sentence. I well remember hearing.him sentence a boy to the House of Correction during one of his terms in Lawrence, and was strongly reminded of his expression and manner, when youth-

ful offenders in his own family, in days gone by, came under his
rebuke or displeasure. He was much amused by the reminiscences
the scene recalled, when I assured him I felt myself the culprit
again, and listened to him as if I were being talked to in the boy's
stead. He admonished him to take time, during his banishment
from friends, to think over his misconduct, to make resolutions to
reform when again at liberty, and to show by a better course of
conduct that he meant to be a better person; and he assured him
that time and reform would wipe away the remembrance of his
error from others, though he might always think of it with regret
and shame."

The death of his venerable and honored mother-in-law
was the occasion of this beautiful letter to his daughter.
She died at his home, where she had long lived : —

SPRINGFIELD, 4th Oct., 1854.

MY DEAR CHILD:

I have just left your mother, sad and lonely, though in health
better than could be expected after all she has passed through.
The funeral of the dear old woman took place on Friday. She
was quietly laid down by the side of her husband, in the town that
gave her birth nearly eighty-five years ago. I wish you and
Charles could have been at home, and looked once more upon that
dear and venerable face. There was nothing of death in it but the
coldness. The expression was one of peaceful loveliness. . . . . .
It is painful to realize that I can no more have the privilege of
caring for her and providing for her wants, and that I have not
done more in *little things* to add to her enjoyment. As in most
cases when our friends leave us, none of us knew how much we
loved and revered her till she was gone. Though her sufferings
were extreme she was patient, peaceful, and lovely, expressing
herself with the most affecting tenderness to all who were about
her. With your mother, the scenes of half a century crowd upon
and almost crush her. True and faithful has she been to that
mother. She will not lose her reward. . . . . .
Hereafter we shall occupy grandma's corner and be old folks.

Your mother has fitted up grandma's room, and we have moved into it. It is very pleasant. The thought that the good old woman is in heaven, hearing its music, seeing its beauties, and enjoying its happiness, makes every thought of her agreeable; but we have lost the blessed privilege of providing and caring for her any more.

Your affectionate father, .

GEORGE N. BRIGGS.

A brief note to his daughter, at Lawrence, is all the trace of him which his correspondence affords in the spring of 1854: —

PITTSFIELD, March 7, 1854.

MY DEAR DAUGHTER:

All well. Sleighing melting away. . . . . . Poor old Uncle P—ly died Saturday morning, and was buried Sabbath afternoon. He was poor and weak and of little account here, but I have no doubt the shining ones were waiting for him on the other side of the river, and joyfully took his spirit to the celestial city. His funeral was well attended, but not by many of the "refined." I never heard Dr. T. more interesting at a funeral, though I think funeral occasions are the places where he appears best. He said the Saviour preached to the poor. . . . . .

Tell George I thank him·for the "Household of Sir Thomas More." *I love Meg.*

YOUR LOVING FATHER.

Before the summer of this year was fairly throned upon the Berkshire hills, the hand of pain was laid heavily upon him. He was prostrated by a severe attack of inflammatory rheumatism. His faithful daughter was at his side in this time of trouble, and her hand draws the curtain which must otherwise have hidden from the public eye the clouded physical life of this noble sufferer, which was yet irradiated by the exceedingly pure light of the life within — the "life hid with Christ in God." She says, —

24*

"This illness produced a marked change in his appearance. Though not made infirm or lame, which is quite remarkable after such utter helplessness, he never regained the look of ruddy youthfulness and firmness which he kept so wonderfully till late in life; and he was long in creeping up to his average health and elasticity. Many weeks of uninterrupted intimacy with my father during this illness, gave me new impressions of his character.

"Always cherishing for him filial affection and respect, we had yet never assumed any relation but that of father and daughter. The ministry and waiting with him in his sick-chamber had made us *acquainted* with each other. We felt that we had become *friends.* We often discussed opinions and events on terms of equality that surprised us when we were separated. It is true, I never so honored and loved him, and never felt so intimately acquainted with him, as during this reunion. I wish it were possible to reproduce some of the incidents of this period. Though very desponding while suffering, he was patient and uncomplaining; and when the hours of repose and delicious ease and peace followed pain and restlessness, when he began to regain the power of motion, his tongue was freed in proportion as his spirits rose. Oh, the *long talks,* and reminiscences of early life and manhood, the *anecdotes* and sketches of public and social scenes at home and abroad! I thought, then, if it were possible, they should be preserved; but alas, that they are forever lost!

"One wakeful night I particularly remember, after watchers had ceased to be required, and little attention was needed, as usual I was resting in his room upon a lounge. He went from one incident and anecdote to another in a certain portion of his life, till we were *tired* out with laughing, and I confess I feared the effect of so much exhilaration upon him. He seemed so rejuvenated in spirit, after his sufferings, that the overflow of playfulness and fun was but the natural outlet of his happiness.

"The profound gratitude which he felt and expressed during this convalescence, and, indeed, when he was suffering most, for the countless blessings mingled with his affliction, was very marked. One of the first times he was able to sit up, after being lifted into his chair and drawn to the window, when he looked out upon the light and glory of the scene before him, he raised his full blue eyes, filled with reverence and fervor, to heaven, and said : ' Can it be that I do not *love Him !* ' As his letters show, he was very self-depreciating, and ever had many misgivings as to his own accept-ance in the sight of God, when he contemplated his own imper-fections in contrast with the spotless holiness of those who dwell in heaven. On one occasion, he had been considering the evi-dences he saw of his being a true child of God, — of having been ' born again,' — and seemed almost overwhelmed with doubt, when, bursting into tears, he said, ' If I know anything, I *know* I love *Christians.'*

"On one occasion, it became necessary to call in from his work the hired man, to assist in raising him, in order to arrange his pillows. He came into the chamber directly from his work, look-ing so brawny and healthful and strong, bringing the air and energy of the working-man into the quiet and hush of the sick-room — almost shocking, though it charmed the helpless invalid, who lay like an infant upon the bed. William, with instinctive ease and gentleness, raised the weary shoulders and replaced the sick man in *most sweet rest,* — and then, standing a moment and looking at him with real pity, the bronzed face bent over the white pillow and kissed the white forehead so reverently and tenderly, that we wept like children. It was one of those impulses which honor human nature. Father asked him to stay a moment as he was retiring, and presently asked, ' William, are you a Christian ? ' ' I am an unworthy member of ——'s church.' ' Then, if a *Chris-tian,* you are rich, William.' After a few words, he then repeated, in tones and expressions which were perfectly melting, the Scrip-ture, 'Come unto me all ye that labor and are heavy laden, and I will give you rest : take my yoke upon you and learn of me, for my yoke is easy and my burden light.'

"One day, after his hands had been powerless for a long while, he found himself able to lift his right hand from the wrist, and, turning it languidly, he looked at its movements, as if gratified with returning power over it, and said, ' It has never been raised against a human being.'

"When sufficiently recovered to see his friends, in the library,

one day Mr. Choate, who was staying in Lenox, drove up to see
him. The moment they met, my father's quick eye read the look
of surprise and pain which the great alteration in his appearance
instantly called up on the face of his friend. The look was quickly
followed by an illumination of Mr. Choate's wonderfully shadowed
and gloomy countenance, and a most inspiring salutation, with the
cordial greeting, 'How well you are looking!' We who saw this
meeting, and remembered the '*alarms*' that had shaken them when
they encountered the pestilence, were much entertained with a
scene so characteristic. After Mr. Choate took leave, my father,
with the melancholy and pleasure with which one faltering with
bodily weakness encounters the freedom and elasticity of health,
said, '*How splendidly he looked!*' — as he really did; for the mountains and pure air of Berkshire had vitalized him; and he never
seemed in more *superb tone* than on that day. My impression is
they never met after."

The date of the next letter is six months later, and just
on the verge of that lovely season when "the time of the
singing of birds is come, and the voice of the turtle is
heard in the land." Sugaring is a part of the April work
of those who live in maple groves; and there is playful
allusion to this rural process and to other very country-
like topics : —

PITTSFIELD, April 22, 1855.

MY DEAR CHILD:

. . . . . Since my return, a week ago, your mother has been
quite well; though when I came, she was nearly "*sugared off.*"
The sap has since been boiled out of the house. Henry got a
quantum-suff. without making much sugar. All glad sap is done
running. We have two calves, though I sold the old cow's
daughter a week ago; we could not raise it. *Lots* of milk; look
out for butter about these days. Turkeys run away dreadfully.
Hens lay lots; fifteen chickens in two broods; occasionally we
have a mammoth great egg, and then a mammoth little one.

Attending court in Springfield, he writes to Lawrence : —

SPRINGFIELD, 6th June, 1855.

MY DEAR DAUGHTER:

. . . . . The heavenly weather, after this most refreshing
rain, I suppose you have in Lawrence as well as we here. Our
little place at home never looked more charming than when I left
on Monday morning. If you could see my acre-and-a-half of
wheat, I *guess* you would think flour will fall soon. Henry's garden looks finely. The good pear-tree promises much fruit. The
corn looks well, and the pastures and meadows are clad in rich
green. I only regret that I cannot be there to enjoy it all, and
more yet that you and Charles are not on, and owning the Merriam
farm,[1] taking comfort and getting health. I am having a pleasant
time here, and am staying at the "Massasoit." The night before
last I was sitting in the parlor, talking with ——, and in the other
part of the room was a party from Boston, very respectable, and,
as the *sequel* shows, very *sensible*. Soon after they left the parlor
to go to their apartments I followed, and, just as I came up nearly
to them at the foot of the stairs, the gentleman remarked, " He
was one of the best Governors that Massachusetts ever had." At
that moment he saw me, and the conversation suddenly ceased.
Now, I was vain enough to suppose that the remark applied to *us;*
and I certainly felt more gratified than I should to have heard him
say, " He was a *scaliwag* of a Governor." To *deserve* the good
opinion of my fellow-men, I am willing to confess, has with me,
all my life, been a strong desire; but to have accomplished so
little to entitle me to their good opinion, is a matter of deep regret.
There is one thing, however, so infinitely more important than the
good opinion of all the world, that if through abounding mercy I
can secure it, all else sinks into nothing in comparison, — that is,
at last to hear those words of eternal blessedness and glory from
the Judge who sitteth upon the throne of the universe: " Well
done, good and faithful servant." Oh! will these ears hear those

[1] An adjoining property, just nearer the village.

words? That they may be addressed to me and all the dear ones I love, is the great desire of my heart, and my daily prayer.

Affectionately, your father,

GEORGE N. BRIGGS.

Early in the winter of 1856 his eldest son, who was recently married, took his lovely young bride to the far South, hoping in the genial climate of Key West, or of Cuba, to find that balm which should check the work of disease in her delicate and fragile frame. The receipt of a letter from his son, with allusions to soft airs and bright verdure and magnificent bloom, suggested to him strange contrasts with the temperatures and aspects around him. He replies to his son's letter from Lenox, where, in the very heart of winter, he was holding court. His reminiscences of that severe winter have special interest for the biographer, writing at this moment in the very heart of a Berkshire winter, and with stinging recollections, not yet a week old, of a temperature, not, indeed, quite equal to that of 1857, but more than twenty below zero : —

LENOX, Jan. 57, 1857.

MY DEAR SON:

Henry came down to-day, and brought your last letter, which gave me great pleasure. The weather for the past ten days has been without a precedent in this latitude. On Saturday, at home, at 7 A. M., the mercury stood at thirty degrees below zero! Dr. Kane's arctic experiences have not much to brag of. Ten degrees below is not regarded as worth an extra garment; but this fellow, that goes down to thirty, puts his cold fingers upon the vegetables in many cellars, where he has not been in the habit of intruding. What a contrast this state of things with the mild, smiling, roseate condition of affairs in which you and Nellie and Cousin M. are regaling yourselves. You are considerably troubled with northers, you say. I wish *we* could have a *southern* breath from your far-off island upon us for a few days. A few weeks, however, will set it all right, and cause beauty and fragrance and joy to smile where now snow and ice and chills prevail.

Nothing new in these Greenland regions. The religious interest continues in Pittsfield. Poor old Uncle Tom, of the cemetery-gate, has moved into the cemetery grounds, and laid down to sleep after about a century of toil outside. He died last Saturday morning. He is believed to be one of the subjects of the revival. How amazing that mercy which, after a hundred years of ignorance, and in disregard from his fellow-men, finds the aged sinner, pardons him, and takes him up to wear one of those crowns of righteousness which the Saviour has in reserve for those who love his appearing. . . . . .

Tell Nelly she must be resolute and active, as though she were well, and as prudent and careful as if she were an invalid. I hope cousin Mary will not think of joining Walker in his present fortunes. I should much prefer to see her joined to a medical gentleman from the border of a northern lake. We think and talk much of you, and hope by the blessing of God, to meet you when the beauties of your climate shall be spread over our mountains and valleys again.

Affectionately, your father,

GEO. N. BRIGGS.

With the summer the invalid daughter-in-law came back, refreshed and somewhat invigorated, but with a hold upon life scarcely more assuring to those who loved her than when she went away. Before the next winter spread its white robes over the hills and vales, she had found, even amid the weakness and fading beauty of this life, a new and wonderful life — the life of faith in the Son of God.

The glad, grateful father thus acknowledges his son's letter, communicating the tidings of her baptism and admission to the church : —

WORCESTER, Dec. 22, 1857.

MY DEAR SON:

We received and read your letter of yesterday with equal surprise and pleasure. We rejoice greatly to learn that Nelly has put on Christ by following Him in baptism, and thus obeying His command. Having taken the yoke of the Saviour, I have no doubt she will find it easy and delightful to bear, and she will find rest to her soul. Those who learn of Him will never be disappointed, but will find fulness of joy. I am satisfied that no one can know the calm and holy joy experienced by those who thus obey and follow the Saviour but those who do it.

I am sure Nelly would bear her testimony to the truth of this assertion. I hope she will have the constant presence of the Master, and that her path will shine brighter and brighter. The good Shepherd has promised to gather the lambs in his arms, and to carry them in his bosom. Not one of his thousand blessed promises has ever failed. Your mother and I feel a new debt of gratitude to our Father in Heaven, that another member of our dear family-band has taken a place in the church of Christ, and enrolled her name among His professed followers. May she adorn that profession more than any of us have done. Though the youngest, may she be an example to the gray-headed ones. The greatest happiness I could hope to enjoy on earth, would be to have the assurance that every member of our family was a sincere and faithful follower of Jesus.

> " That soon or late we reach that coast,
>   O'er life's rough ocean driven,
> We should rejoice no wanderer lost —
>   A family in Heaven."

I am sure the news that dear Nelly had been entirely restored to health, would not have given me the satisfaction that I realized from the announcement of your letter. She might have had health of body, and her soul been left out of the ark of safety. Now I hope she has entered that ark, and is prepared for good or ill-health; for life or death. I wish we might have witnessed the solemn ceremony. We send love to you and Nelly, Charles and Harriet.

Affectionately, your father,

G. N. BRIGGS.

His judicial career is thus graphically and faithfully depicted by the hand of one[1] who not only knew him intimately, but who also had, under a reorganization of the judiciary of Massachusetts, personal experience of the duties and responsibilities of the same position. It will appropriately close this chapter, devoted to his life as a judge : —

"Soon after the completion of his duties as a member of the Constitutional Convention of 1853, Mr. Briggs was appointed a Justice of the Court of Common Pleas. He held his seat upon the Bench during the existence of that Court, a period of about six years.

"Those who were intimately acquainted with him during that part of his professional life in which he gave his time entirely to legal practice, were impressed with the belief that he possessed, in a remarkable degree, some of the most essential qualities of a judge. His quick and clear apprehensions of the facts of a case, his accurate recollections and statements of the evidence in his arguments to the jury; his fairness in giving to his opponents the benefit of all the testimony bearing in their favor; his ability to perceive the real points upon which his case must turn, in the light of the legal principles applicable to the facts; his candor in waiving advantages merely technical, led his friends to believe, that notwithstanding his skill and eloquence as an advocate, his true place would eventually be found upon the Bench.

"But after his election to Congress, and during the twelve years of his Congressional career, and the seven years succeeding them, in which he was Governor of Massachusetts, he was considered as having passed from the law into the arena of political employment, and it was hardly expected that he would return to his profession, either as an advocate or as a Judge. Although, while a Representative in Congress, he continued his professional practice during the intervals between the sessions, he entirely relinquished it upon his first election as Governor. He resumed it again, after

[1] Hon. Julius Rockwell.

voluntarily retiring from political employments, and thus gave
practical evidence of the sincerity of his frequent expressions of
his respect and love for the noble profession in which he had laid
the foundation of his reputation, and from which he had been removed to the high political stations, where he had perfected that
reputation, and made it a part of the history of the State, and of
the nation.

"After Mr. Briggs appeared again in the courts, he exhibited
the same qualities which had characterized his early professional
life, the same ready appreciation of the facts of a case, the same
clear and accurate recollections and statements of the evidence,
the same courteous and generous treatment of his opponents, and
the same power to seize upon the strong and real points of the
case.

"His political pursuits had drawn neither his affections nor his
attentions away from the principles of the legal profession, but
had furnished him with many opportunities for their application.
Yet he was justly aware that the law is jealous of its votaries,
demanding their exclusive attention, and slow to pardon the di-
version of any of the best years of life from legal studies. Upon
his return to the practice of the profession, he employed much of
his time in the perusal of the best treatises, and of judicial reports.
With unaffected diffidence, yet sustained by the confidence of professional friends, he entered upon his judicial duties. In this
sphere, he sustained and increased his general reputation in this
Commonwealth. No party, no counsellor at law, no juror ever
doubted his perfect fairness and impartiality in the trial of cases,
in his rulings upon questions of law, in his instructions to the
jury, in his presentations of contested questions to the ultimate
tribunal for revision and final decision. It is confidently believed,
that the profession throughout the State were satisfied that the
impressions of his personal associates in his early professional
career were correct.

"Mr. Briggs, as a lawyer and as a judge, may safely be presented as in the most essential particulars, a model to young men.
While at the bar, he was kind and courteous to his brethren of the
profession, and to the Court. While on the Bench, he was affable

and courteous in his demeanor to the members of the bar, old and young, experienced and inexperienced.

"During the intermissions of professional duty, he was the most agreeable companion that could be found. Many, very many in the various counties of the State will recollect, with unalloyed pleasure, those evenings of pleasant and instructive conversation, during the terms of court, which they were permitted to enjoy with Judge Briggs.

"The Court of Common Pleas had jurisdiction not only of civil actions, but also of criminal offences. In this part of his duty, the qualities of mind and heart, which characterized Judge Briggs, in all the periods of his life, were often exhibited in a most striking manner. His generous sympathies were never forgotten, even in the stern discharge of his official duty, in passing sentence upon convicted criminals. He remembered always, that the most hardened criminal might be susceptible to kind and Christian sympathy and advice, and that young offenders might be encouraged to reformation. Many instances are remembered, when the Christian judge accompanied the inevitable sentence of the law with kind words and advice. His manner on these occasions will long be remembered by those who witnessed them. His countenance, the tones of his voice, and his whole manner were like those of a father reproving and advising an erring child; and in some instances there is reason to believe, these unpremeditated and heart-felt addresses had an influence for great good upon those to whom they were made."

CHAPTER XXIV.

FOR a period of five years the beloved ex-Governor of Massachusetts had worn the judicial robes with the same single-mindedness and unfeigned love of justice which characterized all his life, whether public or private. Without intentional, and without indeed real disparagement to others who have worthily administered the decisions of the law in this Commonwealth, since his retirement from the Bench, it is only just to say that the State was the loser by the act which removed him from the Bench.

In 1858, under the administration of Governor Banks, a great and radical change in the judiciary of Massachusetts was effected. The Court of Common Pleas was abolished, and the Superior Court organized in its stead. Whatever advantage was gained by this change, much was lost in the needless removal with it of a bench of efficient and honored judges, not one of whom was appointed to the new court, although its functions and jurisdiction were almost identical with those of the Court of Common Pleas.

It is not to be supposed that this sudden stroke fell upon Judge Briggs without the effect of disturbance and annoyance. That he bore these without complaint, is enough to be said in his praise. He did feel the blow, but probably less than others felt it for him, and quite as little, perhaps not so much, for himself as he did for his senior associate, Chief Justice Mellen, whose removal from a place he so greatly honored, was a real grief to his friend.

The end of his judicial service was the end, also, of his public life, except in those aspects of it which were purely philanthropic. At the mature age of sixty-four, and while his natural strength was not abated, and the force of his strong mind not impaired, he finished his work for the Commonwealth, which had honored him for a quarter of a century, and which he had, for all that period, honored in return, by unsullied patriotism, by unswerving fealty to her interests, and by ungrudging toils for her advantage.

He was now and henceforward to work for her in less conspicuous places, and upon less public arenas than those he had occupied. No one who knew him, no one who has formed a just estimate of his unselfish character, will question for a moment, that it was the sphere only which was changed, not the man, not his motive, not the measure of his zeal.

His life became, indeed, richer from the day of his retirement from all public office, in those characteristics and products which most embellish character. He cultivated thenceforward, with greater assiduity, resulting from his greater leisure, the graces and forces alike of Christian benevolence and labor. Never lacking in these through all his service as a statesman, as a Chief Magistrate, as a Judge, he accumulated them grandly in his undistinguished

25*

guise as a private citizen. To this position he was scarcely permitted, perhaps, in one sense, to recede from the public gaze, which followed him eagerly, respectfully, lovingly, into the beautiful fastnesses of the Berkshire hills, and which, when he was drawn out from his farm and his village quiet, to the platforms of great moral and religious societies, rested upon him with admiring earnestness.

To preserve unity in these memorials, the biographer has hitherto kept his public life in view, almost to the exclusion of those accessory labors which were not official, and which were strictly incidental to his position. All through his Congressional career, and no less comprehensively in the terms of his magistracy and judicial service, he did a vast amount of work aside from his public duty, and to this work the Christian reader will assign a measure of importance and a meed of honor, greater than that with which he will invest the official services already reviewed.

It is the crowning excellence, the highest glory of the life and memory of Governor Briggs, that he was, in the fullest meaning of the lofty phrase, a Christian patriot and philanthropist.

His religion vitalized his patriotism, and controlled his philanthropy. He might have been a patriot and a philanthropist without being a Christian, but the difference between his life-work and its results in that case, and these as they now appear, would be so great, that the most superficial glance would perceive it. As they are, they are most beautiful, most abiding, most radiant in their heavenward aspect; as they would have been without Christian love and faith to direct and energize them—they would have had but one side, bright, but evanescent, fair, but passing away. As it is, they are treasures and memories for the home altar, and for the church altar — when they might have been commemorated only in the secular annals of the State and the nation. They have now a double applause — the acclamations of a grateful Commonwealth, and the more enduring affection of a Christian community ; of which if only one could be secured, the latter is immeasurably to be preferred.

The earnestness with which Governor Briggs advocated the cause of temperance, makes his labors in that department of philanthropic service worthy of special review. These labors were indeed contemporaneous with other works of Christian charity, and in the lives of common men would never perhaps bear isolation without disadvantage. But in his case they will not be justly estimated without it.

He was closely identified with that great moral movement against the curse of drunkenness, which marks the second quarter of the passing century, and which in the grand proportions to which it soared, and still more in the wonderful results it effected, will be memorable in history as a mighty reformation.

It began humbly, as such moral movements generally do. The current which eventually poured over the land with the resistless sweep of Niagara's floods, was in the beginning but a trickling drop from the crevice, or a tiny spring gushing up from the land. It gathered force as it flowed. It swept the hamlets, the villages, the towns, the cities, and thus embraced the land within its blessed, and almost omnipotent tide of purgation and purification — whose rolling and resistless surges carried with them those pest houses of existing society, drinking shops of every grade, and finally, the distilleries of the liquid death themselves. The work accomplished was **grand and memorable**, and although

to-day the philanthropist and the Christian look, with saddened heart and tearful eyes, upon the new and far-spread-
ing ravages of intemperance, and feel that the plague was
only stayed, and not uprooted, it is impossible to calculate
the sum of deadly woes which the temperance reformation,
of 'he period alluded to, actually cancelled for that generation and for the succeeding one, which indeed but for its
beneficent sway, might have been born to an inheritance
of physical and moral degradation.

The name of George Nixon Briggs is inscribed upon the
roll of the earliest and boldest and most persistent and
most successful of the champions who went out, in the
interests of desolated families and blighted homes, against
the dragon of strong drink. If he had no philanthropic
record behind that of his devotion and sacrifices in the
cause of temperance, his name and memory would still be
dear to those who love their fellow-men. It would deserve
to be recorded, if not above, yet not below Abou Ben
Adhem's, on the angel's scroll.

When he first drew his sword in this cause — which was
never afterwards sheathed till death found its scabbard
again — he had no inducement to do so save that alone
which sprang from a benevolent heart, under the influence
of Christian principle. He saw the condition of the country
— its desolation and swift coming-doom from the preva-
lence of drunkenness, — and he wept over it.

His own habits of abstinence long ante-dated the great
movement against the evil. They were the result of principle, originating from his experience in early manhood of
the insidious power of appetite over the will.

It is interesting, in a review like this, to catch the first
glimpses of a great progress — to see, as it were, the very

first spark struck out by the dint of the young hero's sword in the conflict into which he went at the bidding, and for the behalf of suffering, weeping, perishing humanity. This first glimpse we may fortunately obtain. It was at Lanesboro', the scene of his student-life, of his resolute strength, nourished on poverty, and cheered by sympathy, of his early religious zeal, of his young and only love; it was there he fleshed his blade for the first, in the great battle with the dragon.

Strange as it may appear, the narrower scene of this first encounter was a small tavern. A temperance meeting was held there, the first of its kind. It was in 1828, far back into the twilight of the great reformation. He had drawn up a pledge to be considered. It was no compromise with the danger. It declared total abstinence from " ardent spirits."

Mr. H., a lawyer present, opposed the adoption of a pledge so broad. He said it was going too far; that there were times when it was necessary to use a little — when washing sheep, in haying, or harvesting; in winter, when cutting wood upon the hills. He did not deny the need of temperance, but total abstinence was an extreme to be avoided.

Mr. Briggs insisted that the only *safety* was in letting it entirely alone as a beverage, that a little, occasionally, was not necessary, but injurious, and he used the following illustration : —

"A rattlesnake lies here on the floor. He is quiet. One man says: 'I can touch him. He won't *bite me.* I am not afraid.' He is told not to do it. There is danger if he touches him; he is safe if he lets him alone. He replies: 'I can take care of myself, I am not afraid of the snake.' Remonstrance is vain; he stoops, he touches him; the snake strikes the presumptuous hand with his venomous fangs; the man dies."

As Mr. Briggs closed his speech, a man, partially intoxicated, who lived near the Hancock line, leaned forward into the room, and, with unsteady speech said, "Squire Curtis' (the chairman), Squire H. has 'spressed my mind 'zacly." A loud laugh followed; when Squire H. arose, and said: "I knew that man when he was a sober, respectable citizen, a man of property. His appearance here to-night has destroyed all my argument. By taking a little occasionally, he has been brought to this condition. I go for the pledge."

That was a bold stroke, and effectively served. Who could see it and doubt that there was a young and able champion springing up to oppose intemperance!

When he was a young man, he used tobacco and snuff, and of the latter, unusual quantities. Perceiving that these habits were injurious to him, he resolved to abandon them. His abstinence from snuff occasioned a severe illness of several days, and consequent depression of spirits. But he was firm in his purpose, and he conquered himself completely; and alleged afterwards, that "there can be no excuse for any person falling into the use of tobacco, and that its use is both unnatural and injurious."

The following extract from a letter to his sons, though written several years later, while he was in Washington, will find an appropriate place in connection with this reminiscence: —

"MY DEAR SONS:

. . . . . "Before I left home, some one told me the boys in Mr. Hotchkin's school had got into the habit of smoking cigars.

I hope neither of you will be so unwise or indiscreet as to allow yourselves to be led into so foolish and bad a habit. I should be very unhappy to know that was the case. There is no excuse for any person to use tobacco, least of all for boys. I beg of you, my dear boys, if you have any regard for your own welfare, and the feelings and wishes of your absent father, never permit tobacco to enter your mouth in the form of a cigar, or in any other shape." . .

To go back a little, chronologically, of the occasion to which allusion has just been made, there lies reserved from his correspondence when he was in Congress, here and there a letter, designed especially to illustrate the phase of his life now under contemplation. One of these letters was written about a year after the Congressional Temperance Society was organized. It was an eloquent commentary on the wisdom and necessity of that organization, which, alas! was not effectual in keeping all the members of the National Legislature out of the way of ruin. Intemperance had, indeed, a fearful hold upon those who of all other men needed to be self-controlled, that they might bring all their faculties unimpaired to the great work of legislation for the Republic and the States, whose servants they were. In not a few letters home from the National Capitol, did Mr. Briggs record and deplore the ravages and wrecks of body and mind wrought by strong drink, within the halls of Congress. Here follows one of these sad memorials : —

WASHINGTON, April, 1834.

MY DEAR WIFE:

. . . . . . We have had to perform to-day the melancholy duty of burying another member — General B., from South Carolina. The circumstances of his death rendered the occurrence, if possible, more shocking than was the death of Judge Bouldin.[1]

1 *Vide* Chapter X.

Just before sundown last night he shot himself in a room, with a pistol. He has for years indulged in habits of intemperance. Like many other unfortunate victims of appetite, his indulgences were periodical. During these spells he became partially distracted, and ferocious. Some time before he came here, last fall, he had united himself to the Methodist Society, not because he professed really to have become religious, but in the hope that, by this means, he might be placed under restraints that would help him break from his vicious habits, and finally become a Christian; but, unfortunately, the power of appetite and the force of temptation proved too strong for resolutions thus taken.

For several weeks past he has been extremely irregular, and, most of the time, mad with drunkenness. Alternating between penitence and passion, reason and insanity, he has given himself and those about him a great deal of trouble. When not under the exciting influence of spirits or laudanum — which, during his debauches, he took in great quantities — he was subjected to the most mortifying reflections. For a few days past he became quite feeble, was confined to his house, and promised that he would drink no more. Yesterday, after the House adjourned, and after dinner, Governor Murphy — a member from Alabama — went into his room, and at his request read a letter to him from his wife. It was full of kind messages, and expressed the most affectionate solicitude for his welfare. Probably, having seen in the public prints enough to satisfy her that he had fallen into his besetting sin, she wished by the language of soothing kindness to reclaim him, or, if he had been reclaimed, to give him consolation and solace. This outpouring of feeling from the heart of his pious and affectionate wife, was too much for him. It overcame him; and, while his friend was reading the letter, he wept like a child.

Doubtless a consciousness of the turpitude of his conduct, which made him unworthy of the warm and devoted affection of his absent and injured wife, threw all the passions and feelings of his soul into commotion; and, in the tumult of their rage, he suddenly arose from his bed, and walked to a bureau in the room, and, although Governor Murphy was looking directly at him all the while (B. kept his back towards him, so as to hide from his view the real object), he took a loaded pistol from his drawer, instantly put it to his head, just above his ear, and drove the ball through his brain. His friend saw the barrel of the pistol gleam as he raised it; but the motion was so sudden that he could not interfere. He fell instantly dead.

How great is our obligation to that beneficent God, who not only surrounds us with the multitudes of His mercies, but who by His grace saves us from the madness and fury of our own passions and propensities.

General B. was one of the largest men I ever saw. He was more than six feet high, and weighed over three hundred pounds. When himself, he was an intelligent gentleman, a noble, amiable, and generous man, and a devoted friend. When under the influence of stimulants, he was a ferocious savage. Let those who advocate the use of ardent spirits, count up its benefits in every possible form, and put them in the scale against this dismal case, produced directly by its use, and see which end of the beam will preponderate.

May peace, health, and happiness fill your cup. Good night.

Thine ever,

G. N. BRIGGS.

Not a twelvemonth later, another of these ghastly sacrifices to the Moloch of strong drink occurred in Congress. It forms the melancholy theme of a second letter from Mr. Briggs to his wife, and was one of the events which fired his soul and made his tongue fervid with that eloquence, before which all classes of his auditors were powerfully moved : —

WASHINGTON, 29 Jan., 1835.

MY DEAR WIFE:

The business of the House to-day has been interrupted by the death of a member — Mr. D., of South Carolina. He has not been in the House during the session. He was sick before he left home, and detained long on the way here. He has been in the city perhaps three weeks. His disease was induced, continued, and consummated by intemperance. It is said that since he has been in this city he has drank a quart of brandy per day. He was a man of brilliant and shining genius, and of a generous, noble, and manly heart, but with all these excellent and high qualities, he lived and died like a fool.

Humanity must drop a tear at his fall from that high and palmy state where his talents and noble qualities had placed him here; but not at his death, for hope of reformation had ceased, and the longer he lived the deeper he would have sunk in shame and ignominy. I should think him forty-five years old — a man of fine face, person, and manners; who by nature had a fine constitution. I am glad to know that he is a bachelor, and leaves no widow and orphans to mourn over his folly and shame, and lament his untimely fate. What a lesson such a case presents to those who yield their reason to their appetite! "Lead me not into temptation, but deliver me from evil," is a prayer that should be always rising from the lips of poor erring mortals. May He whose power and grace is alone sufficient to save us, keep me in the way of truth and peace. May He have you all in His holy keeping.

Thine forever,

G. N. BRIGGS.

It was not long after this that he adopted the principle of total abstinence, and on every occasion afforded him, earnestly advocated it. The meeting-houses and school-houses of Berkshire rang with his manly appeals and his ardent eloquence in the good cause.

From the time of his first entering Congress until he retired from its councils, he was there, as elsewhere, a faithful advocate of temperance. Early in the year 1833, the Congressional Temperance Society was organized; and he was one of the four members of its executive committee. His associates on this committee were the Hon. Theodore Frelinghuysen of New Jersey, the Hon. George Blair of Tennessee, and the Hon. E. Cook of Ohio.

As an illustration of the power of political preferences over the moral inclination and judgment of men, it may be related here that the young Berkshire lawyer, when he was nominated for Congress, lost the vote of his friend, and of his father's friend no less, — the venerable John Leland, — notwithstanding the latter's admiration of his temperance principles, because he suspected he would be a Clay-man in Congress.

Soon after the election was held he met the Elder; and the eccentric old gentleman thus addressed him : " Well, George, you have ridden a cold-water horse to Washington. I am glad you are elected ; but I voted against you, as I was afraid if the election of President went into the House, you would vote for Henry Clay, of Kentucky ; " to which the young representative replied, " You are right, Elder ; I should."

Mr. Briggs was not (for some unrecorded reason) at the meeting of the first National Temperance Convention, held at Philadelphia in May of 1833 ; but at the second convention, held three years afterwards, at Saratoga, his presence, his voice, and his zeal did much to animate the friends of the cause. At this time he took a very decided stand in favor of " total abstinence from every intoxicating beverage," which was then the advanced doctrine of the reform, leaving the original pledge far behind. All the great advocates were not yet up to this point; and Mr. Briggs discussed with a learned professor and divine, the philosophy, morality, and scriptural obligation of the new ground, so eloquently and effectively, that he greatly helped forward the advance movement.

One, who was present upon that occasion, furnishes for these pages the following reminiscences : —

" We call up the yet fresh remembrance of the first time we ever saw Governor Briggs, as furnishing at least one culmination of the eloquence that has been awarded to him.

" It was at a National Temperance Convention, held at Saratoga more than twenty years ago. There was in the convention a large representation of distinguished talents; for it was at that stage of the temperance movement when the advance position was being taken of total abstinence, not only from alcoholic, but from all fermented intoxicated drinks. On the one side were ranged Professor — now Bishop — Potter, and other able conservative men, who were doubtful of the proposed innovation. On the other side were equally able, more bold, progressive men. The discussion rose high; when, at its full tide, near the close of the second day's forenoon session of the convention, a middle-aged, plain-looking man, wearing then, as ever, a simple black cravat without a collar, full-chested, and of a ' ruddy countenance,' arose in one corner, under the gallery of the old Presbyterian Church, and, first in plain, direct argument, then in impassioned and mighty appeal, bore down on the side of total abstinence from all that intoxicates, as the only safe and true ground for all the friends of temperance reform. It is safe to say (all who with us remember that speech — and those who heard have never forgotten it — will second the claim), the hearts of the assembly were swayed by that utterance as the trees of the wood are before a strong wind. The highest tribute to it came at the opening of the afternoon session, from Dr. Potter, who, feeling his position to be fairly assailed, immediately took the floor with the opening remark: ' I had not intended to trespass further on the time of the convention, but for the very gallant assault made on me by the gentleman from Massachusetts.' Inquiry was alive, at the close of the forenoon session, as to who that plain but powerful pleader for total abstinence was. ' That,' said Judge Culver, our informant, ' is the member of Congress from the Berkshire District; his name is Briggs — George N. Briggs.' It was enough to place him as a landmark in my memory; and the remembrance of that occasion, often since, has been revived on hearing him speak. His eloquence not only carried captive the understanding, but the hearts, of those he addressed."

CHAPTER XXV.

IN 1840, the famous "Washingtonian" movement was
one of the most extraordinary impulses of the tidal
wave of reform which was sweeping over the land.
It reached the very lowest classes and cases of inebri-
ates. Multitudes of these crowded the meetings,
which were held almost nightly in many places. In Washington, this new phase of the conflict enlisted all the sympathies of Mr. Briggs, who went — in answer to every summons, to the extent of his strength and time — to hasten
forward the work, to cheer the repentant, to arouse the
stupid, and to lift up the fallen and helpless, by his powerful and persuasive strains.

He did not intermit these labors while there was scope
and occasion for their continuance. It was early in 1842
that he had the extreme happiness of stretching out his
hand effectually to a brother Congressman. The Hon.
Thomas F. Marshall, of Kentucky, was so much a slave to
intemperate habits, that there seemed little doubt but he
would fall a victim to the maddening lust. His brilliant
talents, his fascinating oratory, his personal attractions,

created a profound interest in his case ; and all that friends could do to divorce him from the fiery cup was done, without avail. On the 8th of January he entered the hall of the House in a state of intense nervous excitement and terror, and, rushing almost madly across the hall, to where Mr. Briggs was seated, exclaimed, " Briggs, you must write me a pledge, that I may sign, and live ! "

Mr. Briggs told his daughter, subsequently, that he thought Mr. Marshall was beside himself, and was amazed at his strange request. He said that he perceived, however, the signs of profound distress and earnestness on his fine face, and, without hesitation, he wrote the following pledge : —

" I pledge myself never to use intoxicating liquors as a drink, and request that my name be entered as a member of the Washington Temperance Society."

To this pledge Mr. Marshall instantly subscribed, with a trembling hand and in irregular characters, his name, " Thomas F. Marshall, M. C., Ky. ; " and, having done so, said, " I feel better now ! "

Of his appearance that night at a public meeting, and his repetition of his pledge, the following letter furnishes the interesting details : —

WASHINGTON, 8th Jan., 1842.

MY DEAR WIFE :

It is Saturday night; and, as I am going to our evening meeting, I must be short. Last night I attended a temperance meeting, at which Mr. Marshall, of Kentucky, whose habits you knew something of last summer, came forward and took the pledge, and made a short, but brilliant and touching speech. He is a genius of the first order; but was on the brink of the precipice over which so many have fallen. His case has excited more interest than that of any individual I have ever known. I think he will hold out. Heaven grant he may.

Thine,

G. N. BRIGGS.

In a speech which Mr. Briggs made immediately after Mr. Marshall's eloquent confessions and pledges and appeals, he used these memorable words : " From this hour a new era in the cause of temperance may be dated." To adopt here the language of another : [1] —

" A new spring was, indeed, at once given to the cause. The old Congressional Society, formed ten years before on the ardent-spirit pledge, had died out; and on the 9th of February a new Congressional Temperance Society was organized on total abstinence principles, and Mr. Briggs was chosen president. On the 25th of February a large meeting was held in the Capitol. The magnificent hall was filled to overflowing. Mr. Briggs made an address, in which he gave a history of the old society, which, 'with a pledge in one hand and a bottle of champagne in the other, had died of intemperance.' He was followed by many great men, — Mr. Williams of Connecticut, Mr. Fillmore of New York, Mr. Gilmer of Virginia, Mr. Burnell of Massachusetts, Dr. Sewall, John Hawkins, and Hon. Thomas F. Marshall. Eighty signed the pledge. Soon after, Mr. Briggs retired from Congress; and, losing its head, the society declined. No sooner was he placed in the Governor's chair in Massachusetts than he was chosen President of the Massachusetts Legislative Temperance Society. His speech on the occasion was one of his most eloquent. He hoped before the session closed every name would be enrolled. ' We shall not,' said he, ' do so much for the public good by legislating, as we could by contributing to the temperance reform. If we should all lend our exertions, we might soon say, — there is no drunkard in Massachusetts; there is no wretched family in our State. We would live, then, with but little legislation.' During his whole gubernatorial term, he was most active in sustaining

---

[1] Rev. Dr. Marsh, Secretary of the American Temperance Union.

the temperance reform. We well remember seeing him lead the great procession of reformed men in their mighty march around Boston."

From the day upon which Mr. Marshall signed the pledge, Mr. Briggs felt for him the deepest and most fraternal interest, and was everything to him that a friend could be. Some months later, he received from him the following note, which shows how deeply Mr. Briggs had touched the nature of his friend : —

WASHINGTON, May 2, 1842.

DEAR BRIGGS:

The rain, and other things, prevented my calling. I shall start at six o'clock in the morning. If you love me, follow me at four. I will wait in Philadelphia till Wednesday morning, and thus we will enter the great city together. I shall be lost and dumb without you. Come on, and take care of your proselyte.

Yours, sincerely and always,

THOMAS F. MARSHALL.

Before leaving Washington, at the close of his Congressional life, he received from the Freemen's Total Abstinence Society of the city, an exquisitely-wrought massive gold medal, bearing inscriptions of respect and affection from a large number of his friends with whom he had labored. He always called this and other similar medals, his *crown jewels;* and, when a young girl, it was his daughter's pride to wear one of them, bearing a star in its centre, as a pendent to her bracelet.

This beneficent movement reached, as before remarked, all conditions of the people ; and, perhaps, no single class secured more of its inestimable blessings than the colored people. They were enthusiastic in their efforts to promote the cause among themselves. The letter which follows was written by one of their number, of pure African blood, — which, both in sentiment and style, would do credit to a far more privileged man : —

Troy, July 28, 1845.

To his Excellency Governor Briggs:

Sir, — I have thought it would not be altogether uninteresting to you to receive a little information in regard to the progress of temperance among the people of color. The labor which you have given to this enterprise among all classes of people, both at home and abroad, has emboldened me to address you. If I mistake not, it is as gratifying to the patriot and philanthropist to hear the gurgling of the sweet waters of temperance flowing along the lowly valley, as it is to behold the same streams dashing from the high mountains.

About five years ago several of the temperance men among our people from New York, New Jersey, Massachusetts, and Connecticut, assembled for the purpose of uniting their efforts for the general advancement of the cause. They succeeded in forming the "Delevan Temperance Union." These men immediately went to work in their own neighborhoods, and invited all to come to the crystal waters. Last year the annual meeting was held at the foot of the Catskill Mountains. There were met four thousand sons and daughters of temperance, having good music and appropriate banners. The meeting was held in one of the beautiful groves in that vicinity; "such were God's first temples." It was a happy meeting. A king's palace could not have added anything to our joy. Harmony, peace, and good-will pervaded every rank. We drank from the limpid streams that came leaping down from the glorious mountain whose head is hid in the purple clouds. This year our annual meeting was held in the city of Hudson, and the most moderate estimation made by eye-witnesses has placed the number at eight thousand. Beautiful banners and enchanting music were not wanting. Three steamers, well loaded, moored at the dock that day. The convention was held in the park in front of the Court House. A large concourse of citizens greeted us with their presence. Addresses were delivered by speakers from

New York, Philadelphia, Albany; from Ohio and New Jersey. The singing was led by Richard Thompson, of Albany. There was no rioting, no profane or otherwise indecent language; neither was there an accident of any kind. " Old Berkshire" was most gloriously represented that day. There are about one hundred and fifty societies belonging to the Union, comprising about ten thousand people. The Hudsonians did much to make the meeting pleasant. The progress of the temperance cause among our people, together with the other signs of the times, assure me that "Ethiopia will soon stretch out her hands unto God."

Will the Governor be pleased to accept my solicitude for his health, and permit me to subscribe myself, with respect, his obedient servant,

HENRY H. GARNET,
President Delevan Temperance Union.

To this interesting letter. Governor Briggs sent the following reply : —

PITTSFIELD, 7th Aug., 1845.

FRIEND GARNET :

I have your esteemed favor of 28th of July. I can hardly express the pleasure which your account of the progress of temperance among the people of color has given me. In this great cause, more of human destiny is involved than in any other, except the cause of Christianity. Under the influence of intemperance, men are dead to whatever is noble and good, in this or a future life. I have often contemplated the direful effects of this vice upon your wronged and injured race, with painful interest. When to the injustice and prejudices of their fellow-men, wearing a whiter skin, they themselves add the curse of intemperance, their condition is wretched, indeed. With peculiar satisfaction, I have observed in this, and in other parts of the country, the redeeming effects of the glorious temperance reformation upon their character and prospects. The account given in your beautiful letter more than confirms what I had before seen and heard. In the hands of that divine Master, whose servant you are, you have been instrumental in improving the condition and elevating the character of your brethren of the African family. May He continue to strengthen you in the good work in which you are engaged, and cause your labors to be still more blessed and prospered. God grant that you and those who, labor with you in the cause of religion and humanity, of whatever color or race, may *live* to see the day when "Ethopia shall," indeed, "stretch forth her hands unto God." I thank you for your very interesting letter, and shall ever be happy to hear from you, and to meet you.

Truly, your friend,

G. N. BRIGGS.

Mr. Marsh, before quoted, relates the following anecdotes of his Congressional life : —

"To a gentleman in Washington, who, at a public table, after professing temperance, had put the glass to his lips, and had said to him, 'I only make believe;' Mr. Briggs said, 'Sir, I never make believe.'

"To a lady of high rank and influence, with whom he was on terms of intimacy, he said in his mild and gentle way, 'Do you feel that you are doing all the good you can in this world? Are you doing what you can in your high station for the cause of temperance?' His words were not lost — she banished wine from her table, and her daughter, now a lady of wealth and refinement, has no wine on her table and none at her parties."

The same chronicler says, —

"Governor Briggs was oftentimes truly eloquent, especially in the relation of anecdotes. His story of the poor woman (whose four drunken sons lay in the graveyard) entering the town meeting, and remonstrating with the authorities who were about to resolve upon the issue of licenses, is one of the most eloquent things in the English language, and it is amazing that it has not banished license from the civilized world."

This memorable anecdote may have been repeated by him more than once, as indeed it well deserves to be ; but it is here recorded as it was first related at a great meeting in Albany. It was subsequently printed in two or three forms, with an illustration, by the American Temperance Union, and widely circulated with remarkable effect. It was reprinted also as a page temperance tract in England, under the title of "The Mysterious Woman." It could hardly be omitted from this volume, in a review of the temperance labors of Governor Briggs, without injustice : —

"THE MYSTERIOUS WOMAN.

"At a certain town meeting in Pennsylvania, the question came up whether any persons should be licensed to sell rum. The clergyman, the deacon, and physician, strange as it may now appear, all favored it. One man only spoke against it, because of the mischief it did. The question was about to be put, when all at once there arose from one corner of the room a miserable woman. She was thinly clad, and her appearance indicated the utmost wretchedness, and that her mortal career was almost closed. After a moment of silence, and all eyes being fixed upon her, she stretched her attenuated body to its utmost height, and then her long arms to their greatest length, and raising her voice to a shrill pitch, she called to all to look upon her.

"'Yes!' she said, 'look upon me, and *then* hear me. All that the last speaker has said relative to temperate drinking, as being the father of drunkenness, is true. All practice, all experience, declares its truth. All drinking of alcoholic poison, as a beverage in health, is *excess*. *Look upon me!* You all know me, or once did. You all know I was once the mistress of the best farm in the town. You all know, too, I had one of the best — the most devoted of husbands. You all know I had fine, noble-hearted, industrious boys. Where are they now? Doctor, where are they now? You all know. You all know they lie in a row, side by side, in yonder church-yard; all — every one of them filling the drunkard's grave! They were all taught to believe that temperate drinking was safe — that excess alone ought to be avoided; and they never acknowledged excess. They quoted you and you and you (pointing with her shred of a finger to the minister, deacon, and doctor,) as authority. They thought themselves safe under such teachers. But I saw the gradual change coming over my family and prospects, with dismay and horror; I felt we were all to be overwhelmed in one common ruin. I tried to ward off the blow; I tried to break the spell, the delusive spell—in which the idea of the benefits of temperate drinking had involved my husband and sons. I begged, I prayed; but the odds were against me. The minister said the poison that was destroying my husband and boys was a good creature of God; the deacon, who sits under the pulpit there, and took our farm to pay his rum bills, sold them the poison; the doctor said that a little was good, and excess only ought to be avoided. My poor husband and my dear boys fell into the snare, and they could not escape; and, one after another, were conveyed to the sorrowful grave of the drunkard. Now look at me again. You probably see me for the last time. My sands have almost run. I have dragged my exhausted frame from my present home — your poor-house — to warn you all; to warn you, deacon! to warn you, false teacher of God's word!' and with her arms flung high, and her tall form stretched to its utmost, and her voice raised to an unearthly pitch, she exclaimed, 'I shall soon stand before the judgment seat of God. I shall meet you there, you false guides, and be a witness against you all!'

" The miserable woman vanished. A dead silence pervaded the assembly; the minister, deacon, and physician hung their heads; and when the president of the meeting put the question, 'Shall any licenses be granted for the sale of spirituous liquors?' the unanimous response was 'No.'"

Among the papers which Governor Briggs left, is one of curious interest, as constituting his " brief" for his arguments and pleas in the cause of temperance. It is of considerable extent, and embraces memoranda enough to stock an army of champions, going forth with the weapons of logic and love, against the dreadful scourge of drunkenness.

27

A few quotations will serve to illustrate its value, and the author's methodical habits of preparation for his labors of love, as well as of duty : —

"Produces three fourths of the pauperism in the United States.

"Of 992 inmates of the Baltimore jails last year, 944 were drunkards. In Hartford, seven eights. Nine tenths of the crimes committed are caused by its use.

"Cost of crime in the United States, is $8,500,000 per year; three fourths of it chargable to intemperance, *i. e.* $6,375,000.

"A greater proportion of the suicides and violent and unnatural deaths produced by the same cause.

"Delirium tremens owes its existence to its use. Ten cases in one week in Philadelphia.

"It has produced 30,000 deaths annually in this country. Contemplate this evil. Fills the land with widows, with orphans and mourning.

"A drunkard's grave — what is it?

"Aptly compared to the maelstrom in the Northern Seas; the unsuspecting seaman dreams not of his danger until his ship is brought within the fatal influence of the whirlpool. He gives a scream of despair, and is swallowed up. The next seen is the melancholy wreck disgorged from the vortex, and floating upon the billows."

So conspicuous and efficient were the labors of Governor Briggs in the cause of temperance — especially after his retirement from public office, — and so highly were his zeal and conscientiousness in this great work appreciated, by those who were more immediately in charge of its organized forces and measures, that when, in 1856, Judge Savage resigned his important post as President of the American Temperance Union, no one was thought of to succeed him before him who had in Congress, in the Governor's seat, and upon the Bench for a quarter of a century, and subsequently for several years, stood foremost among the advo-

cates of the cause it was designed to advance. He was
chosen President, and notwithstanding he lived at an in-
convenient distance from the head-quarters of the society,
he was faithful and efficient in the administration of its
affairs — resigning his office involuntarily, only with his
earthly life.

"His speech at the Anniversary in 1860," says Mr. Marsh, " on
the dangers of young men at the present day, will not be soon forgotten. How many have been reformed by him on the principles
of total abstinence; how many turned back from the most destruc-
tive paths, can never be known until the Judgment Day."

The contemplation of no one aspect merely of his active
and invaluable life, suggests more impressively the benevolence and breadth of his humanity, than that of his temperance labors. In these he was indefatigable, and it gave
him more delight to lift a fellow-creature out of the mire
of degradation — out of the "slough of despair" — than it
did to win applause in Congress, or in any public position,
by the force of either talent or tact.

CHAPTER XXVI.

HITHERTO we have followed the career of Governor
Briggs, as he passed through the successive periods
of his professional and official life. Glimpses of
him in private, and at his home, have been all we
could obtain, so brief were the intervals between
his public labors. For this reason, we have not yet reviewed his true, his inner life. This has indeed, ever and
anon, gleamed upon us out of his letters, and out of the
beautiful memorials from time to time offered as descrip-
tions of special aspects of his character.

· Something, however, is yet lacking, and that something
will be found, when it is supplied, so much that, without it,
these Memòirs would be like the statue of Memnon, without the music wakened by the magic of the sunlight on the
stone.

Governor Briggs loved his home and everything around
him there — animate and inanimate. His warm heart had a
place for the humblest creature dependent upon his bounty.
Not his horses and his dog alone knew his voice, and would

come to him at his call, but the cow in the pasture and the fowls of the yard were equally familiar ; and it is told of him, as an authentic story, that his Irish serving man said to him one day, " Please your honor, I have put back the chickens you took from under the hen ; they are not quite hatched enough."

The home he occupied during the last nineteen years of his life, was in striking contrast to the " little green house " in Adams, where in 1818 he commenced his domestic life. Yet were his memories of that humble dwelling-place made so sweet by their long association with his gentle, genial, affectionate nature, that they always had a brightness and a beauty for him, which the multiplied comforts and moderate luxuries of his later home, did not somehow seem to surpass.

He was always simple and unostentatious, and his home, though ample in extent, and bountiful in all respects, was like himself. He indulged in few luxuries, in none, indeed, that were other than true conveniences or comforts. There was no lavish expenditure upon his surroundings, but always enough for simple and natural, and even tasteful adornment.

His favorite retreat was his library, and there he passed many hours of grateful meditation, loving remembrance, joyful anticipation, cheerful intercourse with his family and friends, instructive converse with great minds mirrored to him in books, delightful correspondence with the absent, reverent study of the divine word, and blessed communion with Heaven. This enumeration may not exhaust, indeed, his occupations and delights in his library, but on the other hand, it does not exaggerate them.

One of the secrets of his abundant overflow of thought

27*

and illustration in his addresses — frequently extemporaneous as to their expression — was the diligence of his
habit of reading. His home-library contained few beside
standard books, and he chose the sterling authors in theology and history for his companions. His experience and
public life admirably illustrated the apothegm of Bacon,
" Reading makes a full man." He read to some purpose,
both in his intention, and in the result of his reading.

His fondness for the writings of Robert Hall, indicates
the character of his theology and the healthfulness of his
rhetorical tastes. Macaulay was no less a prime favorite
with him, and one of his incomparable essays was the last
reading, out of his Bible, which he is remembered to have
pursued. He marked the essay, which was that on the
" West Indies, and the Social and Industrial Capacity of
the Negro," with marginal notes and comments of great
sagacity.

He was a devout student of the Scriptures, and carried
into the Bible class and into the social religious meeting
the " beaten oil " which he himself had wrought out in his
library and in his closet. Much devotional reading, besides,
enlivened and strengthened his religious character — of
which, through all his life, he never made a pretentious
show, and equally never glossed or veiled it from a sense
of false and feeble shame.

His was a cheerful, sunny nature, subject to exceptional
moods of despondency, which now and then tinged his religious experience with a gentle melancholy, but rarely, if
ever, availed to mar it with persistent gloom. He was
self-depreciating by nature and habit, and nowhere was
this more apparent than in his Christian life, of which the
model before him was so lofty and so sublime — that he

magnified his short-comings to the proportions of his spiritual ambitions, and by a gentle perversity of spirit looked at his actual attainments in the divine life through the wrong end of the telescope, with which he yet never failed, by a right use of it, to bring heavenly things nigh to him.

His home-life was beautiful for simplicity and sincerity, in every sphere of duty — domestic, parental, and Christian. Once and again the reader has gazed upon some of its manifestations, and the husband, the father, the neighbor, the Christian, has been revealed in these pages.

Of the memories of the departed father held sacred by his children, certainly none are more fondly cherished than those which cluster about the domestic altar. One of those children says, —

" His daily prayers at the household altar were always characterized by earnest asking for wisdom and direction from God. The memory of those prayers, so full of true worship, of gratitude and love, and humble confession of sin, and fervid desire for the blessing of Heaven, lingers with us still, like sweet incense in our dwelling; and the tones of the full, rich, reverent voice, do not cease to our souls. When we kneeled with him in the devotions of the family, we often marked the constant prayer for preparation for death, and acceptance in heaven. He seldom failed to pray that we might ' live the life of the righteous, and die his peaceful death.' "

One memorable incident connected with his prayers at the fireside, though reaching back into his Lanesboro' life, may well find its record here.

A young student of Williams College was teaching school in the village. With amiable qualities of character he united skeptical feelings on the subject of personal religion. Yet he was inclined to visit Mr. Briggs at his home; and the latter said to him, with his characteristic kindness, "If you find it pleasant here, make my house a home."

The young man was often there, and not infrequently at the time of the lifting up of the evening sacrifice, when he listened to the reading of the Scriptures, and to the simple, earnest supplications of the head of the family. Some time afterwards, he said to a young friend: "I have heard Mr. Briggs in court and in public, where human ambition and the love of applause might influence him; but to see him in the quiet of his own home, shut out from the world, with his wife and children, on bended knees, offering prayer in Christian faith, staggers me. I cannot answer that. He is sincere. He is not deluded. There must be something in it." For many years that young man, in mature life, has bowed with his wife and children at their own family altar, in an intelligent Christian faith.

Any portraiture of Governor Briggs, in which the meekness of his soul and of his temper — his Christian humility in another phrase — is not made prominent, must fail in fidelity to its original. He was all his life a man of that lowliness of heart which may have simulations, but can scarcely be found genuine, apart from a truly Christian character.

His frequent and almost painful self-depreciation in his retrospection was not altogether — perhaps not chiefly — morbid in its origin. It was the result of his habitual and unaffected humility. He literally, in obedience to apostolic injunction, "esteemed others better than himself." One of his last utterances was of this nature: "I have done nothing; I have done nothing." It is difficult to

reach that stand-point from which he could thus see himself. These words, and his kindred expressions, in his letters, of the ineffectualness of his life, are to be estimated
in connection with the loftiness of the ideals he cherished.
He aimed so high, that the loftiest reaches he compassed
seemed to have no elevation, when compared with the
heights unscaled above them.

The humility of a truly lofty character is its own veil
only. To others it is an interpretation, an exponent of the
unconcealed stature. It is impossible not to see the moral
and spiritual greatness of Governor Briggs, in the reflections of his life, which to him, undoubtedly, seemed the
images of feebleness and failure.

The meekness of his soul lent a rare gentleness of expression to his features — which were not, however, destitute of a dignity and strength, — blending into an impressive
charm at all times, but chiefly when he was wrapt in
thought, or moved with the passion of impetuous utterance.
He might have been singled out of a group of intellectual
men, by the sign in his face of unpretendingness. In ampli-
fication of this point is the testimony of a friend : —

" Among the dignitaries in the uppermost seats at Harvard Commencement, you might, for successive years, have easily singled
out the Governor, as distinguished by the absence of all pretension in his looks ; not that he had not, otherwise, a commanding
presence, for this he assuredly possessed, but it was such a
presence of benignity, removed from pride and vainglory, as impressed all who came within the circle of his influence. It was so
interwoven into the fibres of his character, that its outward expression was as natural as his walk. It tempered the look of his
blue eye, marked the smile on his face, and made him ever serene,
self-poised, ever equable, drew to him the affections of good men,
nay, even, children, and stamped on him the impress which comes

from no doubtful source, of one 'meek and lowly in heart.' In his case, at least, was illustrated the truth, that 'before honor is humility.' "

It was this unaffected simplicity of his soul, out-shining through his mild blue eyes, and the unavoidable conviction of the truth of his character, that immediately won the heart of the stranger brought into close contact with him, and that with still greater force bound to him those who knew the depths and breadths of his benevolence : —

"Hardly a stranger came to our village," says Dr. Todd, "but was anxious, at least, to see Governor Briggs for a moment; and I know not how often I have piloted them over to his house to introduce them, sometimes fearing he would feel, if he did not say, 'My friend, this is a little too much.' But I never knew him fail to give a warm and welcome reception, and never had one go back with me who did not say, in substance, 'What a beautiful character!' "

A good man, only a few hours before he, himself, passed into eternity, said of him : —

"How much like Jesus! more like Him than any man I ever knew. How much I love him! I thank God that I have known one such man."

This is the language of another, who knew him well : —

"He really loved everybody in such a manner, that he always felt kind and generous and pitiful. I have known him intimately many years at home and abroad, and I never knew him speak unkindly of a human being. He had, by nature, a quick, sensitive temper, and yet I never saw him in a passion, and I do not believe he ever was. I presume he never had a quarrel in his life, and a gentleman who was a member of his Executive Council several years, says 'The perfectly unruffled amiability and suavity of his manner and temper during the tedious and wearisome, and sometimes excessively trying hours in the Council Chamber, where nerves and wisdom are severely tested, were marvellous.'"

" It was my good fortune," writes one eager to bring a stone for his monument, "to make his acquaintance soon after the Gubernatorial election, at the house of one of his warmest friends, Hon. Heman Lincoln, and in all my subsequent interviews I never parted from him, without feeling all the better impulses of my nature stirred within me, to try to imitate his spotless example. The Scripture says, ' When a man's ways please the Lord, He maketh even his enemies to be at peace with him.' The truth of this he fully exemplified. Enemies he had not, even among his political opponents."

His good nature was proverbial, and his politeness in all circumstances exemplary. It was the courtesy of kindness, of a great and yet gentle heart. His kind acts were doubly kind, by reason of his manner in doing them. Of his charities the stream was perpetual. This is no exaggeration. In little things and in large things, he manifested the spirit of his Master, and "went about doing good."

His daughter narrates this instance of his kindness in little things : —

"Going to the village, on a frosty morning, late in the autumn, he overtook a little boy on the way. He was barefooted. My father stopped the carryall, and asked the little fellow to ride. When he had comfortably taken his seat beside him, my father not knowing who he was, asked his name. He rather reluctantly answered,

" ' My name is just like yours.'

" ' What is that ? '

" ' George N. Briggs,' was the answer. He took the boy to a shop and fitted him with a pair of boots and stockings, giving the little pedestrian a more comfortable walk on his return home, than he

expected. This incident came to my knowledge with others of a
similar character, after his deeds of love on earth were ended."

A colored woman, employed in his family when she was
young, relates this simple story of his recent kindness to
her : —

"The last time I saw Mr. Briggs, was down street, last summer. It was a very warm day, and I had walked down from Lanesboro', and felt very warm and tired; and I suppose he saw I was,
for after he saw me he spoke to me so pleasant, and shook hands
and said, 'Lucy, don't you want some soda?' I said it would taste
good, and he took me into a store and gave me a glass of soda
and some cake, and I had such a good time! I never saw him
after."

Here is another of these little kindnesses : —

"Standing in the barber's shop of the village, one day, he saw
a colored girl passing by, on her way to attend a funeral. She
was overtaken by a sudden shower, and was getting very wet.
Without saying a word, he stepped out of the door, placed his
umbrella in her hand, and returned to the shop. Some one in
speaking of it afterwards, said, 'Anybody could have done that.'
'Yes,' said Dr. Todd, 'but only Governor Briggs did do it.'"

An example less of his small kindnesses than of his silent
benefactions, — those gracious deeds done by the right
hand without the knowledge of the left, — is this incident :

"A clergyman whom he very highly-esteemed was unexpectedly
cut short in his income. The Governor, upon ascertaining this
fact, sent an order to his tailor to select the materials and make a
suit of clothes for his friend, with strict injunctions to send them
to him without the least intimation of the source whence they
came. The clergyman must have guessed; but no allusion to it
was ever made by him, until his friend was laid in the grave."

Of much greater breadth, and truly memorable for its extent and duration, is one of his secret bounties to the poor of his village, disclosed to us only since his death, by the admiring friend who was his almoner. This friend was for many years the principal baker in the village; and his business' brought him into close acquaintance with the people. To him Governor Briggs, for several years, never failed to say, just before "Thanksgiving:" —

"See that all the poor families in the village who are not able, in your judgment, to provide it for themselves, are supplied with everything necessary to a nice and bountiful dinner, from a turkey, or fowls, to a dessert and tea and sugar, and be sure let none of them know who sends it. When all is done, send the bill to me, and I will give you my check for the amount."

"This," says our informer, "was faithfully done, until I left the business."

Incidents illustrating his brotherly kindness, and his recognition of the sweet fraternal spirit of the gospel, are very numerous: —

"I think I should never have been a member of the church, had it not been for Governor Briggs," said a plain, laboring man. "I came to this town a stranger, years ago. On Sundays I wandered about, not going to any church, because I knew nobody. One Sunday I thought I would go to the Baptist Church. It was the old building, and the people sat facing the door. I opened the door, and, seeing all the faces turned towards me, was about to close it and go back, when I saw a kind-looking man with gray hair, beckoning me with his hand to come in. I went in and sat by his side. I came again next Sunday; and, when I opened the door, he again beckoned me to him; and it was a long time before I knew that the gray-headed man was the Governor. I found myself going every Sunday, that I might sit beside him. He gave me

28

a hymn-book soon after. Ah! I feel sure I should not have been here had it not been for him."

"The last act he did in health," says his daughter, "was to take to their friends, in his own carriage, two women who had been thrown from their vehicle, as they were driving down the hill near his dwelling. On his return, when he drove into his yard, a few minutes before that melancholy occurrence which ended his life, a member of his household said to herself, when she saw him come in: 'What a good man that is.'"

"He excelled," says Dr. Todd, "in conversation, and seemed to be the centre of the charmed circle wherever he went. In his anecdotes, in which he excelled all men I ever knew, he never said a severe or a wounding word. He would first paint the man so that he stood out before you, and then give you his words, and most likely his very tones of voice, to your great delight. You never forgot a story that he told."

To this testimony to his conversational powers, it may be justly added that he excelled in repartee. A ready and delicate humor marked his utterances whenever the occasion justified it; although no man was more mindful than he of the propriety of his words. In illustration of his felicity in retort — which was always with him "the retort courteous," — the following instance may be quoted, from reminiscences furnished by one who was for some years his pastor :[1] —

"Being rallied by a neighbor on the fact that the vane on the Baptist Church did not correctly indicate the direction of the wind, he instantly replied: 'That is true; but then you know we Baptists do not turn at every wind of doctrine.'"

Spending an evening at the house of a friend in the city, before the company retired, some one proposed dancing,

[1] Rev. J. V. Ambler.

and the movement was adopted. Presently a young lady came forward, and very respectfully said, —

"Governor Briggs, may I have the pleasure of dancing with you?"

He immediately said, with his pleasant smile, "It has been currently reported, that, on a similar occasion, I invited a young lady to dance with me, but she declined because I was the son of a blacksmith. I acknowledge the anvil," said he, "but I deny the pumps; for I never danced in my life; — besides; I am a Baptist, and, as a people, we are not especially favorable to this practice, for the first account given in the Bible of a Baptist, informs us that he lost his head in connection with a dancing-party."

This chapter has run so much to reminiscences of the good man gone from earth, that it may not be amiss, perhaps, to extend this vein yet a little more, and embrace a few anecdotes which, while they may not directly relate to those characteristics specially under review, will yet add something to the reader's knowledge of his many-sided nature, and also of the foundations of his great personal popularity wherever he was known.

He was pre-eminently, as his early life abundantly illustrates, a promoter of peace, and to the last of his public services, whether in the sphere of the world or in that of the church, he labored to restore concord and unity.

"Walking one day from his residence to the village, he heard high words from a house by the wayside, and as he approached it, he saw a woman in the door-yard, crying bitterly, and apparently much distressed. In his pleasant way, he asked, 'What is the trouble?'

"She replied, 'My husband has put me out of the house, and won't let me come in.'

28

"He walked past her, and went to the door, and, after rapping two or three times, was received by the man in possession with a very bland countenance, though a little confused.

" ' What appears to be the matter here?' asked the Governor.

" ' Oh, nothing — nothing,' was the reply.

" ' Why, the woman seems to be out of doors, and she is crying.'

" ' Yes; but she can come in, if she wants to.'

" ' Well, suppose you ask her to come in?'

"The party in power invited the ejected woman to come in; and, the difficulty thus far adjusted, the Governor passed on to the village. A neighbor related this account some time afterward, adding, 'Nine out of ten would have passed on and done nothing; and I have never heard any more high words from that quarter since.' "

The next incident shows the estimation in which he was held by the laboring classes, with whom he was frequently in contact: —

"Two Irishmen were passing a Daguerrian shop, where at the window hung an excellent likeness of Governor Briggs. They stopped to look at it.

" ' Sure as me soul,' said one, 'that's Governor Briggs. He was a good man, and a raal frind to the poor. If iver a man gits square into heaven, it's this same.'

" ' Yis, it's ivery word of it thrue; but, Pat, wasn't he a hiritic?'

" ' I'll dare say he was; but he had the thrue religion in him, afther all; and Saint Pater, as I am thinking, won't mind be asking what he was, when he opens the door to let him in.' "

One whose communications with him up to the last of life were constant and intimate, and who says it "sets his head in a whirl," to begin to call up the interesting reminiscences of him which his own intercourse suggests, related only yesterday, the following amusing account of a practical joke which he played upon him. In this sort of affair, the Governor, he says, was a match for any one, and gave or took with equal zest.

He was summoned one summer morning, by the Governor, to accompany him and his guests to West Pond (not far from the village), for a boating and fishing excursion. Unable to go with them at the time, he promised to join them there, and at eleven o'clock he drove to the pond. The party was out with the boat on the opposite shore, but the Governor was stretched out, fast asleep near the carriages, not literally " *sub tegmine fagi*," but still under a spreading elm.

In a moment, he says, he thought of the lunch in the cart, and found there a gallon stone jug of milk, which he set down close by the Governor's head, and retreated rapidly to join the boat party by making a detour. Presently he landed with them, without having said a word to any one of his trick, and the merriment was unbounded when the proximity of the suspicious looking jug to the mouth of the sleeping dignitary was perceived. It woke him from his slumber, and speedily comprehending " the situation," but without seeing the author of the joke, he joined in the glee, exclaiming, "Ah! that fellow D., is around here, I know!"

The following reminiscence, by his daughter, presents an amusing instance of a mistake of identity : —

"On one of his early visits to Boston, after his election, before he was much known personally, he went as usual to the *barber's*, and found among others who were receiving the attention required, one of his townsmen from Pittsfield, to whom the chief employee was paying most obsequious and marked service, while he, after waiting a while, was given over to the inexperience of a novice in the art, and subjected to the infliction of a dull razor.

28*

He bore it patiently, however, while his neighbor, who had not discovered him, was luxuriating in all sybarite elegances of that portion of his morning toilet. After the neighbor had taken his leave, the barber, turning to the Governor, said, ' Do you know who that gentleman is ? '

"' Why ? did he not pay you ? '

"' Oh, yes, to be sure; that is Governor Briggs,' said the knight of the razor, who had enjoyed the imagined honor of shaving that individual.

"' No; I know that man, and he is not Governor Briggs — that is Mr. M., of Pittsfield.'

" The next time the Governor met his neighbor, he told him the joke was very good for him, but rather sorry work for himself, and hereafter, though he should not object to his being well tonsured, he should not allow his own beard to be torn out by a rusty razor, on his account."

The following reminiscences are from the home treasury, which could not readily be exhausted : —

" He had in his possession several walking-canes, the gifts of various friends, which he valued highly as tokens of kindly regard, though he never used them. One of them made of a shepherd's crook, was sent to him by Mr. Benjamin, the missionary, who cut it for him on Mt. Parnassus.[1] One, wrought out of whalebone, was a gift of General Thompson, of New Bedford. Two were presented to him by Southern members of Congress, — Mr. Sevier of Arkansas, and Mr. Donnely of Florida. One (from the ' old oak ' at Mt. Auburn) the love and memory of Amos Lawrence, made precious; and one was brought to him by Mr. Banvard, which he cut on the Mount of Olives. He told my father that ' he *thought* of him, while he was there.' When showing it to me soon after he received it, and expressing great satisfaction in its possession, and its pleasing evidence of remembrance, he repeated what Mr. Banvard had said, and then, his eyes suffused with tears, added, reverently and tenderly, ' Another Being thought of me there.' "

1 See his letter of acknowledgment in Chapter XVI.

CHAPTER XXVII.

IN an earlier chapter of these Memoirs, an allusion was made to a poor sick girl, who was a grateful beneficiary of Governor Briggs's kindness. Her character was so attractive, and her patience in poverty and pain so beautiful, that scarcely less to present exemplary lessons from her life and death, than to exemplify yet further the loving kindness of him who befriended her, a few pages will be devoted to some simple memorials of their relation to each other.

So far as his ministries to her bodily needs, or indeed to her spiritual nature are concerned, her case is not an exceptional one. It is only in the degree of those attentions, and in those personal characteristics in their object, which made them so impossible to withhold, that it becomes peculiar.

Jane Harrison lived in Pittsfield, in very humble circumstances. She was the eldest daughter of a poor widow. She had a younger sister who was too feeble for work, and their mother was ill, like the daughter, with only a tardier phase of her malady.

Jane did not belong to the denomination with which Governor Briggs was connected, but her sincere piety, her sweet patience, her gentle spirit, and her poor earthly estate were quite as sure passports to his warm catholic heart as any closer church kinship could possibly be.

These lines of the biographer are designed only to introduce her to the reader. A skilful hand has before prepared the pages which her story will fill. In advance of that, however, she shall speak for herself in a letter which she wrote to her benefactor, while he was long absent from home. This letter was found after his death, in one of his private drawers, together with a flower, painted, it is supposed, by her hand, and both inclosed in an envelope, upon which he had written — " Jewels." Other treasures were laid up in the same drawer ; the exquisite gold medal he received in Washington, and a silk purse, the handiwork of Laura Bridgeman, and by her presented to him. The letter which follows, was written in a singularly delicate and dainty style, almost as etherealized as the spirit which inspired its thought and feeling : —

PITTSFIELD, Feb. 13, 1843.

DEAR SIR:

It seems a long time since you left us. I meant to have written before this time, but have been prevented. I would now write you a few lines to let you know I have not forgotten you — for I shall never forget all your kindness to us. I have not been as well for a few weeks. About three weeks ago I had the hiccoughs. I began to have them on Friday night, and had them almost constantly till Sabbath morning. I have not had them since, but have not been as well as I was before. My cough has been worse. I have not raised much lately. I always feel best when I do. I am able to sit up nearly half the time, and walk about some. My pulse is the same it has always been. Doctor called to see me the other day. He said it was faster, by twenty, than it ought to be. I have thought of trying to ride out, but the doctor tells me I must keep out of the air as much as I can. I am in hopes that if I live till spring, I shall be more comfortable, but I don't know how it will turn. I know I *must* die, but I feel it matters not much when the time comes, if I am prepared to go. If I can bid farewell to earth, with the prospect of a better, brighter world beyond the grave. I feel that it is better to die now, than to live till old age, in a world full of storms. I know the *grave* is dark, but I know, too, that light will break through its gloom, and I know that though the body shall mingle with the dust of the earth, it shall rise again, that the spirit shall once more inhabit it, and if it is a redeemed spirit, be clothed in a garment of light and blessedness, and live forever in a world where sickness and death shall never come. We have all got along very comfortably this winter. The worst trouble we have is about a place to live in another year. My brother is to pay the rent till the first of April, but I do not expect he will help any longer than that. We can have the rooms up stairs; they are very comfortable, and I think we shall go up there, if we can manage to pay the rent. We cannot stay below, the rent is so high. I do not know how we shall get along, but when I think how long I have been sick, and how we have been provided for by means unknown to us, I feel that a kind Providence will still take care of us, though it be in ways unthought of now. I hope I shall live till your return; I want to see you once more. I always think of you Sabbath mornings, and it seems very lonesome not to have you come. I have written a few lines, and I hope, in return, you will write me a long letter. Mother and Nancy send their respects to you and your family. Give my respects to your family, and tell them if I never see them in this world, I hope to meet them in a world where there will be no more parting.

Yours with respect,

JANE HARRISON.

Here follows the sketch alluded to : —

"Of many delightful memories of Governor Briggs, there are none that affect me more powerfully than his unwearied ministrations to the poor, — ministrations that were continued with increasing devotion, through all the long course of years wherever

it was my privilege to know his bright example, and to feel its
holy influence. He never pleaded the cares of the State, the
claims of society, or the endearments of a pleasant home, as an
excuse for omitting the frequent personal visits which are so grateful
to the poor. They are thankful for ' *alms*,' — but these, they know,
may be given to appease an uneasy conscience, or from a desire to
be popular, or even to avoid the stigma of meanness; while they
look upon a visit to their dwelling as a recognition of brotherhood,
and a proof of that cordial sympathy, without which, even the richest gifts have no fragrance. Governor Briggs was never satisfied
with the mere giving of money and supplies, — although he was as
generous as he was discriminating in these; — but when about to
leave Boston for a brief visit at home, he would take time to buy
the medicine needed by a poor sick girl in the town where he
lived, and would seize the first leisure moment, after his arrival
there, to carry it, himself, to her sick-room, entering her presence
with as much deference and dignity as if she had been the proudest
lady in the land; inquiring into her wants, and listening with a
fatherly sympathy to her account of her own condition and that
of her family. I went to see her one Sabbath morning, and her
smile, always bright, was unusually glad, as she said, —

"'The Governor came to see us last night. He is to be at home
a few days; and he told me he would come and take me to ride
this morning, if it should be fine.'

"'Well,' said I, 'you will go, for it is very fine weather.'

"'Yes,' said Jane. 'it is three months since I have been out of
this room; the last time I went, he took me; and you don't know
how good it will seem to breathe the cool, pure air once more.'

"Soon we heard steps upon the stairs; and the Governor entered, bearing on his arm a basket, filled with tea, sugar, and other
little luxuries for Jane, which he placed upon the table, saying, —

"'Are you sure you are strong enough to bear the ride?'

"'Oh, yes,' said Jane; 'it will do me good, — I know it will.'

"The Governor bade us wrap her warmly, and assisted in preparing her for the ride; then, standing at the head of the steep stairs,
he lifted her poor, wasted body, and carrying her gently down in
his arms, placed her in the sleigh, tucking the robes around her

carefully, so that no cold winds should creep in to chill her. He drove as long as she could bear it, then lifted her from the sleigh, carried her up the stairs, and placed her in her chair. After this, he went to church, leaving Jane with the sweet recollection of his kindness and sympathy to cheer her until he should come home again. A distressing cough, and the frequent raising of blood, kept her ill many years. She worked in a cotton factory long after her path to.and from the mill could be traced on the snow by the blood that she raised as she went, never telling of it as long as she had strength to walk, because she thought it her duty to support herself and her mother and sister just as long as she could. She never was confined to her bed very long at one time; but she was obliged to keep her room for three years, with the exception of one short visit to some relatives, and an occasional drive, when some friend took her out.

"McMunn's elixir of opium was the only thing that relieved her from excessive coughing, and enabled her to sleep. Of course she was obliged constantly to increase the dose; and for a few months before her death she used a vial-full a week. In all these three years, I do not think Governor Briggs once failed to renew her supply of elixir when he thought it must be expended; and he was in the habit of buying it for her in Boston, a dozen bottles at a time. He was seldom at home for more than one night without going to see her, and carrying her such articles of food as her delicate appetite required, and which her inability to work made her unable to buy. When one remembers that he was all this time oppressed with the cares of the State; that he had numerous relatives and friends whose hospitalities were constantly urged upon him; that his fortune was never large, and Jane was only one of the many recipients of his bounty, — one cannot but revere the Christ-like heart of love that thus followed the Master, remembering His words, 'He that would be great among you shall be your minister, and whosoever will be the chiefest shall be *servant of all*,' for even the Son of Man came not to be ministered unto but to minister.' This path to greatness is so purely the Christian path, and is so little trodden by those whose names are honored by this world, that we welcome every noble name like that of Governor Briggs,

who shines with equal lustre as the faithful servant of his country
and the faithful follower of his Lord.

"At last Jane died, worn out with the long disease, so patiently
and sweetly borne as to make her sick-room seem like 'the gate of
heaven.' Governor Briggs left her, late at night, thinking that she
was 'almost home.' In the morning he went again, 'but she was
not, for God had taken her.' He looked upon her placid face, and
tenderly folded her thin hands upon her breast, as he said to me,
with husky voice, and eyes filled with tears, 'I loved Jane; a more
Christ-like spirit I never knew.'

"Others may tell of his wisdom as a ruler and a statesman;
others may speak of his worldly honors and rewards, — but I
cherish the memory of his constant ministrations to the poor, and
his, tender devotion to that feeble, dying girl, as the proof of a
heart 'unspotted by the world, that *visited* the fatherless and the
widow in their affliction; that did justice, loved mercy, and walked
humbly before God.' "

This touching narrative — as pure a gem of story as any
in "The Short and Simple Annals of the Poor" — is continued in the following beautiful letter from the Governor
to his daughter, whose interest in poor Jane was scarcely
less tender than that of her noble father : —

                                        PITTSFIELD, 7th Nov., 1848.
    MY DEAR DAUGHTER:

Just before eleven o'clock on Saturday night, Jane fell asleep,
and her quiet spirit took its departure. I saw her after dark, and
left H. B. there. She remained until about half an hour before
Jane died. The last thing she said, except to say that she was in
great pain for a moment, she said to H. In a whisper, she began
to repeat, "Though I walk through the valley and the shadow of
death, I will fear no evil; thy rod and thy staff, they comfort me,"
but was unable to go through with it. Helen finished repeating it.

She sent for me just at dusk. I went down, — she was dying.
In a whisper, which had the same sweet and beautiful accent as
her voice, she said, "Mr. Briggs, I want to ask you to be as good

to N. and mother, when I am gone, as you have been to me. N., poor girl, is feeble; nobody knows her; and I fear when I am gone no one will have sympathy for her; and, Mr. Briggs, I want to thank you and your family for your goodness to me. But," said she, "I can't talk much." I told her not to try. I asked if she felt that she was on "the rock." She said, "Yes, I do." She died without a struggle or a groan. She said, when she remembered how kind people had been, how well she had been provided for, she sometimes feared she had had her good things in this life, and should fail of happiness in the next world. Oh, what a beautiful spirit was that, and what a rebuke for the ingratitude of those of us who have an abundance of the things of this life. A respectable number of people attended her funeral. Dr. Todd made some appropriate remarks, and gave Jane a true and beautiful character.

Lovely girl! she is now clothed in celestial robes, and basks in the smile of that Saviour whose beauties she so strikingly reflected in her meek and quiet life. In the last year of her life, it is difficult to say which most honored the Saviour and his religion,—Jane, with her angelic spirit in the midst of poverty and sickness, or H., in health, by her deeds of charity and love towards her.

Affectionately, your father,

G. N. BRIGGS.

The daughter adds, to her transcript of this letter, these fitly concluding lines: —

"His ministry to Jane is ended here; but to the close of his life the mother and sister committed to his care by the dying girl were never neglected or forgotten. Mrs. H. and N. are both living, — the mother many years in her bed, ill of the same disease that blighted Jane in her youth. Often, as I enter the room, the wrinkled, wasted image of the aged woman is transfigured by the angelic vision of her daughter's face, which my soul sees shining through the mother's; and nowhere, as ' seeing Him who is invisible,' do I more truly feel the presence of those ministers of His who do His pleasure, than when sitting beside the bed-side of Jane's mother."

29

His kindliness of feeling was as perpetual as his unos-
tentatiousness of manner; and they were sometimes displayed together in beautiful harmony. Here is an example,
furnished by one who witnessed the incident : —

"During one of those delightful weeks last September, a gentleman and lady from Berkshire County were riding through a retired
village in Connecticut. As they passed a certain farm-house, the
gentleman inquired for one widow Johnson, and was directed to
her place, some two miles distant. As he approached the cottage
of the widow, he saw her walking in the garden. Jumping from
his carriage, he immediately accosted her with the appellation of
'Mother Johnson!' The old lady's eyes being somewhat dim with
age, she did not at first recognize the stranger.

" 'What!' inquired the gentleman; 'do you not know me, whom
you named when a baby, and to whom you gave two silver dollars?'

" 'Ah!' said the lady, 'are you the one I called George Nixon
Briggs when a babe?'

" 'Yes,' was the reply; 'I have come sixty miles to see you.'

"I need not describe the welcome which the old lady gave to
one who, amid the honors and responsibility of public life, still
recollected a poor widow, and obeyed the precept of pure religion."

A little incident, further illustrating this aspect of his
character, occurred while he was Governor of Massachusetts : —

"Several Christian people were waiting at the depot for the cars
to take them to a public meeting. Among this number were Governor Briggs, and other persons of prominence. There was also
there a pastor of a small country church, uneducated, and una-
dorned with eloquence of speech, 'or even with a gold ring, or
rich apparel,'—whose diffidence led him to stand apart from the
more elevated and accomplished. Governor Briggs observed his
embarrassment; and immediately whispered to one of the group,

'If you know that man, please introduce me to him.' The introduction immediately took place, to the gratification of the company; the embarrassment was removed, and all felt that they were
brethren."

The letter which follows is from a friend, well known
under the *nom de plume* of "Godfrey Greylock," addressed
to the eldest son of Governor Briggs : —

"I do not know but the following reminiscences of a trip to
Boston, when your father was on board the cars, may seem to you
of too trivial a nature to be recalled. I know that the incidents
mentioned are such as occurred daily with him, and that the part
which he took in them was the same as in thousands of instances
had given pleasure to those who remembered them, long after
they had probably passed from his mind. It may be well, however, to preserve, for that very reason, a few individual instances
of those minor acts of kindness, which in the mass gave so strong
a color to his character, and, by the love which they gained for him
from all classes, enabled him to accomplish so much good. In the
spring of 1851 I chanced to occupy, one day, the same seat with
your father, in the cars of the Western Railroad. The cars were
excessively crowded, many being compelled to stand; and when
we reached Westfield there entered at the end opposite to us, two
women, evidently much wearied, and one carrying a child. None
of the gentlemen in that vicinity seemed to notice their condition;
possibly the standing crowd concealed them from many. But
Governor Briggs, as the cars moved off, went forward, and invited
them to our seat, and assisted the one with the child to reach it.
At once many seats, which had not been offered to the wearied
women, were offered to the Governor of Massachusetts; but he
continued standing, talking kindly to the women, and, at times,
soothing the child, which had been made restless by its unaccus-
tomed position. There was nothing in this, you may say, more
than any true-hearted gentlemen ought to have done. True; but
in a whole car-full, Governor Briggs was the only one to think of

and do it. Possibly he was the only one who could have gracefully
done it.

"We passed on, and as we approached the Brookline bridge, near
Boston, found that a collision had taken place upon it, completely
blocking the passage with the wreck of two trains, which hung by
a fearfully-precarious hold over the water. It was necessary for
the passengers to clamber over the wreck and through it, to reach
the relief train, while their baggage was sent to the city by the
highway. But among the passengers was an old Irish woman,
one of those wrong-headed and ignorant people who never can be
made to see the necessity of anything out of their ordinary course.
She would not and could not be separated from her trunk — a rude,
hair-covered chest. Most men would have been merely amused —
at least, indifferent to her troubles; but ludicrous as was her grief,
it was piteous and real; and such, however uncouth and ground-
less, never failed to touch the heart of the Governor. So, when,
having passed from one to another, imploring aid, she came to
him, perceiving at once the uselessness of explaining matters to
her, he quietly took hold of one end of the trunk, and helped her
carry it over the tottering wreck. The profuse and quaintly-
expressed thanks of the woman, and her still more profuse and
quaint apologies, when she found who had played the porter for
her, were extremely amusing; but I will venture to say that there
were few present who did not envy your father his promptness and
willingness to confer happiness, by so simple an act, even upon so
rude a creature as this, and that while detracting nothing from the
dignity of his position.

"Continuing my trip from Boston, where your father stopped,
to Martha's Vineyard, I employed a man to carry me from point to
point on that island, — a plain but intelligent and quick-witted person, of much shrewdness and criticism, which he applied freely to
public men as we rode along. But happening to learn, accidentally, that I was from Pittsfield, he checked his horses suddenly,
and exclaimed: 'Governor Briggs lives there!' Somewhat surprised at his apparent emotion, I replied in the affirmative, and he
continued, 'I love that man; I always shall. You know I'm a
Democrat; but I always vote for George N. Briggs. He's got a

heart, — he has!' I asked him how he had found that out; and he said that once, when the Governor was reviewing the militia at New Bedford, I think, he was standing directly behind him, with his little daughter in his arms. The child begged to see the Governor and the troops, and the crowd and his position made it hard to show her either; but the Governor, happening to hear her entreaties, turned round, took her in his arms, and placing her on his horse in front of him, showed her the soldiers, and then, with a kiss, returned her to her father, — a pleased child and a grateful father, as you may well believe. 'I have loved him for that,' said he to me, 'and I always shall.'

"Slight and common as these incidents are, it may not be unpleasant to have them remembered, as occurring in two consecutive days; and one other, which happened since, may be worth recalling.

"Arriving at Pittsfield in the cars with a travelling acquaintance from the West, we found that the train would be delayed a few minutes, and he asked me to show him the residence of Governor Briggs, who then, alas! had passed away. I took him to a point from which he obtained a distant view, and as he seemed deeply interested in it, I remarked, carelessly, 'So you are a hero worshipper.' 'No,' he replied, with feeling; 'I loved the *man;*' I had reason to.' I had no time to learn the reason of this feeling, whether it arose from some of the minor acts of kindness, such as those which I have related, or from some other greater benefits, for which occasion more rarely presents itself; but the tone and manner of the speaker seemed to me more earnest than would have been likely to have been caused by the former. Hoping that what I have written may prove a pleasant addition to your treasury of pleasant incidents, connected with the life of your father,

"I am, as ever, faithfully your friend,

"G. G."

"Governor Briggs," says another witness, "was a real friend to the poor, and to those especially who were crushed by sickness and misfortune; and he felt that among these he had received the most profitable lessons and witnessed the most powerful displays of Divine grace. A member of the church who had attained a

29*

great age, and who lived some miles from the village, had been deprived of sight for forty years; but God seemed to have shut out the outer light that. the inner light, the light of the soul, might shine with celestial brightness. This was one of his favorite visiting places. He loved to sit at his feet and listen to the recital of God's dealings with him. He witnessed his cheerfulness and submission, his overflowing gratitude and love; and felt that this was one of the rarest instances of the power of Christianity to remove all obstacles to happiness, and, literally, to change darkness to light.

"By a previous arrangement, we were to have visited this patriarch in Israel together the day following the accident which resulted in his death. This aged friend soon followed him; and they have met, ere this, in that bright world where there are no accidents; 'where no one shall say, I am sick;' no blindness there; no darkness at all."

CHAPTER XXVIII.

THE religious life of Governor Briggs was so interwoven with every other aspect of his life, that it
can no more be considered apart from them, than
could they be isolated from his Christian experience and practice. They all grew together, — the
natural and the spiritual, the human and the divine, the
secular and the sacred, — and in all these phases the heavenward still controlling the earthward, while the latter afforded
ample scope for the exercise and rich development of the
former.

He was peculiarly a religious man, and his piety was
eminently practical. Its subjective character was profound and thorough. It subjugated, not indeed, by an unwelcome constraint, but rather by a most grateful force,
all the powers of his being taking possession of all, and
transforming them into its own type and image. He was
most consciously not his own, and the recognition in his
soul of his obligations to his Redeemer and Saviour was
unqualified and unintermitted. The entireness of his sub-
jection to the law and spirit of Christianity knew no quali-
fication from his own reason or judgment—and yielded to
none except that which his sinful nature imposed upon it.

343

He loved the cause and the cross of his Divine Master, and if at times he was drifted by the tide of temptation into doubts of his personal acceptance with God, he was never carried into the fogs of impersonal skepticism. His faith in the fundamental doctrines of evangelical religion, of which the vicarious sacrifice of Christ is the centre and soul, was ingenuous and tender. The story of the cross always stirred him to the deepest emotion, and his own loving interest in it made his exhibition of it to others so effective.

His objective piety was consistent with this inner faith. In this respect he was unlike some Christians in whom the two forces of spiritual life are of greatly unequal development. It is this truth that makes it impossible to separate his profession from his practice, his faith from his life. He was everywhere and at all times a Christian, unobtrusive, yet always felt. It was impossible, perhaps, for any one to be long in his society without discovering this inner life from the outer manifestations of it.

The nice balance in his character of the two influences of Christian faith, the interior and the exterior, made him, for the most part, a confident and peaceful believer. Had he been deficient in objective piety or practical religion, his soul would have often sunk into glooms and deep disquietudes — of which he sometimes, even as it was, approached the borders, and trembled in their dim twilight. Generally his active piety, his earnest solicitudes for others, his endeavors to win souls to Christ, his ministrations to his Master's disciples, — especially to the *least* of them, — left him little leisure, and less inclination, perhaps, for those morbid introspections and apprehensions which would have availed to dim the brightness of his view of Christ.

He was never so happy as when his heart and hand were working in sweet unison for the advancement of his Redeemer's cause. His church was dear to him, less for its peculiarities of creed and practice — which, nevertheless, he conscientiously maintained — than for its love to Christ, which binds it to all the redeemed by his blood forever.

Especially was he no bigot. To hold with unwavering firmness peculiar and apparently exclusive and excluding tenets, and yet to have a Christ-like charity, comprehensive and consistent, for all Christians, is the difficult problem which he solved, if not in his speech yet in his deeds, as all who know him well will ungrudgingly concede. His attachment to his own church was exemplary, and his influence in it almost unbounded, as the happy result of his unqualified devotion to all its interests. His presence, his spirit, his council, were each and all productive of harmony and zeal among his brethren.

Nor was he less esteemed among other denominations as a noble and wise and beneficent exemplar of Christianity. Many who had not reached his ecclesiastical stand-point were yet drawn to him, in abiding affection by his great catholic spirit.

Of his religious habits, little need be said beyond the intimations which these memorials everywhere convey of his devotional nature and practice.

At home and abroad he lived in the atmosphere of prayer and praise. He was as fervent in supplication at the parlor worship of the Marlboro' Hotel in Boston, as he was in the conference meeting in Pittsfield, or in his own family circle. Everywhere he breathed the spirit of pure and undefiled religion.

It is both proper and pleasing for the pen of the biographer to give place here to memorials chiefly relating to the Christian character of Governor Briggs, from those who had, outside of his own home, the best opportunity and the best right no less, to know him thoroughly—his pastors in Lanesboro' and Pittsfield.

He understood, better than most Christian men, what is due to the pastor of a church from his people. He esteemed those who were "over him in the Lord very highly in love, for their works' sake." He was his pastor's faithful friend, and held it to be spiritual treason to have two sorts of manners for him, — one before his face and the other behind his back. Hence his pastor was near enough to his person and his heart to understand him, and it is not strange that any one honored enough in God's good Providence to be the pastor of such a man, should have loving testimony to bear for his memorial.

His pastor in Lanesboro', the Rev. J. V. Ambler, contributes the following grateful reminiscences : —

"In the spring of 1837, young and with little experience, I commenced my public ministry in Lanesboro'. I well remember with what trepidation I contemplated the return of the Sabbath when I must preach before our member of Congress. But his appreciative manner, and kind words of approval and suggestion, soon so won my confidence and love, that his presence was *desired* rather than *dreaded.* I felt that when he was present, I had at least one hearer interested in the simple story of the man of Nazareth, and who was in sympathy with the pulpit, understood its difficulties, and would charitably allow for its failures.

"On one occasion, after his return from a protracted session of Congress, he remarked to a friend, 'It seems good to listen again to the simple preaching of the Gospel;' and added, 'many of those who preach before Congress seem to forget that Congressmen, like other men, need Christ.' To the writer he frequently spoke of the lamented Cookman,[1] as a marked exception to this rule.

"His views of religion were eminently practical. With him religion was life, as well as faith and opinions. He believed that a pure and blameless life followed as the effect of religion. After listening to a discourse on 'Common Honesty,' he expressed to me his surprise, 'that a subject of so much importance should be so rarely the theme of pulpit discourse,' and said, 'I regard a religion as worthless, that does not make men just in their bargains.'

"As a public speaker, his earnest manners and his felicitous diction gave him, in a remarkable degree, the power of holding the attention of an audience. I shall never forget how on a Sabbath evening he thrilled the congregation. It was a time of more than ordinary religious interest in town. He addressed himself to young men, and spoke of the young man in the Gospel who came as an inquirer to Jesus, and who, upon learning, as he thought, the hard terms of salvation, went away sorrowful, and after a moment's pause, with subdued manner and voice, he said, 'Young men, unless he repented, he is sorrowful yet.'

"Few men had a keener relish for a good anecdote; and his stock seemed inexhaustible, upon which he had the happy faculty of drawing at the right time and to the right degree, to illustrate and enliven his thought or to clinch his argument. To illustrate the chaffering gift of some men, he was wont, with much good humor and zest, to speak of a Quaker friend of his, who, when told that the potatoes he was offering for sale were *small*, replied, 'Yea, they are small, but they are plump;' and when told that his vinegar was deficient in strength, responded, 'Yea, but thee never tasted so pleasant a sour.'

"His burning words and stirring appeals in behalf of missions will long be remembered by many. But I recall with peculiar interest his first contributions to that cause; and, when the idea of missions as the essential element of aggressive Christianity

---

1 Chaplain for some years to the House of Representatives.

began to take possession of his heart and mind, to remain ever-more a deep conviction.

"My last interview with him was but a few days previous to the accident which terminated his life. At times he seemed much depressed. The woes of his country afflicted him; and the shadow of coming events had fallen upon him. He remarked that he had been thinking over the list of families known to him, where the father had been removed. 'Soon,' said he, 'all things moved on as if they had never been there, and, often, apparently better than if they had remained. These things impress me with the little con-sequence of a man, even in his own family, where he will be the most missed. In the great plan of God Moses died, but the great work did not stop.'

"During the interview I alluded to his pleasant home. 'Yes,' he said, 'it is better than I ever expected to have, and much better than I deserve.' He then alluded to the humble abode and the slender means of the first years of his professional life, and stated that often, when professional duties called him abroad, he saw many things which he desired very much to purchase for the little ones at home and their mother, and that, although his circum-stances were now so changed as to enable him to gratify all reason-able desires in that direction, yet those were the happiest days of his life. He stated, also, that during those early years of struggle several members of the Berkshire bar and himself were conversing on the subject of income and accumulation. 'We unanimously agreed,' said he, 'that ten thousand dollars would be all we should desire.' Then, with a smile and compressed lip, and a motion of the hand peculiar to himself, he seemed to say, 'How little one knows what is in his heart till it is developed by circumstances.'

"As I was about to depart Mrs. Briggs said, 'You will call again soon; remember that we are getting to be old folks.' He quickly interrupted her, and, in his peculiarly pleasant way, said, 'Speak for yourself, if you please, Harriet; *I* am not getting old.'

"The superior of George Nixon Briggs, taking him all in all, is not often seen in this world. If any man ever did, or ever could in truth say of him, 'He has influenced me to evil,' or, 'I trusted him, and he deceived or betrayed me,' I have yet to learn the fact.

In the town where his early years and a portion of those of his prime were spent, his memory is precious as a true man, a Christian, a peace-maker, and a friend to all."

Yet another pastoral tribute to his memory is that furnished by the Rev. Lemuel Porter, D. D., not very long before his own summons came to follow his friend across the narrow sea. Dr. Porter was pastor of the Baptist church in Pittsfield for twelve years; and, from the time Governor Briggs removed thither from Lanesboro' up to his last hours, he ministered to him in spiritual things, loved him, and was beloved by him. The memorial he brings for his life-record cannot, therefore, be without great interest for the reader. It is to us a triple strain of sadness, reminding us of the death of his friend, of that of his own daughter, and, finally, of his own : —

"Passing a few days in Charlestown, Mass., I was invited to meet Governor Briggs, at the house of one of his Councillors. It was then for the *first* time I saw his noble form, his benevolent face, his mild blue eye, and felt the influence of that genial spirit which made his society so charming. The first address I ever heard him make was in Boston, in the Bowdoin Square church, at a meeting of the Missionary Union. He was then Governor in the sixth or seventh year of his official service. His remarks were most impressive and eloquent.

"I next saw him in his own beautiful village of Pittsfield, at a meeting of the Baptist State Convention, and well remember the most touching address he made on that occasion. The *last* time I ever saw him in the street is indelibly impressed on my memory. I had left my dear daughter Clara in my carriage while I went into a shop on West Street. When I came out, there sat the noble man on horseback, cheerfully talking with Clara, — *both* full of life and spirit. Could I then have imagined that within three or four short months both of them would be in eternity! In a few

weeks he had gone to his Saviour's presence, — and in a few weeks
more she, having sung her requiem over his cold form, joined him
in the songs of heaven, 'where there is no more death.'

"The last time I heard him address his Christian friends was at
the covenant meeting, on Saturday, *three* days before the fatal
event which took him from us. It almost seemed as if he had a
secret consciousness that ' the time of his departure was at hand.'
Such spiritual-mindedness, such tender, solemn, affectionate appeals to his brethren to live nigh to Christ, I never heard from his
lips. If he had really known that he was speaking to us from the
threshold of eternity, he could not have been more *tender* or more
earnest. It is no doubt true, that he possessed by *nature* a happy
temperament, but it should be remembered that at the early age
of twelve years his heart was *regenerated* by the grace of God,
and that religion with its elevating, purifying, ennobling power,
became with him a pervading and controlling influence. He
loved the Bible from his youth. His whole spirit, and even his
speech was stamped with the impress of God's word. Underlying
his patriotism, his temperance principles, his kindness to the poor
and suffering, was the Christian disposition. He was the Christian
patriot, the Christian reformer, the Christian benefactor. In religious opinion he was a Calvinistic Baptist, made so by the study
of the Scriptures. His views of gospel doctrines were unusually
clear, yet he loved religion better than theology. His religion was
practical. He judged the tree by its fruit. 'Oh, that Christians,'
he often said, ' were more exemplary in their lives. They ought
so to live, that a Christian profession shall be a passport to
universal confidence.' He had his personal views of revealed
truth, and held them with all the firmness of strong conviction,
yet he respected and loved every one in whom he saw the image
of Christ. He often said, 'Grace be with all them that love our
Lord Jesus Christ in sincerity.' He gave, what he claimed, liberty
of conscience. I never heard him utter a word that savored of
bigotry. He was firm as a rock on any principle, but his manners
were as genial as the aspect of summer foliage on the granite. He
used to engage in all our devotional meetings, especially in those
preparatory to the communion; yet I never heard him pray in one

of them. I used to be surprised at this, and sometimes spoke with him about it. 'I have no gift in prayer,' he would reply. Once, however, several members of our church went to visit our aged, poor, and blind brother Lewis. On this occasion, when called upon, he offered prayer. In that humble home of the poor, amidst that little band of disciples, he poured out his soul in supplication with such unction, such heavenly-mindedness, and in such appropriate language, as made me wonder at his saying he had 'no gift in prayer.'

"There was, indeed, something most unusual and impressive and devotional in his prayers. The tones of his voice — full, tender, subdued, firm, and yet almost tremulous — inspired in others the reverence and awe which filled his soul when he approached God with words of prayer. His prayers were always very short, but every word and sentiment was prayer and worship, flowing in simple, earnest utterance. I well remember at a sunrise prayer-meeting many years ago, on New Year's morning, in the old meeting house in Pittsfield, Dr. Todd called upon him to pray. I see his face and form now, as on that morning, and remember the pathos of his tone, the solemn fervor and humility of his spirit, and the reverent sweetness of his language, and how real and over-shadowing the presence of God seemed, controlling the peculiar influences of this morning hour, while worshippers entered the New Year, — the past receding, the future all unknown.

"He seldom spoke with assurance of his interest in Christ, but rather of his unworthiness. This was, I think, partly from constitutional peculiarities, and partly from his high conceptions of Christian character.

"Well do I remember him in the church, — a wise counsellor, a sure guide, an unostentatious Christian, a liberal donor, and always his pastor's friend.

"He was totally unlike Diotrephes, who 'loved to have pre-eminence.' He was more like John, who 'leaned on Jesus' breast;' like Mary, who sat at Jesus' feet, and learned of Him. He had a winning way in leading his brethren up to difficult duties. A rich brother once seemed disinclined to give generously in an important emergency. The Governor said to him, 'It is hard giving till

you get used to it. If anybody had told me twenty-five years ago
that I should be giving five hundred dollars at a time to the church,
I should not have believed him. But I have been educated up to
it. Giving to the cause of Christ now comes very easy. You
must be educated. The way is to keep giving. The more you
do, the easier it will be.'"

An incident of his life while he was in Washington, will
serve here to illustrate his Christian sympathy and humility,
that had broader exemplifications perhaps, but hardly a
more beautiful one.

He had been apprized that a colored woman was to be
baptized in the river at a given hour. His interest in that
solemn ordinance led him to be a witness of it. As he repaired thither, he met a fellow-member, of popular habits,
who asked him whither he was going. On being told without any evasion, he sneered and said contemptuous things
about the Baptists. The answer he received is worthy of
him who gave it : —

" My friend, the Baptists are the people of my choice, and I
shall be but too happy to encourage and assist, if need be, the poor
slave woman in her noble act of obedience to her Divine Master."

CHAPTER XXIX.

GOVERNOR BRIGGS AND THE MISSIONARY WORK—HIS ENTIRE SYMPATHY
WITH IT—THE FIRST LAY PRESIDENT OF THE A. B. M. UNION—FITNESS
FOR THE OFFICE—TAKING THE CHAIR IN 1848—LETTER FROM DR.
WAYLAND—THE BUFFALO ANNIVERSARY IN 1850—PRESIDENT'S OPENING
ADDRESS—HIS FAREWELL CHARGE TO DEPARTING MISSIONARIES—A
THRILLING QUESTION—ANECDOTES—A REMINISCENCE BY DR. TODD—
HIS FAITHFUL SERVICES—THE "UNION" AT BROOKLYN IN 1861—EX-
CITEMENT ON NATIONAL QUESTIONS—HIS OPENING SPEECH—HIS SPIRIT
AND ITS EFFECT—THE NEXT MEETING AND THE VACANT CHAIR—
TRIBUTES.

THERE is one phase of the life and labors of the subject of this Memoir, of which, important as it was, no direct view has been taken. It is his missionary work. His religion was of quite too practical and objective a character to allow him to stand aloof from the great movements of the Christian world for the conversion of the heathen. He had, rather, the profoundest sympathy with them, and in every possible way helped to advance the cause of his Divine Master in the lands that sit in darkness and in the region and shadow of death.

It was, however, in his own quiet and unobtrusive way that he served the cause of missions during the first portion of his public life, and up to the year 1847, when he was brought prominently before the Christian community as a leader in the sublime work. This was effected by his election, at the annual meeting of the American Baptist Missionary Union, in Cincinnati, President of that great body for the ensuing year.

30*

This society had existed, though under different names, since 1814; and up to the time of the election of George N. Briggs, through a period of thirty-three years, its presiding officers had been all clergymen, five having been successively elected. He was, therefore, the first layman called to that responsible position; and this change of policy in the choice of a presiding officer was the result of much deliberation, and has not since been set aside by the body. ·

The choice then made was universally approved, the excellent name of the new President being familiar to the denomination, by reason of his public distinctions and his connection with the temperance cause.

It was no inconsiderable reason for his selection to this important office, aside from his eminent Christian fitness for it, that he had a high reputation as a presiding officer. It was well known that no one during his Congressional life was more frequently called from his seat to the Speaker's chair, for brief intervals, than he was. He had an exhaustive knowledge of parliamentary rules and points of order; and his dignity, patience, and suavity in conducting business and maintaining discipline, were so well appreciated on the floor of the House, that he at one time narrowly escaped the honor of the speakership — an honor which he unquestionably deserved.

He took the chair of this distinguished body at the annual meeting in Troy, held in 1848, and was then seen, for the first time, by a great majority, perhaps, of the delegates and members composing it, but especially of those from the West and Southwest. A chronicler of the occasion says, —

"His very person and bearing gave him favor; and as he stood up and began to speak of Jesus and his salvation, hearts gathered spontaneously to him; and before he was half done descanting on the blessings of preaching Christ to the heathen, the whole vast assembly was melted into tenderness. It was one of the grandest triumphs of Christian eloquence we have ever witnessed, and it will never die out from the minds of those present. That hour was settled the question who should be President of the Missionary Union for many years to come."

His opening remarks at this meeting were comparatively few, and as yet his soul was not stirred within him. It was in his closing address that he reached and swayed and subdued the hearts of all present, and justified the remark of some correspondent of the press, that " he kept the good wine until the end of the feast." His elevation to the high post was now felt to have been of God. Some who doubted the wisdom of putting a layman and a lawyer into a chair eminently sacred, and hitherto occupied by those lights of the Baptist denomination, Furman, Semple, Cone, Johnson, and Wayland, acknowledged their mistake, and joyfully hailed the new administration as the beginning of a new and blessed era in missionary *management* at home, if not in missionary successes abroad.

The immediate predecessor of Governor Briggs in the chair of the Union was President Wayland; and the following letter from that good great man to the great good man who succeeded him in office, and who has since been followed by him into his rest, will be most appropriate in this sequence.

Both of these distinguished servants of Christ have an illustrious record in the history of foreign missions; and the labors of both in the common field are affectionately and gratefully remembered by the Baptist denomination, and, indeed, by the whole evangelical church : —

PROVIDENCE, June 10, 1848.

MY DEAR SIR:

I have done injustice to my feelings in not writing to you before, to express the pleasure which I, and every member of the Union, derived from your presence and assistance at the late anniversary at Troy. I do not here refer so much to the example which you gave of consecrating your civil station, in some measure, to the service of Christ, or to your peculiar success as a presiding officer, as to the delightful spirit of interest for missions which you diffused through the whole assembly. Those of us who have been for a longer period publicly engaged in the work were delighted to sit at your feet and imbibe a portion of your Christian zeal. I was obliged to return on Friday morning, and thus lost the pleasure of hearing your closing address; but the impression which it left on the assembly was expressed, in the quotation which they made in speaking of it, that the best wine had been reserved to the last.

I know that you will understand the motive which induces me to make these remarks. You have not happened before to be among us; and the situation was new to you. It must, I am sure, be gratifying to you to know that your effort to aid the cause of Christ was attended by a blessing. For myself, I can truly say, that I could have wished nothing in anywise different. I had always believed that the cause of missions would be promoted by placing, in prominent positions, laymen who were interested in its success. Every indication of Providence seemed to point to you; and I rejoice that we all read these indications aright.

Excuse this volunteer commencement of correspondence. Be assured that I rejoice in every instance of your success in your benevolent efforts, and that I remain

Yours, very truly,

F. WAYLAND.

His Excellency GEORGE N. BRIGGS.

In May, 1850, the American Baptist Missionary Union

met on its thirty-sixth anniversary, in the city of Buffalo, where its President made by his addresses, and not less by his whole spirit and bearing, a deep impression upon the great convocation, — never surpassed, unless at the anniversary in Brooklyn, which was the last at which he presided.

The attendance of delegates and members at Buffalo was unusually large, exceeding eleven hundred. In his opening address he said, —

" Men and brethren of the American Baptist Missionary Union, — Under the smiles of Providence we are assembled to hold the thirty-sixth anniversary of this institution on this beautiful May morning. The smiles of Heaven have attended us in our efforts the past year. One year ago we met in the city of Philadelphia, — the city founded by that great and good man, William Penn; the city where that body of men assembled who signed the Declaration of Independence, and where from the tower of Independence Hall went forth the peals of that deep-toned bell that proclaimed us to be an independent people. The year has rolled round, the blessing of Heaven has crowned our labors, and prosperity given success to our churches. And now we are this morning assembled in this young, vigorous, and beautiful city, which has been justly denominated the Queen City of the Lakes, sitting upon the waters prosperous and great. A few years since, all around this spot where we meet was an unbroken wilderness, through which roamed those who knew not God. But now, how changed! Everything in society bears evidence of civilization and Christianity. Here we are, surrounded by natural scenery which is unequalled; inland oceans are spread out before us, and we are within the sound of that cataract which has proclaimed the mighty power of God ever since its creation.

" Brethren and friends, we have come to consult together in reference to the interests of this association. I said last year that we were prosperous; we are still prosperous. I have been told that the past year has been prosperous beyond any in our history.

God has honored us, as humble instruments, in promoting the gospel of his Son. If there is under the whole heaven a work free from the imputations of selfishness, it is that in which we"are engaged. It is the aim of this Union to propagate the word of God, to disseminate the religion of Jesus Christ. And why should we not give this religion to all men? Why should not the religion of that Being, whose enemies, even, acknowledge the purity of his motives and his life, — a religion whose tendency is to elevate human character, to promote its honesty, control its passions, and nurture whatever is lovely and pure, be propagated? If it related only to this life, enforcing all that is just and true in human brotherhood, it should be disseminated. But this is the smallest of its blessings. It not only relates to our interests here, but it reveals an immortality, and shows how we can make that immortality happy. And it is the *only* religion that points men with certainty to eternal happiness beyond the grave. Multitudes are shut out from the blessings of this religion, and why should they not have it? It is our imperative duty to send it to them. And this is the work in which this Union is engaged. We have sent out missionaries, as the report shows, who have planted themselves in countries which a few years ago were enveloped in dense moral darkness. And we look forward to the day when the whole heathen world will be enlightened by the influence of this religion. The work is going forward. The tops of the trees in heathen lands seem to be illuminated by the sun of righteousness, and ere long all nations shall receive the teachings of Christ.

"Brethren, let us not cease in this work, but, under that divine injunction of our Saviour which requires us 'to do unto others as we would that they should do unto us,' let us increase our exertions to give the Gospel to all people. And, at the same time, let us seek to make this Christian land more Christian. One of the best means of accomplishing the work is to have regard to the spiritual feeling of this meeting. I have had the privilege, since our last meeting of attending the anniversary of a similar institution, under the patronage of another denomination of Christians — the American Board of Commissioners for Foreign Missions. It was deeply interesting and instructive. I have seen many persons who were present at that meeting, and all confessed it to be one of the most blessed they ever attended. It was because the *spirit* of the meeting was good. The two meetings of this Union which I have attended were interesting, because pervaded by the same Christian spirit. Let us invoke God to preside over us."

There were present at this great meeting several honored missionaries, fresh from the field of their work, and, besides these, others who had just been accepted for the service, and were now to receive their instructions. Following these from the Secretary of the Union, came what may be called the farewell from the President. The occasion itself was full of interest, and some who were not specially attracted by the spirit and aim of the meeting, came to hear what the popular Governor of the Commonwealth of Massachusetts would say. The great church edifice was thronged. He felt the inspiration of the opportunity, and rose to it grandly.

The following extracts from his impressive speech on that occasion, will indicate the spirit of the whole, but the most exact report of his language without the fire and fervor, the pathos and power of his almost impassioned manner, will not reproduce the effect it wrought : —

"You go on an embassy compared with which all the embassies of men dwindle into utter insignificance. You go forth as the ambassadors of Christ. You go to crumble idols — to convey light to benighted minds—to kindle love to God in the souls of ungodly men. Who can over-estimate the qualifications requisite for such a work? But your Lord has not left you without the instruction you need. In his precepts you will find all you want. Especially remember what he said to his immediate disciples, as he sent them forth, —'Be ye wise as serpents, and harmless as doves.' Let the heathen see by your daily deportment; by your every word; by the very air and motion of your persons, that you are filled with love and good-will towards them. Be harmless, be courteous,—full of good works.

"You have been told that you know not what is before you. And true, you do not. But the great Captain who, on so many occasions heretofore, has so signally interposed in behalf of his servants, is able to carry you also safely through. Never forget that no evil can befall you like that of betraying your Master. And doubt not you will be remembered by those you leave behind. Thought shall speed its way through the globe to meet you. The fervent, effectual prayer shall ascend to the mercy-seat for you. You shall never see the day when your brethren who sent you out will turn their backs on you. But look higher. The Saviour has told you, 'Lo, I am with you always, even unto the end of the world.' That almighty Friend will always be at your side to sustain you.

. . . .

"You go, brethren, to carry to perishing men the glad tidings of salvation. You go to hold up that crown before them, and rouse them to the holy ambition of wearing it. You go, under God, to work such changes that those dark skins shall make the snow to blush. Thousands and thousands of now benighted heathens shall, we trust, through the labors of missionaries, come up from every part of the globe to receive that crown in the last great day.

"I am instructed, brethren, to give you the parting hand in the name of this Union. Accept it as a pledge of the warm interest with which we shall follow you to your respective stations. Farewell—farewell!"

The felicitous illustrations and incidents made use of by the speaker, greatly moved the audience. Speaking of the great missionary, Apostle Paul, he quoted his language, " Henceforth there is laid up for me a crown of righteousness." Then pausing for a moment, till all the vast audience were breathless with expectation of his next words, he said, in full, deep, thrilling tones, —

" Is there any one in all this vast congregation who will not on that day wear this crown of righteousness? "

The effect was almost electric — and excited feeling, in hundreds of throbbing hearts, was relieved by gushing tears.

Some one after the meeting spoke to him of the solemn spell produced in the congregation by his question. He replied, —

" I saw it. It flashed into my mind, and it produced the precise effect upon the audience which it did upon me."

As he was leaving the church after the adjournment, he overheard a gentleman on the pavement remark to a companion, —

" It is strange, I think, that the Governor of Massachusetts should be President of a Baptist Missionary Society."

The Governor immediately turned and said, with his own affable smile, —

" Sir, I think it more honor to be President of a Baptist Missionary Society, than to be Governor of Massachusetts."

And he did. There was no affectation, no exaggeration in this remark. He counted all the honors which had been bestowed upon him by a grateful community and Commonwealth as absolutely inconsiderable, when compared with that which the denomination he loved had put upon him in calling him to preside over its greatest benevolent organization. It thrilled his ingenuous, humble soul more to be counted worthy to lead his brethren in the great spiritual advance of Zion against the kingdom of darkness, than it did to represent Massachusetts in Congress, to sit on her proudest seat of power, or on her judicial bench. He was never more profoundly — while yet humbly, — happy, than when he was doing something for his Master.

31

The meeting of the " American Board of Commissioners for Foreign Missions," to which he alluded in his opening address, was held at Pittsfield, and was a very interesting session of that venerated body. Of his presence and influence there, his friend and neighbor, Rev. Dr. Todd, gives this pleasing reminiscence : —

"It was while he was the presiding officer of this Missionary Union that the American Board of Missions, in a kindred denomination, met at Pittsfield. And here, surrounded by many venerable and glorious fathers and many burning missionaries, he took a lively part, and made an address which will never be forgotten. With inimitable good taste he made not the remotest allusion to his civil office or honors, but greeted the Board as a sister, and older sister to his own."

Year after year, with that fidelity which characterized his official service in every sphere, he was in the chair at the opening and the close of the Union, aiding greatly by his wisdom and moderation the work of the sessions, and in times of excitement growing out of discussions of missionary policy, proposed amendments to the Constitution, or other causes, his firm but gentle hand guided its affairs successfully, and his peace-loving spirit soothed the rising gusts of strife to rest.

Eleven years after the scenes in Buffalo, at which we have glanced, the Union met in Brooklyn, and the distinguished ex-Governor and now ex-judge, went to the solemn convocation with an unwonted solemnity of feeling. It was in the spring of 1861. The first exciting events of the rebellion and the war had stirred the souls of all classes of citizens, and created in all thoughtful minds profound solicitude for the future of our beloved country.

A great gloom was upon the hearts of many, and Governor Briggs was of this number — though seldom suffering his apprehensions even to dim his simple confidence in God, who was his " Rock of Salvation."

The meeting of the "Union" followed other anniversaries of Baptist Benevolent Societies, and also a general meeting of ministers and laymen, held to consider the state of the country. This meeting had greatly excited the feelings of some, and the waves of passion threatened to overwhelm that measure of discretion and judgment which is essential to right action.

In these circumstances the Union convened. The President rose in the pulpit. His face and manner betrayed the deep excitement of his soul, and the conflict of hope and fear, through which he had been passing since the guilty rebellion, had plunged those who should have been brethren into dreadful strife.

He was greatly changed, and those who knew him saw and marked the change with sorrow. He was himself still in his calmness, benignity of expression, and gentleness of manner and speech ; but his face was thin and blanched, and his expressive eyes were sunk. Even his voice was changed, though perhaps only in its vigor.

Not a few then present looked upon him with sad forebodings that he would perhaps never again call the Missionary Union to order for a new anniversary ; that if his days were not ended before it met again, he would be too feeble to preside.

All this visible decay of his robust strength was not the direct result of mental anxiety and care. He was still physically feeble from a slight experience of sunstroke the previous summer, which he took reverently as a summons

to him to "set his house in order," and to do his work as
if he must speedily render an account of his stewardship.
He was preparing even now to do this.

The very tones of his voice had something of eternity in
them, while he directed all hearts and thoughts and desires
to God as the only source of wisdom, strength, and salvation.

He prefaced the opening exercises by narrating, in a
most impressive manner, the following anecdote, which
was communicated to Stephen Gillett, the Quaker preacher,
by a friend in Russia : —

"Shortly after Napoleon entered Russia, and a cloud of darkness settled on that empire, when the Emperor was about yielding,
some one reported to him that a certain prince was acting the part
of a traitor; for, while all St. Petersburg was in anxiety and
terror, he was fitting up and repairing his magnificent palaces.
The Emperor sent for the prince and inquired into the matter.
'It is not so, your Majesty,' said he. 'How, then, are you making
these preparations for future prosperity?' 'Because,' said he, 'I
trust in God, that everything will yet be brought about, and peace
and prosperity will be restored.' 'How is this?' 'Because the
Bible instructs me to put my trust in Him.' 'What do you mean
by the Bible?' He took a Bible which lay near him, and which
accidentally dropped on the floor, and opened as it fell. He took
it up, saying, 'I will read to your Majesty the chapter which has
opened, and this will show you what I mean by the Bible.' He
then read the ninety-first psalm. The reading made a deep impression on the Emperor. Before leaving St. Petersburg, the Emperor
repaired to the largest church in the city. Much to his surprise,
the priest read the ninety-first psalm. After the service, the Emperor sent for the priest, and inquired how he came to select
that chapter. 'Who directed such a selection?' 'Nobody, your
Majesty; I sought direction from God what to read, and I thought
He directed me.' More confounded than before, the Emperor left

and proceeded on his journey. At night, arriving at another town, he entered a church, where, behold! the priest read the ninety-first psalm. Amazed at the occurrence, he sent to this priest also, and inquired, 'Who directed you to read that psalm?' 'Nobody, your Majesty; I did it because I thought I was directed to it by God, as appropriate to the times.' The Emperor was overwhelmed; and from that day became a religious man. And ever after he kept a Bible in his room, which he read morning and evening. The narrative was printed in a tract, with the psalm in question, and millions of copies were distributed throughout Russia."

He then read, with great effect, and in an almost audible silence, the ninety-first psalm; after which, he made the usual address of greeting, marked by wisdom that, to the thoughtful, seemed freshly inspired from heaven. His allusions to the state of the country were most impressive, displaying a firm and lofty patriotism, blending with profound sorrow for the unhappy misconceptions of Northern spirit and temper, which had led the South to rebellion, and constrained the Government to the dread alternative of war for its defence. We quote a part of this admirable address : —

" By the kind providence of God we are brought together to attend another anniversary. The simple purpose of our organization is the promotion of the religion of Christ. It is declared by our constitution to be the sole object of the society to extend the Redeemer's kingdom, by means of missions among the heathen. Can we meet for a higher, a holier, a better object? It becomes us, then, to act in the spirit of the Gospel which we aim to promote; to come in the spirit of Christ, the author of the Bible, which is indispensable to success in the propagation of the Gospel as it is in the progress of the religious life. 'For if any man have not the spirit of Christ, he is none of his.' If we are assembled to promote the work of the Holy Spirit, we must be influenced,

31*

directed, and controlled by that Spirit, or we have no hope of success. In the peculiar circumstances of the country we may expect that our assembly will be smaller than usual; but we have the sweet consolation that those who are here have come with hearts devoted to the great purposes of the Union. And I may ask that the time be sacredly, honestly, sincerely, and earnestly devoted to the claims of the missionary cause. It is not unkind to say that for several years past, the great and solemn objects of our association have been kept in the background, while other and collateral subjects have absorbed our attention. For the sake of the cause, for the sake of its Author, I beg that no more time may be so consumed.

"We are assembled here to-day under such circumstances as never before. I hope I shall go down to my grave before such a state of things occurs again. The country is flooded with armed men; families are leaving their homes; soldiers with their guns are flying to the field of conflict; the American flag floats over every street and village and community in our land. Patriotism sways the heart of every youth and every man of every age. All are rallying to the support of the Government, of law, and of order. I am amazed and excited at this outburst of patriotism. Oh, while we gather around the standard of our country with such enthusiasm, shall the standard of the Prince of Peace be deserted? It is not right. I would that the Christian host, wherever the standard of Christianity waves, might gather to its defence. How ardently is this to be desired. If our cause is just in this conflict with the South, as we believe; if it please God, He will cause it to succeed. Let us so conduct that we may compel our brethren in arms to respect us. I feel that the great difficulty is an entire misapprehension of our brethren of the South of the feeling of the North toward them. I wish the heart of the North could be uncovered to the South. If it were so, the trouble would end at once."

One of the returned missionaries of the Union, who met Governor Briggs for the first time at this anniversary, afterwards said of him, " That good man seemed to have more of the spirit of the Master than all the ministers present." It was, indeed, the spirit of Christ that characterized him, and, perhaps, especially during that session of the Convention, when the foundations of the Republic seemed to him to be shaking under his feet.

When the Union met again,[1] he was not in the chair. The forebodings of those who saw the change in him at Brooklyn were realized. His earthly work was then well nigh done, and before the anniversary returned he had gone to render up his account. His absence from the chair and from the scenes he was so closely identified with, threw a veil of sadness over that occasion.

The new President,[2] in his opening remarks, made the following allusion to his distinguished, but departed, predecessor : —

"When I remember who it was that for fifteen years, by your willing suffrages, occupied this chair, and how he honored it, and how you delighted to honor him, — especially when I remember the affluence of his virtues, his unostentatious piety, the beautiful simplicity of his life, his blameless innocence, his ardent devotion to the cause of missions, his active yet modest benevolence, exhausting itself in deeds of charity and love, — deeply conscious of my own inferior qualifications, I tremble at my own temerity in venturing to assume the position.

"It is not for me, on this occasion, to pronounce the panegyric of my lamented predecessor. Others have already performed that sad but grateful office. Eloquent lips have portrayed his exalted virtues. Your tears and sorrows have embalmed his memory.

"For more than half my life it was my happiness to enjoy the personal friendship of Governor Briggs. I cherish the recollection of his great and varied excellences with the tenderest reverence. Happy would it be for us all, if from the fading vision we could still catch a more holy enthusiasm."

[1] In Providence, May, 1862.
[2] Hon. Ira Harris, of Albany, N. Y.

When the Committee on Obituaries, in their report, paid a beautiful tribute to his memory, the Rev. Dr. Stow, of Boston, moved its acceptance and publication, and closed his personal tribute to his worth with these words : —

"All remember his opening and other addresses at these meetings, — tender, kind, genial, and eloquent. We shall never forget his opening address at Brooklyn last year. He has gone to his rest, more honored for his usefulness in the church, and having a larger amount of respect in Massachusetts, than any son who sleeps beneath her soil."

The suavity and equity of his rulings and decisions, in the sometimes excited sessions of the great representative body over which he presided for fifteen years, were the theme of grateful and general acknowledgment. One of the secretaries of the Union[1] at the time of his first taking the chair, said of him, in a funeral memorial : —

"Our relations to the Missionary Union, and to him as its presiding officer on that and several subsequent years, gave us the best possible opportunity to see and to know him in circumstances that would be likely to test some of the great qualities of his mind and heart; for those were years in which questions of missionary organization, of policy, and of administration, agitated our churches and public meetings as they have not done at any later period. We know that he had very positive opinions of his own upon these questions; but we can testify that we never knew him, in all these years of trial and peril, to swerve in a single instance from the line of an honorable impartiality in discharging the delicate and difficult duties of presiding officer.

"His ability to preside well was pre-eminent; and the consciousness on all sides that this ability was combined with the highest integrity, and the largest measure of practical good sense, gave

[1] Rev. Edward Bright, D. D., editor of the "*Examiner.*"

his decisions the weight of oracles. No man ever appealed from them, however much he may have regretted that they were not more favorable to his side of the question. Indeed, from the year 1848, no one arrangement was deemed so essential to a good meeting of the Missionary Union, as to be sure of having the President himself in the chair."

This chapter might be extended with many other pleasant and profitable reminiscences of his interest and labors in the great cause of missions. But here, as in all the special aspects of his life-work, a circumscribed selection of incident and material has been necessary to prevent the growth of this Memoir into too large a bulk.

His missionary spirit and efforts were alike memorable; and the church inscribes them in its records, and holds them in its remembrance, with unfeigned gratitude to God.

CHAPTER XXX.

THE year 1861 dawned upon the land in gloom and trouble. The rebellion, forever memorable hereafter in the annals of history, for its vast extent, its great persistence, its terrible accessories, its wonderful moral results; and all these surpassed in the wanton criminality of its design and origin, was really inaugurated in the secession of South Carolina. Each successive step of the melancholy progress excited fresh wonder and apprehension in the minds of patriots throughout the States, uninfected by the breath of treason.

These conditions of gloom and alarm affected Governor Briggs very deeply, as the reader has already gathered from the preceding chapter. In his own quiet home especially, every fresh rumor of trouble and every new measure of incipient revolution assumed, to his excited and nervous temperament, proportions of terror.

It is remembered that when he first saw in print the fiery, wicked message which Senator Toombs, of Georgia, sent from Washington to his constituents, he rose and paced the floor of his library in exceeding agitation of spirit, deploring the madness which as he expressed it, would " fire the magazine."

From day to day his depression increased, doubtless aided by his physical weakness. On one occasion he said to his children, speaking of the condition of public affairs, " The die is cast, and we are all gone."

Although he took at times more hopeful views of the case, he passed the early months of the year in a despondency of mind, from which nothing but the consolations of religion availed effectually to rouse him. For weeks he heard the mutterings of the approaching storm, and could find no comfort except in prayer and meditation upon God's faithfulness.

At these times he read, continually, such psalms as the seventy-seventh,[1] and in his favorite Bible the fourth verse of this psalm was marked completely round with his pencil, " *Thou holdest mine eyes waking. I am so troubled that I cannot speak.*"

His son says that this was literally his experience, and that his apprehension and grief, in reference to the progress and prospect of the national troubles, seemed, at one time, likely to produce serious illness.

His letters of this period, however, reflect but little of this gloom. He seems to have assumed a cheerfulness he did not feel, that he might not cast shadows upon the hearts of others.

He writes thus to his daughter : —

PITTSFIELD, Feb. 6th, 1861.

MY DEAR DAUGHTER:

Your mother and I are in the library *solitary and alone.* Both

---

1 " I cried unto God with my voice, &c."

families, by the blessing of our Heavenly Father, are in usual health. Henry is much engaged with his company,[1] resolved to be in readiness for any demands the country may make upon him. I hope it will be with him, as General Root, of New York, wished it might be with the militia of New York. On the occasion of a military dinner, a captain arose and proposed as a sentiment, — "The militia of the State of New York; may they never want, and ——" he hesitated, stammered, and repeated, "The militia of New York; may they never want, and — and ——" till the suspense becoming painful to the company, General Root roared out, "*never be wanted.*"

Nothing new in town. Dr. T. has been quite sick with diphtheria. He is doing well. Several persons were talking about the good things that had been sent him, naming, especially, brandy and port-wine. C. R. was present, and said he guessed the doctor would get along, if he did not die of delirium tremens! The joke delighted the Doctor. Love to Charles.

Affectionately, your father,

G. N. BRIGGS.

The following letter was addressed to a Southern gentleman with whom he had formed an agreeable friendship, and maintained a correspondence for years. It possesses great interest, as a reflection of his opinions at that critical juncture, and also as an expression of his views as to the moral position of Massachusetts towards the disaffected States :—

PITTSFIELD, Feb. 20, 1861.

DEAR SIR :

Your letter of last July was received. I did not answer it because I was in poor health most of the summer, and scarcely had the spirit to answer a letter, and because, if I had, I could not have concurred with you in your views of the questions of the

---

1 The Allen Guard. This was the first company from Western Massachusetts, to march for the defence of Washington. It was under the command of Capt. Henry S. Briggs.

day. The reception of it gave me much pleasure, for it was evidence that I was remembered by one whose views I had much respected. Yours of the 25th ult. was also received, but by some accident I did not get it until some days after it arrived. I was gratified at its reception for the same reason that I was with the other. The pleasure was mingled with deep sadness — you told me you wrote from a "foreign country!" Then you and I have no longer one common country! As soon as those who fought and bled for a common country are in their graves, their children have rent that country asunder! The bones of Greene now lie in a country foreign from that of his birth! Can these things be? and yet you say it is settled! You stated in brief, what the South regarded as justification for so important a procedure of breaking up this Union. I thought at first I would, in reply, state to you what we at the North regarded as the true state of the case, but on the whole concluded it would not be useful, and do not do it.

But, my friend (for such I trust I may truly call you, until we shall meet in a world where the question of *slavery* will not mar our Union or alloy our happiness), I will say to you that I believe and am quite sure that the people of the South are entirely misled and deceived as to the intentions and feelings of the people of the North towards them. The people of the North are opposed to slavery because they believe it to be morally and politically wrong. They believe it to be a local institution, belonging entirely to the States where it exists, and that they have not only no right to interfere with it there, but they have no intention, wish, or desire to interfere with it there. To its extension into free territory they are opposed, because they believe it wrong, and because they believe also that the South has no constitutional right to demand that it should go there, and they believe that she has no right to ask it on the ground of good neighborhood; because they believe that those who formed the Constitution expected and believed that before a very long period the institution of slavery would, by the action of those who then sustained it, become extinct. That is the reason why there is nothing in that Constitution from which any strangers to our institutions could have known there was such a one as slavery.

32

When the Constitution was adopted, slavery, by almost the unanimous action of the four Southern slave States, had been forever abolished from every foot of territory that belonged to the United States. Thus the Union and the Constitution began. Has the South any ground of complaint of the action of the General Government towards her since then? Nine new slave States have been admitted, and five of them out of territory acquired since the adoption of the Constitution. Has not the South had her full share in every department of the Government? Is the election of a President according to the forms of the Constitution, without an official act on his part, good cause to dissolve the Union? Massachusetts is probably as anti-slavery in opinion as any other State; and yet I declare to you, I have never heard any man in Massachusetts express an intention, or wish in any manner, to interfere with slavery or the rights of slaveholders in the slave States. In Massachusetts, at this moment, there are no feelings among her people but those of kindness and good-will towards the people of your State. Any citizen of Georgia could at this moment pass through, mingle with our people, and express without reserve his opinion upon any of the topics of the day, without receiving any incivility or interruption. Even Toombs might again speak in Faneuil Hall without interruption. Massachusetts has heretofore passed a Personal Liberty Bill, which has never been put in force. The law was not passed with the intention of opposing the Fugitive Slave Law, bad and offensive as that law is, — but for the protection of our own citizens. Parts of that personal liberty law I believe to be unconstitutional, and ought not to have been passed, and ought at once to be repealed for that reason. Those parts of it, I believe, would not be sustained by our courts, if questions under it should ever arise. The South has never been injured by it, and in my view it furnishes no reason for breaking up the Union. Massachusetts believes the South under the Constitution is entitled to a reasonable fugitive slave law, which ought to be carried out. But she believes slavery is wrong, and will go no further in that matter, or any other, than to fulfil her constitutional obligations. With these views, the South had no right to ask them to go any further. I tell you again, my friend, the people of

Georgia are mistaken as to the feelings and intentions of the people of Massachusetts towards them. If you could mingle among them at this time you would be satisfied of the truth of this assertion.

But you say the die is cast, and you wish to avoid war. I fully concur with you. Let me say to you, my dear sir, in all this matter, it is the South who has talked and acted violence. Has she not with violence seized the forts, arsenals, and magazines of the Government, plundered its mint and seized its money and threatened blood? The North believes the Government has the right to protect its property and execute its laws, — with all the provocation received, has it done any violence? I think the general sentiment of the North is against war and blood. God grant it may always be. With all the excitement and warlike movements at the South, you would be surprised to witness the quiet of the North.

Compare the calm, conciliatory and friendly language of the President elect, on his way to his official station, with the language and tone of the new President of the new Confederacy. What a contrast! I need not ask you which accords best with your own feelings. Mr. Davis may some time learn that such language neither excites fear nor creates respect at the North.

Our national condition is sad and gloomy. I fear that we have all so under-estimated our numerous blessings, and been so forgetful of the bountiful Giver, that He is about to leave us to bring upon ourselves, by our own madness, the chastisement which we deserve. But He reigns and will reign. He can make the wrath of man to praise Him, and the remainder of wrath He will restrain.

Let the political commotions be what they may, my dear sir, may you and I cherish love for our Master and love for each other.

Very truly, your friend,

GEO. N. BRIGGS.

Here is one of his birth-day letters. It was his habit to commemorate these occasions in his correspondence with those dearest to him, and to make them times of spiritual retrospection. His habitual self-depreciation is apparent in this letter : —

PITTSFIELD, 12th April, 1861.

MY DEAR SON:

Henry received your letter last night. He expects to leave for Lawrence at 3 P. M., with Mary and Harry and Mamie and little Nelly. I suggested to your mother that she had better go with the goers; but I suppose she thinks I shall not be able to keep house without her.

This day I am sixty-five years old. How old! and yet how little have I done that I ought to have done — nothing! And, yet how good and merciful has God been to me and mine. If *One* who is worthy were not our Advocate, how desperate would be human hopes! Rowland Hill said, if he ever got to heaven, it would be by crawling in on his hands and knees. How inspiring the thought that we may one day, with Bunyan's Pilgrim, look upon Him who was spit upon, and who wore the crown of thorns — wearing the diadem of the universe! To be the humblest, and to occupy the lowest place in the numberless throng of the redeemed, will be all that I could ask.

Good Dr. Humphrey's funeral was numerously attended, on Monday. Dr. Todd preached an excellent sermon. On Monday night the widow of John Humphrey, who was visiting at the doctor's late residence, died very suddenly. She has been ill a long time; but no immediate danger was apprehended. She went without a moment's warning. S. said yesterday, she could not but think with what a sweet smile of surprise her father would meet her in heaven as he would say " Why, daughter, have you come so soon!"

The doctor, all things considered, I think, was for worth and wisdom second to no human I being I ever knew.

Affectionately, your father,

G. N. BRIGGS.

His daughter here becomes, again, his biographer. She says, —

"The blows that had fallen on Fort Sumter and our dishonored flag there, had passed, every one of them, like electric throbs through every fibre of Massachusetts.

"The first call of President Lincoln for seventy-five thousand troops was heard at Bunker Hill, though it had not reached the hills of Berkshire. Returning at an unusual hour in the afternoon of April 18th, from his customary walk to the village, my father brought, open in his hand, a long, narrow ribbon of paper, inscribed by the telegraphic fingers with words which were among those that thrilled the hearts of many who dwelt in peaceful New England homes. They ran thus: —

" 'BOSTON, April 18, 1861.

" 'GEORGE N. BRIGGS, Pittsfield, Mass.:

" 'Probably I shall pass Springfield, not coming home. Come to Springfield with mother and the children. Get Georgie's and Harry's Daguerreotypes on one plate, for a locket.[1] Bring my uni-

---

[1] This locket was the occasion of an interesting incident at the Battle of Fair Oaks; and gave rise to the following correspondence between General Briggs and Colonel Jenkins, — the latter, a youthful and gallant soldier, was killed in the Battle of the Wilderness: —

"HEAD-QUARTERS PALMETTO SHARPSHOOTERS.
"COLONEL:

"Having obtained from one of my men a medallion, containing, I presume, the likenesses of your family, I return the same to you. The medallion was found in your camp, in which my regiment slept the night after the battle of the 31st ult.; and, though willing to meet you ever in the field while acting as a foe to my country, I do not war with your personal feelings; and, supposing the medallion to be prized by you, I take pleasure in returning it.

"M. JENKINS, Col. Palmetto Sharpshooters.
"Col. H. S. BRIGGS, Colonel 10th Mass. Vols."

"IN CAMP NEAR SHARPSBURG, Md., Oct. 7, 1862.
"GENERAL:

"On a visit, yesterday, to head-quarters of the 10th Regiment Mass. Vols., formerly commanded by me, and from which I had been separated by wounds received at the Battle of Seven Pines on the 31st of May last, I found a note from you, as commander of the Palmetto Sharpshooters, accompanying a much-prized locket, containing, as you conjectured, the likenesses of my family. By some unaccountable negligence on the part of those to whom it was committed, the execution of your kind intentions has been delayed. I trust the delay in the

32*

form. Coat, sword, belt, sash, hat, epaulets, are in the office; fatigue-coat and cap in the armory; pants in the wardrobe at home. Let Georgie find them.

" 'H. S. BRIGGS.'

"But few words were spoken in the household. Children's heads and hearts grew suddenly old, and were busy, as were older hands, in making hurried preparations for departure. In the mean time, the young fair faces were copied, with the shadow of pain upon them which the hour had left there; and at evening our father and mother, with Georgie and Harry, were hastening to Springfield, for the meeting and the farewell. A train from the east brought its throng of stifled, struggling, resolute souls, — soldiers and citizens, men, women, and children.

" My brother was not in his place when a cause in which he was engaged [1] was resumed, in the Supreme Court in Boston, on the morning of the 19th of April. 'Where is Mr. Briggs?' demanded the Chief Justice; and the response was, ' Gone, at the head of his company, to Washington.'

" That morning, with wife and little children and his brother, he had taken the cars from Boston to Springfield. Awaiting him

receipt of the locket and your note, will be a sufficient apology for my long delay in acknowledging the favor you have conferred upon me.

" I beg to assure you of my high appreciation of the generous magnanimity and delicate courtesy of your act, and to thank you, with all my heart, for the restoration of that, in comparison with which all other loss of effects on that day was of no consequence.

" You will pardon me if I say, in alluding to a paragraph in your note, that I cannot, without pain, contemplate the meeting as a *foe*, even on the field, one who has performed so honorable an act, and conferred on me so great a favor.

" I cannot say that I desire the opportunity to requite the favor under similar circumstances, but I will assure you, that, should *any* opportunity ever occur, I shall improve it with pleasure and alacrity. Until then, and ever, I shall hold you and your deed of kindness in grateful remembrance.

" I am, sir, very respectfully, your ob't serv't,

" HENRY S. BRIGGS, Brig. Gen. Vols. U. S. A.

" Gen. M. JENKINS."

[1] This cause was the famous Elephant case, to which allusion is made in Chapter XXII. It was now on trial in the Supreme Court, and Henry S. Briggs, Esq., was conducting the case for the plaintiff.

there, were his own 'Allen Guard,' summoned, only a few hours before, from the farms and workshops and stores and offices and homes of beautiful Pittsfield; and, without delay, they hastened to Baltimore, for they had heard of the *baptism* of blood there on the 19th of April.

"A 'bruised reed' was our father that day. Our mother was tearless. Death could not have made the cottage home on the hillside more empty, when they, with the soldier's wife and children, kindled among the ashes of happier days the fire on the deserted hearth.

"*At home* there was only patient waiting, earnest praying, *faith in God*, and life's daily duty. *Joy* had gone! hope, alone, whispered of safety and of a future reunion with the absent one. Those who sent father, husband, son, or brother, at that call of danger which came from the heart of the nation, will know forever what patriotism is, and what an all-devouring passion it becomes when such a sacrifice is required and made, and they will know, too, how hearts can bleed and love.

"The effect of this great strain upon my father's health was alarming. He never, for a moment, faltered in the firmness with which he gave his son, as his own right hand, to his country. How could so true a patriot falter! But his suffering overpowered his nervous system, so that, at one time, we dreaded a paralyzing overthrow. The next morning, after the departure of the 'Allen Guard,' he could read at family worship only in a husky whisper. Within a few days afterwards he was summoned to Boston on business, and went as a necessity, returning as soon as possible to Pittsfield. He was there, witnessing and sharing in the excitement and confusion of those first dreadful days of rebellion, and said he felt in danger of losing his reason. There, so changed and enfeebled was he in appearance, that his eldest son felt the parental claims upon him to be irresistible, and resolved, as soon as practicable, to change his business arrangements in the city of Lawrence, where he was residing, and take up his abode with his father in Pittsfield. That father's voice sunk into a feeble whisper, instead of the full rich tones so peculiar to him; and in three weeks he lost, without being ill, twenty-five pounds in weight. I never saw such ravages made by purely mental distress. However, there came to him at length a stimulus, in the daily excitement of the news, and the best of tonics in letters from his son. So wonderfully are we organized to suffer, when we *must*, that time, while it does not remove or efface the grief of stricken ones, yet brings solace, and teaches us day by day how constantly and calmly we can endure an abiding sorrow. Accustomed to the cloud into which we enter, as into a great darkness, we learn to walk not seeing whither our steps are led. The tramp of armed hosts shakes the ground, and we sleep peacefully. Vacant places confront us everywhere, and yet we *smile*. God has made us so that we *cannot* be miserable, unless we *forsake* Him and wander as orphans in His world."

CHAPTER XXXI.

OF the letters from his son in the service of his country, which proved such happy tonics to the depressed and sinking spirits of Governor Briggs, the following is an example. It possesses a special interest, moreover, as coming from on board the gallant ship whose name is linked with the earlier naval glory of the Republic. It is addressed not to his father but to his wife : —

U. S. FRIGATE "CONSTITUTION," April 22, 1861.

DEAREST MOLLY :

You will doubtless be greatly surprised to have me hail from the glorious old ship so famous in our history. My last to you was a hasty note from Philadelphia, on the eve of our departure from that city.

On our journey to Hayre de Grace, where there is a ferry railroad across the Susquehanna, Captain Devereaux's company and mine were selected for what proved to be exciting business. It was known before we left, that the rebels had laid a plan to seize the ferry which we must cross ; in which event the two companies were ordered to retake it, the rest of the regiment being able only to act in support. by reason of the narrow approach to the boat.

Now, for the first time, the two companies loaded with ball car-
tridges under the inspection of the Brigade Major. You may well
imagine that all hands were not so steady as usual, and that some
of the men, who at home are quite familiar with the use of fire-
arms, exhibited, under the observation of the staff officer, unusual
awkwardness.

But the Pittsfield boys behaved nobly, and not one of them
flinched. We had a pretty fair test of our pluck in the opportunity
of coolly contemplating for two hours all the dangers of a charge
with the bayonet. There were some watery eyes as the chances
were calculated and contingencies provided for; but there never
was a more enthusiastic response than was made in the shout of
assent which the men gave me, when, after stating to them fully
the nature and danger of the undertaking, I asked them if they
were ready to stand by and follow me.

One incident I must detail. Before reaching the place, I told
the men I proposed to lead them with bayonet in hand, as did
Lieutenant Richardson; and that it would be necessary for us to
take two of the muskets from the privates, of course relieving the
men thus disarmed from participation in the enterprise. I asked
some one to lend me a gun. Not one was offered. I turned to a
fair-faced boy of nineteen, — whom we have often seen about C.'s
carriage establishment, — and told him I would take his musket, as
it was left for me to make a choice.

He withdrew his gun as I reached forth my hand for it, and immediately burst into tears; clinging to it with the devotion of a
veteran, and pleading with me not to deprive him of a part in the
dangerous service. His conduct was as noble and heroic as though
the enterprise had been carried into execution, and we had met
the fate of a forlorn hope. His name is Richard Powers.

We were agreeably disappointed in being suffered to take peace-
able possession of the steamer; the outlaws having retreated,
after occupying the locality the same morning, and burning the
dwelling-house of the president, or superintendent, of the railroad company.

The whole regiment, to the number of something more than
seven hundred men, embarked immediately, and instead of pro-

ceeding to Baltimore by rail, steamed directly for Annapolis, the capital of Maryland, and the site of the Naval Academy, where the ship in which we now are was moored, and threatened with capture by the rebel authorities.

We arrived before daylight, and twice the troops were called to arms by apprehensions of an attack. At an early hour yesterday (Sunday) morning we got alongside and made fast to the old ship, with the purpose of towing her over the bar and out of the bay (the Chesapeake) towards her destination, which was New York. But both vessels got aground, and we are yet within full view of Annapolis and the wharf we left about noon yesterday.

Last night, fifty of my company were ordered on board the ship with Captain Devereaux's men. I learn the intention is to keep us on board until she is towed to New York, for her protection from the enemy. Had we reached her six hours later, the dear old ship would have been in the hands of the rebels, as yesterday was the day they had fixed upon for seizing her, and a body of six hundred of the secession force is just behind the hills on the shore, intending to take the ship. Indeed they desired to attack us and attempt to take her yesterday, but were dissuaded. This morning a tug from New York has arrived to take her on. The "Boston," a steamer from Philadelphia, has also just passed us with the Seventh Regiment on board, bound for Washington, *via* the Potomac. The Seventh left Philadelphia about the time we did.

I have been well, though the fatigue has been very great — having so constantly to be on the alert, and in such close quarters on the Havre de Grace ferry-boat. . . . . . I need not tell you how much I thought yesterday of the quiet home and the dear ones there, and how little I could realize the object of our expedition, or that the day was Sunday. I cannot write more now. Love to all.

Affectionately yours,

H. S. Briggs.

After the receipt of this letter at the homestead, Governor Briggs wrote to his son as follows : —

PITTSFIELD, April 24th, 1861.

MY DEAR SON:

I have nothing special to communicate. I only write to say that by the blessing of God, we are all in health, at both houses. Lonesome and anxious, we are, of course. In this respect we are situated like many of our neighbors and great multitudes of our countrymen. Ferry[1] came on Saturday night. He says he had the account of the occurrences in Baltimore when the Sixth Regiment of Massachusetts troops passed through. On the part of the sixty men who marched *two* miles, opposed by a mob of four thousand, there was a manifestation of cool bravery, which was very uncommon. A man told him, that after that company entered the cars, and were moving off, one of the rioters said, "It is no use to try to do anything." "Why?" asked another. "Because," said he, with an oath, and pointing to the cars moving off, "Because there goes Bunker Hill."

We should be glad to see you, but if you cannot leave so that all will go on well, *don't come.*

In this time of gloom, may we trust in God.

Affectionately your father,

G. N. BRIGGS.

Forwarding the letter from Captain Briggs just quoted, to his daughter at Lawrence, he writes : —

PITTSFIELD, April 25, 1861.

MY DEAR DAUGHTER:

Inclosed I send you a letter from dear Henry. Its details show that he has true courage, and that his men are of real *metal.* The story of the young man is very touching. I read it to Mr. C. His lips quivered and his eyes filled with tears. What times! If God did not rule the world, I should despair and die; but I hope to acquiesce in His good and right government. If He designs to humble us by sad reverses, He will do it; if not, we shall be sustained. In my sadness the other night, I opened a letter and found

---

[1] Then a member of Congress from Connecticut; since Brig.-General of Volunteers, and now U. S. Senator.

a tract, which detailed a conversation between Cromwell's Ambassador to Sweden, and his servant. In a storm he was waiting to start on his mission, and was sad over the condition of his country, and could not sleep. His servant said, "Please sir, may I ask you a question?" "Certainly," said he. "Then, sir, don't you think God governed the world very well before you came into it?" "Certainly," said he. "Please, sir, don't you think he will govern it as well after you have left it?" "Certainly." "Then, sir, won't it be as well for you to be content, and let Him govern it while you are in it?" The ambassador made no reply, but turned over and slept till he was called to go. How just and beautiful the rebuke! May I take it and profit by it. We look for George and Whitey[1] to-morrow. Love to Charles. Come as soon as you can. All well as usual, except your mother. God bless you both.

Affectionately, your father,

G. N. BRIGGS.

The reminiscences of Mrs. Bigelow, again help the biographer in his pleasing task : —

"The last time my father was in Boston, he went to the Tract Society's[2] rooms, as he always liked to do when in the city, and went into the private room of the Secretary to tell him how valuable the little tract[3] of two pages had been to him; and at the same time he had with this friend a delightful talk of a few minutes on the presence of God in human events, and of the peace which real faith in Him inspires."

Inspirited by his son's letter, he seeks, with noble words, to inspirit him in return : —

PITTSFIELD, 28th April, 1861.

MY DEAR SON:

We were glad to hear from you yesterday. Since you left, the

---

[1] A favorite horse more than once mentioned in these Memoirs, and still cared for by the family.

[2] He was President of the American Tract Society up to the time of his death.

[3] The tract alluded to in the foregoing letter.

excitement here and throughout the State has been at fever heat. P—— has generously deposited a thousand dollars for another company. The "Allen Guard," with their commander, have been much in the minds of our people and much on their tongues, since they left. You must have had stirring times all the while till your arrival at Annapolis.

I think, so far as we are informed, Butler's course and conduct do him credit, and elevate him in public estimation. I believe, if this contest continues, he will make his mark so that his name will live. I heard him make a short speech at Springfield, which I think was exactly the thing. I was never more gratified with anything of the kind.

Massachusetts has early gained a prominence in this war, which is very remarkable. At once she is placed high in the estimation of sister States, and I hope she will continue to deserve the credit she has won. I still hope that God, in His great mercy, will order this most unprovoked rupture between the States of this Republic to be rightly adjusted. But if the wrong-doers persist in their madness, and the contest goes on, fully believing we are on the side of good government, law, and right, I trust He will give success to the right and rebuke the wrong. I hope those who will have to fight, if fight we must, will look to God to give strength to their arms in the hour of trial. What an example the brave and good Havelock is to Christian soldiers! Allow me to express the hope, my son, that while you do all your duty as a soldier, you will as faithfully do your duty to the Captain of your Salvation. Nothing sustains me in my regret at your absence but the cheering belief that, while you march under the banner of your country, and bravely support it, you will never cease to feel that the banner of your Saviour waves always over you, and that His strong arm will sustain you. God have you and all of us in His holy keeping, and give success to what we believe to be the just cause of our country.

Affectionately, your father,

G. N. BRIGGS.

In one sentence of the next letter he gently reproaches his son for what it is manifest from his whole life, was

something like an inherited trait — that of self-depreciation : —

PITTSFIELD, May 14, 1861.

MY DEAR SON:

Your long and most welcome letter came to hand yesterday. It
broke up some water fountains, but nobody was drowned. We
are getting on very well, considering the absence of one who
thinks he would be of no consequence here. We should be quite
willing to try to live with him. I hope, my son, you will hereafter
forego remarks so under-estimating yourself, and be willing to let
the opinions of your friends have their proper weight in the estimation of your worth. I have little news to write. The spring is
late, — no planting, so far as I know, in the fields, and but little in
the gardens. *Greylock* looks fluely. The patriotic feeling keeps
up. The "Allen Guard" is not forgotten. Whittlesy is going on
to join them. I hope there is room for him. I rejoice greatly to
learn that your health is so good, and that the Father of mercies
has preserved the health of your company. Above all, I hope that
the morals of your company will be preserved, and that they will
show that soldiers in the service of their country can maintain the
character and morals of good citizens, and thus do a double service
to their country. I feel the deepest interest in their success, desir-
ous that by soldierly, manly, and upright conduct, they honor their
town, and show themselves to be true sons of Massachusetts.
God *bless* you all. His protecting care has been signally over you
all. I pray that it may continue to be so. Show yourselves to be
men.

A day or two later he writes again; and there is a
gleam of his old playfulness in the lines : —

PITTSFIELD, 16th May, 1861.

MY DEAR SON:

Since you and your company left home, you have not been permitted to halt long enough to wash your face and hands. We had
hardly finished your letter giving an account of your improved
condition at Fort McHenry, before we received your telegram

announcing that you are at Federal Hill; and this morning it is
said General Butler and the Massachusetts troops are ordered to
Fortress Monroe. These, I suppose, are the chances of war; and,
as cousin Richard Briggs said when it rained hard and he wanted
fair weather: "There is no use saying a word." . . . . .

God bless and preserve you, my son.

Affectionately, your father,

G. N. BRIGGS.

The grandfather's heart keeps all the freshness that filled
the father's, twenty years before; and it wells out in this
extract from another letter to his son: —

. . . . . "Little Harry went to church this morning, and
slept through. After we came out, he asked if he had not behaved
well? He is a *dear* little fellow. Little Nelly is as healthy as a
doe. Your brother George procured a pole more than forty feet
long for a flag-staff, and Georgie has painted it ready to be raised.
Mary has draped your full-length portrait with *the colors.* The
other day, I whittled out a sword for Harry. He painted the blade
white and the handle black, and has placed it across and under the
picture, and it sets it off very well. My best wishes to all the
'Guard.' God bless you. Much love from your mother."

His daughter's hand guides us yet again along his declining pathway: —

" As the summer advanced, he gradually regained his health and
usual tone of spirits, and was actively interested and occupied in
passing events. Indeed, he seemed in more elastic and firmer
health than for many years. He was vigorous in thought, cheerful
and hopeful for the country, and his social, genial nature seemed
never to find so many sweet expressions and ministries. He had
a pleasant word for everybody; his good stories were never better
or more ready. All of us who knew him best saw that he dwelt *in
the light.* Many passages in his letters written during the summer
have *now* a thrilling significance. We see *now* that the exceeding

peace which flooded the evening of his life, while tempestuous scenes were passing around him, was the dawning of heaven upon him; so kindly was the veil suffered to rest over the event of death; and yet so evidently was his spirit made ready for the approaching ho ir of its departure from the body with which it had dwelt more than sixty years. How often after the departure of the beloved, this heavenly preparation becomes manifest to us, not discerning it fully at the time.

" Sitting down one calm evening, he said to my mother, ' I wonder when I shall go home.' A few days before he was stricken down, he visited an intimate friend in his office. He entered it in a playful mood. Breathing quickly after mounting the stairs, he said, ' I am growing old,' and then his countenance suddenly assumed an earnest expression, and he said, ' but, brother Francis, I don't feel as I used to about growing old. Death has lost much of its gloom,' and proceeded to discourse of *dying*, and the realities and occupations of *another life.*"

Under date of June 25, 1861, he writes : —

"How fast we are all hastening to the other world! What manner of persons ought we to be !"

The incidents of the war were now the most engrossing of earthly things to his mind. He writes again : —

PITTSFIELD, 18th July, 1861.
MY DEAR DAUGHTER:

On Monday morning, all of both families accompanied Henry to Springfield, with the intention of seeing him and his regiment off. Previous to their going, there was a very interesting ceremony of presenting the state and national colors to the regiment, by the ladies of Springfield.

I was impressed with the power of Henry's voice when giving orders to the regiment. It was clear, distinct, and penetrating, and distinctly heard at a great distance. I suppose I was not an impartial judge of his appearance. His labors are very severe;

33*

and if the cause he is engaged in was not the most just and sacred that man can be engaged in, I could not be reconciled to the labor and fatigue and anxiety it costs *him*, to say nothing of the solicitude of his *friends*. God bless and preserve him. I know He does all things well.

Your affectionate father,

GEO. N. BRIGGS.

A little later he writes again, the influence of things to come — beyond the narrow sea — prevailing now over the disturbing influences of earth. How manifestly, although unconsciously, he is ripening for heaven and its felicities :

"We shall very soon, in the course of nature, be where the anxieties, solicitudes, and glooms of this life will not disturb us. If, then, we shall be so happy as to be in that joyous world, where no one will say ' I am sick,' and all tears will be wiped away from the eyes of its peaceful inhabitants, where He who groaned on Calvary will be the delight and admiration of blissful myriads, no matter what may be our transient uneasiness here.

"I hope you and Charles will be able to see Henry before he leaves. With kindest love for Charles,

"Affectionately, your father,

"G. N. BRIGGS."

Father and son never meet again : —

"The vision of the beloved face," writes Colonel Briggs, "upturned to heaven, peaceful and fair as a child's, while he stood on the wharf in Boston, was my last, until the silence and sacredness of death rested upon him."

"At that last interview," says the daughter, "each was similarly impressed with the appearance of the other, and both seemed to have discerned a peculiar glow of ' the inner countenance of the soul,' — a glimpse, perhaps, of what we shall be when ' this mortal shall have put on immortality.' In speaking of the departure of his son, standing under the evening sky, his head uncovered, on the wheel-house of the steamer, which was veiled in clouds of cannon-smoke, rolling up to blend with sunset clouds, he said, 'H. looked angelic with the serene smile that lighted up his face.' Shall they not meet again?

> " 'Oh, the rest forever and the rapture!
> Oh, the hand that wipes the tears away!
> Oh, the golden homes beyond the sunset,
> And the hope that watches o'er the clay!' "

Under date of August 14th, he writes to his son at Camp Brightwood, just out of Washington : —

" This morning we hear of the great battle in Missouri and the death of General Lyon. The disproportion of forces was very great. . . . . . We are glad to hear you are better, and well established in your new camp. I hope the sickness among your men is diminished. Saw the Governor and staff at Commencement,[1] but did not talk with them. Colonel L. spoke of you in the kindest terms; said that you had the reputation of standing up for the rights of your men. Do your duty faithfully as an officer. Be kind and true to your men. Trust in God. Daily bear the yoke of the Saviour. Live *near* Him and all will be well. The Saviour has said ' My yoke is easy and my burden is light,' and He will give rest to those who come unto Him. This is as true in the camp as it is in civil life. Make my kind regards to Mr. Blair, and my respects to your officers.

" Affectionately, your father,

"G. N. BRIGGS."

A letter from one who met him on that Commencement occasion, brings him back to memory with welcome truthfulness : —

" The vivid remembrance of our delightful Christian intercourse at Williamstown, a little more than a month ago, comes up in con

[1] In his remarks at the dinner of the Alumni, he was conciliatory in his tone, and inculcated kind feeling towards our enemies, " though," said he, " my right arm is given to fight, if fight we *must.*"

templating his departure, — so kind, so gentle, so loving, was all he
said and did. It was mainly owing to his benevolent efforts in
the Board of Trustees, that the delinquencies of a student were
overlooked, and a degree given to him. 'We must not sacrifice
the young man,' he said, 'perhaps, by kindness, we can win him
into the right path.' "

The last letter he wrote was addressed to his son in the
army. For all who loved him it possesses a deep and
almost sacred interest. It is dated, —

PITTSFIELD, Aug. 20, 1861.

MY DEAR SON:

We are glad to hear that the health of your men is improving,
and that you are well. We are well. While this intelligence can
be mutually communicated, how grateful should we be to that
blessed Providence who has been so merciful and good to us as a
family. I saw a letter to-day from young Hemmingway,[1] of the
Pollock Guard. It was a well-written letter, in which he said
some agreeable things of their Colonel. . . . . . A strict discipline, with kindness, and a proper regard for the welfare of the
men, will secure respect and love. I rejoice to see the rigid and
excellent rules which McClellan has proclaimed for his army. The
observance of temperance in his camp, which, it is said, Butler has
enforced among his soldiers, and prescribed for himself and officers, cannot but be useful and honorable. It is a *fact* too well
proved to be denied, that intoxicating liquors are not useful to
men in health, and should be used as medicine with great caution
and wisdom. But I will not give a lecture on temperance, as I
have promised Sayles to go to South Adams and give one on
Thursday night.

Your mother sends "a dear mother's love," and you know what
that is.

I have taxed you with a long letter, when you have so little

---

[1] Sergeant Haskell Hemmingway, of the 10th Regiment, a noble and youthful
soldier, who fell bravely fighting at Malvern Hill, and one of three sons from a
neighbor's family who were victims of the war.

time to read one. *Remember, it is from a father who in the course of nature will not tax you to read his letters a great while longer. Never forget or neglect, my son, the best friend you have in the universe, who will never forsake you, if you do not forsake Him. I think every day of my fleeting life I more and more love "Him who is altogether lovely, and chiefest among ten thousand." I hope one day to be with Him, and to see Him as He is.*[1]

With kind regards to all your officers who think my regards worth having. God bless you.

Affectionately, your father,

G. N. BRIGGS.

P. S. Yesterday little Harry, gun in hand, went through the manual exercise for Grandmamma Bulkley's benefit. For shoulder arms, he very *emphatically* said, "*soldier*" arms.

During the last six weeks of his life, he was much more cheerful than he had been for months. He made several addresses, short public speeches, which are vividly remembered by all who listened to them. A nephew wrote to him, during the political campaign preceding the fall election, urging him to make a speech in New York. He wrote in reply, —

"My dear boy, I have put off my political harness, and cannot put it on again. After such a speaker as Lincoln, I should fail, and that would mortify you."

In the month of August, after the return of the Allen Guard to Pittsfield, at the close of their three months' service, the company attended religious service at the Baptist church, on which occasion Governor Briggs addressed them in his most eloquent and feeling and impassioned manner. One who heard him, says of the address, —

---

[1] These italicized words are engraved upon a marble scroll drooping over his tomb.

"He spoke to them of patriotism, declaring it to comprehend love of home and love of country, respect and obedience to law, and the fulfilment, with a loyal and true heart, of all the duties of the citizen to the Government and to the country. The opposite of patriotism, is spoken in one word — *treason!* and the opposite of the patriot is the *traitor.*"

These latter words were pronounced with a most impressive emphasis and solemnity. He then applied the principle of patriotism to religious obligation to the benign and exalted government of God, and exhibited the sin of man in his rebellion against such a government and such a God. He closed with an affecting and earnest appeal to every one to make the Saviour his friend, and to seek him with all the heart, and without delay.

Among the latest public utterances of his eloquent lips, was a brief address of welcome to the Hon. Joseph Holt, who made a brief stay in the village, and to whom the citizens gave a cordial reception. Not long afterwards, the names of these distinguished gentlemen were associated together in the public prints, as umpires in the question which had arisen between our Government and that of New Grenada. The anticipation of service on this important commission, stirred in his heart not a few of the old and apparently extinct pulsations of interest, and he spoke with a keen zest of the pleasure with which he should mingle, yet again, with public men and things.

It is not a little remarkable that upon the very day on which the newspapers thus revoked him to public life, a fiat, more resistless than that of a mighty human government, interdicted him from obedience to that call, and bade him leave forever the busy theatre and the shifting scenes of earthly life.

As the veil is now to drop over the activities and achievements and honors, which so broadly and shiningly marked his career, the biographer is glad to give place to one whose intimacy with him entitles him to the privilege of letting it fall, with few but fitly chosen words of retrospect and commemoration : —

"It is now, I suppose, considerably more than thirty years since I became acquainted with him, and every year has added to the strength of my early conviction of his various and distinguished excellences. Nature endowed him with the finest powers of mind. But to me his great mental endowments were less attractive than his geniality, kindness, and the frank and open impulses of his nature. He was *strictly* and *ever* a man of probity and truth. Long in public life, a part of the time mixed up with bitter political contests, — how few men pass through that ordeal, and *preserve the original* purity of their character! Over him the temptations of political life and public station seemed to exercise no *unfavorable influence* whatever.

"His heart and reputation were as pure and unspotted the day he left as when he first entered office. His course was always firm, open, and manly. He denounced fraud and corruption in high and low places with unsparing energy. Many have felt the sting of his eloquence, and yet I never heard, and do not believe, that either as a politician, legislator, Governor, or Judge, it ever occurred to any one to question his integrity or the purity of his motives. For many years I have been in the habit of speaking of him, and thinking of him as one of the most perfect characters that I have ever known, and one of the *safest models* for young men just entering life, to imitate. Weakness and failings he may have had, for that is the lot of humanity, but these, if they existed, it never fell to my lot to discover. It seems but a short time since I first met him. At that time he was *overflowing* with life and spirit, not fully conscious of his strength, but yet indulging in hopes of future eminence and usefulness. These hopes I have seen fully realized.

" He attained to distinctions and honors, surpassing the dream of his youth, and yet he looked upon all these things as vanities, and poor and worthless illusions in comparison with a conscience void of offence towards God and man, — a lesson which the world has been learning and forgetting from the beginning."

CHAPTER XXXII.

ON the morning of the fourth of September he awoke from the last night of healthful, refreshing slumber vouchsafed to him in life. He was daily gaining in health and spirits, and took so lively an interest in passing events, that the newspapers engaged his attention as soon as morning worship was over. On this memorable morning he read, at family prayer, the eighty-fourth psalm, "How amiable are thy tabernacles, O Lord of hosts." Those who enjoyed that occasion of worship are thrilled to this hour with their speedy, subsequent, and profound realization of the significance to him of the beautiful promises in that sacred lyric, — "Blessed is the man whose strength is in thee. They go from strength to strength. Every one of them in Zion appeareth before God."

Almost his next reading was the announcement, alluded to in the previous chapter, of his recall to public duty. His son's filial devotion treasured up the events of that morning, as if by some presentiment of the extraordinary interest with which, before night, they would be invested.

His last service at his library table was one of kindness, in writing a letter of introduction for a young man. His usual walk to the village — from the business centre of which his dwelling was distant something over half a mile — had this distinction from all others, that it was his last! He visited a familiar haunt, — the insurance office, — and was so genial in his manner and so cheerful in his tones, that, after he left the office, a friend remarked, "There is the old ring in the Governor's voice to-day."

It is remembered of this last visit to the village, that he was more than usually playful, and told several stories on the street with much zest. "He came home," says his son, "on that pleasant sunny day, without a single sigh for the world to which he would return no more."

This almost exhilaration of feeling continued, and was displayed at the dinner-table, where, with much vivacity, he rallied a guest. After dinner he prepared to complete his kind attentions to some ladies — who, by the breaking down of their carriage in front of his house, had been thrown upon his hospitality — by carrying them to their home. For this purpose, he had borrowed of his son his favorite horse "Whitey" and his chaise, — now ready for the benevolent expedition.

In his own room he exchanged some pleasant words with Mrs. Briggs, and entered a closet to take down a light overcoat. While stretching out his hand to do this, he threw down a loaded gun which had been moved from its wonted corner, into what was considered a safer place. While he was picking it up from the floor, it was in some way discharged with most melancholy and fatal effect.

His wife, who was sitting with her work in the room, saw nothing, and, for an instant, in the blinding, suffocating smoke and stunning explosion, thought herself hurt. His voice aroused her, —

"It has burned my face, Harriet," he said; and, turning instantly, she saw him lift his hand to his cheek, and, as he did so, he added, "It is all gone."

The noise brought his son into the room just in time to aid him to reach his bed. Cordials were immediately administered, and efforts were made to staunch the flow of blood from the dreadful wounds. While this was doing he said, faintly, to his son, —

"You placed the gun in the wrong place;" and, after a moment's pause, he added, "I shall soon die; but it is all right. Now, my dear son, pray with me."

As his son knelt to comply with this request, the father took both his trembling hands in his own, and during all the heart-broken supplication his face wore an expression, no longer of agony, or even of unrest, but rather of perfect peace and of the most serene devotion.

When the prayer ceased, he said, again, "I shall die;" and, looking up, added, "It is strange, that in my own peaceful home I should meet the fate of the battle-field. But it is all right."

His son attempted to divert his mind from this dreadful conviction, by calling his attention to the torn brim of his hat, and to the large number of shot that had entered the ceiling, indicating that he had escaped quite a large part of the fatal charge.

As the physicians, who were instantly summoned, gathered about his bed, he noticed them, and said, "Dr. Cole is our family physician. Dr. Childs, and all of you, are my friends. God bless you. What do you think? I wish I could clear my throat a little."

"Those," says his daughter, "who were with the sufferer during the dreadful hours which followed cannot dwell upon the agony borne so patiently and quietly. His own blessed spirit seemed to inspire those ministering to him with strength and calmness, equalled only by their tenderness and pity. The hour of his keen suffering under the hands of the surgeons being passed, he called for a slate, and wrote, 'Ma, it has come! "Be still, and know that I am God." ' Then, drawing his son's ear close to his lips, he whispered, 'One hundred dollars to little Harry from his birth;' and this was all the arrangement he suggested, so completely was 'his house set in order.' "

Mr. D., one of his kindest friends, and for whom Governor Briggs cherished a sincere regard, was standing nigh, and his son, pointing to him, said, —

"Father, you have no better friend."

"Yes, my son; there is *one* better friend I have;" and his eyes were lifted heavenward as he spoke feebly. He then whispered, "Charles — Harriet — Henry?" as if he would ask if they had been informed.

His grandchildren, Harry and Nellie, entered the room, and stood, hand-in-hand, looking at him with childish surprise and sorrow depicted in their tearful eyes. The sight overpowered him, and he motioned to have them taken away.

Speaking, afterwards, of the first fearful night which followed the disaster, he said to his physician, "What a night that was, doctor! *He* scourged me, and then He bound up my wounds;" and, bringing his hands together, the back of the right hand into the palm of the left, — a gesture which his children and friends remember his using frequently when he was greatly moved, — he added, "How good He is." Of the same time he said, also, in his expressive manner: "Dr. C.'s face told the story."

The first and only superficial examination of his wounds did not indicate the real peril of his situation. The surgeons pronounced his case serious, but not dangerous. The subsequent probing of the hurts caused them to reverse this opinion; and indeed before midnight, such alarming symptoms appeared, that the chief surgeon thought he would sink and die immediately from loss of blood. He admonished the only son present of the danger, and suggested the importance of his father's immediately making any needful arrangements of his affairs. When the son answered that there were none needing to be made, the surgeon said, —

"Then I want the power of hope in his own bosom to help save him. We *may* stay the blood; and, if he has the stimulus of hope, it may be the feather whose weight will turn the scale in his favor."

To enforce his view, he instanced the case of General Shields, who was shot through the lungs, in the Mexican war, and who was saved from sinking by precisely this mental power.

This measure of suggesting a false hope to the sufferer occasioned some perplexity to his children. The son reasoned aloud, with himself rather than with the surgeon, — "Father is ready; there is nothing to fear for him; but, can we see him go with no word of farewell and blessing?" The exigence seemed great, and not a moment was to be lost, when he added, "Doctor, I leave him in your hands," and the stricken son turned to his only Helper.

The doctor returned to the crimsoned bed, and bent over the fainting, gasping sufferer, who looked up into his face with a gaze which those only can comprehend who stand

34*

betwixt the living and the dead, and, with stifled accents, said, —

"Doctor, I shall die!"

Calm and hopeful, the dark eyes of the physician returned his gaze, and, with a quiet, confident tone, his lips answered the touching appeal, —

"Oh, no, Governor, you will live many years, we hope."

The momentary inspiration of *hope* had the desired effect. With God's blessing that crisis passed, and a week of peaceful life succeeded, bequeathing to his family priceless memories, which transmute sorrow into thankfulness.

His daughter was at her home in New Bedford when the accident occurred, and did not reach the melancholy scene of it until the next evening. She was accompanied by her husband, and when they entered together the father's chamber he was lying quite tranquil, and without pain. But alas, "his visage was so marred!" His soul yearning towards his children with all the energy and tenderness of his loving nature, he pointed up and uttering only one word, calmed with it their tumultuous agony, which was ready to overwhelm them. "None," says his daughter, "none who saw it can ever forget the marvellous expression of his eyes as he uttered that one word — 'God!'"

From the moment of her arrival, his daughter was constantly at his side, and to her faithful memory and pen the biographer is indebted for the mournful, but yet deeply interesting, details of his last days on earth. Her narrative of her tender vigils would be given without modification, if some abridgment of its details were not quite necessary. For the most part her own words will be employed:

"After the first forty-eight hours," she says, "he had *no* suffering, and so entirely healthful was his condition, that there was nothing but quiet waiting for the processes of nature to go on. Few anodynes were needed, and nothing checked or changed the perfectly vigorous play of every faculty. There was, perhaps, never more of sweetness or of dignity in his presence, than when he lay on those white pillows which were yet to support his dying head. He was not allowed by his surgeons to speak *much*, but his whispered utterances, though sometimes checked by our anxiety, were of unspeakable value to us. The surgeons and his own family physician never gave us reason to hope for his recovery, after the extent and nature of the wound were fully understood; yet so firm was the nervous tone of his system and so unimpaired his constitution, that when no unfavorable symptom appeared, the thought would arise in our hearts, that with such a pulse and with such general health and vigor, he might pass the critical point, and survive."

The day after the terrible disaster, Mr. Scofield, a most experienced nurse, came to attend him; and no one gave him more real comfort than this faithful helper, who early and late was at his bedside, and whose ministrations did not cease till his body was laid in the grave. The sick always enjoy the assistance of the strong and cheerful, and this man, six feet tall, broad-chested, with a genial face, had most rare skill as a nurse. The daughter, recalling his ministrations to her beloved and suffering father, says, —

" His action, though firm and decided, was never sudden, and he would move about the bed, and if need be take his place *upon* it, with the nimbleness of a kitten. He would place his strong arms beneath the noble form, and lift him steadily and tenderly as a mother might raise a sleeping babe.

" The pillows were always 'just right,' and the bedclothes folded smoothly across the bed, when S. was there; and no one, like him, could *always* arrange the bed so that there should be 'no bad place in it.' 'The bed is just as nice in the morning,' he said to me once, ' when S. watches, as when he first makes it.'

"Father had frequently, during the last year of his life, met S. in the sick-rooms of several very dear friends, as one followed another to the grave. So, while in health, he had become attached to him as a nurse, besides being interested in him in his business, which was that of a machinist. Only a short time before my father received his injury, Scofield came to summon him to the bedside of one of these departing friends, and of this occasion the former related to me this reminiscence: 'As we walked along together, your father looked very grave, and did not smile as usual. He said, "We meet often in the sick-room, Scofield. It is a blessed thing, in a sick-chamber, to have those about us in whom we have confidence." Then he turned to me and said, "Scofield, I shall want you before long.'"

"'What for?' I asked.

"'If anything happens to me I shall want you to take care of me. I shall want to see you about me. You always seem cheerful.'

"'Well, Governor,' I replied, 'I will come if I possibly can.'

S. was inclined to be amused with the request, 'and when I went home,' he said, 'I told my wife I had another place engaged; the Governor wants me.'

"'Why,' said she, 'is the Governor sick?' 'No; but he says he shall want me before long.'

"'Well,' she replied, 'he has spoken in season.'

"'Of course this conversation was recalled with singular impressiveness when I was so soon reminded of my promise. When I first came into the room, the day after the Governor was hurt, he grasped my hand and looked up into my face without saying a word; and as I bent over him and was looking at the wound, he patted my head and said, "I am glad to see you." I said, "Governor, I little thought you would want me so soon." The first thing he asked me to give him was water. He was quiet for half an hour, and then I asked him when he looked up at me, "Governor, are you in pain?" "Not in the least," he said. I said, "Governor, it looks *bad*. I am sorry to see it." He replied, "It is all right, Scofield." He then added, "I wanted you last night when I couldn't make them understand."

"'I was always welcomed with a happy smile, and though he often insisted upon my leaving the sick-room for rest and sleep, he never rested so sweetly as when I was near him. When it was proposed to send for another attendant, the Governor said, "You want rest, Scofield, but I want you to be with me *all* you can be." Two days before he died, I said, "Governor, it is hard to see you suffer so." He replied, "S., I have had no pain." The day before he died, he beckoned to me to him, and laying his hand over my head, he said, "S.," will you do *all* for me, everything? Dr. C. will help you, but I want you to take charge of everything; *you* know how." I said, "I will, Governor." "Well, you are a good man; and you know how."'

"And he did *know how*,—lingering to catch his faintest whisper, and to anticipate *every* want; and he did for my beloved father the last offices that human hands can perform."

Friday, Sept. 6th, while his son-in-law was sitting beside him, he wrote on the slate: "I thought that day I should be in eternity in *one minute!* I *think* I was perfectly calm. Your poor, feeble mother was wonderfully calm, and saw everything as it was."

His daughter affords us here, a glimpse of such a death-chamber — as that of which the Christian poet so expressively says:—

> "The chamber where the good man meets his fate,
> Is privileged beyond the common walks,
> Quite to the verge of Heaven."

"On Sabbath morning, September 8th, Capt. Bigelow came down a little late and found him comfortable, and meditating upon his bed. The sun shone brightly into the window. He greeted him lovingly with the large, full tones of his voice, and said, 'I have been thinking what a *morning* this would have been in Heaven;' meaning that it would have been his first Sabbath there

" Another morning, as I was bathing his face and hands, as he lay calm and quiet in the pleasant stillness of the dawn, he asked for the slate and wrote, ' Oh, how I want to be in Heaven.'

" ' Yes, father,' I said, ' we ought to be willing to have you go, but we want to keep you here.'

" The trees in the avenue leading to the house were every one to him like a friend. One large, benevolent-looking maple-tree I always called *his* tree, because among the other trees, stately and graceful as they are, this well-rounded, wide-spreading maple, yielding its sweetness in the spring, and drooping its deep, restful shadows over our path in the summer, — where so many birds found a home, — made me *think* of him. I once told him so, and he said that it was pleasant to be associated with such an object in nature. In the early autumn, this tree alone held out one bleeding, deep-dyed coronal of leaves for the wreath we laid upon his coffin. On this pleasant morning I told him the only bright leaves were on *his* tree. We were looking upon the beautiful prospect, half hidden, half revealed, through the mist that overhung the river as the sun was rising. With a radiant countenance, he wrote on the slate, —

> " ' Sweet fields beyond the swelling flood,
> Stand dressed in living green ;
>
> .   .   .   .   .
>
> There everlasting spring abides,
> And never-withering flowers,"

and then he pointed up, with a rapture that made me feel Heaven was very near."

At one time, his wife had the impression that he was desponding, which led some one to make a remark about it, and he replied in writing : —

" How you all misunderstand me. No low spirits ! You are all *so* kind. But Heaven, Heaven is much better."

His daughter then recalled the cheerful views Mr. Amos Lawrence, when in his usual health, cherished of the other life ; and assured him that he was not misunderstood, but that all his family knew his feelings were the emotions of a man stricken of God, and who felt that he was in the hands of a pitiful Father. He *looked* so happy, replying only by his silence.

"When," continues his daughter, "we were arranging his pillows, he said, 'How much trouble you have.' Then he wrote, 'How I *love* you all. I have not seen little George or Mary or Nelly to-day.' To Dr. C. he said, 'I am afraid you are going to cure me, doctor; I want to be in Heaven.' He *said*, at another time, 'Dear Henry!' (and the tears gushed into his eyes, and the poor, wounded chin quivered), 'If I should go,' pointing up and raising his eyes, ' and he should be killed, *what* a meeting it would be!' 'I have done nothing, *nothing*,' he said one day when he seemed very comfortable, and we were all very hopeful. He had been happy in having us in his room and hearing us talk. He said, 'Perhaps He will restore me. If He does, for what?' 'He will show you for what, father,' one of us said; '*He* will guide you with His eye.' With a confidence that surprised me at the moment, because so unlike his prevailing doubtfulness in other sicknesses, he said, 'I am His forever.' Then, with great emotion and solemnity, moving his hands and raising his eyes to Heaven, he added slowly, 'His forever;' and as if breathing vows of consecration, he continued, 'Life or death, sickness or health, *I am His forever.*' Once speaking to mother, with a firm and rapturous anticipation of Heaven, he said to her, 'You never heard me say this before.'"

He strenuously advised that his son Henry should not be summoned home, as he knew McClellan's army, with which he was connected, was in hourly expectation of being called into action. He occasionally inquired concerning events that were passing in the world, but usually preferred not to be excited with such tidings. He seemed to have surrendered all anxiety concerning human affairs. Only a few hours before he fell asleep, a message from the absent and grieving son reached him: "Tell our dear father how much I love and honor him." The dying father received the greeting of his heroic son with a heavenly expression of pleasure.

"A few days after he was hurt," says the daughter again, "the most natural and loving expression came back to his face; all the discoloration and swelling disappeared, and the lips were flexible and flushed as in health. One morning, when I bent over and kissed them, and told him the old smile had come back to them, a single tender word and a tear in his eye, told me how sweet life was, even then, standing, as he did, on the verge of heaven.

"When his eldest brother came in to see him, the head covered with whitened locks was bent tenderly over him. My father received him most lovingly, saying, '*Once* more this side of heaven;' then caressingly, and almost like a mother fondling the head of her little boy, he wound the silver curls around his fingers, and added, 'White hairs.' He trusted himself to say no more.

"When his youngest sister came, with her husband, and could not keep back her tears, her whole frame shaken with the tremor of her soul, he said, with a firm voice and a most serene expression, 'Clouds and darkness are round about His throne; His ways are past finding out.'

"September the tenth," continues Mrs. Bigelow, "was a day of great peace and quiet. He said to me, 'It is calm below, but, oh, how calm and great and good above! Oh, that this poor, frail, unworthy one were there.' Again he said, 'I must necessarily be much alone henceforth; why should I wish to live?' Thinking he might be dwelling upon the change in his life which would be likely to follow in consequence of his injury, I suggested the resources which *art* has at command for repairing the mutilations and losses of the human frame; when he shook his head, and said, 'No, no,' evidently choosing not to contemplate any contingency of that kind.

"About noon the wearisomeness and feverishness became quite marked, and his tones and manner grew languid. Patient and quiet, he seemed to be withdrawing from all around, to rest with perfect peace in God, his Refuge.

"When the surgeons came, about four o'clock P. M., to dress the wound as usual, Dr. H. Childs[1] accompanied them; and never, in his brightest days, was their meeting more cheerful; and before parting, they exchanged the liveliest expressions of delight in the prospect of another life, which, in the course of events, must not be very distant.

"When wakened, an hour later, from a quiet sleep, he wrote, thus, for his son George: —

"'I am at the lowest point of animal existence. Don't see how I can be saved. Have no wish for it. God and Christ are my all. I love you. Do what you think best. Leave all to God — God — God.'

"That night passed without pain, but with more restlessness; and the morning found him feeling not quite so strong. Mother, with her unfailing and quickened perceptions, saw a change in his general tone which I had not perceived, though he must have been conscious of it himself. Larger doses of quinine and an increase of stimulants were thought to be necessary. He gently remonstrated, saying, 'I have not in thirteen years so sensibly felt the effects of medicines as to-day.' When Dr. C. said, pleasantly, 'You must consider yourself a *sick* man, now, and allow us to judge what is best for you,' he acquiesced, and gave himself no more anxiety, though he kept his medicines in his own charge till no more were administered.

"This was the critical day; and we were not surprised that it seemed likely to be a less favorable day. Though we had not allowed ourselves to be encouraged with hope of his recovery, yet unconsciously we felt a slight depression as the morning wore on. Yet it was impossible to realize that death was now approaching. On this last day, after he was conscious, no doubt, that all would soon be over, he did not trust himself to speak much with mother. His eye followed her all day with closest attention; and I have

---

[1] The father of one of his surgeons, for many years an eminent practitioner, and still, as then, President of the Berkshire Medical College.

never so fully realized, as since he is gone, how fondly the dying
cling to their beloved ones. For who, —

> "'This pleasing, anxious being e'er resigned, —
> Left the warm precincts of the cheerful day,
> Nor cast one longing, lingering look behind?'

"Quite late in the afternoon, he called attention to the temperature of the room. Asking for the slate, he wrote to one of his
attendants, 'Look at the mercury; how is it?' From the hushed
voices and movements in his room, when the surgeons paid their
last visit, at four o'clock in the afternoon, it was evident a change
had passed over all the scene; and when I entered, as they were
taking leave, I met his earnest, saddened, and inquiring gaze. I
met the look with the cheerful response which my lips were then
able to give, speaking encouragingly to him of *rest*. He looked so
tired, as he lay, panting, in the great conflict, the stress of which
was now very near. Soon his physician, Dr. C., arrived, and, on
entering the room, saw that his friend and patient was much
changed since morning. He was in a raging fever. He wrote
upon the slate, in answer to some questions, 'I have taken twenty-
five drops of quinine every three hours.' Presently the doctor sat
down by his bedside, and felt his pulse. My father asked, 'How
is it?' 'A little more frequent,' was the reply, the physician's
face revealing more than his words to the searching, silent ques-
tioner. My father then asked for the slate, and wrote, in as fair,
firm words as his hand ever traced, 'I want to be placed in a plain,
metallic case,' — the last words he ever wrote. He gave the slate
to the doctor, looking at him with a firm, tranquil countenance.
Not a word was spoken. The doctor handed the slate across the
bed to me. Oh, the silence and agony of that moment! After
,ite a severe paroxysm of coughing which immediately followed,
the weary sufferer sunk into a refreshing slumber. When he
awoke, about six o'clock P. M., he was again disturbed by coughing. I was summoned hastily, by mother, to his side. I sat down
beside him, when he laid his hand in mine, and, opening his eyes,
looked *full* into my face. His expression was sweet and calm.
The anxious look was all gone. He said, firmly, 'It will come

pretty soon.' I could not make my heart believe his words, and instinctively said, ' *What*, father, do you say?' Then he looked at me again, just as calm and loving as before, but he changed his voice into a most pitying and tender tone, repeating, ' It will *come* — pretty soon.' ' Why, father,' my heart answered, hopefully, 'your pulses are better than they were an hour ago. We don't think so.' Then he said, ' You won't leave me again, will you?' ' No, father, I shall stay here *all* night.' Then he fondled my hands with his own, *never* so tenderly, I thought, gave a little nod, very characteristic of him when he felt entirely satisfied, and immediately sank into a gentle sleep. *He never woke again.* Sixteen long hours that dear hand lay motionless in mine, warm as his dear heart through life — till life was gone. The dear Lord had kindly closed, in painless sleep, the eyes of him who once so much feared to meet death. And so, not the suffering of beloved ones, sleepless through all that night of dying; not the heart-rending sob of the devoted wife, bowed on the pillow beside him; not the cold drops that returned as fast as loving hands could wipe them from his white forehead; not even the laboring breath and poor, fluttering heart in his own bosom, — brought one pang of suffering to his serene spirit, as he passed through the dark valley. There is a peculiar sense in which was fulfilled to him the promise, ' Verily, verily I say unto you, if a man keep my saying, he shall not *see* death.' The prayer of his life was fully answered at last. He lived the life of the righteous, and died his peaceful death. At nine o'clock on Thursday morning, September 12th, his breathing ceased, and the seal of death was set upon his placid face and noble form. ' Having believed, he entered into *rest.* ' "

CHAPTER XXXIII.

HE tidings of his death spread rapidly, and carried sorrow to many hearts in widely-separated regions of the country. The telegraph flashed the sad news from city to city, and the religious and secular press alike commemorated the event. The following tribute from the columns of the *Watchman and Reflector*, a leading Baptist journal, — a contribution by a correspondent in New York, — will indicate the spirit and tone of the eulogies which expressed, rather than directed, the sorrow of the great Christian public : —

"Towards the close of last week the hearts of thousands in this State, as well as far abroad through the land, were saddened by the intelligence of the great loss sustained by Massachusetts, in the death of Ex-Governor Briggs. Few men in this nation were more truly honored, more profoundly loved. Few men in public life have ever exhibited a combination of intellectual and moral qualities so well adapted to inspire universal confidence. His character was transparent. His aims were high and honorable. Every one who approached him trusted in him. Every one felt assured that he was incapable of deception. As a man, a citizen, a statesman, and a Christian, he stood far above all partyism, and commanded respect from men of every class of society and every grade of political opinion. He was 'a mighty prince amongst us;' he swayed a potent sceptre; in an important sense it may be said that his honors were undisputed, because men felt proud of conceding them; and in many a contest he gained an easy conquest, because no man felt humiliated by yielding him the palm of victory.

"While in Congress his influence over men from every part of the country was very great; gentle, but effective. The decided and earnest advocate of temperance, he revolutionized the sentiments of many with whom he associated, while the most dissipated, who were wasting the finest gifts of genius 'in riotous living,' attested his sincerity, and greeted him as a manly and honest friend. Hence it has been seen that in the most stormy times, when the elements of discord were raging with the utmost fury, no chairman could so well rule the House in committee of the whole, because all alike confided in his sagacity, his firmness, and his impartiality. Never did true Christian manliness win triumphs more enduring.

"At the same time this man, so honored in his place within the halls of legislation, might be seen, at the set hours, occupying his place in a very different sphere, namely, the meeting for prayer and conference. It was there that he seemed to inhale a new life, and receive new strength for his great life-battles. At Washington, Governor Briggs was the same man and the same simple-hearted Christian that he was in his own town and his own family circle.

"Regarded as a whole, his character was of that sterling kind which always appears with some particular advantage in every new position from which it may disclose itself to the eye of the most critical observer. A memoir of him, fairly written, without any attempt at embellishment, would be a most valuable gift to every young man in America, especially to every one who may be commencing a professional career, and intent upon carving out his fortune with his own sturdy hand."

The feeling throughout Berkshire was of a still profounder type. The people universally deplored the loss of

35*

a personal friend or of a public benefactor. The manifold excellences of him who had been so suddenly and strangely removed from them, shone out with surpassing effect from the deep shadows of death that encompassed him. There was unfeigned grief throughout the village; and slowly or swiftly it rolled its tides along the beautiful valleys, and climbed the hill-sides, until every home, lofty and lowly alike, was invaded by the presence of almost a household affliction. Old men and children, young men and maidens, felt themselves personally bereaved.

During the few days which elapsed between his death and the funeral, great numbers of all classes and conditions of the people came to gaze upon his lifeless remains. Their sorrowing looks were answered by no sadness on his clay-cold face.

"As if it were," says one who beheld that face in death, "a last expression of kindness, a benignant smile, returned the gaze of sorrowful ones who looked upon him as he lay 'asleep in Jesus.' There was no desolateness in the room where the pale form reposed. The gloom of death was banished, and Death himself seemed awed by the majestic, solemn presence of that body which in the morning of the resurrection shall be raised incorruptible, when shall be brought to pass that saying, 'Death is swallowed up in victory.' "

The funeral rites were performed on Saturday afternoon, — first at the family residence, and immediately afterwards at the Baptist Church in the village, where he had been for so long a time a reverent worshipper and a revered pattern of practical piety.

The services at both places were conducted by his beloved pastor, Rev. Lemuel Porter, D. D. At the house, Dr. Porter was assisted by Rev. Dr. Todd, whose personal rela-

tions of social and christian intimacy with Governor Briggs
entitled him to share in those preliminary obsequies.   In the
public services, the pastors of the village bore appropriate
parts.

The attendance of personal friends at the home services
was large, and unusual solemnity and sacredness marked
the scene. Besides the reading of the Scriptures, and
prayer, the following hymn was sung by those present : —

> "Asleep in Jesus ! blessed sleep
> From which none ever wakes to weep —
> A calm and undisturbed repose,
> Unbroken by the last of foes.
>
> "Asleep in Jesus ! oh, how sweet
> To be for such a slumber meet,
> With holy confidence to sing,
> That Death has lost his venomed sting.
>
> "Asleep in Jesus ! peaceful rest,
> Whose waking is supremely blest, —
> No fear, no woe shall dim that hour
> That manifests the Saviour's power.
>
> "Asleep in Jesus ! oh, for me
> May such a blissful refuge be ;
> Securely shall my ashes lie,
> And wait the summons from on high."

A long procession accompanied the body to the church.
Deacon Daniel Stearns, Hon. Henry Hubbard, Hon. H. H.
Childs, Hon. Henry W. Bishop, James Buel, Esq., and
Calvin Martin, were pall-bearers. Deacon Almiron Fran-
cis, Hon. Thos. Colt, Hon. E. H. Kellogg, Robert Colt,
George H. Laflin, Henry Colt, T. G. Atwood, and William
M. Walker, Esqs., were coffin-bearers. The hearse was

drawn by the favorite horse which had long drawn the family carriage of the Governor. Among the strangers from abroad who were present, were Ex-Governors Washburn and Clifford ; Hon. Joel Hayden, of the Governor's Council ; Oliver Warner, of Northampton, Secretary of State ; Collector Goodrich, of Boston ; Gen. H. K. Oliver ; John Morrissey, Sergeant-at-arms of the House of Representatives ; Senator Branning ; Chief Justice Bigelow ; Hon. Increase Sumner ; Rev. Israel P. Warren, Secretary, and Edward S. Rand, Chairman, of the Executive Committee of the American Tract Society, Boston ; Rev. Jonas G. Warren, D. D., Secretary of the Baptist Missionary Union, and Rev. John Marsh, Secretary of the American Temperance Union.

In the village, flags were displayed at half-mast, the places of business were closed, and all the bells tolled as the procession moved along the street. The pulpit, and indeed the church throughout, and the *vacant* place in the Governor's pew, were draped in deepest mourning. Everything about the building was in harmony with the feeling of the people. The services here consisted of reading the Scriptures, by Rev. Mr. Yates, of the Methodist Episcopal Church ; prayer, by Rev. Mr. Dimmock, of the South Street Congregational Church ; sermon, by Rev. Dr. Porter ; prayer, by Rev. Dr. Todd, of the First Congregational Church. The following hymns were sung : —

I.

"Brother ! though from yonder sky
Cometh neither voice nor cry,
Yet we know, for thee to-day
Every pain has passed away.

"Not for thee shall tears be given,
Child of God, and heir of heaven ;

For he gave thee sweet release, —
Thine the Christian's death of peace.

"Well we know thy living faith
Had the power to conquer death;
As a living rose may bloom,
By the border of the tomb.

"Brother! in that solemn trust,
We commend thee dust to dust;
In that faith we wait, till, risen,
Thou shalt meet us all in heaven.

"While we weep, as Jesus wept,
Thou shalt sleep, as Jesus slept;
With thy Saviour thou shalt rest,
Crowned and glorified and blest."

II.

"My Father's house on high,
    Home of my soul! how near,
At times, to faith's foreseeing eye
    Thy golden gates appear.

"I hear at morn and even,
    At noon and midnight hour,
The choral harmonies of heaven
    Seraphic music pour.

"Oh, then, my spirit faints
    To reach the land I love, —
The bright inheritance of saints —
    My glorious home above."

One who participated in the sad obsequies, and in the grief they awakened, says : —

"The occasion drew together a large concourse of people from the town and Berkshire County, as well as from distant parts of

New England and New York, — all moved by one common sentiment of sympathy and sadness, that a great and good man had
fallen.

"All classes were there, — ex-Governors, judges, distinguished
civilians; the representatives of benevolent and philanthropic
societies with which Governor Briggs had held high official connection; clergymen of note in the different denominations; lawyers, merchants, farmers, mechanics, laborers, — men, women, and
children from every walk in life were there, to drop a tear and
take a last look of him whom all rejoiced to claim as a friend.
Perhaps no man was ever so completely the common property of
humanity at large, — and hence the whole people came to his burial.
It was a solemn moment, when strong men, with slow and meas-
ured step, passed up the aisle, and deposited in front of the pulpit
all that was mortal of George N. Briggs.   Nor did our hearts feel
less when our eye fell on the widow, leaning on the arm of her
eldest son, George P. Briggs; on the second son, with his wife
and children, — the officer who had that morning arrived from
the seat of war; on the only daughter, with her husband; and
then on the smitten pastor, as he ascended the pulpit, and, with
suppressed emotion, opened the service.   To us, everything was
in mourning, and everything said and done was in keeping with
the occasion.   Never before did it appear, in our view, so great
and good a thing to live and die a Christian.

"Certainly never did a truly Christian burial service — for the
precious truths it embodied — seem fraught with such excellence.
Dr. Porter opened his discourse [1] with a free and fervent exposition of those words which the Governor had written upon the
slate soon after the fatal disaster, 'Be still, and know that I am
God,' filling up the remainder of the hour with a simple and just
portraiture of the character and acts of the departed.   This done,
the coffin — 'a plain, metallic case' — was opened.   It was *he*, in
the embrace of death, — but still, it was he, the noble man we had
all seen and greeted so lovingly, robed in citizen's dress, — his
head resting as if in sleep, partly on one side, so concealing from

view the terrible wound, and presenting to the eye an object of real attractiveness. Death, and yet there was the same manly form, the same benignant expression, we had met so many times amid the activities of life. How could we give such a treasure to the grave! We leaned over the desk as the multitude passed by, made up of every grade of society. One person fixed our attention. It was a boy ten or twelve years old, in poverty — almost in rags, with nothing but a shirt and trousers to cover his nakedness, and yet, if his face was an index to his heart, he was in full sympathy with the most richly dressed and sincere mourners. He came to claim his share in all that was left of his friend, the lover of men. We looked, and as we looked we understood the secret of the greatness and power of Governor Briggs. We understood, that, as nothing in human form felt itself repelled from his person when dead, so nothing wearing that form, however degraded and lost, was repulsed from his presence when living. In that was found his goodness, and his goodness was his greatness. That made him like Jesus, the 'friend of publicans and sinners.' There flashed upon us in that instant a conception of the character of 'God manifest in the flesh, and of the spirit of the Gospel.

"The sun had already sunk behind the western hills when we reached the place of burial. It was a secluded spot, in the valley of the 'West Branch' (one of the streams which unite to form the Housatonic), a mile or more away from the centre of the village of Pittsfield — a very gem, set in the bosom of the mountains. Here, on a slight elevation, within a neat hemlock inclosure, amid sighs and songs, prayers and tears, and beneath the moon and stars, we laid to rest his mortal remains, in the full hope of the resurrection, and with the comforting assurance that already his spirit had realized the exceeding blessedness of those who hunger and thirst after righteousness."

The profound reverence and affection which were cherished for him by all classes of his fellow-citizens, originated the call of public meetings in both the villages he had honored and blest with his residence while he was in the ser-

vice of the State. These meetings were thronged by the
people, and are yet remembered, as occasions of deep and
tender interest. Prominent gentlemen in both places paid
tributes to his worth, and indulged in personal reminiscences of his goodness and genial manner.

The Berkshire Bar also held a special meeting of commemoration and condolence. At all these meetings resolutions were passed, embodying the public estimate of the
noble man and citizen gone to his reward, and conveying
to his family expressions of unfeigned sorrow for their
common loss.[1]

This volume might be greatly expanded by testimonials,
biographical notices, and letters of condolence from prominent men in all the departments of public life, and
especially of philanthropic and Christian labor, — but the
greater part of such matter is necessarily excluded.
There was reason for the universal sympathy and sorrow
which his death created, for in that death the noblest causes
that engage men's hands and inspire their hearts lost a
zealous and judicious promoter, and the poor and needy
and afflicted lost a loving and ministering friend.

He was pre-eminently one of those of whom the inspired
seer, looking through the veil of time into eternity, proclaimed their beatitude, in the immortal and comforting
words, —

"BLESSED ARE THE DEAD WHO DIE IN THE LORD FROM HENCEFORTH.
YEA, SAITH THE SPIRIT, THAT THEY MAY REST FROM THEIR LABORS, AND
THEIR WORKS DO FOLLOW THEM."

[1] See Appendix III.

HIS MONUMENT IN PITTSFIELD CEMETERY.

APPENDICES.

APPENDIX I.

THE BERKSHIRE JUBILEE.

OF the copious records of this festival, so beautiful in itself, and so memorable to all the sons and daughters of Berkshire, more were marked to be included in this Appendix than the bulk to which this volume has grown will admit. To exclude all account of it would be doing injustice to the occasion itself, and especially to the eager interest and prominent part which Governor Briggs took in its progress. The following brief abstract therefore of the memorials, including nearly all the Governor's speech, with a poem by Oliver Wendell Holmes, and Miss Sedgwick's very entertaining chapter of its "Chronicles," is offered to the readers of this Memoir, with regret that there is not room for more: —

Berkshire is the large western county of Massachusetts, extending from Connecticut to Vermont, something like fifty miles in length, and containing somewhat over forty thousand inhabitants. On the east lie the Green Mountains, which shut it away from the rest of Massachusetts. On the west are the Taghcannic Mountains, which separate it from New York. It is a region of hill and valley, mountain and lake, beautiful rivers and laughing brooks — the very Piedmont of America. Till the railroad was completed, and the iron horse came puffing and snorting up over these mountains, Berkshire had very little intercourse with the rest of "the Old Bay State." Most of its business was done at New York, while with New York people it had none but a business intercourse. A community thus secluded, and educated amid scenery surpassingly lovely, breathing the mountain air, and drinking the waters which flow in thousands of rills down their mountain-sides, till they form the Housatonic, or "river of the hills,"—must love the home of childhood. For the last fifty years Berkshire has been constantly sending out her sons and daughters to other parts of the land to find new homes. In the mean time her own college has grown up, officered almost wholly by her own sons, till its name is among the first in the land, and the old homestead has been steadily advancing in wealth, enterprise, education, and morals. Probably it would be impossible to find a county in the whole land, in which there is more of the home feeling than in Berkshire; and, wherever you go, if you can hail from this " garden of the Bay State," you are sure to find a warm welcome. Her sons are everywhere filling the highest posts of influence and respectability. No less than eight of these sons have been in Congress at the same time; and we believe the same number were on the bench as judges, in a neighboring State, at the same time. Scattered over the land, these emigrant sons have ever yearned towards the homes of their fathers. By a sort of electrical excitement they seemed ripe for a gathering at once. A committee was raised in New York to correspond with a similar committee in the county, and to make preparations for celebrating a jubilee. The arrangements finally made were, that on Thursday, the 22d of August, 1844, the committee from New York and the county committee should meet at the Town Hall, at eleven o'clock A. M., where greetings and courtesies should be passed. The preparations to receive the new-comers were, —

1. Every house, table, room, and chamber in Pittsfield was to be at the service of the guests, and even in the neighboring towns the same was done. No pains, time, or money was spared in making the fires burn brightly on the hearth-stones of each family. This part, like many others, cannot be printed.

2. Preparations were made to have the stranger-guests call on the citizens of Pittsfield without ceremony, and meet old faces as they passed from house to house.

3. A register was prepared, in which the emigrant sons of Berkshire might insert their names, time of living in the county, present place of abode, or any other memoranda.

4. A stand and seats, sufficient to contain between three and four thousand people, were erected on a beautiful hill just west of the village, and which commanded an enchanting view in all directions. " The river of the hills " (Housatonic) kissed the foot of the hill, while the lofty " Greylock," on the north, seemed to look down upon us as if he was the stern guardian of the valley, and father of all the beautiful mountains which lay around.

5. The Rev. Mark Hopkins, D. D., President of Williams College, was appointed to greet the returning sons and daughters in a sermon.

6. The Hon. Joshua A. Spencer, of Utica, was appointed to deliver an oration.

7. Music, secular and sacred, was provided. Odes and songs had been written in great abundance, and of superior excellence. One of the first bands in the county was secured and brought on the ground for the occasion.

8. A poem was assigned to the Rev. William Allen, D. D., of Northampton, and also minor poems to others of acknowledged poetical talents.

9. Provision was made for speeches, sentiments, &c.

10. A dinner (at which his Excellency, Governor Briggs, was to preside), all dressed and cooked in Boston, and transported with all necessary furniture on the railroad, was provided on the delightful grounds formerly known as "the Military Grounds," and now occupied by the Young Ladies' Institute. The tables were spread under a canopy, and capable of seating over three thousand people. The whole to be conducted on the strictest principles of the temperance reformation, sobriety, cheerful and dignified friendship.

Such were the measures adopted to welcome hearts that had been throbbing at the thought of the gathering all over the United States. In every part of the land little plans had been laid by which to bring families and friends together, and have friendship renew the oil in her lamps. It was to be the gathering of a great family.

The dinner was not only the central, but, very reasonably, the most attractive point of the three days' occurrences. According to the plan, it was provided in a spacious tent erected upon the grounds of Maplewood, and plates were laid for three thousand guests. Probably that number sat down to the bountiful and excellent entertainment—about equal numbers of both sexes. Grateful as the viands were to the appetites of the happy throng, most were impatient for the after pleasure,—"The feast of reason and the flow of soul,"—which was yet to come.

At the head of a raised table in the centre, were the President, Governor Briggs, Joshua A. Spencer, Esq., Judge Bacon, and others. A blessing was asked by Rev. Dr. Shepard.

The cloth having been removed, his Excellency, Hon. George N. Briggs, Governor of the Commonwealth, rose and addressed the immense audience as follows:—

"Brothers of Berkshire,—I should do injustice to my own feelings, if I did not in the outset declare to you the deep feelings of gratitude which pervade my bosom at the expression of your kindness which has placed me at the head of this family table. The committee of arrangements have put into my hands a schedule marking out what remains to be done at this family gathering; and, as the respectability of all families depends very much upon their good order and conduct at at the.table, you are requested to observe during the residue of the ceremonies the strictest order; for, if I am not mistaken, in such a family as this, before the sun goes down you will have first-rate speaking. There are some boys here that can do that thing up well. I see by this arrangement that there are to be some introductory remarks by the President. I hardly know, my brothers and sisters, what to say to you. Foreigners have said, that when we get together here in this Yankee land we always talk about ourselves. Now I

36*

should like to know, upon this occasion, what else can be talked about; for I
think it is very bad policy for families when they are together to talk about
other folks! (Laughter.) It is very right for the children when they come
home, to talk about the old home and fireside, and when they cluster about the
old people, they have a right to talk of what has taken place during their
absence. They have a right to inquire who is married, who is dead, and who
is — run away! if they please.

"Here have come together, around this family board, sons and daughters,
whose residences are scattered over the surface of eighteen of these twenty-six
States. We may well say to ourselves (and if there are strangers here they will
indulge us in saying so), that we must be rather a promising family, to have our
children spread thus far and wide over the four quarters of this great land, and
gathered together again on an occasion of this kind. We have heard, brothers,
from our friend, yesterday, in sober prose, and from our other friend in cheerful
poetry — we have heard much about the history of our good old mother Berkshire. They went back to her origin as a county, alluded to some events in her
history, talked of her loved and interesting children, spoke of her beautiful
scenery, and of the spirit and enterprise of her sons and daughters, — and they
had a right to talk so. It was said to-day, that within twelve hours after the
news of the first act of aggression at Lexington reached this valley among these
mountains, the sons of Berkshire were on their way to the point of danger. That
is matter of history. And it is no less true, that from that moment till the surrender of Cornwallis at Yorktown, there was no day, no hour, no battle fought
of any consequence in that great struggle for independence, where not only Massachusetts men were not found, but where there were not found, also, Berkshire
men mingling in the fight.

"A little incident relating to that bold and fearless attack upon Ticonderoga,
I will name to you. The Connecticut Legislature, or some of the dauntless ones
there, conceived the idea of surprising Ticonderoga; and they sent up some right
men through this region of country to hold consultation as to what plan of
arrangements should be fixed upon. They came here to the village of Pittsfield,
and in an old house where Willis's store now stands, and where lived the maternal grandfather of my friend at this end of the table (Dr. Childs), they held consultation, and there his grandfather James Easton, John Brown, and other
faithful men, matured a plan of operations. Some were to go to Jericho, now
Hancock, and secure some choice spirits; and before the country knew it, Ticonderoga had surrendered at the demand of Ethan Allen, on an authority which
they dare not question. Col. John Brown was a citizen of this town; he went
to Quebec, and was there with *Benedict Arnold*; while there, with his sagacious
eye, he pierced through the covering and discovered the traitor. Before he
returned home, some difficulty arose between them, and Brown published him as
a *coward* and *traitor*. Afterwards his true character was developed. You know
the history of John Brown; he sleeps at Stone Arabie, where he fell in that
murderous attack of the Indians upon the Mohawk. And he sleeps not there
alone; many a Berkshire boy fell with him. From our little sister town of

Lanesboro', three of her sons perished in that bloody conflict; many a Berkshire mother's heart sunk within her at the news of that day's work. Bennington! they were there, too; Berkshire was alive when she heard that her neighbors on the north in the Green Mountain State were in danger, and she poured through the gorge of the mountain beyond Williamstown her brave sons; and many of them were in the fight, and many Berkshire men fell there. That same Lanesboro' lost three worthy soldiers in that battle. And so it was, as I said before, they mingled in all the great fights, they flew to every portion of the country where danger bade them. Out of the sixty-nine thousand soldiers which Massachusetts furnished to that war (and that was one third of the whole number—two hundred and twenty thousand—furnished by all the States in the American Revolution), this, our native county, furnished her full proportion. Berkshire men were at the surrender of Cornwallis at Yorktown. I knew a good old man, — peace to his ashes!—who was through that whole revolutionary struggle. He was a brave soldier and a true son of Massachusetts; and was as honest and just in peace as he was firm and courageous in war. In that dreadful winter, at Valley Forge, he suffered with his fellow-soldiers. The last time I saw him, he gave me the whole history of the battle of Yorktown. He was there during the preceding summer, and discharged many an important and confidential trust confided to him by Lafayette. And I saw that good old man meet in this village his brave and generous old commander. Fifty years had passed since they fought together; the old man had toiled away in his shop at Lanesboro', — and when he heard that Lafayette was to be here, his heart beat high with the pulsations of youth, and he said he must see his general once more. He came down and met him under yonder elm; and when he mentioned an incident which served to awaken old associations, they clasped each other and wept like children. His name is David Jewett, — a name which has never gone abroad on the wings of fame, but he was one of those who resembled more the corner-stone of the building, which the world never sees, than he did some more ornamental but less important part.

"And so we went through the Revolution. Well, in the last war (for I am now talking about the soldiers of Berkshire), so long as the name of the 'Bloody Ninth' shall endure, so long the valor of the Berkshire soldiers will be borne in mind. We have had an Indian war in Florida; and, oh, what a rich and costly sacrifice Berkshire has offered upon that altar! Our own young Lieutenant Center, from this Pittsfield, fell by a bullet from a Seminole rifle; and our Childs spent some three or four years amidst the bogs of Florida, and almost fatally impaired one of the finest constitutions in the world. During all his course in that most inglorious war he never did an act of unnecessary cruelty, or was guilty of perfidy towards the hunted Indians of the Florida everglades. . . .

"Here all denominations of religion exist. Who has ever seen among the different persuasions more harmony and Christian good-will prevailing than in this very county of Berkshire?

"I was admonished by the committee that one part of the arrangements is, that speeches must be short. We should make the best speeches in the fewest words. My heart is too full for connected thought or studied speech. Brothers, we have come together (and thank Heaven that we have lived to see this happy occasion) to mingle our feelings and rekindle our affections at this family altar. We have come in the fulness of our joy, to talk to and of one another, to inquire of each other's welfare, to say how we have fared during our long separation. We know that our brothers from abroad bring back good tidings of the counties where they dwell; strangers have shown them kindness. Our hearts have been made glad to hear of their prosperity in every part of this goodly land. The South and the West have dealt kindly with them. During the time I was honored with a seat in the House of Representatives of the United States, I met, in every Congress, Berkshire men. In one House of Representatives there were eight members who were sons of Berkshire. Wherever her sons are found, whether in honor or humility, they remember their good old mother with affection. Well, here we are once more together in the old homestead, amidst all the joyful and endearing associations which have been so touchingly described yesterday and to-day.

"In the freshness of this gushing joy, a sad reflection comes over the mind, that this glad jubilee will be the last that many of us will ever witness. Of the present we are secure; and for its blessings we thank Heaven around this family table. You have come, my friends, to walk in the green meadows over which your boyish feet once ran with the lightness of the roe; to ramble over the pasture where once you lingered after the returning cows; to look into the old well and see its dripping bucket, to gaze upon that old apple-tree where you gathered the early fruit, to walk on the banks of the winding stream and stand by the silver pool over which the willow bent and in which you bathed your young limbs, to visit the spot where with your brothers and sisters you gathered the ripe berries; to look upon that old school-house where you learned to read and to spell, to write and to cipher, where sometimes you felt the stinging birch; to reascend that well-remembered rock upon which in mirth and play you spent so many happy hours, to see if it looked and appeared as it used to; to walk once more up the aisle of that old church where you first heard the revered and loved pastor preach and pray; and you have come to visit the peaceful graveyard, to walk among its green mounds and drop the tear of affection and friendship upon the silent resting-place of loved ones who sleep there. You have come here to rekindle at this domestic fireside the holy feelings of youth. To all these we bid you welcome! Welcome to these green valleys and lofty mountains! Welcome to this feast, to our homes, to our hearts! Welcome to everything! Once more I say, welcome!

"I give you for a sentiment, —

"*The County of Berkshire*, — She loves her institutions and her beautiful scenery, but, feeling the sentiment and borrowing the language of the Roman mother, she points to her children and exclaims, 'These are my jewels.' "

The President announced that a poem would now be delivered by Dr. Holmes, of Boston.

Dr. Oliver W. Holmes rose in his place, but was greeted with cries from various parts of the audience, to come to the centre of the ground, so as to be heard by all. The President said, —

" And I suggest to the gentleman to follow the example of our good friend who preceded him, and get *upon* the table, which is an advancement upon former feasts, where the tendency was, rather, to get *under* the table. (Cheers.) "

Dr. Holmes accordingly took the *table*, and requested to be allowed, before he opened the very brief paper in his hand, to advise his friends of the reason why he had found himself there : —

" It shall be short," said he; " but inasmuch as the company express willingness to hear historical incidents, any little incident which shall connect me with those to whom I cannot claim to be a brother, seems to be fairly brought forward. I will take the liberty to refer to one. One of my earliest recollections is of an annual pilgrimage made by my parents to the west. The young horse was brought up, fatted by a week's rest and high feeding, prancing and caracoling to the door. It came to the corner, and was soon over the western hills. He was gone a fortnight; and one afternoon — it always seemed to me it was a sunny afternoon — we saw an equipage crawling from the west towards the old homestead, — the young horse, who sat out fat and prancing, worn thin and reduced by a long journey, the chaise covered with dust, and all speaking of a terrible crusade, a formidable pilgrimage. Winter-evening stories told me where — to Berkshire, to the borders of New York, to the old domain, owned so long that there seemed a kind of hereditary love for it. Many years passed away, and I travelled down the beautiful Rhine, — I wished to see the equally beautiful Hudson. I found myself at Albany; a few hours' ride brought me to Pittsfield, and I went to the little spot, the scene of this pilgrimage, — a mansion, — and found it surrounded by a beautiful meadow, through which the winding river made its course in ten thousand fantastic curves; the mountains reared their heads around it, the blue air, which makes our city pale cheeks again to deepen with the hue of health, coursing about it pure and free. I recognized it as the scene of the annual pilgrimage. Since that I have made an annual visit to it.

" In 1735, Hon. Jacob Wendell, my grandfather in the maternal line, bought a township not then laid out, — the township of Pontoosuc, — and that little spot which we still hold is the relic of twenty-four thousand acres of baronial territory. When I say this, no feeling which can be the subject of ridicule animates my bosom. I know, too well, that the hills and rocks outlast our families; I know we fall upon the places we claim as the leaves of the forest fall, and as passed the soil from the hands of the original occupants into the hands of my immediate ancestors, I know it must pass from me and mine; and yet with pleasure and pride I feel I can take every inhabitant by the hand and say, if I am not a son, or a grandson, or even a nephew of that fair county, at least I am allied to it by an hereditary relation. But I have no right to indulge in sentimental remarks." (Cries of "Go on, go on.")

Dr. Holmes read the poem, as follows, which was received with continued and hearty cheers: —

"Come back to your mother, ye children, for shame,
Who have wandered, like truants, for riches or fame!
With a smile on her face and a sprig on her cap,
She calls you to feast from her bountiful lap.

"Come out from your alleys, your courts, and your lanes,
And breathe, like young eagles, the air of our plains;
Take a whiff from our fields, and your excellent wives
Will declare it's all nonsense insuring your lives.

"Come you of the law, who can talk, if you please,
Till the man in the moon will allow it's a cheese,
And leave ' the old lady, that never tells lies,'
To sleep with her handkerchief over her eyes.

"Ye healers of men, for a moment decline
Your feats in the rhubarb and ipecac line;
While you shut up your turnpike, your neighbors can go
The old roundabout road to the regions below.

"You clerk, on whose ears are a couple of pens,
And whose head is an ant-hill of units and tens;
Though Plato denies you, we welcome you still,
As a featherless biped, in spite of your quill.

"Poor drudge of the city, how happy he feels
With the burs on his legs and the grass at his heels;
No *dodger* behind, his bandanas to share, —
No constable grumbling, ' You mustn't walk there!'

"In yonder green meadow, to memory dear,
He slaps a mosquito and brushes a tear;
The dew-drops hang round him, on blossoms and shoots, —
He breathes but one sigh, for his youth and his boots.

"There stands the old school-house, hard by the old church;
That tree at its side had the flavor of birch;
Oh, sweet were the days of his juvenile tricks,
Though the prairie of youth had so many ' big licks.'

" By the side of yon river he weeps and he slumps, —
The boots filled with water, as if they were pumps;
Till, sated with rapture, he steals to his bed,
With a glow in his heart and a cold in his head.

" 'Tis past — he is dreaming — I see him again;
His ledger returns as by legerdemain;
His neck-cloth is damp, with an easterly flaw,
And he holds in his fingers an omnibus straw.

" He dreams the shrill gust is a blossomy gale,
That the straw is a rose from his dear native vale;
And murmurs, unconscious of space and of time,
' A 1, extra-super; ah, isn't it prime!'

" Oh, what are the prizes we perish to win
To the first little 'shiner' we caught with a pin!
No soil upon earth is as dear to our eyes
As the soil we first stirred in terrestrial pies!

" Then come from all parties, and parts, to our feast,
Though not at the 'Astor,' we'll give you at least
A bite at an apple, a seat on the grass,
And the best of cold — water — at nothing a glass."

Passing over all the rest of the dinner speeches, and more prominent exercises of this festival, this Appendix will be appropriately closed with, —

THE LAST CHAPTER OF THE CHRONICLES OF THE BERKSHIRE JUBILEE.

BY CATHARINE M. SEDGWICK.

Now George, of the tribe of Briggs, being of a goodly stature, and, moreover, having an upright mind and a pleasant speech, gained the hearts of his brethren.

And the dwellers in Massachusetts chose him to be their head and chief ruler. And George dwelt in the goodly land of Berkshire, and his dwelling was in that upper valley of the Housatonic which our fathers bought of the red men, and called it Pittsfield.

Now in the first year of the magistracy of George, a good spirit entered into the hearts of the sons of Berkshire, both of those who dwelt in the homes of their fathers, and of those who were dispersed abroad.

And to these last came visions and dreams, and the homes of their childhood rose before them, and they saw in vision the green and dewy hills of Berkshire, with their maple groves, and the wide shadowing elm which hath no equal for beauty and gracefulness among all the trees that the Lord hath made; and also the firs and the pines of their mountain-tops; and the smiling valleys standing thick with corn, and the pasture and the orchard, and the skating and the coast-ing-ground.

And there appeared before them in vision, also, the fair daughters of their people, even as they had seen them in the freshness and the beauty of their early days.

And the ripple of the lakes sparkling in their valleys, and the gushing of the streams from their hills was in their ears, like far-off music.

And their kindred who had been gathered to their fathers, the mother who had rocked their cradle, and he who had toiled for their youth, and brothers and sisters and friends, rose before them, and beckoned them to the land in which they were born.

And their hearts were faint within them, till a goodly purpose was breathed into them and they spake with one voice, and said, "Hath not the Lord given us rest on every side? Now we will proclaim a jubilee! we will go up to our Jerusalem! We will worship in the temples of our fathers! We will kiss the sod that covers the graves of our kindred, and we will sit ourselves down in the old places where their shadows will pass before us!

"And we will rejoice and make merry with our brethren; and Memory and Hope shall be our pleasant ministers. And we will lay our hearts together and stir up the mouldering embers of old friendships till the fire burns within us, and this, even this sacred fire will we transmit to our children's children."

And even as they said, so did they; and in the summer solstice with one heart and one mind they came together.

The pilgrims from afar and the sojourners at home. Even from the valley of the Mississippi came they; and from the yet farther country of the Missouri — and from the land of the sun, even from the south land, and from all the goodly lands roundabout Massachusetts.

And strangers who honored them, and whom they honored, also came; not intermeddling with their joy, but greatly augmenting the sum thereof.

And they gathered together a multitude of people, old men and elder women, young men and fair young maidens and much children — and a very great company were they.

They came not, like the Queen of Sheba, "bearing spices, and gold in abundance, and precious stones," but, instead of these, sound minds well instructed, hearts of gold, loyalty to the land of their fathers, imperishable friendships, religious faith — all pearls of great price.

And a great heart was in the people of Pittsfield, and they opened the doors of their pleasant dwellings and bade their brethren enter therein. And they spread fine linen on their beds, and they covered their tables with the fat of the land; for the Lord had greatly blessed the people of Pittsfield.

And they said to all their brethren, "Come now and enter in, and freely take of our abundance, for, lo! have we not spread our tables for you; and hath not the angel of sleep dressed our beds, that our brethren may sleep therein?"

And the faces of their brethren shone and they entered in; and they said, "It was a true report we heard of thee; thy land doth excel, and thou hast greatly increased the riches and the beauty thereof. Corn aboundeth where, in the time of our fathers, the ground was barren. Thy flocks and thy herds are multiplied. Many goodly dwellings, such as were not aforetime, hast thou set up. Thou hast enlarged the bounds of thy fruitful fields, and thou hast gemmed thy gardens with flowers. Walks hast thou laid out and planted them, and thou hast done well to cherish that stately elm, the monument of the past, the last relic of the forests where the red men hunted.

"And moreover, here do we behold a wonder such as Solomon in all his wisdom conceived not of, when he said, 'There is nothing new under the sun.' Here, in this land, the wilderness to which our fathers came but as yesterday, have ye builded a work which was not done, nay, nor was it so much as conceived of, by the cunning artificers of the East, nor by the many-handed labor of Egypt, nor by the art of Greece, — and even now is the report of its ponderous engines and passing multitudes in our ear!"

And many words were spoken, cheering the heart and lighting up the countenance.

And all the people went up together into the temple of the Lord. And there spake unto them Mark, the son of Archibald, and this was the same Archibald, albeit a tiller of the ground, honored among his brethren of the lower valley, for he loved much, and was an honest man, but now he was gathered to his fathers, and Mark his son was set up to be a light in the land and an instructor of the young men. And his brethren had chosen him to speak unto them, he being of an excellent spirit and knowledge and understanding, and noted for showing of hard sentences and dissolving of doubts. And he spake wisely and he greatly pleased his brethren: are not his words written in this Book of the Jubilee?

And William, the son of that priest of the valiant heart, who in the days of the oppression of the kings, ministered unto the people of Pittsfield, he also spake unto his brethren.

And Joshua, of the tribe of Spencer, a wise man and learned in the law, spake to them. And he brought forth to them from their old chronicles lost and forgotten treasures, and he pleased them with the sayings and doings of their fathers.

And a goodly tent was spread, and they did eat together, both men and women, with great gladness, but they drank not save of the pure water of their hill-country, for George, their ruler, said unto them, "Touch not the wine-cup, for there be of our brethren who have perverted this good gift, and drunk of it to their own destruction, and thereby causing us shame, and also much sorrow, — therefore we will put away this evil from among us."

And they listened to the voice of their ruler, for they loved him, and they did the thing he desired.

And now all that Joshua spake, and also the sayings of the wise and the witty men, and the speech of the eloquent, and the salutation of the stranger, and the word spoken by the simple and loving heart, and the song sung to the stringed instruments, behold they are written in this Book of the Jubilee!

Now the time of separation came, and they blessed the Lord for that he had greatly blessed the land of their fathers.

And a spirit of meditation fell upon them, and they said in their hearts, "Our days on the earth are a shadow and there is none abiding.

"One generation appeareth and passeth away and another cometh, but the good that we do, that shall remain.

"Have we not this day listened to the words of Mark and Joshua, and have we not delighted to honor George, whom our brethren have set up to be a ruler over us? Whence come they forth—Mark, Joshua, and George? Not from the rich nor the learned; lo, did not their fathers labor among us even with their hands? Now, seeing this is the order of our land, shall we not call on the son of the humble man to be diligent,—shall we not multiply for him instruction, and open to him the fountains of knowledge, and remove far from him vanity and corruption?

"We pass away, but our hills and our valleys they remain; in beauty hath the Lord made them. His creations are fair to look upon,—shall not the work of our hands be in harmony with the Lord's work?

"Therefore, where the hand of the feller has felled the goodly trees, we will plant and water, and the Lord will surely give us increase.

"And when we build our temples, whether they be for the worship of the Lord our God, or for the instruction of our young men and maidens, or for the meeting of the rulers and judges of our land, we will seek a goodly pattern therefor of men cunning in art.

"And also for the houses in which we dwell, and the barns, and whatever is builded with men's hands will we ask a pattern of men skilled in these matters, lest, following the devices and desires of the ignorant, we mar and burden the lovely land the Lord hath given us.

"And our bridges, and our fences also, shall be pleasant to the eye, and order and neatness shall be manifested about our habitations; and in all these things will we heed the warning which Benjamin, of the tribe of Franklin, hath given us, in the parable of the 'speckled axe,' thereby warning us not to sit down content with imperfection.

"And we will enlarge our gardens and plant therein the fruits and flowers of divers countries; and our daughters shall tend them, as Eve dressed the garden in the days of her innocency.

"And also we will not forget our burial-places where our kindred lie, and where we shall soon be gathered among them. We will extend the borders thereof. We will plant around them trees and fashion walks, that our young men and maidens may love to come thither to think on their fathers. And there shall be seats there, for the old man at noon-tide to sit under the cool shade and meditate on the life and immortality which the Lord our Saviour hath brought to light.

"And, moreover, we will plant flowers there, that our little children may come to pluck them, and the soft music of their feet may be on the sod that covers our graves."

And this good and much more did they purpose to the land they loved, even the pleasant land of Berkshire.

And when the hour of parting came, the bands of their early love were straitened. And they said with one accord, "HENCEFORTH AND FOREVER WE ARE BRETHREN!"

APPENDIX II.

FUNERAL SERMON.

BY REV. LEMUEL PORTER, D. D.

"BE STILL, AND KNOW THAT I AM GOD."— *Psalm* xlvi. 10.

SOON after the deceased received his fatal wound, he wrote for his afflicted wife these words, "It has come; '*Be still, and know that I am God.*'" He recognized the solemn truth, that he was soon to leave this world; and he would sustain his family by considerations drawn from the Divine character. He believed that God is infinitely *wise;* hence, that mistakes and accidents are impossible under His administration. *We* are to be still, in a spirit of Christian submission, when God's hand is on us, lest we arraign supreme wisdom. He believed that God is infinitely *good,* even when apparently severe, chastening those whom He loves; therefore we should be perfectly resigned to His discipline. He believed God is a *sovereign,* rightfully dealing with men, according to his good pleasure; therefore it becomes the bereaved to say, "The Lord gave, and the Lord has taken away; blessed be the name of the Lord." He believed in God's Providence,—that He acts in human affairs by agencies which are often invisible, but closely connected and arranged to affect His purposes. We are to be still, though some afflictive event discloses that we were links in the invisible chain that caused it. He believed in Christ, as the only Saviour of sinners, having heavenly glories in reserve for believers; and that death is the passport to his presence. It becomes us, then, to be still, when dear Christian friends die, for the road to heaven passes through the tomb. He trusted, with all his heart, in that character whose wisdom, goodness, sovereignty, and Providence are so exquisitely blended. His first impulse was to send those he loved to his source of strength. He knew that philosophy was a vain helper. Its highest lesson is, that repining is useless. It cannot open the eyes of the dead, nor vitalize the heart that has ceased to beat forever. Philosophy is an opiate; trust in God is a cordial. The lacerated soul cannot find peace in the stoic's creed or in the Indian's fortitude. It comes only from the hand that smites us. Christian submission is consistent with a full knowledge of our loss, and with such tears as Jesus shed. When God says to a mourner, "Be still," he means, "Be not discouraged, indulge in no murmurs." When he says, "Know that I am God," he means, "Confide in me, — I will arrange this trial for your good." The Christian sees in this command no tyranny; it is the authority of love.

We need faith in God to-day, for *we are all bereaved.* While George N. Briggs lived, every one felt he had a friend. That friend has been summoned above. As the tidings of his death still spread, in widening circles, multitudes exclaim, "Is that good man dead? shall we see him no more? shall we never hear his voice again?" The poor have lost a benefactor; his charities distilled like the dew, silently, beneficently. The erring found in him a kind adviser. The young regarded him as a father. Who ever had a better neighbor? What citizen was ever more beloved? In the councils of our nation, was not his influence as a statesman and a patriot most salutary? As the Chief Magistrate of this Commonwealth, who was his superior? As judge, who feared to trust a righteous cause to his decision? He passed the ordeal of public life with honor, thus proving there is a straight path through the labyrinth of politics. Honors and responsibilities sought him, not he them. It might be chiselled on his monument, "An honest statesman," and no man would wish to erase the inscription. God spared him nearly sixty-six years, to the serene evening of his life. He had earned the right to retire to the bosom of his family and to his home in the church. Yet though he was retired from public service, he continued doing good. Twelve years in Congress, seven years Governor of Massachusetts, three years judge, he was not weary of toil. At the time of his decease he was president of several important organizations, over which he presided with great acceptance. Among them, the American Tract Society, Boston, the Baptist Foreign Missionary Union, the National Temperance Alliance, the State Sabbath School Union, and the Berkshire Insurance Company. He was a trustee of several colleges. He had recently been appointed umpire in a most important case, pending between our Government and that of New Grenada. He declined many high positions; among them, that of Secretary of the American Sunday School Union, Secretary to the American and Foreign Bible Society, and Chancellor of the Madison University, New York. His death has created many a void. Forty years he was the firm and eloquent advocate of temperance. At Washington, at Boston, — everywhere he was consistent. "*Total abstinence* from all that can intoxicate as a beverage," was his motto and his practice. A gentleman who was strictly temperate, asked him, one day, "What is your course when wine is offered you here, in fashionable circles, in the capital?" "I decline it," said he, "and drink water." "I just put the glass to my lips," said the gentleman, "and then set it down, without tasting the wine." "But," replied this inflexibly-honest, consistent, and morally courageous man, "I decline it openly, for example's sake."

He had a true American love of liberty. He believed that the normal condition of all men was freedom, and saw no good reason for excepting the colored race. His benevolence and sense of justice made him long for the termination of slavery. He understood the difficulties of emancipation better than most

37*

men. He was honest in upholding the South in all their constitutional rights; but he believed that God would not suffer an
institution so opposed to the spirit of our Government, so un-
Christian, so detrimental to the republic, so compact with inex-
pressible evils, always to continue. If all men were like George
N. Briggs, drunkards and slaves would be as impossible here as
in heaven.

He was a firm friend of popular education, and often lectured
upon it. How he extolled the Holy Bible in those lectures!
How he quoted its sacred contents! how he affirmed that it
afforded the best discipline for the mind, and the best culture for
the heart; that it created a correct taste, and laid the foundation
of excellence — in character! Who can remember any address
of his, whether to legislators, to judges and jurors, to educators,
to patriots, to Sunday-school scholars, to Christians, which was
not enriched by quotations from the book of God. He was an
extemporaneous speaker; hence, to our great regret, very few
of his speeches are preserved. I need not say that such a man
as Governor Briggs was a lover of his country. The Government is sure of support from such men. It had his prayers, his
gifts, his influence, and he freely gave to it his son. These
walls still echo [1] with his patriotic eloquence on a recent occasion.

There are two places which he loved, above all others, — his
home and the church of Christ. I hardly dare speak of his
home. Can I allude to him as the husband and father and
grandfather? Can I open his doors and show you how his presence shed happiness on the domestic circle? Can I go with you
from room to room, and point you to the numerous tokens of regard, the gifts of friends from both sides of the ocean? Can I
lead you to the family altar at which he worshipped? Ah, no!
Not to-day. Bereaved friends, you all profess to be Christians.
God has sustained you by his grace. Oh, submit cheerfully to
His will! This precious book which your husband and father
loved, is full of promises. "Be still, and know that I am God."

1 Address to "Allen Guards."

How shall I speak of his bereaved *church?* There is his *pew* from which he was seldom absent. *There* is the *place* where he taught in the Sabbath school. Here is the place where he so often stood and advocated some good cause. Here is the table from which, for many years he reverently received the communion. Below are the rooms where he delighted to meet his brethren for prayer and praise. Here are the walls to whose erection he so liberally contributed. Who, of us can ever forget his words at our last church meeting, preparatory to communion? Oh, how melting! how heavenly! "It is well," said he, "to be sound in gospel doctrines, but oh, it is *better* to have the Spirit of Christ." Can it be, dear brethren, that he will walk those aisles no more? Can it be that his noble form and mild blue eye and benevolent face will not be seen again in this sanctuary? Can it be, we shall never hear his voice again? Can it be that his pastor, who has leaned on him eleven years, shall have his support no more? Let us *be still*, for the Lord — he is God.

Governor Briggs loved *his* home, but he made many homes happy. He loved *his* church, but he was the friend and brother of *Christians* in all churches. His political and Christian opinions were very clear and settled, but all men felt, in his presence, that patriotism rose above party, and christianity above church. His work is done. He has gone to his reward, but his influence will live, while the memory of the just is precious.

I have tried to avoid eulogy, for I know it is opposed to the simplicity and humility of his character. Everything has been plain at his funeral, for he was a plain, though great and good man. I know that instead of praise for him, *he* would have this occasion lead our thoughts to *Christ*. He always wanted the crown on the Saviour's head.

In some circles he will be remembered but as a statesman, in others as a philanthropist. Here, he will be remembered but as a Christian. He had long been ripening for heaven, and for two years past the process had been rapid. He united with the church when only twelve years old, and has been fifty-four years a growing Christian. Brethren, he is with Christ, and we have his work to do as well as ours. On whom shall his mantle fall?

It is interesting to learn how a man like Governor Briggs approached the eternal world. He did not converse much, after his wound. He wrote upon a slate, and many of these brief writings have been copied, for preservation. It is gratifying to know, that the fear of death, which was a constitutional peculiarity of his, was completely removed. " It has come. Be still, and know that I am God," were his calm words to his wife. To his son-in-law, — " I thought that day I should be in eternity in one minute. I think I was perfectly calm." Immediately after reaching his bed, he said to his son, " Strange I should meet the fate of the battle-field — in this quiet place. It is all right." That son knelt by him and prayed. The father folded his hands on his breast with a most devout and placid expression of countenance. His soul was in peace. His love for his family was frequently expressed. " How much I trouble you!" " How I love you all!" " I have not seen little George and Mary and Nelly," his grandchildren. To his physician he said, " I am afraid you are going to cure me." After a moment's thoughtfulness he added, " What a night that was, doctor!" " Your *face* told the story." " God scourged me, and then He *bound* up the wound." How good He is! We all know his Christian humility. " My life," said he, " seems useless. I have done nothing — nothing!" His submission to God's will, and his longing for heaven, were constantly manifested. " Why do I linger here? it is to prepare me." " Joy and calm below, but oh, how calm and quiet and good above!" " Oh, that this poor, frail, unworthy one were there!" A dear friend stood by his bed. His son said, " you have no better friend than this." " I have *one* better friend," he said, looking up. To his daughter he said, " Oh, how I want to be in heaven!" The day but one before his death he said to his son, " I am at the lowest point of animal existence. I don't see how I can be saved from dying." " I have no wish for it; God and Christ are my all." " I *love* you." " Do what you think best. Leave all to God! God!

God!" On Wednesday evening he sank into sleep. On Thursday morning his spirit gently ascended to his Saviour and his home.

[1] Honored and loved he passed away,
  As sinks a summer's day to rest.
The brightest when the radiant clouds
  Of silent evening, gem the west.

'Twas not when youth's bright morning beams
  With glowing crimson flushed the sky,
But crowned with glory and with years,
  God called him to his home on high.

And calm as evening's jewelled zone,
  The valley dark, he fearless trod;
His words breathe peace and trust alone—
  "Be still, and know that I am God."

Like some fair tree on mountain's brow,
  Which braves the whirlwind in its might,
So, firm, he stood on Zion's Hill,
  A noble champion for the right.

Alike he trod the halls of State,
  And lowly cottage of the poor;
While every place his presence blessed,—
  Seemed brighter than it was before.

All called him friend: all mourn to-day,
  For silent, he is sleeping now;
His still hands crossed upon his breast,
  And death's pale signet on his brow.

1 "This requiem," says Mrs. Bigelow, "was composed by the gifted young girl, Miss Clara Porter, the daughter of the preacher, who a few months later, and after a brief illness—herself entered her 'glorious home on high.' When her father had nearly completed his sermon on the death of his friend, she entered the study and said, 'Father, I wish you would read me the conclusion of your sermon. *I have been composing something which may be appropriate.*' When he had finished what he had prepared, he read it to his daughter, and she sitting on a low seat at his feet, then repeated the words of the foregoing requiem, which he copied from her lips, she not having put pen to paper. It was the touching utterance of her gentle soul, inspired by the delicate and fervent affection she felt for my father, and her intense grief for his loss. She was entirely overcome at his death, and unable for many hours to leave her bed after it was announced to her."

No more his beaming smile we'll see
    Which sunshine always seemed to shed·
No more within these walls he'll bow,
    Now draped with mourning for the dead.

Crossed is the surging flood of death,
    Gained is his glorious home on high;
There, free from every earthly ill,
    He lives to-day; he cannot die.

Then trusting in the God he loved,
    We'll bow beneath the chastising rod,
For lo! a voice celestial speaks —
    " *Be still, and know that I am God.*"

APPENDIX III.

PUBLIC MEETING AT PITTSFIELD.

A meeting of the citizens of the town was held on Sunday evening, in order to express the sentiments which filled every heart. The spacious church of the First Congregational Society was filled, and hundreds were unable to find entrance. Besides our own citizens, several distinguished gentlemen from various parts of the State were present, and took part in the meeting.

Rev. Dr. Todd presided, and speeches were made by Hon. James D. Colt, Hon. Oliver Warner, Secretary of the Commonwealth, Rev. Dr. Marsh, Secretary of the American Temperance Union, Rev. Dr. Warren of Boston, James Francis, Esq., Hon. Henry H. Childs, and Hon. Thomas F. Plunkett.

We cannot report fully the speeches, but give a few prominent facts stated.

James Francis, Esq., senior deacon of the Baptist Church, and long a personal friend of Governor Briggs, said, —

MR. CHAIRMAN :— In consenting to occupy a few moments this evening, I do not presume to be able to say anything that might not be better said by any individual who should have enjoyed the same acquaintance with Governor Briggs as myself. If I were to speak, sir, of the first thing that arrested my attention in the early part of my acquaintance with him, it would be the power that he possessed of attracting all persons who knew him to himself. From the little ragged boy, with a single suspender over his shoulder (I refer here to a touching incident at his funeral), in all the gradations of society to the most elevated and refined, all, all felt this strong impression that here was a man to be trusted and loved. The secret of this universal power I wished to discover. I perceived that with high intellectual endowments, he had a cheerful face and a noble heart; but I had seen other men of brilliant talents, of generous hearts, and genial countenances who had gathered around them from certain classes admiring friends. On farther acquaintance, I seemed to see that the measure of his happiness was the measure of the happiness of all around him; that wherever there was suffering, whether it was the poor drunkard, approximating in his degradation near to the lower order of animals, or in the higher walks of life, he instinctively fled to their relief; and so powerful was this passion that it seemed to me at times as though he could not do otherwise if he would, thus illustrating the beautiful sentiment of one of the English poets,—

> " The heart that bleeds for others' woes,
>   Shall feel each selfish sorrow less;
> The breast that happiness bestows,
>   Reflected happiness shall bless."

No one who knew him could doubt his love for the Bible, its spirit and its author. While the beautiful symmetry and loveliness of his Christian character excited the admiration of all who knew him, yet how often has he, with a gleaming eye and a swelling countenance, said to me, " When I think of the wonders of redemption, and what the great Master has done for the redemption of mankind, and for me, it is then I distrust the genuineness of my hope that I am a Christian."

I remember, sir, it was said by those most intimately acquainted with the celebrated Robert Hall, of England, that the reason why some of the finest productions of that wonderful mind were lost to the world, was that, erecting before his own mind so high a standard of excellence in composition, and contrasting that with his own productions, they sank so far below, in his own estimation of that inimitable model, that he utterly refused to give them to the world.

When Sir Isaac Newton was on his death-bed, a friend, standing by, said to him, " It seems to me, Mr. Newton, it must have been a source of exquisite joy to you now to think how useful has been your life; how much you have done for the advancement of science and religion, and for the highest interests of your race!" He replied, " I seem to myself like a little child who has gathered a few pebbles on the shore, while the vast ocean lies before me yet unexplored."

Mysterious and accidental as seemed to be the chain of events that led to his death, yet it has been observed by members of the church with which he was connected, during months previous to his death, that he was rapidly advancing in the divine life. When the summons came so suddenly, he seemed like "a shock of corn fully ripe unto the harvest." And although he has left us, to return no more, yet the influence of his bright example will live until earth's last inhabitant shall have passed away, and then onward undiminished forever.

Hon. Thomas F. Plunkett said that although always opposing the political party to which Governor Briggs belonged, he had always had the highest esteem for him personally. In this connection a fact mentioned by Mr. Plunkett has much interest: he said, —

It gave him great pleasure to add his testimony upon one single point in the character of Governor Briggs, in addition to what has already been said by others, and that is as to his character for official integrity. In the early part of the year 1857, he spent several weeks in Boston analyzing the expenses of our State. He had full access to the public documents in the Treasurer and Auditor's department, and he employed a competent accountant to assist him. They examined all the expenses of the State from 1832 to 1856 inclusive, a period of twenty-five years, and every item of expense for that long period was classified under its appropriate head, for the purpose of ascertaining when and how the expenditures of the State had been so largely increased in the five last years preceding 1856. Governor Briggs was in the executive chair from 1844 to 1850, inclusive (seven years), during that time he found no item of expense that could be justly criticised. The ordinary expenses of the State were, in 1844, $413,000, and at the end of seven years they had increased to $560,000, making about $20,000 annually, just about in proportion to the increase of the population. In the next five years, the ordinary annual expenses had reached $1,400,000, or three times as much as they were under the administration of Governor Briggs.

Governor Briggs had not the reputation generally of having great memory of statistics, but in one instance he much surprised him. In 1857, Mr. Plunkett published a small pamphlet on our State expenses, giving in tabular form the expenses of each year for twenty-five years preceding. He handed Governor Briggs one of these pamphlets; he cast his eyes over the column of the total expenses of each year, and when he came to 1845, he said at once that was wrong. It should be about so much. He thought he was mistaken, but examined the item over and found that Governor Briggs was right, and that there had been a mistake in adding. Considering that it was eleven years afterwards, it was remarkable that he should have recollected the amount. Whatever mismanagement and extravagance we may have had since he left the gubernatorial chair, we are certain that there was no prodigality or plundering under the administration of George N. Briggs.

Hon. Thomas Colt, on introducing the resolutions, said, —

I will not, at this late hour, detain this audience with any lengthy preface to the resolutions that I propose to offer. Now, sir, that there is nothing left to us of Governor Briggs, but the memory and the grave of one in whose heart the love of us, his fellow-men, was only weaker than his love of God, I desire to offer for the consideration of this large assembly the following resolutions, that they may be placed upon the public record, in token that this community appreciates the character of such a patriot, philanthropist, and Christian as was George N. Briggs. There can be no stronger proof of the affectionate esteem that this whole people had for him than the occurrence of this occasion :

Whereas, It has pleased the Wise Disposer of all events to remove suddenly and mysteriously by death, our fellow-citizen, George N. Briggs, formerly our representative in Congress, then the Governor of this Commonwealth, and afterwards the Judge of the Court of Common Pleas, and who during his life has held many other offices of public trust, —

Resolved, That this community entertain a high estimation of the character of our late friend and fellow-citizen; a man who, in social and private life, had the power to draw all hearts to him; who, in charities, ever had a heart so large and a hand so noble that the poor blessed him while living, and many will rise up and call him blessed now that he is gone; a man who in all the relations of private life, as a friend and a neighbor, has seldom had an equal; who, in all the relations of public office and public life, was never accused of wrong or unworthy motives; who met the expectations of all, fulfilled the most arduous and delicate trusts and responsibilities so as to be entitled to the gratitude of all; who, during the very long period which he served in Congress, and as the Chief Magistrate of this ancient Commonwealth, made a deep impression upon his associates of his honesty, sincerity, and lofty moral principles; who, as an advocate and example of temperance, made a deep impression on his generation; who, as a Christian gentleman, was a bright example of all that was courteous ·in intercourse, all that was humble in self-estimation, and all that was pure and lofty in hopes; the man in whom were so united the grave and the cheerful, the strong and the lovely parts of human character, — that we might truly say

> " the elements
> So mixed in him that nature might stand up
> And say to all the world, *this was a man !*"

Resolved, That we are grateful to that Providence which has so long spared us a fellow-citizen so much beloved, so widely known, so long and so extensively useful, so cheerful in life and so happy and blessed in death, and that his memory will forever remain precious to this whole community.

AT LANESBORO'.

A public meeting was held in Lanesboro' Sunday evening, September 15, with reference to the death of Governor Briggs, long a resident in the town. Various gentlemen have interesting reminiscences of his life, and all bore emphatic testimony to the excellence of his character. Afterwards the meeting, by vote, adopted the following preamble and resolutions : —

Whereas, It having pleased God, in His inscrutable providence, to visit the community with a sudden and terrible stroke in the death of the Hon. George N. Briggs, it seems fit that the citizens of the town in which he studied his profession and began his public career, should give some united expression to their sense of his worth; therefore,

Resolved, That, having known George N. Briggs from early life, we long ago learned to esteem and love him as a man, a neighbor, and a friend. And as the young lawyer of Lanesboro' went on and up till he had for many years held a seat in Congress, we still found him, and have, since he filled the highest offices in the Commonwealth, ever found him affable, genial, warm-hearted, and true.

Resolved, That from the time he entered upon public life we observed his course with peculiar interest, and believe that he passed through the trying ordeal of politics unscathed; that he never sold his vote, or sought popularity by base or dishonorable means; and that, whether in the halls of national legislation, in the executive chair of the State, or upon the judicial bench, he maintained a noble integrity.

Resolved, That we regard him as having been a true philanthropist and a sincere Christian. The poor found in him a sympathizing and efficient helper, the cause of temperance an able and consistent advocate, and all who love our Lord Jesus Christ, one ready to greet and co-operate with them in paternal love.

Resolved, That while his family, his friends, the county in which he resided, the State, and the nation have suffered a great loss in his death, and that at a time when they would seem least able to bear it, we have occasion to be grateful for that precious legacy which he has left in his unsullied name and bright example. And as we tender our profound sympathy to his bereaved family, whom many of us count among our personal friends, we rejoice that they have solid ground of consolation in evidence that the high excellences which marked his life were the fruit of religious principle, early implanted, but developing new power and shining with added grace as the evening of life drew on, till it became serenity, perfect resignation, and triumphant faith upon the bed of death : —

> " Weep not for *him* the sainted one,
>   He treads a happier shore;
> His own and all his country's woes
>   Can touch him now no more."

Geo. T. Dole,
Justus Tower,
J. V. Ambler,
  Committee.

ACTION OF THE BERKSHIRE BAR.

At a meeting of members of the Berkshire Bar, held at Lenox, September, term, e861, Hon. Increase Sumner was chosen chairman, and Henry W. Taft, secretary.

The chair communicated to the Bar the intelligence of the recent decease of Hon. George N. Briggs, when, on motion of Hon. J. E. Field, Messrs. H. W. Bishop, Increase Sumner, and Geo. J. Tucker were appointed a committee, who subsequently reported the following resolutions, which were adopted by the Bar: —

Resolved, That in the death of George Nixon Briggs, we deplore most deeply the loss of one who, throughout his professional career was the ornament and the beloved of this Bar; who, in the outset of life, by his sound and vigorous understanding, moral excellence, and incorruptible honesty, won the esteem and confidence of an appreciative public, and received from it the honorable recognitions due to eminent virtues and endowments.

Resolved, That there is due from the whole country, and particularly from his own State, a debt of lasting gratitude for the many useful and able public services discharged and fulfilled by him, with a Christian's loyalty and a patriot's devotion.

Resolved, That, as a member of Congress, he studiously consulted the interests and fully met the just expectations of those whom he represented; was capable, faithful, and true at all times to his constituency and his country. As a Governor of the Commonwealth, he was judicious, firm, and exempt from the influences of political animosities and personal considerations; and, as a judge, just, intelligent, and impartial.

Resolved, That in the various offices with which he was charged by a confiding people, he sought earnestly for what was good and right, and was more solicitous to deserve, than to receive, the approbation and honor of his fellow-citizens.

Resolved, That the rare excellences of our departed friend were particularly conspicuous in his social and domestic relations. He was studious of the happiness of all about him; he loved his friends; he had no enemies to hate; although sentiments and opinions which he regarded as erroneous and pernicious received his emphatic censure, they never produced feelings of personal hostility to him who might entertain them. His genial nature; his ardent and confiding attachment; his chaste and delicate pleasantry; his apt and charming narration of anecdote, never without point, and often wonderfully illustrative; his social powers, admitting unconstrained familiarity, but repressing offensive readiness by manly dignity; his active kindness, quiet almsgiving, and his hearty co-operations with good men in all the measures wisely devised for the good of the race, are all well known to those with whom he has been associated in public and private life.

Resolved, That we will cherish the memory of Governor Briggs as a faithful friend and exemplary Christian, a public benefactor, and a model of moral excellence and social and domestic virtue.

At the request of the Bar, these resolutions were presented by the committee to the Supreme Judicial Court, then in session, with the request that they might be entered in the records of the court. The presentation to the court was accompanied by appropriate remarks from Messrs. Bishop and Sumner. Mr. Sumner said, —

May it please your Honors, — The resolutions just read, prepared by Brother Bishop, so fully embrace what is fitting on this occasion, that I dare not presume, I can add to them acceptable remarks.

When tidings of the sad occurrence to Governor Briggs came, as it did, suddenly upon me, I felt that I should faint and fall prostrate upon the earth. But I am calmer now. The agony is over, and the pure and gentle spirit of George Nixon Briggs, quit of its tegument of flesh, is in heaven.

There are instances, when men eminent for great gifts and powers and public services are taken away, the event so bewilders and overwhelms that we cannot at once composedly dwell upon their history or speak of their lives and character. Not so of Governor Briggs. The entire scenery of his life, so rare and picturesque and lovely, opens upon us instantly as his presence departs, and we can at once look upon it with admiration and pleasure, and speak of it, not only with composure, but delight. Just as when we stand on some commanding hilltop, at the close of a serene summer's day, and see the sun retiring in glory, leaving a vast space of the horizon aglow with tokens of his blessing upon the day, and with promises of a goodly morrow, the quiet beauty and calmness of the scene prompts alike to contemplative humor or to discourse; so now, at the closing of the good man's day, we look calmly upon his life-scenes, and speak of his deeds.

Of humble but respectable origin, dependent under Providence upon his own efforts, he acquired a legal education and admission to this Bar. He found the ground occupied by distinguished members of the legal profession, — such men as Dwight and Jarvis and Mills and Howe, in the freshness and full vigor of their powers, were his competitors, — but such were his talents that he at once took rank with them as their peer, and succeeded in sharing with them successfully the patronage and business afforded in the courts. His fellow-citizens saw and appreciated his many and excellent qualities; they discovered in the analysis of his mind and character a strength of understanding, a strict and intelligent regard to duty, such as springs from sincerity, integrity, and faithfulness, and a laudable desire to promote the best interests and welfare of all. No marvel was it, therefore, that he should have been selected and retained for twelve long years as a representative from this noble section of the State in the national legislature, during all which time those who from the restraints of political associations withheld from him their suffrages, were not less earnest and ready than those who bestowed them, in expressing their satisfaction, and pride even, that in the halls of Congress there stood, as the representative from this district, one so blameless in his life, so truly honest in all his aims and efforts, and so capable for the discharge of his trusts.

He was a native of this county, and he loved with all the ardor and affection of a son this, our ancient Commonwealth. He studied its interests and welfare, and well understood each, as well the grandest and noblest objects it presented, as those humble and minute. The mariner, whether he furled the sails of his bark at our wharves, or afar off upon the deep spread them to the breeze; the success of the humble mechanic or laborer, or of the opulent merchant upon 'change; the great enterprises of the manufacturer, or the toils of the poor factory boy; the prosperous agriculturist with his rich acres and flocks, or the humble ploughman upon the hill-side; the noble designs of charity; the associations and efforts promotive of the stability or advancement of morals and christianity; all institutions of learning from least to greatest, and all engaged in the cause of education, from the young cottage child, with primer in hand, seated upon the lowest form in the school-room, to the distinguished professors and governors of our colleges, — in a word, all which could tend to make our beloved Commonwealth truly great and prosperous, and its people virtuous and happy, received his earnest attention and solicitude. So manifest was all this to his fellow-citizens, and so correctly did they judge of his capacities, that most natural was it, they should instinctively, as it were, elevate him to the highest place in their gift — the Executive chair — which had been filled by such men — his predecessors — as Hancock and Samuel Adams, Sullivan and Strong, long since gone, and by Levi Lincoln and Edward Everett, still living, and whom may kind Heaven long preserve. It is comment enough to add, that the expressions of confidence in his ability and merits as a Chief Magistrate were repeated, and deservedly so, at six successive elections after he was first chosen.

He was a just man, in the highest and best sense of the term; he possessed correct perceptions of the difference betwixt right and wrong, firmness and excellent judgment, and legal attainments adequate for discharging the duties of a judge. Hence, after his retirement from the office of Governor, he was called to the bench, and it is not too much to say that he left an honorable record of his judicial labors.

A survey of the life and character of this eminent and excellent man, how like is it to the viewing of some vast landscape in which no single deformity or ruin exists, but filled with objects that, whether seen singly or in groups, are alike charming and captivating; no broken surfaces nor rugged features, no dreary wastes nor darkened caverns, but everywhere, far and extended as the eye can reach, all verdant and beautiful, illumined with balmy sunshine enamelled with flowers, and fragrant with the sweet breath of heaven. It would be pleasant to linger yet awhile upon the scene, and depict the lovely images everywhere discernible, but the hour allotted us requires me to be brief. Over all the landscape

38*

there is only one place of which we may not speak, except with subdued voice and few words,—the place dearest to him of all, and which his presence so blessed,—compared with which in his affection neither honorable position in the halls of legislation, nor elevation in the judicial forum nor chair of state, were even of remote account,—his own loved home. We may not speak of it now, for his departure is too recent and this occasion is too intense. There also rests what of him was mortal, and thither upon the morrow we may repair, with silent tread and bowed and uncovered heads, and with rites fitting Christian sepulture, take up the precious remains and lay them in their resting-place, where angels will watch their repose until the sounding of the last trumpet shall thrill him with its warning.

And thus upon earth we part with him; in the solemn, impressive, and appropriate language in the burial service of the Church of England, "Looking for the general resurrection in the last day, and the life of the world to come, through our Lord Jesus Christ, at whose second coming in glorious majesty to judge the world, the earth and the sea shall give up their dead."

His Honor, Chief Justice Bigelow, replied as follows:—

Gentlemen of the Bar,—The Court respond most cordially to the sentiments contained in the resolutions of the Bar which have just been read, and unite with a sorrowful satisfaction in paying a tribute to the virtues, both public and private, of your late beloved associate. The death of a member of a Bar, whom we have been accustomed to regard as one of the circle with whom we are brought closely in contact in the discharge of our duties, is always an event which arrests our attention and "gives us pause," even amid the pressure of our constant labors. But that impression is deepened and our sensibilities are quickened, when, as in this case, we are called on to deplore the death not only of a professional associate and brother, but also of one who sustained towards each of us the closer and nearer relation which results from strong personal friendship and regard.

The death of Governor Briggs will be widely and deeply felt throughout the Commonwealth. During the many years which it was his fortune to pass in public life, he became more generally known to the people of the State than most persons who are called to fill high official stations. His great affability and kindness of manner, and the republican simplicity which characterized his intercourse with others, allowed every one to approach him with perfect freedom, and he won the hearts of all by the genial traits which distinguished him. He was indeed a remarkable example of the fostering influence of our institutions upon men who enter into life without adventitious aid or early opportunities to acquire knowledge. Employed in agricultural and mechanical pursuits until he had attained his majority, he never had opportunities to enjoy the benefits of early and careful training and study. With a scanty education, such as could be acquired in our common public schools at the period when he entered life, more than forty years ago, he not only attained distinction as a member of this Bar, but he filled the many high public stations to which he was called by the confident regard of the people with signal success and honor. He was a faithful, consistent, patriotic representative in the national councils, who never forgot the interests of his constituents, or was false to his duty to his country. He was an upright and impartial judge, who administered justice without fear or favor. He was a dignified, independent, firm, and enlightened Chief Magistrate, who shed lustre on our beloved Commonwealth by his long and faithful services. In all the stations which he filled, exposed as he was to the shafts of political rancor, his integrity was never impeached or called in question. Detraction, it is said, finds its most "acceptable quarry in the failings of the good man;" but it may be said with truth that it never ventured to assail him.

And this leads us to notice what, on this occasion, we most delight to recall—his personal character and virtues, which endeared him to us as a man. Where can we find in the circle of our friends and acquaintances one who had a warmer or purer heart? Where shall we seek for a more sincere and disinterested friend, a wiser counsellor? Who can point to a more consistent and devoted Christian?

His death was sudden, and was accompanied by severe physical distress; but it did not find him unprepared or unwilling to meet the great and final change. Although we feel keenly the shock, we cannot doubt that to him, who relied so confidently on the promises of the Gospel, and who was so well entitled to inherit the blessings in store for the pure in heart, his death was only a translation to the higher and happier mansions above.

In compliance with the request of the Bar, the resolutions which have been offered will be placed on record.

Finis.